THE MYSTERY SHOPPER & THE HOT TUB

First published in the UK in 2020 by In Jest

This is a work of fiction. This novel's story and characters are fictitious. Certain historic properties and businesses are mentioned and with the exception of Alastair Curbuun, the characters and events involved are wholly imaginary or used in a completely fictitious manner. Any mention of or resemblance to actual persons, living or dead, or actual events is purely coincidental or contextual within the story.

Paperback ISBN: 978-1-8382692-3-4
.epub eBook ISBN: 978-1-8382692-1-0
.mobi eBook ISBN 978-1-8382692-2-7

Cover design and typeset by Spiffing Covers

THE MYSTERY SHOPPER & THE HOT TUB

HELEN E. FIELD

BOOK ONE OF THE DE'ATH FAMILY ANTICS

Contents

AUTHOR'S BIOGRAPHY

Helen Field is a business woman, writer, publisher of greetings cards, funny poet, speaker, traveller and author of The Mystery Shopper & The Hot Tub.

She was born and brought up in Waltham Abbey in Essex and currently lives in a small village in North West Essex, so it would be fair to say she has earned her "Essex girl" badge!

Helen has had a varied and interesting career in retail and hospitality in UK, Europe and USA, including setting up and running her own restaurant. She runs her own training consultancy to the hospitality industry. One element of her business has been designing and implementing mystery shopper programmes all over the UK for some of the most well-known organisations. With inside knowledge of the industry and armed with thousands of funny mystery shopping incidents, she was inspired to write her debut novel, The Mystery Shopper & The Hot Tub.

Helen has recently spent time combining work and writing with travelling with her husband, including four months in Europe in a 20 year old campervan, a completely wild four-month ride round India by train and a month in an isolated log cabin in Finland.

She rides a motorbike and has three talented and amazing grown up children.

P.s. She doesn't have a hot tub… yet!

AUTHOR'S NOTE

For those international readers, who may not be familiar with UK regional dialects and colloquial language, it is worth explaining that Essex is a home county very close to London. Over the years, many Londoners moved out to Essex and their language and accent followed – sometimes referred to now as Estuary English. It is spoken to this day in the county. You may also find the occasional strange word or phrase in some of the dialogue, with which you are unfamiliar. Cockney rhyming slang, which originated in the east end of London in the 1840s, was a means by which market traders, hawkers and possibly criminals would hide what they were saying from passers-by and the authorities. It is also still used to this day and my characters use it from time to time in their speech.

See https://www.cockneyrhymingslang.co.uk/ for further information.

For my dear late Mum and Dad - Vera and Jack Field, without whom I would never have been an Essex girl.

1

Desires, Motives and Means

'It's only seven and a half grand,' Brooke commented.

'Yes, love, but we haven't got seven and a half grand and, besides, you've got high blood pressure…and flat feet,' Dean responded wearily.

As the eight-seater hot tub glistened under the burning sun, Brooke sauntered around it, caressing the sides as she went, aware that she was being stared at by some chaps a few metres away.

She possessed almost white-blonde hair, cut to precisely vertebrae T2 as specified by Dean, and it fell in Goldilocks ringlets that bobbed up and down her spine, like out-of-control Slinky toys. She was unusually tall, and her black and gold body con dress looked as though it'd been painted on, as her luscious curves filled every millimetre. Her stock four-inch stiletto heels (painted red underneath) had been slipped on, as usual, before she and Dean had left the house – as any self-respecting Essex girl does when they'll be spending the afternoon at the garden centre. Brooke slinked as she walked. Impossible to ignore. A stunner!

A mass of sweaty bodies, pushing huge flat trolleys, shuffled up the aisles and checkouts of the garden centre. It was a scorching summer day and it looked as if the whole of Essex had decided that going to the garden centre was the best possible way of spending it. There were no seats left in the restaurant, where people were scoffing down a plated roast dinner for £9.99 and tables were covered in debris. The tree houses on display were being wrecked by a group of unruly, dirty children doing moonies out the windows.

Dale Farm, thought Brooke turning her little nose up.

The hot tub section bustled with social climbers and creaking retirees, working out repayment plans with the overly familiar salesmen.

'What's my blood pressure got to do with anything, anyway? And my flat feet?'

'I remember reading something once in the *BMA Home Medical Guide* that hot tubs aren't good for people with high blood pressure. And you'd be slipping all the time getting in and out, with those plates of meat.' Dean nodded towards her feet.

'You and that bloody medical book. I could kill your mum. I'm not an invalid, you know.' Brooke paused before continuing, 'Well, if you can't buy me one, Dean, I'll just have to get myself a job, won't I?'

Clever girl.

'The twelve-seater's only another two grand. Just imagine the parties we could have in that! Come on, Dean!

For God's sake, look a bit more enthusiastic.' For Brooke, a hot tub would be the epitome of success amongst their social circle.

Dean was dog-tired. Paige, their eleven-month old baby, had kept him up all night on a regular basis since she was born; screaming with pain – allegedly from colic. Dean had his doubts. Any baby dragged around Lakeside shopping centre for hours on end needed an outlet for their anger and frustration. Unfortunately, Paige's outlet was frequently at night when Dean was on 'bottle duty'. Brooke was still breastfeeding (almost all her girlfriends bottle fed or had given up after only a few weeks and thought she'd gone doolally). She'd been the only one of her friends to join the NCT, who were entirely responsible for her persistence in the matter. She'd express milk into a bottle for poor Dean to 'do his bit' in the middle of the night.

Dean's designer ripped denim shorts rested just below his paunch (he liked his food) and his pink Ralph Lauren polo shirt was untucked. His Adidas Originals were as pure white as an Arab's kandura, having been given a microscopic once-over before leaving the house. One could almost see the dark stubble spreading across his face as the minutes ticked by. Unusually, Brooke had let him lie in so he'd not had time to shave. As a child he was nicknamed Super Mario by his chums, due to the dark moustache that he appeared to have been born with. When he was twelve, his mother noticed half his moustache had disappeared and then found a razor in his bed. His father had reluctantly taught him to shave after that.

He absent-mindedly dunked his hand in the hot tub water and swished his fingers to and fro, watching the patterns they made and vaguely thinking how lovely and warm it was. Within seconds he realised what a stupid mistake he'd made. Schoolboy error! He yanked his hand out, looking around, as though he'd committed some sort of crime. Too late! Brooke was grinning at him, with that sort of expression that young ladies display when they're about to declare they're expecting.

'You're warming to the idea, aren't you? I can tell.'

'No.'

'I'll give you a blow job if we get one.' Brooke leaned forward and positioned her tongue hard into her cheek as she stared at him.

She possessed an irreverent sense of mischief and revelled in the controversy and chaos created if she managed to cause a reaction.

'No, Brooke!' Dean whispered it between his teeth, furtively checking no-one was listening.

'OK, a blow job every day for a year then!' She raised her voice slightly and smiled.

'NO! Now pack it up, you're embarrassing me.' Dean continued to look around to check no-one could hear.

A rather grubby old man walked past Dean and whispered, 'Well, I'd sign on the dotted line right now if I was you, mate.'

At least a dozen people were gathered around The Romanesque twelve-seater by this time, listening with various degrees of interest to the salesman, who had a middle-aged couple within his grasp, with his enticing description of the musical functions and his enthralling knowledge of PH increasers and bromine.

The woman pointed at the intriguing design that ran around the sides of the hot tub and asked, 'What's that picture meant to be, then? It looks a bit saucy to me.'

The salesman stammered and muttered something about Roman emperors and orgies.

'No. That's not right, mate,' Brooke called out.

The entire group looked over to her.

'For a start, they're not emperors (who were actually real live people by the way). That's the gods Venus and Mars in Pompeii that is; you know, that place where the volcano blew up and turned everything into stone.'

Everyone stopped doing whatever they were doing, mouths slightly ajar, and stared at Brooke as she spoke.

'But they did bathe starkers, I'll give you that.'

Dean was inexplicably ruffled and yanked her away from the crowd. 'Whatever. We're still not getting one.'

With the corners of her mouth turned down in an exaggerated fashion and a voice steeped in disappointment and hope, she continued, 'But you looked so thoughtful just now; as though you were thinking about how great it'd be to get in…lie back with a cold beer…with all your mates and…'

Her mock sales pitch fell miserably flat.

'Brooke. I'm fucking knackered! That's all that look was, so don't start getting any ideas. We can't afford a hot tub; I can't even afford to keep you in nail varnish.'

Brooke's face, shoulders and mouth dropped like a small child who didn't get her way. She hated the fact that the purchase of a hot tub was vetoed effectively because she had no money of her own. She'd reluctantly accepted that her financial security and the life she wanted (and believed would make her happy) wasn't in her own hands – at least not as long as Dean insisted on treating her like a china doll. And yet…she quite liked the idea of not working, because that showed people she had a husband who could afford to keep her, like all those D-list celebrities with glamorous wives she read about in *OK!*. Dean quite liked that too. Except he couldn't. At least not in the lifestyle she was so desperate for, fed by a diet of *Cosmopolitan*, *Love Island* and Kim Kardashian's backside on Instagram.

Brooke snatched a hot tub brochure off the side and slid it into her Michael Kors shopper next to a copy of *The Spectator* she'd stolen from the doctor's surgery the previous week. She stormed off, catching one of her heels in between the pavestones and tripping as a result. She was forced to bend down, much to the delight of the old man who'd been watching the entire event, before hurriedly pushing it back on and continuing her diva exit.

The old man hobbled after her until he caught up with her, 'Hey! Love! I think this is yours.' Brooke turned around and retrieved the zebra-print false nail from his outstretched hand. 'It was floating in the hot tub.'

'Bloody cheap shit glue! Thanks, mate.' Brooke smiled at him before noticing that his flies were undone. She leaned forward and gently put her arm on his and whispered, 'I don't want you to think I normally go round looking at men's private parts, but your flies are undone, mate. Wouldn't want you to be embarrassed now!'

'Oh gaawd. We don't want the beast making an unexpected appearance. Thanks, love!'

Dean was left to push the obscenely expensive Bugaboo back to the car, just as Paige let rip with one of her infamous screams. He'd never have paid a thousand pounds for a pram, but Brooke's Mum Jackie (spelt in the same way as Jackie Kennedy as she never tired of telling people, yawn yawn) had insisted that Paige only had the best. Image was *very* important to Jackie and she went to great lengths to keep up appearances. Brooke had been the archetypal spoilt only child.

As Dean approached the car park, the irony of the scene ahead didn't pass him by. His stunning wife, dressed top to toe in Versace (from Freeport Outlet Centre in Braintree, needless to say) and groomed to perfection, was leaning against their ten-year old, battered Peugeot 306, aka Edna, after Dean's cantankerous old grandma, and flicking through a hot tub brochure. His heart collapsed like a soufflé. Brooke was so precious to him, and Dean believed she needed protecting from the rigours and stresses of working life. She suffered not only with high blood pressure, but she'd suffered a mild uterine collapse after Paige was born. All most unpleasant. And then, of course, there were her flat feet. She couldn't possibly be standing up all day! He loved her and wanted her to be proud of him, but the sight before him made him want to bow his head in shame. There was this niggling something inside him which made him feel like it was his duty, his obligation as man and head of the household to provide his wife with whatever she wanted; not like his father, who'd deserted his mother, their five daughters and Dean and then buggered off when Dean was just thirteen. Such a cad. His mother's life had been hard and so he was determined he'd be different. In his late teens he'd been the envy of all his friends when Brooke had made it obvious that Dean was 'the chosen one'. They'd all thought they stood a chance with the best-looking girl in their group, but, in the end, Brooke chose Dean. He walked around for months grinning almost permanently. He owned a bright-red Triumph Dolomite Sprint back then, which was his pride and joy ('classic car, my Dolly is' he used to say) – well, until Brooke came along anyway. She didn't care for it and declared that if he really worshipped her, he'd dispose of it and purchase something more upmarket. So he did. A Mitsubishi Lancer Evolution. She was happy enough with that, but he didn't have it long, after racing his best chum Martin along the A127 to Southend one Friday evening and crashing it outside Tots nightclub. An unmitigated disaster! He actually wept, wailing, 'That car had a skimmed head and a Janspeed exhaust!'

As Dean gently lifted the yelling Paige out from under the pram's umbrella, it occurred to him that, up until just now, Paige had miraculously stayed asleep the entire trip, exhausted from no morning nap. As he started to put her in the car seat, his mind momentarily turned to work. Soon…very soon, he hoped that he'd finally get the promotion he'd worked so hard for. Six months, maybe three if he was lucky. Then he could get rid of Edna; a most undesirable vehicle. If he didn't use it for a couple of days, it didn't start; the driver's window was broken and would fall down inside the car door at speed, requiring a coat hanger to get it back up again. If he got the promotion, it'd come with a company car.

A company car!

Dean had always dreamed of getting a company car. In his eyes, that'd be the moment he'd show the world he'd made it. The moment his friends would envy him once more, his wife fawn over him and any children he ever had wouldn't be embarrassed to be picked up from school by him. He thought of the time he'd implored his father not to drive right up to his school, but to park down the road a bit. The ancient, clapped-out Ford Sierra that the family had was the most revolting green and grey colour, the front bumper had come off in an accident and they could never afford to get it replaced. The exhaust was held together with a Schweppes tonic can and gaffer tape and made a noise like a tractor. How he'd longed for his father to turn up in a Mercedes like his best friend Matt's family owned.

'Dean. What are you doing?'

'Sorry, love, just having some trouble getting Paige in.'

Dean ran round to Brooke's side of the car and bowed deeply. Before opening her door, he looked at her meaningfully, grabbed her round the waist and yanked her towards him, giving her a lingering kiss on the lips. She didn't fight.

'By the way, how did you know all about that picture and stuff on that hot tub?'

'That Mary Beard woman. Bloody brilliant, she is.'

Dean had no idea who Mary Beard was.

'I love you, Mrs De'Ath. If I get this promotion, I promise I'll at least *consider* a hot tub.'

She squeezed him and looked him in the eye with an intensity that Dean knew meant only one thing.

'Thanks, babe. I know you won't let me down. I love you too… I can't wait to tell Stacey.'

'Tell Stacey what?'

'That we're getting a hot tub soon! She'll be so jealous!'

Brooke got out her iPhone, pinged a message, then retrieved *The Spectator* from her bag and began reading where she'd left off: 'The Rise and Fall of Australia's First Female Prime Minister'.

***

All applicants must be reliable, observant, discreet, have high attention to detail, excellent written English, with good spelling and grammar. Must have own car, be willing to travel and ideally be available at short notice. All expenses will be reimbursed and, additionally, some assignments are paid. In return you can expect to be allocated a range of interesting and exciting visits to restaurants, hotels, golf clubs, pubs and health and leisure centres. Full training will be given.

The advertisement in the *Evening Standard* that Monday caught Dean's eye. He read it and at once knew he had many, if not all, of the qualities they were looking for. He enjoyed food and travelling, it'd be great fun *and* Brooke always said he was as fussy as Sheldon from *The Big Bang Theory*. Maybe he could get that hot tub sooner than he'd thought. Several weeks had gone by since their garden centre visit and he'd not heard the end of it. Every other day Brooke would hold forth about it and talk about buying matching furniture from Debenhams and it'd made him feel despondent. This advertisement cheered him up enormously.

He delved into his pocket to get his phone out and ring Brooke, but suddenly stopped. He sat back in his chair and chewed the inside of his mouth, thinking, hesitating, procrastinating – his favourite pastime. Not only might this be a fabulous surprise if he was able to do enough paid visits to help him get the hot tub before the promotion, but – he was almost frightened to think it – but maybe…

it could give him a break from Brooke and the baby now and then. It was the least he deserved! If Brooke got wind of it, she'd almost certainly persuade him to let her do the best assignments or at the very least go with him if the assignment permitted that. And that just wouldn't do at all!

Dean knew he had a reputation with 'the lads' of being henpecked by her. On the outside, it looked as though he brushed off their comments admirably, but, deep down, he knew they were right. She could be a tad dominating at times. Most of the time he really didn't mind. He was a simple chap with simple needs and was happy to do whatever made Brooke happy. But every so often, the worm felt like turning. And this was one of those moments. He put the phone back in his pocket and sat pondering for a while.

The silence of his daydreaming was soon punctured by a gravelly voice that sounded as though the owner had smoked fifty Woodbines a day for twenty years.

'A penny for them,' said Chloe.

'Uh?'

'You look like you're away with the fairies, Dean. A penny for your thoughts.'

Chloe was a colleague who'd always rather fancied Dean. She sat down next to him in the small work kitchen/canteen.

'What's that you've circled? You're not looking for another job, are you?'

'No – it's nothing really – just an advert for mystery shoppers. I saw it and thought it might be a laugh, but I dunno whether I'll actually apply.'

She read it quickly. 'Why on earth would you *not* apply?' she asked, startled that anyone wouldn't take up such an exciting opportunity! 'I'd apply if only I could drive!'

Dean went on to express his weariness at Brooke's insistence that he bathed Paige each night and told her bedtime stories, when all he actually wanted to do was crash out with a beer on the sofa.

'But I could do with a bit of extra wonga, though I haven't got a clue how much they pay.'

Dean stretched out and put his hands in his pockets. 'Her ladyship wants a hot tub.' With a look of hopeless resignation, he rolled his eyes.

'Oh does she now? Well I doubt mystery shopping pays enough for stuff like that. Still, free meals in fancy restaurants and stays in posh hotels can't be bad.'

Chloe leaned over confidentially. 'It could be a good excuse to get a break from "her indoors" for a few nights.'

Dean laughed and mirrored Chloe's actions. 'Don't tell anyone, but that did actually cross my mind. Isn't that awful?!'

'No. Completely understandable, if you ask me. I feel sorry for all those poor guys who arrive home from work knackered, to a wife that's been at home all day with a baby and expects them to immediately take it from them so they can have a rest. What about the poor guys? Don't *they* need a rest? Aren't *they* the ones who have been actually *at work* all day?' She thoughtfully added, 'Mind you, not having kids myself, I'm probably not the best person to judge!'

'No, you're right. You're not, you silly cow!' replied Dean.

'D'ya know I once read in a book by Allan Pease that women have six areas of their brain that enable speech and that they speak on average 24,000 words a day. Guys only have two areas and speak only 8,000 words a day. Do you realise what that means?'

Chloe sidled up closer to Dean, revealing more thigh as she did so. 'All around the world, women at home all day with 23,000 words to use up, but with only a baby for company, use only two or three words. Men at work all day with adults use up all 8,000 of their words. Man arrives home with nothing left of his 8,000 words so can only grunt and woman has 23,997 words still to use up, so she starts as soon as he arrives and doesn't stop until he goes to bed. No wonder so many guys get pissed down the pub before they go home!'

Dean burst out laughing. 'Oh my God, that's so funny but so true. I'll have to get that book!' Then he looked at his watch and, picking up the paper, said, 'I've got to get back to my desk now before "you know who" is on my case. See you later.'

He smiled at her warmly and walked briskly back to

his desk, thinking about Allan Pease's statistics. It occurred to him that Chloe was a rare female indeed! He couldn't think of any other woman he'd ever met who'd shown such insight and understanding of the predicament of the man who's both husband and new father, as well as… well…just ordinary chap. He smiled and shook his head, then carefully placed the paper on his desk in a way that implied he'd made a decision.

What harm could it possibly do?

2

Dean's First Mystery Shop

Angie stared at the used condom pinned on the noticeboard. In what way did a degree in Geography at Cambridge prepare her for this kind of work, she wondered.

'What the fuck is that?'

'Eliza sent it in. Don't worry it's quite fresh – it only arrived about thirty minutes ago. It was in her bed at The Swan Hotel on Monday night. She thought we wouldn't believe her so she felt compelled to send it in with her report.' Pete looked at Angie as he explained the arrival of such an unexpected item on their ARSE board (Assessor's Returned Special Exhibits).

'Well that's gotta win first prize this month. I must admit I didn't think we'd ever beat the sheet with the hole, but I think we just have.' The whole team of assessor coordinators giggled.

These were the patient individuals whose job was to source and allocate which mystery shopper was going to undertake what assessments, where and when and then chase them for their report afterwards. It was like herding sheep, spinning plates and painting the Forth Bridge all rolled into one.

Angie recalled the day she received a recorded delivery in the office a few weeks after she joined. Its contents were what'd started the ARSE board. One of their regular assessors had stayed at a 5* hotel in the centre of London and the sheet on his bed had a hole in it, so large that he could pull it over his head and body and down to the ground. He'd also sent a photo of himself performing this bizarre act.

'No, no no no!' Pete shouted above the raucous laughter, 'the toenail clippings in the sink in that hotel next to Heathrow Airport – that's got to beat the sheet with the hole!'

'I'd vote for the spider in the Caesar salad in that restaurant in Fulham, personally,' said David with a screwed-up face.

The whole team cackled at the memory of these precious items arriving in the office. Their job was difficult, to say the least, if not downright stressful at times. Anything that relieved the tension and pressure was most welcome.

Angie had worked for Sonny Global Mystery Shopping Ltd for a couple of years; ever since she'd left university. She saw an advert for a temporary job in a business that organised mystery shopping visits. It sounded intriguing, so she applied and, much to her amazement, was offered the job on the spot. She was unaware the directors had wanted her because they believed her Geography degree would be 'tremendously helpful' in the team. What they actually meant was, they thought she'd at least know that Aberdeen was north of Kingston upon Thames and that visiting Newcastle and Enfield Town on the same day was probably not realistic. Little did she know quite what she'd let herself in for.

Angie was single and suffered with bipolar, but she got the job done in her own inimitable style anyway. Her phone was already ringing as she walked towards her desk.

'Sonny Global, Angie speaking, how may I help you?'

'Oh hi there. My name is Dean De'Ath and erm… I'm just ringing to find out what my first mystery assignment is? You left a message on my voicemail to let me know my application had been successful and asked me to ring you today?'

'Oh yes. Hi, Dean. Welcome to the mad house – and congratulations! We don't take just anyone here, you know. You must've read our training manual very thoroughly. You got one hundred per cent in your test. No other assessor's ever done that. Bloody amazing.'

Dean was pleased, but laughed nervously.

Angie riffled through a heap of documents on her desk as she spoke.

'Right. Well, we desperately need a visit doing tonight. Someone just cancelled. Can you do that? You'll seriously be in our good books if you can.'

'Oh God, I wasn't expecting something quite so soon.

What would I have to do?' implying that there was a possibility that if it was too tough, he might refuse.

'It's not difficult, but you do need to have a good appetite,' Angie replied, intriguingly. 'You need to go to Nous Geraldine in Covent Garden with one other person and have drinks and dinner.'

'Oh! Well that sounds alright, I'm sure I can manage that,' Dean responded quickly and breezily. (Just in case they thought he was going to be unwilling or difficult and therefore not ask him to do anything else.)

'Well…yes and no,' said Angie with just a hint of mystery. 'The visit brief is very specific.'

'Sorry but I'm new to this, don't forget. What's a visit brief exactly?'

'Of course – sorry. It's what our client has specified they want you to do on your mystery assignment.'

'Oh, OK. So what's the visit brief for this dinner, then?' Dean asked with his usual healthy dose of wariness.

'OK, well I'll send this all to you in writing, but as you're a visit virgin, I'll run through it with you on the phone first and also what you've got to do afterwards.'

'Sounds good to me,' Dean offered more hopefully.

'So, you need to phone the restaurant and make a booking. Then the whole theme of this visit is assessing the staff's ability to upsell. They've been specifically trained to do this at various stages of the customer experience. So, when you arrive, they should offer you a Bellini cocktail. You mustn't ask for a drink, but wait to see if they do this.

Assuming you get offered one, you must drink it as quickly as possible to see if they offer you another.'

'But I'll be driving,' Dean interrupted with some alarm in his voice.

'OK, well not to worry then, we'll have to give the visit to someone else,' replied Angie in a matter-of-fact way.

'Hang on a minute. Let me see if I can get my wife to pick me up from the station. I'm sure she will,' Dean said eagerly.

'OK. Once you're seated, they should immediately offer you water – sparkling or still.' Angie clearly assumed he'd be going. She spoke at lightning speed and Dean had to concentrate hard to make sure he both heard and understood everything.

'You must order a bottle and drink it as quickly as possible to see if they offer you another bottle. Accept it if they do. Order just a main course with no sides to see if they try to persuade you to have a starter and dishes to go with your mains. Accept their recommendations of starter and side dishes. Don't order any wine. Just wait and see if they offer. If they do, just order a glass each, but if they try to sell you a bottle, you should accept. Drink this quickly so the staff have an opportunity to offer you another. Don't ask for dessert or coffee. Wait and see if you're offered this. Accept whatever they offer. Drink your coffee quickly to see if they offer you another. Note if they invite you to have a dessert wine, liqueur or a port with dessert.'

Jesus, slow down!

'Blimey, that's a lot of food and drink in one night!' Dean half joked.

'You'll be fine,' Angie stated confidently. 'After the visit, you write up your report and send it in within twenty-four hours. Any questions?'

'I don't want to seem disinterested, but I'm not sure. It's a lot to take in and I don't want to do anything wrong and let you down on my first assignment. Can you email it to me now, so I can have a read-through and check if there's anything I don't understand before going ahead?'

'OK, but you need to be speedy, because if you can't do it, I need to find someone else PDQ.'

'Right, well let's just say that *unless* you hear from me in the next half hour, assume it's all fine.'

'Great stuff. Thanks, you've gotten us out of a big hole tonight. Ring me tomorrow and let me know how you got on.'

With that, she hung up and Dean was left holding the phone and staring into it as though something was crawling out of it. He finally put it down.

How was he going to explain this to Brooke? She'd not be able to find a sitter for Paige at such short notice. Who on earth was he going to take with him? The visit had to be for two people. He suddenly realised he might've bitten off more than he could chew. He panicked. It was only 10am, he tried to reassure himself; he'd think of someone before the morning was out. His phone rang and he picked it up with his head a million miles away.

'What's all this about you getting a hot tub?'

'Martin! Thank god. Are you free tonight?'

Ha! What impeccable timing – Martin must have a sixth sense!

'That depends. Free for what?' asked Martin.

'I've gotta go out for dinner.'

'What do you mean *got* to go out for dinner? No-one's *got* to go out for dinner.'

'Well I do. Just say yes, mate, and I'll explain later. Should be some half decent grub, to be fair.'

'Well, as it happens, I'm doing sweet FA tonight so, yeah, I can go. Where?'

'Fantastic. Meet me at The Nag's Head in Covent Garden at six-thirty for a pint first and I'll explain what we've gotta do, but we're going to a place called Nous Geraldine. I'm late for a meeting now so I've gotta go. I'll see you later.'

'Sounds intriguing, mate. Yeah, see you later. Bye.'

Within a minute, Martin's phone started vibrating, notifying him of a message.

Don't mention this to Brooke for now – will explain later.

***

'That's Death for two people at 7pm?'

'No. It's De…Ath – two separate syllables,' replied Dean tersely.

Dean had read Angie's instructions multiple times before making the call and he still forgot to ask if they could have a seat overlooking the piazza. He ummed and ahed about calling back again but decided he'd just ask when they arrived.

As the afternoon wore on, Dean began to think more about the imminent mission he was soon to undertake. Being very conscientious, as well as a food lover, he started to look forward to it in a slightly nervous kind of way.

It got to 6pm and he started clearing his desk, writing his to-do list for the next morning, prioritising and deciding on anything that could be delegated – which wasn't anything as far as he could see. Delegation wasn't one of Dean's strong points; not helpful for an IT manager in a busy call centre.

At 6.30pm, on the dot, he arrived at The Nag's Head and spotted Martin sitting on a stool at the end of the bar with a pint in his hand; a common sight over the years he'd known him. Dean waved to him above the heads in the crowded bar. As soon as Martin saw him, he ordered Dean a pint from the disinterested barman.

By the time Dean had pushed and shoved his way through the crowd, it was too late to stop the pint. He knew what Martin didn't; that they were going to have more than enough drink tonight.

'Cheers!' Martin shouted as they clinked glasses. 'So, what's this all about then? It's all a bit mysterious!'

Dean glugged down half the pint, licked his lips and

laughed. 'Well, actually, that's exactly what it is, mate – mysterious.'

'What d'ya mean?' Martin screwed up his face.

'Tonight, you and me are going to do a mystery shop.' This was a declaration.

'What's that then?'

'Exactly what it says on the tin. We're gonna have dinner in Nous Geraldine round the corner, but none of the staff know why we're there. They just think we're two blokes having dinner. We've got to ask for and look out for very specific things, which are all written down in this questionnaire I've been given. Tomorrow I've got to write up a report about how it all went and then I get paid twenty quid, plus the cost of the meal is reimbursed.'

'How the hell d'ya end up getting to do that, then?' Martin asked, wide-eyed and with a hint of jealousy in his voice.

'I saw this ad in the *Evening Standard* for mystery shoppers who worked in the area and thought I'd give it a go.'

'Bloody 'ell, can I join?'

'This is the first time I've done it, so I don't even know how it works yet. Let's do this one and see how it goes.' Dean leaned forward confidentially and went on, 'The original reason I applied is that, as you well know, Brooke's been on about that fucking hot tub again and I thought I could earn a bit extra towards it. She's absolutely determined she's gonna get one. I can tell by the look on her face. It was dead embarrassing at the garden centre the other week. She dragged me round there just to show me and when I said no to her, she loudly offered to give me a blow job every night for a year. You should've seen this geezer next to us. He was laughing his bloody 'ead off.'

Martin had known Brooke since they were teenagers at the same secondary school. He'd always fancied her, but then so did all the other chaps. He was portly and had a skin complaint, so he had no hope! He just used to drool at her, which gave her the creeps and made his chances of a cheeky fondle even slimmer.

'Well I wouldn't hesitate,' said Martin matter-of-factly. 'I'd have signed on the dotted line there and then!'

'God, that's what he said! I do have bills to pay, you know. It's seven and a half grand!'

Martin thought seriously for a moment or two.

'Well if you have it for at least ten years that's only a couple of quid a blow job. That's good value, if you ask me. That's assuming she gives you one every day for ten years.'

'Yeah and pigs might fly! Do you know she actually threatened to get a job?'

'Ooooh – get a job? Well we can't have that, can we? Your precious Brooke actually having to work for a living? Like normal people? You treat that girl like she's made of bleedin' glass you do.' Martin took a gulp of his pint.

'*And* she said she'd withdraw my conjugal rights!'

'Oh blimey. Well *that's* well out of order, that is. You'll have no choice but to satisfy your manly urges elsewhere then!'

Dean ignored Martin's comments, looked at his watch and pulled out the questionnaire from his man-bag. He leaned over towards Martin and talked him through what they had to do. He felt like one of those spies who have to learn their legend. He had to have a plausible story of why they were having a meal, where he worked etc. – just in case the staff tried to engage him in conversation.

'Fuck me, that's a lot of food and drink,' Martin said.

'I know, that's what I said. Oh shit, that reminds me, I completely forgot to ring Brooke to tell her I'll be late. She's gonna have to pick me up from the station.'

He sent her a short message and then immediately put his phone on silent – one sure way she couldn't get hold of him to argue:

Gonna be late, babe. Going out with Martin. Will need u 2 pick me up at station later. Will ring u.

'Why don't you want her to know what you're doing?' Martin asked, surprised.

Dean thought long and hard before answering. Martin knew him so well and quickly gauged that whatever he was about to say might incriminate him. He shuffled from one foot to another awkwardly. He just couldn't hide his guilt, but then once a Catholic…

'Well,' Dean offered up cautiously, as if he weren't sure about whether to trust his trusted old friend. 'I soon realised the money I might get isn't exactly gonna contribute much to a hot tub, but…the company says they often have hotel visits, which involve an overnight stay—'

'You dirty little rat! I'll bet your manly urges'll be satisfied there!' Martin shrieked indiscreetly.

'No, no no – not what *you're* thinking,' Dean said defensively. 'It's just that every so often I'd love a break from always having to do Paige. The thought of being able to go to some posh hotel somewhere occasionally, with a spa and stuff and be paid to do it… Well, you can see what I mean? I just thought it might make a nice change and give me a bit of a break now and then.'

'I bet. I don't know how you do all that nappy changing shit. But you could still tell her – she could come with you.'

'You must be bloody joking. She'd get the right 'ump. Or even more likely, demand to take my place! So, I just thought that as I'm going for this promotion, I could tell her that I'm gonna be expected to go to more meetings and conferences away from home!'

'Right. Well. Your secret's safe with me, mate. For now, anyway!' Martin teased with an exaggerated wink.

Dean stood up, signalling they had to go or they'd be late for their booking. They both downed the rest of their pints and made their way out of the pub and over to the restaurant.

3

The Customer Journey at Nous Geraldine

Dean and Martin walked towards the restaurant looking around surreptitiously, like a couple of petty criminals.

Just as they reached the door, without warning, Dean put his hand over Martin's arm. 'Stop!'

'Why? What's the matter?'

'Are the window boxes attractive and well cared for?' Dean asked with concern.

Martin realised that the assessment had started. His head took on a slight lean to one side as he looked meaningfully at the evergreen plants in the window boxes. He frowned and moved closer to them for further inspection.

'I dunno – what do they mean "well cared for?" They're not dead. The leaves look pretty green to me and the mud looks wet.'

'Mud? Do you mean soil? Plants aren't put in mud, you idiot,' said Dean disdainfully.

'Well whatever. They look alright to me.'

'So that's probably a yes then,' said Dean as he and Martin stood staring, long and hard, at the window boxes, much to the amusement of the staff inside.

Dean realised they'd been observed looking at the window boxes and felt a mild rush of panic.

Not rumbled already – please!

He and Martin strutted through the doors and Dean noted that no-one had come to the door to open it for them.

That's a 'No', I'm guessing. Maybe we should've hung around outside a bit longer to give the staff a chance to open the door? God, this is hard.

'I like your window boxes, love,' Dean blurted out, trying to sound natural.

'Thank you. I'll tell the manager,' said the waitress with a wry smile. 'Do you have a reservation?'

'Yeah. Table for two at seven-thirty under the name of De'Ath.'

'Oh yeah, I see you right here,' she said as she ran her slender finger down the reservations page. Dean noted the small enamel flag pinned to her shirt underneath her name badge. 'Lena'. He recognised the flag as Poland. He'd been a flag boffin since he was seven, his mother having persuaded him it'd come in useful.

'Please, let me take you to your table.' She waved her hand, beckoning them to follow her. When they arrived at the table (happily overlooking the piazza), she asked if she could take their jackets, which they duly handed over.

They seated themselves at the table while she hung the jackets up. She returned and gave them a cloakroom ticket, followed by a menu.

'Can I get both of you one of our fabulous house Bellini cocktails to start?' she asked, the moment they took their menus.

Oh my God, thought Dean, *that's exactly what the visit brief says should happen.* And it also said that, *If one is offered, you have to accept.*

'Er. Yeah. That sounds bonza!' said Dean quickly.

Martin shot a look of wide-eyed horror over to him.

For a moment, Dean was torn between knowing that his best friend did not under any circumstances want a Bellini – he wanted a pint – and knowing he was meant to accept the invitation. This was awful! So much harder than he'd expected and they'd barely started. Well, he certainly wouldn't be bringing Martin again. He clearly needed someone submissive who'd assist him, not someone who was going to debate every instruction.

The waitress had been carefully examining the faces of both men during those moments and had come to the conclusion that she should just return with two Bellinis.

The second she left the 'in earshot' area, Martin challenged Dean as to why *he* had to have one.

'It's only *you* doing the mystery shop. Surely *I* don't have to live by the same rules?'

Dean thought about this and then tried to educate Martin in the ways of the mystery shopper, by which time the waitress had arrived at their table with the cocktails. She smiled an overly sweet smile and placed them on the table.

'Are you ready to order or would you like a few more minutes?'

Dean and Martin hadn't even looked at the menu and indicated so. She tersely offered to give them a few more minutes.

That's not good. We shouldn't be made to feel rushed.

As soon as she'd left the table, Dean chastised Martin and reminded him that he was there to help as a non-paying guest and as such he'd no right to complain about anything at all. He had to do precisely as Dean asked or he'd never ask him to do anything again. It then struck Dean that, considering Martin didn't want a Bellini, he'd practically downed the entire glass.

'OK, OK! Don't blow a gasket!' Martin was rather surprised at Dean's overly professional tone with him. 'I'll have whatever you want me to have – OK? So, what do I have to eat?'

'Whatever you like.'

They both stared grumpily at the menus and Lena soon returned with her notepad and pen, poised to take an order, looking decidedly unprepared to come back a second time. 'Are you ready yet?' she asked, this time with no smile.

She's not treating us in a friendly manner and she hasn't told us about the specials or made any recommendations either.

'What can you recommend?' asked Dean, putting on

his best work telephone voice.

'Well that depends what you are in the mood for eating. Fish? Meat? Vegetarian?'

'Mmm, I feel fish, I think.'

'The sea bass is good,' offered Lena in a voice devoid of any enthusiasm and without so much as a glance at him.

'OK, I'll have the sea bass then and a…' Dean suddenly stopped talking.

Shit! She's meant to suggest what side orders go best with the main course.

'A…erm…er…'

'New potatoes and kale would go well with that,' she finally proposed with a sigh.

'OK then, new potatoes and kale it is.' Dean felt relieved for her that she'd done what she was supposed to.

'What about a starter?'

The server should offer you a starter, you must select one and ask a question to test server's knowledge.

'Are the eggs in the eggs Benedict free range?' Dean enquired.

Lena looked stunned 'I have no idea. I'll have to go and find out.'

Dean and Martin looked over in unison to the kitchen door through which she disappeared.

'Why are you talking funny?' Martin sneered at Dean, knowing perfectly well why. Dean didn't bother replying.

The door swung open numerous times and they caught sight of a chef and Lena on their knees, peering at some boxes inside the door to the kitchen. A few moments later, they saw them arguing openly and loudly.

'What the hell are they doing in there?' Dean whispered in a perplexed tone. 'I only asked if the eggs were free range!'

Lena returned looking flustered and seemed reluctant to speak.

'So…are they free range or not?' Dean enquired.

'I'm sorry, sir, but I cannot say for sure.'

'Huh? How can you not be sure? They either are or they're not – surely?'

'Well, the chef insists that they are, but the boxes do not state they are free range, so I would not like to guarantee. Maybe you would like to choose something else?'

'No, don't worry, I'll risk it.'

Did the server have good product knowledge? That's got to be a no, but then again she did seem bothered and she did try to find out and maybe it was the chef who was lacking in product knowledge? Damn, it's a tough call.

She turned to Martin, raised her eyebrows and tilted her head upwards, as if to say 'And you? What do *you* want?'

Was the server's body language, demeanour and overall manner attentive and positive?

Dean couldn't decide. He thought she seemed rather stroppy and disinterested as he watched her take Martin's order. But then again, he thought maybe all Poles were a bit like that. He worked with one once – Piotr – who'd told Dean: 'We are a miserable nation and have no reason to smile.'

Bloody hell, this is hard.

'I'll have the same starter and that please, love,' Martin stated with glee, and, not knowing how to pronounce it, pointed at the Chateaubriand on the menu with a grin and an energetic rub of his hands. 'Lovely jubbly!'

'I'm sorry, sir, but that is for two people.' She merely stared at him in expectation, until he finally made up his mind on an alternative.

'Oh. That's a bugger. Well then, I'll just have the sirloin steak, medium–rare please.'

'OK, that's one sea bass with new potatoes and kale and one sirloin steak. Would you like some wine with your meal?'

If you're offered a bottle of wine, ask for a glass instead and see if they try to upsell you a bottle. If they do, you should accept.

'We'll just have a glass of house red each.' Dean replied in a sort of embarrassed tone, as though real men don't order just a glass of wine.

'You know it is better value to buy the whole bottle if you are thinking of having another glass later,' she confided.

'OK, well in that case, let's have a bottle then,' Dean responded rather too quickly.

'OK, good choice – and bottled water?'

That's good, she's meant to offer that. And I have to accept.

'Yes, sparkling please.'

'And can I get you another Bellini while you are waiting?'

Dean shocked himself as he became aware that, in a matter of minutes, he and Martin had almost finished the drinks, despite neither of them particularly even wanting one.

You should drink your Bellini quickly so the staff have an opportunity to sell you another.

'Yes, why not?'

'Great!' exclaimed Lena with a delighted smile. And off she trotted.

Bread! Where's the bread?

Dean panicked for the third time in an hour.

Am I meant to ask or is she meant to offer? Hell, I just can't remember.

Without a second thought, he bent down and rifled through his man-bag to get the visit brief.

'What you doin'?' asked Martin, laughing at Dean's panic-stricken face.

Dean explained that he couldn't recall some of the details of the brief and needed a quick look. Right on cue, Lena turned up with the second round of cocktails and the bottle of sparkling water.

Like someone in a cartoon, Dean saw her out the corner of his eye, immediately stopped rummaging and sat bolt upright, smashing his head on the table on the way up.

She completely ignored Dean's uninhibited cry, left the Bellinis on the table and walked off.

'Bloody 'ell, that hurt!' exclaimed Dean, rubbing his head. Martin laughed.

He had the hard copy of the questionnaire in his hand.

'I'm just gonna pop to the loo and check out where we are. I wanna make sure I haven't forgotten to do or ask anything. I'm desperate for a piss, anyway.' Dean was beginning to look a tad anxious and flustered.

Martin wasn't in the slightest bit concerned. But then he naturally didn't give a damn and never had. He proceeded to glug down his second cocktail.

A few minutes later, Dean came out having folded the questionnaire up small and shoved it in his pocket, giving his lower region a rather deformed appearance. When he got to the table, Martin stood up and declared that he too needed the lavatory.

You should drink the bottled water quickly to see if you're offered another.

Dean opened the bottle, poured himself a glass and downed it in one. He promptly forgot where he was and let out the most unfortunate burp – one of those right from the gut, that seems to go on for eternity.

Two immaculately dressed chaps, holding hands, on a neighbouring table both glanced over at Dean in disgust.

One was sporting a dark-green velvet suit and the other wore pointy grey shoes, which worried Dean. His mother had always said never to trust a man wearing grey shoes.

When Martin got back to the table, Dean poured him a large glass of water.

'Get that down your Gregory.'

'For Christ's sake, mate, I've already had two of them Bellini things and two pints, give us a break. I'll be pissing all night at this rate.'

'You must – we've got to give her the opportunity to sell us another bottle.' Dean explained.

Martin shook his head in disbelief. 'What're they trying to do to us? No normal human being could keep up this level of fluid intake!' He looked at the large glass of water and took a few gulps.

'More – quickly!' said Dean with a wry smile as he was beginning to see the funny side of the situation.

Suddenly Lena appeared at the table and picked up the now almost-empty bottle of water and smiled at them both.

'Would you like another?'

Oh God. I think I should be saying yes, but I really don't want another one. We'll end up just leaving it. What a waste of money!

If there's one thing Dean couldn't bear it was wasting anything. Brooke called him mean, but he really wasn't. There it was again. Once a Catholic…

Surely normal people don't order this much? It'll look

suspicious if I say yes. She'll realise we're mystery shoppers if we order another one.

'Is that a yes or no?' she finally blurted out, looking exasperated at Dean's seeming inability to make a decision about something so trivial.

'Erm…er.'

'No thanks, love,' Martin finally declared. 'We're alright.'

Well let's hope that's not a problem. She hasn't brought the bread and she should've brought it with the water. Make a complaint at some point during the meal to see how your server deals with it. This seems like as good a time as any.

Just as the waitress turned to leave the table, Dean took a deep breath, sat very upright, puffed out his chest and said in an unnaturally annoyed voice, 'Can't we have some bread around here? We've been here at least ten minutes and we haven't even been given bread!'

She looked aghast at this outburst from a man she'd originally written off as a wimp and a walkover. Dean retreated immediately back into his chair, like a teenager who suddenly realises that he's gone too far.

'I'm sorry, sir, I will get some for you straight away.' She rushed off.

Martin stared at Dean and scolded him for being a tad harsh. 'It's only bread, mate, we can wait.'

'That's not the point!' Dean said viciously between his teeth. 'If we don't follow this bloody brief to the letter, I won't get paid!'

Within seconds, the waitress arrived with bread and the wine which she placed carefully in the centre of the table and proceeded to open the bottle and pour wine in both glasses.

The server should show you the bottle label and ask you if you'd like to taste it. Oh dear, well she's not doing that. I don't mind not tasting it. I never do when me and Brooke go out. Is that even relevant though? I dunno. Aaaaaaargh!

Martin raised his glass, by now ever so slightly tipsy. 'Cheers, mate! Thanks for inviting me – this is gonna be a right laugh!'

Dean smiled nervously. He looked at it, sniffed it, swirled it and finally sipped it. Then he took a large mouthful, theatrically swirled it round in his mouth and sucked it through his teeth before finally swallowing and licking his lips hard and loud. 'Great vintage!'

In unison, velvet man and grey shoe man threw another disdainful look, but swiftly went back to their clearly intimate conversation, as if they merely wanted their disgust to be registered.

Martin and Dean chatted away, mostly about a strategy for coping with the possible withdrawal of his conjugal rights. The restaurant began to fill up, making it feel less like an assignment and more like a night out. The booze made it surprisingly easy for Dean to forget that he had a job to do. Within a matter of minutes, he'd taken his eye off the ball and all sorts of undesirable behaviours and service errors were happening all around him without him even noticing.

Lena finally arrived with two plates of eggs Benedict and placed them down carelessly on the table, making one of Dean's eggs slide right to the very edge of the plate.

How many minutes did you wait between the server taking your order and receiving your starter? Oh damn, I should've checked my watch when she took the order. I haven't got a clue when that was.

'Martin, how many minutes ago do you reckon she took our order?'

'I dunno; five?'

'No must be more than that – must be at least ten or fifteen.'

For some inexplicable reason they both put down their cutlery and looked at their watches – as though this act would make it clear to them how long they'd been waiting. Lena was over like a shot.

'Is everything alright, sir?' she asked anxiously.

Oh shit, she knows. That was just too quick and caring. It's not normal for people to look at their watches during a meal. We must look so bloody suspicious. What can I say to put her off the scent?

'Yeah fine, thanks. We were thinking about the football score – West Ham are playing and it's half time.'

'Up the 'ammers!' shouted Martin, pumping his fist in the air to try and help. Dean glowered at him.

Lena smiled sweetly, nodded and left them to it.

'Fucking genius, mate! I'd never have thought of that.'

Martin roared laughing.

'God, this is so stressful. There's so much to remember and so much to keep your eye on. I can't believe how hard it is. I don't want to mess up on my first visit, they might not give me another one.'

They tucked into their starters and rapidly finished the wine in their glass.

'We need to see if she comes and offers us another bottle,' Dean whispered. This time, Martin picked up the bottle of wine and filled their over-large glasses until there was no more wine left in the bottle. He banged it purposefully on the table.

They sat gawping at Lena as she moved swiftly, clearing tables.

'Out of two, I'd give 'er one!' said Martin as he winked at Dean, who closed his eyes and recalled their lads' holiday in Torremolinos.

She finally realised they were staring at her and hurried towards their table.

'Yes? Can I get you something?'

They both continued to stare at her with silly smiles. They were waiting for the offer. She looked from one to the other and then to the contents of the table.

'Oh, I'm sorry, would you like another bottle of wine?'

If you're offered a second bottle of wine, you should accept.

'Is the pope Catholic?' Dean asked before bursting out laughing.

Lena just gawped at them for a moment, waiting for further clarification. None came. 'Yes, of course he is, but I'm sorry I do not understand.'

Martin and Dean looked at each other and exploded into an uncontrollable fit of giggles at their cultural faux pas, as the confused waitress looked on in utter incomprehension.

'Would you like another bottle?' she repeated, slightly irritated.

Dean pulled himself together and answered politely: 'Yes, thank you.' He carried on sniggering with Martin.

Lena wandered off, shaking her head. She returned looking slightly anxious this time and offered the wine for tasting. Dean waved his hand dismissively and said that was unnecessary. She poured wine again into two glasses, smiled a false smile and left them to it.

'I need a slash,' said Martin suddenly.

'Me too.'

Then, like a couple of schoolgirls, they shuffled through the now-crowded restaurant together to visit the lavatory.

A few minutes later, Lena glanced over at the table. Her face sank as she clocked the empty chairs. Her eyes, wide and manic, rapidly scanned the restaurant and then over to the door. No sign of them.

She ran to the entrance and was about to run out into the street, when she noticed the jackets she'd taken still hanging on the coat stand by the exit. She breathed a huge sigh of relief and put her hand to her heart. Once bitten, twice shy.

When Martin and Dean returned to their table, their starters had been cleared and they started on their second bottle of wine. Dean leaned over and whispered loudly, slowly and with obvious amusement to Martin. 'Do you realise we've had four pints, four Bellinis and a bottle of wine between us already?'

The world was beginning to appear to them in slow motion. The sounds in the restaurant seemed to go from a sort of dampened crashing to echoing banging.

Finally their main courses were brought over. They were so bloated by this time that the food really didn't appeal too much, but Dean diligently persevered.

Did the server give the correct food to the correct person?

When Dean looked, it was all correct. He was glad. He wasn't in the mood for kicking up a fuss. In fact, he felt a tad nauseous and was rather hoping it wouldn't take too much longer as he'd quite like to go home.

He ate his main slowly with just a fork, as though it were a TV dinner that didn't require much more than shovelling it in – sort of getting it where it needed to be without any thought or consideration of its flavour along the way.

Was your food tasty, the correct temperature and presented attractively?

Hell, how did my sea bass look when it arrived? I can't

remember and I've eaten most of it now.

'What's the matter, mate?' Martin asked, looking mildly concerned.

'Would you say your food was attractively presented?'

Martin looked down at his half-eaten sirloin and tipped his head to one side and then the other, as if this in some way was going to remind him of what it looked like when it was first put down in front of him. 'It was alright. It's just a steak. How attractive can a steak look?'

Dean looked up to the ceiling and screwed up his nose to help him decide whether this was a fair and accurate comment.

Come on, Dean, for God's sake. What would it have had to look like on the plate for it to be any more attractive? Garnished? Vegetables on the plate instead of in a side dish? Oh Christ, I dunno.

Dean started eating more quickly.

'I need to go to the loo again, Martin.'

'What?' Martin exclaimed. 'You've only just been!'

'Yeah, but not actually for a slash – to write some notes. I'm beginning to forget some stuff. I need to get it out of my head and onto paper.'

He proceeded to get up clumsily and dashed out to the toilet. Velvet man glanced over, tutted and shook his head.

In the lavatory, Dean took some moments to prise the folded-up questionnaire out of his pocket and to flatten it out near the sinks, so he could read it and write on it.

Instead, he soaked it in a coagulated mess of liquid soap and water.

'Oh shit!' He waved it around vigorously to try and shake the water off. In so doing, it escaped through his fingers and flew towards the urinals and onto the floor. He reluctantly bent down to retrieve it from the stinking pool of urine in which it now rested.

The door opened and in walked grey shoe man, who stopped in his tracks, as he clearly struggled to decide what to do about the vision in front of him. Dean leaped up and felt compelled to explain his somewhat bizarre position. 'I dropped something,' he offered by way of explanation, as he continued to shake the questionnaire and half-heartedly push it towards the man.

'So it would appear,' the man said snootily as he navigated around him, like Dean had some sort of contagious disease.

Mortified, Dean moved into an enclosed toilet. He sat on the seat and tried to flatten out the damp, crumpled document onto his lap and find his place on the visit questionnaire. He found it and began to transfer what he had in his head onto the paper. The letters he formed using his Berol liner pen soon resembled ink on blotting paper – the blue colour spreading slowly across the page so the words became almost illegible.

'For fuck's sake!' Dean exclaimed through gritted teeth in sheer frustration.

Grey shoe man looked sideways with a frown and a

curled lip, revolted. Behind, Dean was still mumbling all manner of curses as he tried desperately to read what he'd written and read the questions he'd yet to answer. After washing his hands, grey shoe man shook his head and walked out

Dean did his best in his semi-inebriated state and eventually appeared back in the restaurant and returned to the table leaving a faint whiff of stale urine in his wake. On sitting down, he looked intently at Martin, then buried his head in his hands and looked like he was about to break some seriously bad news.

'What's the matter now?' Martin asked with some impatience. He knew his friend well and Martin was always telling Dean to 'lighten up' and not get so worried about things.

'Oh, mate, it's a right bloody mess. I dropped the questionnaire in the loo and now I can hardly read it.' Dean ran his hands through his hair.

'Stop worrying, mate; it'll be fine. We'll remember it. What's next?'

'Well, we need to wait and see if they ask us if we want pudding,' Dean said wearily.

Just then, Lena came over and cleared the table, looking discreetly at Dean and Martin, to see if they were still in that strange mood.

They waited for her to return and offer them a dessert they didn't want. Crème caramel was their choice as it was the least filling of everything on the menu. They were also offered and ordered coffee, which arrived before the dessert. This confused Dean, but he couldn't remember whether it was meant to be delivered before or after – or maybe even with dessert. He racked his brains but simply couldn't recall.

He and Martin just stared at the crème caramel. To anyone watching, it'd have appeared that there was immediately and obviously something terribly wrong with it; the look of resignation on their faces and the way they blew air out from their mouth through pursed lips – a bit like people do when they're facing a truly daunting task.

Dean picked up a spoon and instead of eating his dessert, he prodded it, moved the plate three hundred and sixty degrees, lifted it up on the tip of the spoon and looked underneath it, in the way that children do when they're examining a new food presented to them and deciding whether they're going to eat it or not. Lena was immediately back over.

'Is there something wrong with your dessert, sir?' she enquired with a worried look.

Martin replied. ''s fine.' He then proceeded to scoff the whole thing down in under ten seconds.

Dean watched him, astounded that he seemed so able to swallow – never mind digest – more food. Lena walked away, quite clearly not entirely satisfied with Martin's answer. The cappuccinos sat untouched on the side and the froth got less frothy as the minutes went on and stuck to the side of the cup.

By this time, Martin and Dean had stopped conversing. They couldn't face the coffee and Dean finally caught Lena's eye and made that universally known air sign for the bill.

Are they meant to bring it without asking, or are they not supposed to bring it until I've asked for it? Oh well, it's a bit bloody late now.

Lena nodded and, within a matter of minutes, brought the bill with a beaming smile .

'Did you enjoy your meal, gentlemen?' she enquired, ensuring piercing eye contact with Dean.

There were no flies on that girl!

'Yep. Great.'

Do I leave a tip? Maybe service is included?

Dean put his glasses on and looked at the blurred bill on the table in front of him. The letters and numbers seemed to be dancing all over it for some reason. He realised he wasn't sufficiently compos mentis to go through the bill in detail to check it was correct.

He put his hand in his pocket but couldn't manage to pull out his wallet. He made several attempts, but it was as though it was stuck to his pocket's inside lining. Dean looked at Lena looking at him and winked at her with a fixed grin on his face. She waited patiently, all the time staring at him.

'Do you do extras?' Martin sniggered as he undressed her with his eyes – down and up, up and down. Dean slapped him on the arm and told him off for being so uncouth. He paid the bill with a credit card and finally left a twenty-pound tip – it was all the cash he had.

In her native Poland, Lena was an architect. Newly qualified and smart. She'd been unable to secure a job so had come to the UK, ostensibly to improve her English. She'd ended up at Nous Geraldine, which had been an eye-opening experience. Too many times she'd seen City boys this drunk. Many times she'd smiled sweetly in order to secure a good tip, when all she actually wanted to do was inflict pain to their private parts for treating the waiting staff with such a lack of respect.

She tersely thanked Dean, quickly processed the bill and left them to get their act together before clearing their table for the last time.

Dickheads.

Dean and Martin swayed from side to side as they exited the restaurant, both tripping up over the small step on the way out.

4

The Aftermath

'WHY DIDN'T YOU ANSWER MY MESSAGES? HOW CAN YOU DO THIS TO ME, DEAN? I've had to wake Paige up to come and get you. I still don't understand why you couldn't get a bloody taxi from the station?'

'Sorry, my phone was on silent. I had no money.' Dean groaned and, looking green, proceeded to throw up spectacularly over the bonnet. Brooke got out, her face screwed up with contempt, then carefully looked around to see if anyone else had witnessed this shameful incident. She showed not one ounce of compassion or empathy and ran around to the bonnet, waited until he'd finished vomiting and then hit him rather pathetically several times over his upper arms, with alternate fists, palms first, as women often do, leaving him embarrassed as opposed to physically damaged in any way. A couple of chaps nearby were laughing at him and one shouted out, 'That was me last week, mate! Don't worry, she'll get over it!'

Dean didn't have the strength to argue or defend himself, so, once he'd finished and wiped away the regurgitated sea bass with his sleeve, like any man in the dog house, he bowed his head and crawled into the car. For the next six minutes, Brooke sounded like a howling banshee. He hadn't a clue what she was saying and he really didn't care.

When they arrived home, Brooke left Dean to fend for himself in the car.

Sometime later, he opened the car door, hung his head out over the bumper and threw up again over the drive, before deciding he needed to get inside. In his inebriated state he staggered to the front door, barely able to get his key in the lock. He teetered straight into the lounge and toppled onto the white leather sofa.

There he stayed for the next five hours.

At 6am, Dean's alarm went off. It seemed the cruellest sound imaginable. He fumbled around to find his phone and was physically shaking as he struggled to swipe the alarm off. Predictably under the circumstances, he fell straight back to sleep, until two hours later when Brooke came downstairs and barked at him that he'd be late for work. He ignored her and went back to sleep.

At 9.30am, his mobile rang. Disoriented, he picked it up with a rough 'hello'.

'Dean. Where are you? You're meant to be at the brainstorming session at nine o'clock?' Brian from the office sounded concerned but annoyed.

When Dean realised the time, he leaped up, but tried overly hard to sound serious. 'Oh sorry, something came up at home and I'm afraid I just had to stay here – I'll be with you in an hour, I promise,' he said apologetically. 'Start without me and I'll join you as soon as I get in.'

Just then a message came through from Martin saying he thought he had food poisoning and did Dean feel bad too? Dean ignored it, collapsed back onto the sofa and threw his phone to the side. He sat on the edge of the cushion, buried his head in his hands and tried to muster up the wherewithal to shower and change.

The front door opened and in stomped Brooke with eyes of steel and a hump as huge as Quasimodo himself. The house phone rang and Brooke answered. Dean was having difficulty pulling himself together and was only vaguely aware that she was talking to someone.

'It's for you,' she said abruptly and walked off, turning around before she got to the kitchen to say, 'Don't you forget that we're going round Sharon and Dave's for tea tonight. And, by the way, you stink.'

'Hello?' Dean had no idea who'd be calling him on his house phone at this time of the morning midweek.

'Hi, Dean. This is Angie from Sonny Global, I just wanted to check that you did your visit to Nous Geraldine last night?'

'Ohh…er …yes I did.'

'Great. Well, just to remind you that we need your report by the end of today.'

Oh fuck. Where are my notes?

'Yeah…no problem.' He fumbled around in his trouser pocket and retrieved a wet, smelly, virtually illegible bunch of notes.

Well at least it's something.

Dean barely managed to perform his ablutions and get dressed. Tentatively he looked about for Brooke and found her in the conservatory reading *Hello!*

'I'm sorry, Brooke,' he offered. 'Me and Martin had a bit too much to drink last night and I ran out of money so I couldn't get a cab.' Silence. 'Look, my moped's stuck at the station and I'm really late for a meeting.'

She didn't move, but carried on apparently digesting the details of Victoria Beckham's in-growing toenail operation.

'*Please* can you take me?' As he slid over to her, she turned her cheek away but let him kiss it gently, looking full of remorse as he did so.

She'll come round – she always does.

Brooke let the magazine fall to her lap.

She hated it when Dean got drunk, although she herself was not always blame-free in this regard!

'Got no choice, have I?'

She drove him to the station in silence.

***

Dean pretended to walk assertively into the brainstorming session, despite still feeling nauseous, but the team had finished. They all just stared at him as Chloe declared, 'Too late, we're brainstormed out! We're going for a coffee;

come and join us and we'll update you on where we've got to.' She gave Dean a knowing wink, which momentarily threw him, then he remembered that he'd told her he was doing the mystery shop. He forced a smile and tried to convey that he was grateful for her discretion in front of the team.

For the rest of the morning, Dean hunkered down in a side meeting room to give himself the time he needed to recover. But he was anxious about the completion of the questionnaire, especially given the illegibility of his notes. He knew that he had to write it up ASAP before he forgot the details. In fact, he was very concerned that he already had. He fretted as he began to think about the visit. Did they really have to drink that much? Did he remember to ask all the right questions and do all the right things? His heart started pumping as he thought about the two hundred pound bill. He really needed to check that and get the questionnaire completed ASAP. He only had five and a half hours to hand it in.

As soon as he could take lunch, he disappeared to the park near the office, where staff often retreated when they needed a break from customers unable to stop their stairlift going up and down. He sat on a bench and picked up his phone. Brooke had called a couple of times but left no message. He knew that if he got involved in a call with Brooke, he'd not get a chance to do the questionnaire, so he just ignored it.

Even after spending his lunch hour deciphering his

notes and racking his brains to remember whether Lena helped them on with their coats when they left, he didn't quite complete every section of the questionnaire. He'd have to check a few things with Martin to see if he recalled some of the finer details.

Suddenly Dean checked the time on his watch – a fake gold Rolex given to him the previous year by Brooke for his thirtieth birthday. Brooke would get upset if he didn't wear it, so he accepted it as part of his 'uniform' for work. It was just over an hour since he left the office, so he jogged back, the near-completed questionnaire flapping precariously as he went. He felt much better after some fresh air, but hadn't been able to face any food. As soon as he sat down, his stomach made a loud gurgling noise indicating it needed feeding. Martha looked over at him and raised her eyebrows. Dean apologised and explained he was hungry. 'But you've only just been out for lunch, Dean. Didn't you eat anything?'

'Long story but, no, I didn't. If you're going out, you couldn't get me an egg and cress sarnie, could you? But only if you're going to Pret?' Pret appealed to his sense of perfection – the fillings always spread evenly and fully right up to the edges of the bread on all sides. This gave him a real sense of satisfaction. He was exactly the same with scones.

Martha smiled and returned half an hour later with his sandwich, which he nibbled in small sections, rather than take his usual four mouthfuls. She'd worked with him for years and knew him very well. Something was definitely wrong with Dean, nibbling like that.

As the afternoon drew on, Dean looked forward to getting home and going to bed. He'd three hours fifteen minutes left to finish his questionnaire and decided he'd do it on the train on the way home. As soon as his team had gone, he left the office. On the train, however, the chugging proved too soporific for Dean and within minutes he was kipping.

'This train will shortly be arriving at Brentwood. Please take all your belongings with you!'

As the train drew into the station and the doors opening made that ubiquitous sound 'beep beep beep beep', Dean leaped up with a start and shot a look outside.

Shit shit shit!

He ran towards the door, but his sprint was so out of control he nosedived and crashed face down onto the floor right in front of the doors, which began to close in front of his eyes. All he could see in front of him on the other side, was a hairy par of legs topped off with a disgracefully tight pair of Lycra cycle shorts. Dean was vaguely aware that arms (presumably belonging to the legs) were holding the doors apart for him. 'Hurry up!' Lycra man shouted impatiently. Dean simply couldn't make it to his feet, so Lycra man gave up and let the doors go, trapping Dean inside the carriage.

Now I'm up shit creek without a paddle!

He could either ring Brooke to come and collect him

at the next station or cross over to the other side and catch the next train going back. He dithered as he pulled out his phone. Unable to decide what to do for the best, he glanced at the screen on his phone and noticed he had seven missed calls from Brooke.

Oh Christ, my phone's been on silent since lunchtime! She'll kill me.

He traipsed over to the platform on the other side and waited twenty-five minutes for the next train back. He dreaded explaining to Brooke why he'd not answered her calls. She hated it when Dean didn't ring her back within the hour. She put an inexplicable correlation between how long it took him to reply to her messages and how much he loved her.

He decided to leave his phone on silent and claim he'd forgotten to turn it back on after his meeting. As he walked up to the front door, it opened and Brooke was standing there with Paige in her arms screaming her little lungs out.

'Where have you been and why haven't you answered my calls? What's got into you? You'd better hurry up because Sharon and Dave are expecting us in half an hour and you need to get changed.' This wasn't a request but an instruction.

'Oh my God!' Dean let slip out. 'I've got some paperwork that I've absolutely gotta do first, babe.'

'Why didn't you ring me? I bet you haven't picked up my message to bring some M&S Prosecco back with you, have you?' It wasn't really a question so much as an accusation.

'What paperwork anyway? You never do paperwork!' Brooke didn't wait for an answer. 'Well you'll have to do it later; I don't wanna be late.'

Dean was worried he couldn't survive another late night, so he had one of his worm-turning moments and shouted back, 'Brooke, I *can't* come until I've done it. Now then. You go on without me and I'll meet you there.'

Brooke was taken aback at Dean's rare display of assertiveness but she was furious, nevertheless. She stormed outside, slamming the front door along the way, tucked Paige up in her car seat and wheel span out the drive. Trouble with a capital T!

Dean knew he'd have to focus for just enough time to complete his questionnaire and then he'd think up something wonderful for Brooke so that she'd forgive him. He delved into his jacket pocket, but there was no sign of it, he felt inside both pockets of his trousers. Nothing. He went to look in his man-bag. Where was his man-bag? Dean was sure he brought it with him when he left the office. He mentally retraced his steps.

Oh shit!

He remembered placing it on the overhead luggage rack.

Oh shit!

His man-bag and the questionnaire were now almost certainly sitting on a train somewhere in Shenfield.

Dean began to wonder what he'd done to deserve

all this. He tried to telephone the station, but there was no option button for what he wanted. He couldn't even leave a message. All options kept informing him to go on their website and leave details of his lost property there. He slammed the phone down in utter frustration and shouted up to the heavens, 'I JUST WANT MY FUCKING QUESTIONNAIRE BACK!' No reply.

Dean sat for a few minutes before finally deciding to ring Sonny Global and come clean.

'Well you won't get paid and, depending on the quality of the report, the client may not reimburse your expenses, so let's hope it's a good report when we do get it and then they might pay. Not a great start to your mystery shopping career though, is it, Dean?' Angie said somewhat patronisingly. He'd liked her the first time he spoke to her. He wasn't so sure now.

Well at least they didn't say I couldn't do any more visits.

He vowed he'd not get drunk like that again and talked sternly to himself as he got changed. As he sped round to Sharon and Dave's house, he just prayed that someone had handed in his man-bag.

***

At 9am sharp the next day, Dean rang the lost property number. This time there was a human being, not a nine-option answering machine. He was relieved and immediately went on to explain his predicament.

''ang on,' came the nonchalant reply.

The wait was agonising and Dean felt rather sick.

'Yeah, it's here. You'll have to come and collect it within the next twenty-four hours and there's a three pound charge.'

The relief swept over Dean in a slow motion wave. Now all he had to do was work out when and how he could go to Shenfield. He did the only thing he knew would persuade Brooke to pick it up; promised a nice meal out, but she still berated him, reminding him what an idiot he was. He agreed to it all, apologised again and said he'd make it up to her. He just prayed she wouldn't go rifling through his bag.

As soon as he got to work, he asked Brian if he could 'work from home this afternoon to type up some reports'. The company allowed senior people to take work home if they thought they could do it more productively there than they could in the office. In light of his missing the brainstorming meeting, he was relieved to be given the thumbs up and so, at lunchtime, he found himself on the train back home.

When he got back, the car wasn't in the drive so he knew Brooke wasn't at home, although he didn't know where she was. His pungent bag was on the kitchen table and the questionnaire safely inside. He hurried to type in the last of his wretched notes online.

Within half an hour he'd completed it and telephoned

Angie at Sonny to inform her. He repeated his grovelling apology for what'd happened and the subsequent tardiness of his report. He asked her to advise if it was satisfactory. Being a rookie and not wanting to spoil his chances of further visits, he was most anxious to get it right.

'OK, Dean, I'll ring you if we've got any queries and once I've processed the data.' Angie seemed back to being all best chums again now. He couldn't make her out.

Within the hour, she'd rung him back and wanted to know how many minutes passed between them asking for the bill and them receiving it. Dean racked his brains yet again, but had to confess that he'd failed to observe for this critical piece of information but said it didn't seem very long at all.

'Mmmm. OK, well, we'll have to hazard a guess – five minutes?'

'Oh no, much quicker than that.'

'Under a minute?'

'No. Definitely more than that.'

Angie snapped. 'Right, let's say two minutes. The rest of the report was very comprehensive though – especially since you're a mystery shopping virgin. Well done! We usually have lots more problems and queries with the Nous Geraldine reports…how's your bladder?' The question was spoken with just a hint of a smile in her voice.

'What?'

It suddenly dawned on Dean that they'd sent him on a known difficult assessment; they knew exactly the challenges that sort of visit put on the poor unsuspecting assessor!

What a bunch of bastards!

'Ah, so it wasn't my imagination then, we really did have to drink all that stuff? You've no idea how much trouble I got into with my wife!'

'Oh dear! Well we'll try to make it up to you – and her! How do you fancy a hotel visit?' Angie was back into 'let's get down to business mode' and suddenly started speaking at machine gun speed.

'You could take her on that! We've got a nice one coming up. Client is very particular though. Gotta be done by the end of next week. What d'ya reckon?'

Dean was surprised they were offering him something else again so soon, especially given his less-than-perfect first visit. But a hotel visit? Now that sounded fun – well less stressful anyway. If only he knew!

He was pondering her invitation and wondering whether there was payment for this one. Chloe's words were ringing in his ears '*they don't pay you enough to buy a hot tub*' when she said impatiently, 'So come on, Dean, do you want to do it or not? Trust me, we've got assessors lining up waiting for this one!'

The trouble was, Dean didn't trust her. 'Do we get paid for doing this one?'

'You must be joking. I've been offered bribes by one assessor to allocate it to them!'

'Mmm. So which hotel and where is it?'

'It's The Hempel in Paddington. It's a mid-week visit.'

Dean had never heard of it, but reckoned that if an assessor was prepared to offer an inducement to do it, it must be worth doing.

'OK. Please can you send me the brief ASAP? I'd like more time to look over this one.'

'Blimey, you are conscientious. Yeah, I'll email it to you right now.'

She was spot on. Dean was very conscientious. He always had been; even as a young child. Punctuality was in his DNA and, well, if a job's worth doing and all that…

The call came to an end, with Dean beginning to feel a bit nervous about what he'd just let himself in for. Then he reminded himself that this was one of the main reasons he signed up. Peace and quiet!

But then it'd been offered as a kind gesture by Angie so he could take his wife – to make up for the Nous Geraldine night.

What to do?

He tried to persuade himself that Brooke probably wouldn't want to go anyway; it'd be difficult with Paige, and on a weekday, and the additional expense of her coming up to London, there'd be no point would there?

Just then Dean's mobile went off. It was Martin.

'Mate. Where have you been? Why haven't you answered my calls or messages?'

Dean didn't need this. It was like listening to a male version of Brooke.

'I've been so bloody ill – throwing up for the past twenty-four hours or more and I've never had diarrhoea like it. Worst bout of food poisoning I've ever had. Haven't you been ill too?'

'Yeah, but let's face it, Martin, it's not food poisoning, we got seriously hammered.'

'Well you might've been; you only have to look at a glass of wine and you're pissed. I definitely got food poisoning. Anyway, can you and Brooke come over to ours for a BBQ next weekend?'

Dean had to stop and think when he had to do the visit again. It'd be much more fun with Martin. But that would be most undesirable – they might have to share a bed. Dean shuddered at the thought of snuggling up to a fart machine. He decided to wait for the visit brief, see what he had to do and then decide who to take.

'No, I think we're going to Jackie and Rick's, sorry, but let me check with Her Ladyship and I'll let you know. You're not alone in being ill though, mate. I threw up all over the car bonnet. Brooke went mad! D'ya know she even hit me in front of a couple of blokes in the car park?! So bloody embarrassing.'

Dean then went on to describe the series of unfortunate events with the questionnaire. Martin found the entire thing extremely amusing and Dean became irritated at his lack of empathy.

As soon as their call was over, Dean googled The Hempel. As he clicked from one page to the next, it was as if he'd been transported to some paradisaical world.

Fuck me! How can I not bring Brooke here? She'd die to come to this place. Seven hundred and fifty quid a night?! Oh my God.

And there began The Hempel dilemma.

5

Desperate Measures

'Well fifteen pounds per hour is terribly expensive; significantly above market rate. No-one else is charging anything like that.'

Letitia Townsend tilted her chin up as she spoke into the phone, with an air of dismissal.

In her early seventies and no more than five foot tall, she was slim and dressed elegantly in a DVF pink linen shift dress and flat open-toe leopard-print sandals. Her nails, makeup and simple grey bob were understated and her whole demeanour reeked of old money. She spoke with an affected voice, which many would describe as condescending or patronising. But she didn't mean it to be. It was just the way she'd been trained.

'But I'm not like anyone else. I'm as fast as hell. If ever you're not happy I'll leave and you won't have to pay me a penny. I'll even do a trial day for free. There. I can't say fairer than that. What d'ya say?' Brooke grimaced as she prostituted herself.

'Well, I'd like to meet you in person first. I need someone honest, discreet and flexible. I think you need to see the house and make sure that you're comfortable with everything that'll be expected of you.'

'No worries. How about tomorrow morning?'

'Alright, let's say eleven o'clock, by which time I'll be back from riding. When you arrive at the front gate, press the buzzer, announce yourself and someone will let you in. Drive up to the main house and park just to the right in the staff car park. It's signposted. If you have a sat nav, the postcode is CM13 3JF and the house is called Purses.'

Bloody hell – staff car park? How many staff does she have? What do they all do?

'OK. See you then. Oh…er…do I need to bring anything with me?'

'No, but if you've any references, that'd be most helpful. OK, I look forward to meeting you tomorrow.'

Brooke said goodbye, put the phone down and bit her lip as she stared at the ground for a moment. She let out a deep sigh. Was this really what she wanted? Had it really come to this?

***

'Well how long are you going to be?' demanded Dawn

'I'm not sure, but no longer than an hour I reckon. Please, Dawn, I'm desperate.'

'Well where are you going? What's this all about? You're not having an affair, are you?'

'Don't be so bloody daft. Course I'm not. I promise

I'll tell you when I get back. I really can't be late.'

Without further discussion, Brooke unceremoniously dumped Paige in Dawn's arms, with her nappy bag and a bottle of milk.

'Thanks a million, Dawn – I owe you. Love ya!'

She ran as quickly as her stilettos would carry her back into her car and sped away, leaving Dawn still at the doorstep holding the baby and wondering what on earth she'd let herself in for. Although her friend, Brooke was always one to push her luck. Dawn was a sort of ad hoc unofficial child minder and Brooke always used her when she needed to leave Paige with anyone. She trusted her implicitly and knew she would do whatever Brooke asked of her – except when she'd had too much to drink that is. Cider by the pint was her tipple of choice. Dawn's own children were a bit older so did not need quite the same level of supervision as a one year old. Dawn's husband Shane had left her last year and she was having to raise all three of her children on her own. Shane had the children three weekends in four so she could do some shifts at the Harvester to earn a bit of extra cash. Brooke admired her. She was in awe of her 'can do' attitude in the face of so much heartache and difficulty. Dawn was a good few years older than Brooke, who hoped that she would cope with any adversity she might suffer in the future as admirably as her friend.

As Brooke pulled up at the grand wrought-iron front gates of Purses, her heart sank. She was looking at *the* most beautiful house she'd ever seen; well, for around these parts anyway.

How can I possibly drive my shitty old car through those gates and park in there?

She couldn't do it. She drove a few metres past the entrance, parked Edna further up Warley Road and walked back down to the gates.

She stood transfixed and scared; on the outside looking in. She took a deep breath and pressed the buzzer.

'Hello…er… I'm here to see Letitia Townsend?'

'And who are you?' came back the rather gruff and unfriendly reply.

'Oh sorry. I'm Brooke.'

'Brooke who?'

Brooke rolled her eyes. 'Brooke De'Ath.'

'Ah yes, Lady Townsend is expecting you.'

Oh shit! She's a Lady. I thought she sounded a bit posh.

The gates slowly drew back inside.

Brooke waited until they were fully open before stepping over the threshold, heart thumping loudly in her chest. She was sure it could be heard a mile off.

She took her time, taking in the glorious gardens. The gravel beneath her feet crunched as she ventured her way up towards the main house, wobbling slightly in her heels. Purses was magnificent. The space around it and the sheer size of the frontage filled her with awe. She admired the vast oak front door, the brass knocker and bell and she even recognised the beautiful lantern hanging from the storm porch as a Jim Lawrence original.

She glanced over to the staff car park. In it were a couple of Range Rovers, a Nissan truck and an Audi A3. In another, sectioned-off car park nearby was a clapped-out old Ford Fiesta, which looked as out of place as a Porsche on a council estate.

Thank God I didn't bring Edna in here.

As she walked towards the front door, it opened and a man in his thirties came out.

'Hi, you must be Brooke. I'm Hugo.' He put his hand out to shake the three limp fingers she offered. This didn't seem to be the same grumpy person who'd answered the buzzer. Brooke was uncharacteristically nervous.

'Oh hi. I'm here to see Letitia…er…Lady Townsend?' She appeared and sounded unsure.

'She won't want you to call her that. She prefers Mrs Townsend,' he offered helpfully.

'Ah. Right. Thanks for that.'

She was then led through the black and white tiled chequered hall, where her stilettos click-clacked painfully loudly, and into a large and exquisitely decorated drawing room. She gasped as she noticed the huge swags and drapes at every window.

They must've cost thousands.

There was a stunning view into an enormous back garden. She caught sight of what looked like a vegetable patch over to one side and it wryly struck her that it was bigger than her entire garden. In fact, the room she was standing in was almost certainly larger than the whole ground floor of her house.

Hugo offered her a seat and a cup of tea or coffee.

'Oh I could kill for a brew…if that's not too much trouble.'

'English breakfast or Earl Grey?'

'Oh just bog-standard builders' for me, thanks.'

'English breakfast it is. Mrs Townsend will be with you in a few minutes. She has the auctioneer with her at the moment.' Hugo left the room.

Auctioneer?

Brooke sat perched on the edge of the damask sofa, which she immediately knew to be a Sanderson fabric and picked up one of the silk colourful cushions that adorned it. She stroked it and turned it over to try and find the label. Osborne & Little.

Oh my God. Osborne & Little! That's a hundred quid straight off, just in that one cushion!

Brooke's many hours spent browsing *Homes & Gardens* magazines for the last seven years or so had ensured she had first-hand knowledge of the best designer makes, the most exclusive fabric designers and the latest trends in all home accessories.

Suddenly, Mrs Townsend strode purposefully through the door and Brooke threw the cushion down.

'I'm so sorry to have kept you waiting, Brooke. The wretched auctioneer got our appointment date wrong and it seemed churlish not to see him as he was here.'

Brooke leaped to her feet and, without thinking, performed a clumsy semi-curtsey, much to Mrs Townsend's amusement.

'What on earth are you doing?' she laughed.

'Sorry, I didn't know what I should do; the man who answered the door called you Lady Townsend.' Brooke was mortified and felt stupid. She offered three fingers to shake.

'Well I wish he hadn't – he's completely up himself, my dear. Please call me Mrs Townsend. And, for heaven's sake, never curtsey; that's only for those with the title HRH. By the way, your handshake is far too limp. You need to crush my bones. Like this,' Lady Townsend took Brooke's hand and squeezed it so hard, she let out a yelp. 'Now then, onto business. Let me show you around.'

Just then Hugo arrived with Brooke's tea and a coffee for Mrs Townsend. Brooke's mobile suddenly went off with an unexpected call from Dean, but she cut it off.

'Please do answer that if you'd like, dear.'

'No, no, you're alright.'

The next hour was taken up with the most heavenly stroll around every room in the house; including the Mark Wilkinson kitchen, the impressive swimming pool and the stables. Brooke mentally noted seven bedrooms, seven bathrooms and five reception rooms. Each one was decorated with such taste, Brooke was beside herself. She was desperate to take some pictures, but managed to keep her phone in her pocket.

Mrs Townsend was the most curious woman, Brooke decided. She was well-heeled, yet she swore frequently, cracked jokes with the gardeners and seemed very grounded for someone with so much wealth. She told Brooke funny little anecdotes at certain points during her tour and seemed to be waiting for Brooke's reaction, which was uproarious. Mrs Townsend seemed to like that. She asked Brooke a lot of questions about her life and circumstances. Brooke showed her a photograph of Paige being held up by Dean – both with big grins on their faces. They found themselves chatting quite naturally with each other towards the end and Brooke eventually forgot who she was talking to and why she was there. She asked a lot of questions about the house, the furniture, paintings and the many objets d'art.

After returning from the lake at the bottom of the garden, they walked back into the living room and Lady Townsend invited Brooke to sit down.

'Brooke. I really do like you. You're easy to talk to, you're English thank the Lord, and you're the only one of six people I invited for an interview who's actually showed up. But I don't understand why you want to do this. You're a bright, intelligent and resourceful young woman, it seems to me, and I think you deserve something better. You're certainly capable of something better. In fact, I'm quite sure that if and when something better did come along, I'd lose you and that wouldn't do at all.'

Brooke was stumped. No-one had ever called her

bright and intelligent before. She felt a lump come up in her throat.

'Thank you, Mrs Townsend. No-one's ever said anything like that to me before. But I think this house is awesome and I'd love to work for you…honestly! So, if you're up for it, based on what I said on the phone, then I can start next week.'

'Well if you're quite sure, my dear, then I'd like to offer you the post. Did you manage to bring any references with you?'

Brooke averted her eyes and fiddled with her ringlets.

'I'm sorry but it's been two years since I had a job and the last company I used to work for went bust so there's no-one I can ask. I did work on the Clinique counter in John Lewis up town, but that was seven years ago now.'

Mrs Townsend looked at her inscrutably. 'Then I'll have to take the risk. How about Monday morning at eight-thirty?'

Brooke gulped, wondering if it was feasible to get Paige up, ready and out by 8.30am without causing suspicion with Dean.

'Could we possibly say nine-thirty?' Brooke asked, looking awkward at having to start negotiating so early on.

'That's absolutely fine. One other thing, darling, please don't come to work in those stilettos, you'll ruin the flooring.'

Brooke now realised, for the first time in her adult life, that there were times when high heels were simply not appropriate. She smiled and promised she'd wear flats.

'Let me walk with you to your car.'

Brooke froze.

'No. No. I er…I er…didn't actually come by car. I walked.' She winced to herself as she told the lie.

'What?!' Mrs Townsend asked incredulously. 'In those heels?! You must be mad.'

'Well not all the way, I got a lift partway here.' Brooke felt fire rise up in her cheeks.

'Please let me drive you home, my dear. Brentwood's only two minutes from here in the car. I insist.'

Brooke was in a pickle and unable to handle this totally unexpected situation. She wished she hadn't lied now, but it was too late and Mrs Townsend was walking over towards the staff car park. Brooke followed haplessly. She really, really didn't want Mrs Townsend to see where she lived.

'Well if you're sure you don't mind, that'd be fab. If you don't mind dropping me off in the high street though, that'd be even better; I just need to get some milk and one or two bits.'

As they approached the staff car park, Mrs Townsend took a sharp turn and headed towards the clapped-out Ford Fiesta. She stopped, pressed the button on her key fob and opened the doors.

'In you get, dear!'

As Brooke's mouth fell open, she got in, not quite computing that this was Mrs Townsend's car. Why, Edna was in better condition than this one! They drove slowly down the gravel driveway and out the gates. Brooke looked wistfully at the sight of her Peugeot, abandoned down the road.

She tried to keep up cheery conversation whilst feeling anxious and frustrated at the situation she found herself in, but which she knew was of her own making. A few minutes later, they came into Brentwood High Street and Brooke pointed out the little convenience store a few metres ahead of them.

'If you pull over here, that'll be great, thanks. My house is just around the corner. Thanks a lot and I'll see you Monday.'

'Are you sure you don't want me to wait and drive you home?'

'No honestly. No probs. Thanks a lot for the lift. Bye.'

Mrs Townsend waited for a gap in the traffic before she could pull out and so Brooke felt compelled to actually go into Paradise stores and buy milk, just in case she was still there when she came out! But she was gone.

Brooke stood in the middle of Brentwood High Street with no car, her baby a mile away and holding a pint of milk she didn't need.

For God's sake. Brooke pulled out her phone.

Babe, where R U? Been ringing.

Oh God, that's all I need.

Sorry Babe, fone on silent by mistake. Whats up?

Nothing really. Just fancied a chat.

I'm at the checkout – can I call you back?

No worries – c u tonite.

Ok xxx

Brooke rang Dawn.

'Dawn, it's me.'

'So much for one bloody hour. Where are you? Paige hasn't stopped crying since you left.'

'Sorry, Dawn, I'll explain in a few minutes. Can you do us a favour and come and pick me up from the High Street? I'm outside Paradise Stores and I haven't got my car.'

'What? Why not? I haven't got a bloody car seat, Brooke.'

'Oh shit shit shit! Can't you just put her in the play pen? You'll only be a few minutes.'

'No I can't!' Dawn sounded incredulous at the suggestion she should leave Paige for even one minute.

'Right, well then I've gotta walk. I'll be as quick as I can but I've got my heels on.'

Brooke pressed the End button firmly and bit her lip. She knew she was responsible for the circumstances she was in, but she'd helped Dawn out numerous times over the years and she was most disappointed that Dawn wasn't prepared to help in this monumental crisis! On the other hand, she knew it was unfair to expect Dawn to leave Paige on her own.

With pint of milk in hand and beginning to regret putting stilettos on, she marched towards Dawn's house, chastising herself all the way.

When she arrived, Dawn let her in silently, her face demonstrating her disapproval of whatever Brooke had done. Brooke went straight to Paige and tried to soothe her; she was red, hot and distressed. Paige wrapped her tiny arms tightly around her mother as best she could.

Dawn made a cup of tea and placed the mugs down firmly and meaningfully while looking Brooke straight in the eye. She sat back, folded her arms and legs, eyebrows raised and just waited for Brooke to speak.

She spent the next hour filling Dawn in, not knowing whether she'd laugh or cry. She laughed. Just as well!

'The only problem is, Dawn, I've now gotta get back to pick my car up, with Paige and no car seat, before Dean gets back.'

'Mmm.'

'How about if you drive yours and I'll sit in the back next to Paige on some cushions – like a booster seat and strapped in with a seat belt? I can hold her nice and tight.'

'I dunno, Brooke, it seems a bit risky to me. Is that even legal?'

For the next half an hour or so they Googled page after page, but remained unsure.

'Come on, Dawn, if I'm happy to risk it and she's my kid, then surely you will? We're talking minutes, for God's sake!!'

Dawn tapped her fingers and her eyes flitted from side to side, then with a look of finality on her face she said, 'Alright then, let's go. C'mon.'

They gathered all of Dawn's rather gaudy scatter cushions and took them out to her hatchback, leaving Paige in her travel cot.

Brooke arranged the cushions in the back seat. She quickly ran inside to get Paige and carried her to the car, but, as soon as Brooke attempted to put her in, she arched her back.

'Paige. Don't do this to me now. Please,' Brooke was hissing under her breath.

Dawn's neighbour Jane was in her front garden peering on with a 'Just what I'd expect from your type' expression. They didn't get on. A full-on raging battle for three years – just over a car parking space. Jane used to be a social worker and was very earnest and nosy. From the do-gooders' brigade, as Dawn used to say.

'Is *you know who* watching us, Dawn?' Brooke enquired through clenched teeth and sounding a tad worried.

'Stupid cow. Just ignore her.'

The husband, Doug, was the greater concern as he ogled Brooke's fabulous derrière as she bent over to get Paige in; saliva practically dripping down his chin. He'd a pock-marked face, wore 1970s-style tinted glasses and his hair styled in a greasy combover. They deserved each other.

Brooke deployed her favourite tactic of tickling Paige at the bottom of her tummy, which then made her – for just a split second – arch the other way. As quick as a flash, Brooke belted her up. Dawn handed her the other large cushions which Brooke stuffed either side of Paige under the seat belt. It was all a bit Heath Robinson and little Paige resembled Alice in Wonderland after sipping some 'Drink Me' liquid.

Never the quiet, shy retiring type, Dawn shouted over to Doug, 'What you looking at, you perv?' She didn't care what people thought of her.

Doug quickly looked away, pretending he didn't realise she was talking to him.

Dawn fetched their belongings and peered in the back seat.

'Mmm. Well she looks reasonably safe. It'll have to do…but I'm not happy, Brooke.'

Brooke manoeuvred herself into the unfamiliar territory of the back seat. Paige looked quizzically up at her, wide-eyed and mouth open.

Throughout the four-minute journey, Brooke kept glancing around, looking decidedly furtive. At one point she saw someone she knew, so threw a blanket over Paige (much to her chagrin) and then calmly proceeded to look the other way.

Paige had yanked it off again in seconds with a loud 'Na, Maammeee!'

'So where exactly is this place then? We're coming up to Great Warley Road now.'

'It's called Purses, about another five hundred metres

more; but I parked a bit further along, so just go straight past it and drop us off there.'

'You must be joking! After everything you've put me through and what I've done for you today and you expect me to not even take a nosy at this gaff?'

She recognised Brooke's description of the black wrought-iron gates and pulled in; not quite in front of them, but far enough off the road that she could take a sneaky peek.

'Bloody 'ell!! I see what you mean!'

'Dawn, that's enough, please just drive on. I don't want her to see me.'

'I might just get out and take a little wander—'

'NO!' Brooke screamed. 'Just drive on, Dawn!'

Dawn was a big tease and she'd found the entire episode extremely funny, unlike Brooke who was just weary and wanting to get back home.

Dawn parked in a space just in front of Brooke's car. They both got out and retrieved Paige from her almost certainly illegal velvet and sequinned den, stood in the road and had a quick hug.

'Thanks a million, Dawn. I owe you.'

'Yeah, like you said that this morning. It's all adding up, Brooke. It's gonna be the mother of all favours you're gonna have to do for me!' She laughed, walked off waving as she got back into her car.

Brooke expertly put Paige in her proper car seat and felt huge relief as she did so. At the right moment in the traffic she did a U-turn, but, as she completed it, came to a halt as the traffic was slow-moving. There, at the side of the road, was Mrs Townsend, just beginning to cut some roses growing over a hedge outside her house.

Brooke screamed silently to herself and begged the car in front to get a move on. The seconds passed, but it seemed like many minutes. She even felt herself sliding down the car seat as though this would make her invisible – like when people duck as their car goes under a low road bridge. Completely pointless!

As luck would have it, the cars started to move, but within seconds had halted once more. Brooke screamed silently again as she was practically in front of Purses' gates. 'C'mon, c'mon, c'mon!'

Mrs Townsend got off her ladder, turned it round and placed it down facing the road; as she went to step up onto it, she caught sight of Brooke. Their eyes met for a split second; Brooke couldn't pretend that she hadn't seen her.

She took a deep breath, smiled the biggest smile and waved cheerily at her as though they were best buddies and that it was the most natural thing in the world for her to be there.

C'mon traffic…bloody move…move!!

Mrs Townsend waved back with a slightly perplexed smile and continued to do so as she watched Brooke's car gradually glide past her and off into the distance.

For God's sake! What a waste of time that was! All that palaver for nothing! Aaaaaaaagh!

It then dawned on Brooke that it was always going to have been a waste of time. She should've realised that if she was ever going to be driving there regularly, it was always going to be in Edna. She was only ever delaying the inevitable day when Mrs Townsend would see her car.

And now that doesn't even matter anyway because her shit heap is way worse than mine!

I can't bloody well believe it – I just can't believe it!

Paige started getting tetchy, so the used and abused music CD came out and Brooke drove home to the sound of 'Wheels on the Bus'.

When they arrived home, Brooke put Paige upstairs for a nap and plonked herself down on the sofa, exhausted with the strain of it all. After only a short while, however, a smile crept across her face. She very much hoped that next week would be the beginning of a new chapter in her life, albeit one she had very mixed feelings about.

Needs must, when the Devil drives. Anyway, it doesn't have to be for ever.

6

The Hempel Dilemma

As Brooke walked into the kitchen, Dean immediately clicked on the top right-hand cross on his screen. He hadn't even heard her come in the back door.

'What are you doing home?' snapped Brooke suspiciously, whilst surreptitiously glancing over his shoulder.

Dean tried to sound casual.

'Oh, I needed to get some reports typed up, but I realised some of the documents I needed were in my bag, so I asked Brian if I could do it from home. Thanks, babe, for picking that up for me. I know it was probably a pain.'

Before he knew it, he'd already spun a lie. He put his arms around her waist and pulled her towards him so she couldn't see his face. His heart had started thumping. She pushed him away and looked at his sorry face; suddenly she couldn't be angry with him anymore.

'It'll cost you a hot tub.'

He groaned internally but managed a forced smile and promised her he'd do his best.

'Let's go to the Toby Carvery for tea – make up for my

bad behaviour on Monday.'

'You actually gonna give those moths in that wallet of yours a day out? What about Paige?'

'Let's bring her with us. If we go early, she can stay in her car seat at the table.'

This was a compensatory act of guilt, pure and simple, and he knew it. He knew that even by suggesting this, he'd subliminally already made up his mind that he'd not be taking Brooke to The Hempel. The apparent ease with which he made the decision worried him. In typical Dean De'Ath style, though, he soon became anxious and fretted about it all evening.

Brooke sensed something wasn't quite right, but for once she let it be.

***

On returning home, Brooke immediately went to put Paige down and Dean logged into his email and saw the visit brief from Angie for The Hempel.

'Book, arrive, check in, eat in the restaurant, drink at the bar, visit public toilets, stay o'nite, order full English breakfast, check out.'

He sat staring at the brief summary and kept picturing himself walking into this minimalistic haven… but Brooke always kept appearing by his side! He couldn't get the vision of her out of his mind. Oh the guilt! He tried to imagine Martin by his side and inadvertently burst out laughing at the thought of him coming to such a sophisticated place.

But who else could I take? One of my sisters? Mum? What an opportunity. I might never get it again. Seven hundred and fifty quid a night!! I don't wanna waste it. But who? Maybe I should go on my own? Ah. Yes. Why not? But such a waste!

Dean had always been a procrastinator. Planning and thinking things through were a necessary part of his life so nothing could be done on impulse. This would drive Brooke to distraction. She loved doing things on impulse and got really annoyed at what she saw as his lacklustre and unenthusiastic response to her many exciting suggestions…in all departments of their life. (She once bought a nurse's outfit from Anne Summers – just for a hoot. Dean was mortified and merely remarked on the cheap nylon and how the buttons were falling off.)

'You're not still working on that bloody report, are you?' Brooke asked.

As his heart banged against his chest, he managed, 'Yeah, but I'm almost done now – five more minutes and I'll be finished.'

Brooke went to the kitchen, poured herself a glass of Chardonnay, lay down on the sofa and switched on the TV.

'You really shouldn't be drinking while you're still breastfeeding, you know. It said in the *BMA Home Medical G—*'

Brooke was irritated and cut him short. She knew he was right but she just fancied a glass.

'It's only one. That's not going to harm her. Besides, I'm gonna stop breastfeeding soon. She's had more than enough from me. All my mates gave up after a few days!'

She carried on sipping as she put her feet up to watch *Big Brother*. She loved that programme and it was her ambition to try and get on it one day and win.

Brooke was surprised Dean didn't pursue his chastising, but she wasn't complaining. His mind was definitely elsewhere.

Bloody hell look at that bed!

'Dean, can you massage my feet? They're killing me.' She waved her feet and wiggled her toes at him, milking what was left of this period of Dean's dog house status.

'DEAN!'

Dean snapped out of his dream world and started massaging.

As he rubbed her immaculately manicured but humungous feet, he looked so preoccupied that she waved her hand in front of his eyes. 'Anybody there?' she enquired jokingly.

Dean just smiled. 'Sorry, babe, I'm a bit knackered.'

Big Brother began and Dean knew Brooke would be glued to the TV for the next hour, so he slowly stopped his massage and went to the kitchen to make himself a cup of tea. He leaned against the cabinets, mug in hand, eyes looking up to the ceiling as if it was going to shout out advice on his predicament.

God why's this so hard? Why can't I just make a decision? What's the worst that could happen if I went on my own? Brooke might find out and kill me, Martin might find out and give me a hard time. But how would they find out? Nobody would know about it to even tell them… Bugger it… I'll just go on my own.

Brooke padded across the kitchen floor and said, 'Your brain looks like it's working too hard.'

Yet again, Dean smiled.

'I think I'm gonna have an early night, babe. Is that OK?'

'Well as long as you get your energy back for next weekend.'

Dean gulped; what was happening next weekend? He racked his brain but couldn't recall what was happening. Brooke sensed by the rabbit in the headlights look, that he'd forgotten.

'Paige's first birthday party, remember? We've got my family coming round and all our mates with their kids. I did tell you.'

'Yeah yeah yeah, I remember, I remember. No worries.'

Oh holy shit!

Brooke then went on to explain how this party was going to be organised. Dean was given a list of all the jobs he'd have to do after work the following week to make sure the house and garden were ready in time.

'Why the hell do I need to paint the front door?' exclaimed Dean as he perused the list with alarm.

'And I'm not erecting that bloody gazebo thing again, please spare me.'

Brooke just stood there, leaning on one leg, the other in front, arms folded and daggers flying from her eyes. 'STOP MOANING!' she shrieked. 'It's only once a year.'

'But they're babies; they won't notice or care!' shouted Dean back, exasperated.

'No, but Katie, Chelsea and Stacey will – and Chelsea's husband's a right snob. We'll show them we can put on a good party for our kid. Now, I've ordered a pretend shop as Paige's birthday present, but it won't be here until the day before the party, so you'll need to put it up the night before, after she goes to bed. You can pick up the birthday cake on the way home from work; I've ordered it from that fancy baker's on the high street. It's a one-metre green caterpillar in green icing. I'll be too busy cleaning the house. You can get Martin to help you on Saturday morning to put the gazebo up and mow the lawn. You'll need to get the weeds up and give the garden furniture a good scrub. There's some pigeon poo on it and it ruins my nails when I try to get it off.'

There was no point in arguing. Dean could tell by her voice, her stance, her lack of eye contact and how the sentences just sort of merged into each other without pausing for breath. These were the all-too-familiar signs of his wife on a mission. Unstoppable, uncompromising, determined.

He gave her one of his resigned looks, let out a deep sigh and gently enquired how many people were coming, as a one-metre cake seemed a little large.

'Eighty.'

'What? We haven't got room for eighty people. Not even in the garden, we won't get them in. Who the hell have you invited? We don't even know eighty people. Brooke, I really think this isn't a good idea.'

'Well it's too late, they've all been invited and accepted now. Anyway, we'll manage.' She smiled cheekily at him, not in the slightest bit perturbed by his protestations, pinched him very hard on the cheek, wobbled it side to side, pecked him on the lips and returned to *Big Brother*.

Dean was left dumbfounded. How in God's name was he ever going to fit The Hempel in around that lot?

***

Dean walked into work the next day looking somewhat downtrodden and weary. It didn't go unnoticed by Chloe, who was making tea in the office kitchen.

'You alright, Dean? You look spaced out.'

Dean looked up and smiled. There was something about Chloe that was so immediately calming, reassuring and more likeable in many ways than Brooke.

'Don't even go there.' Dean shook his head, looked down at the floor and shut his eyes. 'Her ladyship has only organised a birthday party for Paige for eighty people. We don't even know eighty people.'

Chloe carried on making her tea. 'Well *you* mightn't, but *she* probably does – that whole mother and baby scene is huge, I hear.'

Dean ignored Chloe's remark and carried on in despair '...and we haven't got room. What if it rains? And you should see the list of stuff she's given me to do before the party. I don't know how I'm gonna do it – and with The Hempel stuff as well, it's all just too much.'

Chloe turned her head sharply. 'What do you mean "The Hempel stuff?"'

Dean stared straight at her, blew air out slowly and looked up again at the ceiling that never spoke.

'Well you know that mystery shopping company I've started with? They've asked me to do a visit to The Hempel Hotel – and it's got to be done next week.'

'O...M...G. Dean – that hotel is awesome!'

Dean realised that she must know the hotel, but he couldn't think how.

'That's one of the smartest hotels in London. The Beckhams and people like that go there. I can't believe they've given that to *you*!' She shook her head in disbelief.

The emphasis was definitely on the 'you'. Dean was rather hurt by this. 'Why wouldn't they?' he enquired quizzically.

Chloe suddenly realised how her comment came out.

She shuffled around and attempted to explain herself.

Mmm.

Dean allowed himself to be persuaded.

'Can you hide me in your suitcase?' Chloe joked as a way of changing the subject.

Dean laughed, saying how he wished he could – just as something to say really, not because he actually meant it. Another schoolboy error!

Chloe stopped what she was doing and came and sat down next to him. Close; not taking her eyes off him for a moment.

Dean moved back into his chair. Chloe was a good-looking girl, about the same age as Brooke, but less curvy and shorter – definitely not as stunning as his wife. But she flirted unashamedly with Dean and he couldn't deny that he found her attractive.

'I mean it, Dean. Why couldn't I come? We wouldn't… you know…*do* anything…it'd just be for a laugh. I've always wanted to stay in that hotel; ever since it opened.'

Dean said nothing, but felt compelled to clasp his hands in front of his crotch to hide the evidence of his most primitive manly thoughts.

'I expect you're taking Brooke though.' Her tone suddenly swapped to one in which she indicated that this was completely to be expected.

Dean was paralysed by indecision. Turned on but terrified, tempted but guilty, (once a Catholic…), excited but anxious, his head racing and filled with lustful visions of Chloe's breasts, while his trousers filled with something far less desirable. Naughty boy!

Chloe picked up on Dean's indecision.

'Aren't you?' she asked inquisitively and with a wry smile. When no answer was forthcoming immediately, she gasped.

'Are you planning on being a bad boy?' Chloe teased. She was getting visibly excited now.

'I haven't decided who I'm taking yet,' Dean responded, in that way people do when they're being rather superior about catching someone making an incorrect assumption. 'I don't think Brooke would want to come, because she'd have to leave Paige and she hates doing that, so I thought I might ask Mum if she wanted to come – as a treat.'

'You're joking, Dean. You've been asked to mystery shop The Hempel and you're thinking you'll take your *mum*? You've lost your marbles, mate.'

Chloe laughed and went back to her desk. 'Well, if you change your mind let me know.' She winked at him and purposefully sashayed down the corridor in full view of Dean. What a bad girl!

Jesus. What do I do, what do I do?

As usual, the ceiling didn't reply and nor did Jesus for that matter.

I'm a married man, I love Brooke, I've got a baby daughter.

The evil little gremlin sitting invisibly on his shoulder was whispering in his ear...because you can....and because it'll be fun…and because no-one will ever know. Dean's adrenalin began to gush through his veins. He returned to his desk and logged on. The phones started immediately. He just wanted to ignore them and think about 'other things', but the pressure was on. He'd not been performing as well recently and his Operations Manager, Brian was getting rather too interested in analysing Dean's statistics for some reason. Dean tried explaining that he had a new baby daughter who still didn't sleep through the night and so he wasn't getting enough sleep himself.

'Not interested and not my problem,' came the terse reply.

What tosh! Brian *relied* on Dean!

Brian was a bastard with a serious BO problem. Everyone loathed him and his wretched clipboard, checking how many calls were waiting in the queue. It was a standing joke that Brian, who was single, would be more lenient on the girls in the call centre if they flirted with him. So he'd lean over their screens in that rather pervy way that sexually deprived elderly gentlemen do, when they haven't had any rumpy-pumpy for years, rubbing themselves up against the girls whenever possible. What was worse is that he genuinely thought the girls were interested in him and he'd relay tales of supposed 'near dates' with all of them, to anyone and everyone who'd listen. Little did he know that one of his team had written a little poem about him which had gone round the whole office on email to everyone but him.

Brian the lion loves the lasses
Especially those with big black asses
Groping any girls in his path
Who simply wish he'd have a bath.
He likes to look closely at their screens
But it's just an excuse to rub and lean
He only succeeds by pulling rank
Why can't he stay at home and wank?

One April Fool's, the entire team decided to have the poem as their screensaver, illustrated with a cartoon of him watching porn with his hands down his trousers. There were bets going round to see who managed to have it up for the longest without him realising. He must've circled the office a hundred times that day and never noticed, despite the fact that the team were in hysterical laughter most of the day.

Brian suddenly appeared at Dean's desk. The man had no sense of personal space. Unfortunately, Dean's hoped-for promotion would always be influenced by what Brian told the big bosses about him, so, to some degree, Dean was forced to be nice to him. It seemed to Dean that no-one else had a 'Brooke' at home cracking the whip to climb the ladder, get a company car and earn more money…and a hot tub of course.

'Hello, Brian, what can I do you for?' Dean asked with as much of a smile as he could muster.

'IT Support's closed cases are down by twenty per cent this past month. I like you, Dean, but if you want that promotion, you're gonna have to do better than that.' Brian did like Dean, but he misguidedly liked to present a 'tough boss' image to the team. Silly old fool!

Dean's ardour evaporated instantly and he allowed his head to drop down and bang his forehead onto his desk. He had to focus.

The Hempel.

What was he going to do about The Hempel?

He stared into the darkness of his desk and Chloe's breasts once more appeared in front of his eyes. His ardour returned with a vengeance.

Suddenly his mobile pinged. It was a message from one of the company's clients asking Dean to get over there quickly. They'd apparently discovered an urgent technical issue they needed to speak with him about. He looked perturbed and went straight away to see Brian to let him know he was going to have to leave the office – for the rest of the afternoon by the sounds of it. As he got close to Brian's office door, Dean's mobile rang and he answered it, forgetting momentarily where he was. Without realising, he'd accidentally pressed the loudspeaker button. Before he had a chance to rectify the situation, Brian heard loudly and clearly,

'Hi, Dean, it's Angie, have you booked the hotel yet?'

Dean fumbled about for the volume button hopelessly, as Brian looked up from his desk, first with surprise and then with a salacious grin and a wink and an invitation to: 'Come and sit down and tell Uncle Brian all about it.'

Dean just wanted to curl up in a ball and die. He tried in vain to explain that what Brian heard wasn't what it sounded, but Brian was having none of it. In his mind, this was the perfect porn fantasy and he wanted verbal detail of this imaginary event which he'd created in a matter of moments.

Dean eventually managed to tell him about the client's urgent request for a meeting at their office, after which Brian joked with him that a client meeting was a 'crap alibi for a secret shag'. He made Dean promise to go out with him for a drink after work some time, to tell him 'all about Angie'.

Dean collected his man-bag, retrieved the client file and walked towards the exit door, where Chloe's desk was situated. He tried to avoid her gaze, but as she looked up she smiled and winked, then cooed, 'Don't forget my offer.'

7

Trials and Tribulations.

Being the ultimate diplomat and technical wizard that he was, Dean dealt admirably with the client. It turned out that they'd been sending incorrect technical advice to the call centre operatives at TrussInUs, the company Dean worked for.

On the way home, he decided to make a list of all the things he had to do, as he was beginning to feel extremely stressed. He was a man of order and control, but today he'd felt as though he was totally out of control.

He made his list and prioritised it using H for High, M for medium and L for Low:

Have drink with Brian	L – avoid at all costs/put off
Book The Hempel	H – Today
Decide who to take, if anyone	H – Today
Read visit brief	M – Thursday
Conduct visit to The Hempel	H – Thursday night
Erect gazebo	M – Saturday
Pick up cake	M – Friday
Put together Paige's shop	L – Friday night

Paint front door first coat	H – Monday
Mow lawn	M – Wednesday evening
Weed + second coat on door	M – Tuesday evening

He couldn't escape the fact that he had to make up his mind about The Hempel right now before booking. He was having heart palpitations just thinking about it… and the deadline. If he didn't do this now, they mightn't even have a room left. Chloe's breasts, Martin, Mum …or just no-one?

He finally plumped for no-one. He was already exhausted and next week hadn't even started. He needed a rest and this was going to be well deserved. He'd tell Brooke that he was going to a business meeting in London and TrussInUs's IT provider had arranged to take him (as the man with special responsibility for IT) and a few suppliers out for dinner and put him up in a hotel for the night so he didn't have to travel home late. He believed that sounded perfectly reasonable.

He telephoned The Hempel and made his reservation for Thursday the following week. That way, he'd be home for all the stuff Brooke would inevitably add to his list of jobs for Friday.

When Dean arrived home, Brooke was lying on the sofa. She stretched out her arm and waved her fingers at Dean. This normally indicated that she wanted a kiss or a cuddle. He immediately sat next to her and kissed her on the head. She smelled of Jimmy Choo perfume. A wave of shame and guilt came over him about his seeming inability to control his manly and primitive urges earlier in the day. How could he have even begun to contemplate taking Chloe to The Hempel? He was either mad, bad or stupid. He decided he'd still do the visit without telling Brooke. He sensed that it'd be just more hassle than it was worth.

He tried to get himself into a more casual, chatty mood and told Brooke about his client meeting; they both giggled as they pictured OAPs around the country riding up and down on their stair lifts for hours on end because they wouldn't stop and they were unable to get off!

Then Brooke wanted to talk about her preparations for Paige's party.

'I talked with the baker's earlier and they said that Paige's birthday cake will be ready on Thursday next week, so can you pick it up on your way back from work?'

Dean closed his eyes and prayed to a god he'd been assured existed, to help him out.

'Actually, babe, I meant to tell you but…I'll actually be away on Thursday night.'

'What d'ya mean?' Brooke turned around with a look of genuine shock and surprise on her face.

'Well, I've been asked to go to a meeting with one of our suppliers in town and they're taking us all out for dinner afterwards. They've offered to put all of us up in a hotel for the night, so we don't have to go home.' It came out like a well-rehearsed script.

Brooke stared him straight in the eye. Dean swallowed

hard.

'Blimey. Which hotel?' she asked, as sharp as a pin.

Dean was thrown. He wasn't at all prepared for this conversation. He hadn't had time to think about the detail of what he would say; to check that his story made sense.

'Errr, that's a very good point; he hasn't told us yet. I'll find out and let you know. You don't mind, do you, babe? You know what? I think it might just be the beginning of my path to promotion.' It slipped out of his mouth as easy as water down a plughole. He felt sick. He was perplexed as to why such a little white lie caused him so much heartache. He was trying to analyse his own thoughts at the same time as responding and attempting to act naturally.

'Oh God, Dean. That'd be so fantastic. You must go. Who else from the office is invited?' Brooke asked grinning, cosying up next to him as if preparing for a whole evening of intense conversation about this thrilling turn of events.

This wasn't the reaction Dean was expecting. On the one hand he was relieved she didn't kick up a fuss about taking a night away from home so close to the party. On the other hand, he was alarmed at the direction of her questioning and it began to make him very nervous. His face felt like someone was holding a flame to it. He immediately got up and walked out to the kitchen to get himself another beer, talking as he went.

'I don't know that either; it's all only just been decided,' he shouted out as he opened the fridge.

'I expect I'll hear more detail early next week. D'ya

fancy a glass of wine? I'm getting a beer.' He desperately tried to change the subject and tried overly hard to sound casual.

'Yeah. We should celebrate.'

Dean was beginning to see that his story was already going to cause him trouble.

'Celebrate what?' Dean enquired, slightly worried.

'Your imminent promotion, of course!'

'I think that's a bit premature, babe. It's only a meeting.'

'Yeah, but if they're inviting you for dinner and to stay in a fancy hotel afterwards, they must think you're worth making a fuss over.'

'It's our IT people who have invited me – not the company, and who says it's a fancy hotel? We don't know anything yet. I wouldn't get so excited if I were you,' Dean responded with his usual healthy dose of caution.

In her head, Brooke was already imagining a new car, a pay rise, the white leather sofa she'd seen in DFS, and two weeks at Center Parcs for them all.

'Dean. Why are you so fucking negative?! This is the first time in all the years you've worked at that bloody place, that you've ever been invited to something so obviously important and you're making out it's nothing. Why can't you just get a bit enthusiastic for once?' she retorted.

Oh shit, what have I done?

Dean walked back into the lounge and sat down, taking a gulp of beer.

'Wine?' Brooke demanded, tilting her head and with

the palms of her hands facing upwards.

Dean leaped up, apologising. He then stopped, coming to his senses suddenly, but made the crucial error of reminding her yet again that maybe she shouldn't be drinking. He'd read on the internet all about the evils of alcohol in mothers who were still breastfeeding. The internet fed his already overcautious, overprotective nature. Since Paige had been born, he'd convinced himself that she had an anal fissure, whooping cough, an obstruction of the intestines and meningitis on three separate occasions. Brooke was a very maternal sort of young woman and there was no questioning her love and care for Paige, but it paled into insignificance when compared to Dean.

'Dean, will you please just get me a glass of wine. I'm not a baby. I know what I'm doing. Besides, you're the one who bloody well offered it to me!'

She knew she probably drank a bit too much wine, but wasn't prepared to be lectured about it.

Dean refused to be drawn on further discussion about the meeting. He was purposefully vague, which only made matters worse. The vaguer he was, the more questions Brooke asked. In the end, he got so worked up about it, he told her that she was stressing him out and putting him under too much pressure and would she just shut up about it until he knew more details.

She sat there like a sulking child, looking straight ahead, nursing a small glass of Chardonnay for the rest of the night. Niggled. Annoyed. Resentful. Powerless. But secretly she was thrilled at what she'd convinced herself was the beginning of a new chapter in his career, although she wasn't going to hold her breath.

Dean sat there in a state of unadulterated turmoil, made so much more unbearable by the fact that he had to hide it.

8

Brooke Ventures Out

At 7.30am, Dean sprang out of bed like a spaniel. He'd always been an early bird (unlike Brooke) and preferred to get into work early so he wouldn't be home late. Brooke, on the other hand, would lie in bed until Dean had gone and then she could go about her ablutions without bothering him. He hated being moved on out of the bathroom and toilet and got irritated when trying to get his breakfast if Brooke got in the way. She was generally only just beginning to rise as Dean left the house at 8.15am.

But not today.

Today, she had her eyes on the clock. She'd estimated it'd take her at least an hour and a half to get them both ready and to drop Paige off in enough time to get to Purses. She had to start before Dean left. It got to 7.45am, after which she couldn't lie there any longer.

Dean did a double-take as Brooke sauntered casually down to the kitchen with her dressing gown on.

'Blimey, you're up early. You feeling alright?'

'Yeah I'm fine, I thought I'd go to Lakeside today and see if I can get a few things for Paige's party. I wanna be back before tea, so I need to get off early.' Brooke turned away with kettle in hand so Dean couldn't see her face.

'I need to buy shares in that place and you should have a second home there!'

Brooke laughed, but her mind was elsewhere.

What shall I wear?

Dean carried on with his breakfast and Brooke tried to keep out of his way. She made herself a tea and took it upstairs. She opened her wardrobe and was confronted with around fifty pairs of stiletto heels. The couple of pairs of flat pumps she owned were hiding right at the back. Plain black, flat, suede ballerina pumps with a little bow on the front, hardly worn.

They'll do.

She'd decided on jeans and then pondered a while over which top. Comfort was the priority, but not any of those garments which she wore to potter around the house in, or wear when she was feeling sorry for herself. She had to look reasonable and she didn't want to look hard-up or desperate.

She picked out a stretchy long-sleeved shirt from H&M.

Is it worth showering now or shall I have one when I get back?

She took off her dressing gown to reveal her long, curvy body, not a hair in sight. She was the first of all her friends to have The Hollywood and she did her best to keep herself as smooth as a baby. She lifted her right arm into the air and sniffed under her armpit and then repeated it with the left.

They'll have to do.

She dressed and went to see if Paige was awake yet. She peeked through the bedroom door and observed her happily sitting up in her cot, playing with a fluffy rabbit toy.

Alleluia!

Brooke stared at the contents of her dressing table. A huge jar of cotton wool balls, tubes, pots, creams, brushes, nail varnish and makeup covered every centimetre. Dean despaired over it. He failed to understand how a woman could want or need two lipsticks almost identical in colour. Her argument was always the same. He didn't understand subtlety in colour, but then he was a mere man!

With the speed and precision of a pro, she set to on her makeup routine; sweeping, wiping, contouring and drawing. It took her twenty minutes and she looked like a model on the front cover of *Glamour* magazine by the time she'd finished. Not once did it occur to her that this look really wasn't appropriate or of any benefit for what she'd be doing. For her, though, it was habit. She had to be ill not to put her makeup on.

Dean came running up the stairs to say goodbye. He looked over at Brooke's reflection in the mirror as she put the finishing touches on. He smiled, put his arms around her and pecked her on the top of her head.

'I can't remember the last time I saw you up and about

this early. You look really nice,' he said genuinely. 'Don't spend too much money!'

'Thanks, babe. See you tonight. Don't forget you've got to paint the front door!'

She breathed a sigh of relief as she heard the front door bang. 8.15am. She walked fast into Paige's room and plucked her out of her cot. From then until she left the house it was like a military operation.

In the car, Brooke lifted the flap on the sunshade mirror and checked her makeup. She couldn't decide if it was a little OTT. She'd observed that Letitia Townsend's look was very natural with minimal makeup. Then again, she'd no need to look like her; she was more than twice her age! She talked herself into feeling comfortable with her look.

She arrived at Dawn's and dropped Paige off. Dawn gave her an exaggerated 'nudge nudge wink wink' look and laughed. As Brooke thanked her, kissed Paige and waved, Dawn shouted down the drive, 'It'll cost ya!'

Brooke laughed and was suddenly very grateful to have a girlfriend like Dawn. She might have her faults, but then don't we all?

Within a few minutes she'd arrived at the gates of Purses. Once again, she took a deep breath; only this time, she pressed in the code she'd been given and drove Edna up the driveway into the staff car park. She parked next to the Audi A3 with mixed feelings. The thing Brooke couldn't get her head round was that the state of Lady Townsend's car didn't seem to bother her in the slightest. She was at a loss as to why she'd drive around in that when she clearly could afford something very smart.

As she went to the front door, Hugo appeared from nowhere and greeted her warmly.

'Morning, Brooke, you need to come in the staff entrance from now on. Follow me and I'll show you where it is.'

'Oh sorry, I didn't know.'

'Not a problem. How are you feeling about your first day with us?'

'I'm a bit nervous, to be fair.'

'No need. The old girl's alright as long as you do your job properly. She treats us all well. She already loves *you*.'

Brooke raised her eyebrows, genuinely surprised that Lady Townsend would've shared such early thoughts about her with her staff. 'Really? I can't think why; she doesn't even know me.'

'Ah, but she reckons she's a very good judge of character and it has to be said she's rarely wrong.'

They walked through the back entrance and Hugo showed her where she could put all her personal belongings. He briefed her as to what she was expected to get through that day and showed her the relevant storage cupboards, saying that if she'd any particular requests for equipment or products, she was just to ask. He said he'd come and find her at about 11am so they could have a coffee together.

Brooke thanked him, looked at the list and then rummaged thoroughly through the storage cupboards. She'd never seen or heard of half the paraphernalia that was in there, but she gathered what she thought she'd need and headed off to the kitchen. By 11am, she was halfway through her list and Hugo found her in the drawing room.

'How are you getting on?' he asked.

Brooke took out her list and showed him how far she'd got.

'That can't be right. Are you sure?'

'Why not? You can check if you like, but it's all done. I don't mess about, me.'

Brooke put her hands on her hips indignantly. Hugo could see that he'd offended her and was quick to diffuse the situation by suggesting they talked through her schedule over coffee.

Hugo was tall with clean-cut dark hair. He wore a smart suit, shirt and tie. So elegant! Brooke was intrigued by him as he sat and briefed her about everything that needed to be done. Although she was listening, she couldn't help but gawp at him as he spoke.

Bet that's an Armani. Why does he speak so posh? Don't come from round here, that's for sure. What is his job here exactly? Wonder how long's he worked here?

After their coffee and as Hugo walked with her to Letitia Townsend's bedroom, he asked Brooke if she had any questions.

'Yeah, I do as it happens. What's it you do here exactly?

You haven't told me.'

'Well it's a good question with a rather vague answer. A whole array of things, really. I'm a sort of mix between a butler and an executive assistant.'

'Bloody 'ell, I didn't think people had butlers these days. You only think of them when you watch *Downton Abbey*!'

'I know, but modern butlers are rather different. I went to the British Butler Institute where you learn all about the services required of the wealthy, famous and high-profile people who recruit them. I applied for the role here after my gap year travels after uni in Oxford and got the job. I'd initially intended for it to be a stepping stone to a bigger and better role at a larger country house, but I actually love working here and Mrs Townsend's smashing to work for, so I've been here for seven years. I have my own accommodation here; you might've noticed there's a small cottage right at the end of the drive past the main house. That's where I live.'

'You went to Oxford University? Oh my God, you must be so clever!'

'Sadly not. I went to Oxford Brookes – not the same thing at all. "Playschool", my eldest brother calls it; he went to *the* Oxford University.'

Brooke became aware of butterflies in her stomach and a wobbly feeling she'd not experienced since school. Hugo had piercing-blue eyes and he didn't take them off her for one moment throughout his explanation. She kept averting his gaze.

'I do everything from her diary appointments and travel arrangements through to picking up dry cleaning, instructing the groundsmen and posting letters. I've also taken her breakfast in bed!'

'God, I just can't believe people still live like that! It's like another world.'

Hugo laughed. 'Trust me, this is nothing. I've got friends from the institute who are butlers for Russian oligarchs. That's a whole different ball game.'

Brooke was fascinated and could've listened to him for hours.

'One more question and then I'll shut up, I promise! Where are you from? You definitely don't sound like you're from round 'ere?'

'Oxford. That's where my parents still live. I go back and see them fairly frequently.'

At that point, Hugo said he'd see her later; they were both conscious they'd chatted for a bit too long and so went back to their respective tasks. He checked her work and was astounded at how much she'd got through in such a short space of time.

As Brooke opened Lady Townsend's bedroom door, she jumped back with a yelp, startled at the vision in front of her. There was Lady Townsend, standing absolutely starkers in front of the bed.

'Oh my God! I'm *so* sorry, Mrs Townsend, I didn't think you were in here!' Brooke was horrified and immediately turned round to face the door, like a child who's caught their parents having sex.

'Oh don't worry about me, dear – you just carry on. I'm sure you've seen it all before. How are you getting on, on your first day?' Letitia Townsend's voice was calm, smooth and completely unruffled. She was actually just deciding what to wear for a meeting she had later that day; she was a trustee of a number of charities and was going to London to meet one of them later.

There, on the bed, was a set of the most exquisite set of ivory La Perla silk lingerie.

That's way too sexy for an old lady! That's just not fair!

Next to it were a pair of navy-blue, ankle-length Jaeger trousers, a Paul Costelloe white, pleated skirt, a red, silk, long-sleeved Ralph Lauren blouse and a short-sleeved floral top by Erdem. Brooke's eyes swept swiftly over it all.

Oh my God this woman's got taste!

'I simply can't decide what to wear for this trustees' meeting.'

Without even thinking, Brooke went straight over to the bed and blurted out, 'Oh definitely the Erdem top and the Paul Costelloe skirt. It's far too hot for a long-sleeve blouse – it'll show your sweat patches.' She picked them up and sort of presented them as her recommendation, but then put her hand to her mouth realising that she shouldn't have spoken; it wasn't her place.

Lady Townsend watched her and roared laughing.

'You're quite right, my dear – and what knowledge

of fashion you have. And taste!' She paused. 'I know what you're thinking, but you're quite wrong. I don't mind in the slightest taking your advice. You're younger and probably see things that I don't even think about any more. I think you're going to be very good for me, Brooke.'

Brooke was stunned. She watched Mrs Townsend's wrinkly but still quite pert little bottom pootle off to her en suite; she'd have to come back to that room later.

Brooke couldn't stop smiling. For the rest of the day, she found herself thinking about Mrs Townsend's bottom, butlers and Oxford University, chortling to herself with a combination of disbelief and excitement. Working here was almost certainly going to be much more interesting than she'd originally thought.

And she couldn't say a single word to Dean.

9

Party Preparation

'Babe, do you know where the tin of white paint is?' Dean was on his hands and knees in the garden shed.

He'd left work early, which threw Brooke, who'd only been back from her first day at work a short time and was still reeling. Dean wanted to start wading through the list of jobs Brooke had insisted must be done before the party. He decided to paint the front door first, as it needed a couple of coats. He'd already sanded it down the evening before in preparation.

Their house was a tiny two-bedroomed 1980s terraced estate house in a small cul de sac called Elephant Close. Brooke despised the name and, within a matter of weeks of arriving, was desperate to move just so she'd never again have to recite it as her address. Their house looked the same as the two hundred others that surrounded it. Neat front lawn, room to park a car, two windows at the front, a small garden out the back and a front door the same as everyone else's. I.e. white.

'No worries, we're not gonna use the same colour anyway. You need to pop to Homebase and buy a 2.5-litre tin of Farrow & Ball… Cooking Apple Green, satin finish,' Brooke shouted back.

'Why can't we just use what we've already got? Why d'ya want to paint it a different colour? None of the other houses have painted theirs a different colour,' Dean protested.

'Dean!' Brooke yelled, exasperated. 'Why can't you just do what I ask? I think they look cheap and I want ours to be different.'

Dean recognised this 'not to be argued with' tone and dutifully crawled out of the garden shed. It was late, so he'd need to hurry. As he walked through the kitchen Brooke thrust a piece of paper in his hand, with the paint details.

***

In Homebase, Dean looked up to the ceiling at the array of hanging signs that promised to make life easier by guiding you in the right direction for your purchase. He wandered over to the Paints aisle, only to be confronted with wicker boxes and dustpans.

He ventured down the 'Decorating' aisle, to find cleaning products. He sighed and walked up all the aisles, unable to find paints. Eventually he accosted a young lad called 'Arthur'. Dean found himself pondering that the lad just didn't look like an Arthur somehow. He'd been walking aimlessly across the shop floor when Dean asked him where the Farrow & Ball paints were. The slovenly youth dutifully escorted him to the aisle that said 'Paints', only to discover wicker boxes and dustpans.

'They must've moved 'em,' he said, scratching his head.

Dean was getting a bit irritated as he didn't have that much daylight to get the first coat done.

'Jeannie' (clearly a supervisor of some sort) was just passing and Dean took the chance to ask her where the Farrow & Ball paints were. She found them on a gondola unit at one end of the paint aisle, pointed at it and left Dean to it. He inspected all the colours, sizes and finishes on offer. He didn't recognise the tin and had never heard of Farrow & Ball. He thought it looked a bit old fashioned, but Brooke was the boss, so he took the right one up to the customer service desk as all the checkouts were closed.

This time he was served by an apathetic woman whose name badge stated 'Rose'. She looked about seventy and like she might be a bit of a lush; dressed like a sixteen year old, all short skirt and cleavage bursting out of her too-tight blouse.

'That'll be forty-three fifty.'

'You what?'

'Forty-three fifty.'

'That can't be right. Hang on a sec, let me just check the ticket on the shelf.'

Dean wasn't worried. He knew she must've made a mistake. No paint cost that amount of money. He just needed to show her the ticket on the shelf. Before the assistant had a chance to say anything, Dean ran back to the shelf and there it was in bold black print: £43.50.

For fuck's sake, she's lost the plot this time! Forty-three quid for a bit of paint?

He stormed back to the desk and told the cashier he'd leave it as it was too expensive; he'd find a cheaper alternative. The woman shrugged her shoulders 'That paint is expensive, love – it's for them period 'ouses.'

But we've got a bloody terraced box, not a country mansion!

Dean forced a smile and nodded, then navigated his way back to the paints and selected the one he thought looked most like the Farrow & Ball Cooking Apple Green.

Cuprinol Willow: £15.50.

That's more like it.

When he got back, Brooke was in the shower; she'd put Paige to bed and so he got straight down to work. He quite liked painting. He found it therapeutic and it suited his careful and precise nature. He put his iPod and headphones on to listen to some music, without disturbing Paige.

He hummed away to himself happily, 'ooh yeah... baby... baby', but every so often thoughts came into his mind about his imminent hotel visit and his stomach went into knots. Brooke had tentatively asked a couple more times about it, but he'd just kept fobbing her off. Originally, he'd thought he'd tell her it was a completely different hotel, but then he knew what she was like. She'd want photographs. So he'd made up his mind that he'd keep it as real to life as possible; like the spy-type legend he'd had to create for his first visit.

He suddenly felt a sharp finger prodding him in the back.

'Ouch! What're you doing? What was that for?' Dean wailed as he looked up.

'WHAT…is that?!' Brooke asked, pointing at the nearly finished first coat on the front door and looking absolutely furious.

'I've nearly finished the first coat and, yes, before you say another word, I didn't buy that Barrow & Fall Brooke.' He carried on painting and sounded firm. He wasn't in the mood for one of her tantrums. He was tired and didn't want to be painting at 9.30pm.

'Why not?'

'Because it was a ridiculous amount of money and we can't afford it. That's why not.'

'But it's good-quality paint and much nicer colours than normal paint. It's worth paying that bit more. All the posh houses round 'ere use it, I know.'

'Yeah well, we haven't got a posh house. We live on an estate. I bought one that's virtually the same colour but a fraction of the price and, as you can see, I've nearly finished, so don't push me, Brooke. It looks just fine.'

Brooke had been shut down. She wanted to argue with him, but just like Dean knew her tone and look, she knew when he wasn't to be argued with. She turned away, picked up the tin and turned it round. 'Cuprinol exterior wood paint "Willow" for sheds and fences.' She visibly crumpled.

'Dean. Did you realise—'

He interrupted. 'Brooke, I told you, don't push me, I've had enough and I'm knackered.'

She walked away feeling hopeless and miserable, but didn't dare say another word about it. She collapsed on the sofa, and stared at the floor. She couldn't escape the fact that her front door was going to look like a fence.

Within ten minutes, Dean had finished and carefully put his brushes in white spirit in the kitchen. He felt a bit guilty as he walked past Brooke staring at the floor; she looked genuinely unhappy. When he came back into the lounge, he leaned over the back of the sofa and cuddled her from behind.

'It looks great, babe, honestly, go and have a look.'

Brooke shook him off, mumbled something incoherent and stomped upstairs to bed. Dean hated the atmosphere created when Brooke doled out her silent treatment. He tried snuggling up to her, stroking her hair and tickling her back. She usually relented fairly quickly, but this time she was different. All over a tin of damn paint. Women!

The next morning she stayed in bed and Dean brought her up a cup of tea. He kissed her on top of her head of tousled hair. She thanked him reluctantly and asked him to bring Paige in. She then spent the next hour enjoying playing with her; momentarily forgetting about the front door. She could never decide whether she wanted a large brood or whether she might stick to just one. Paige's birth was very difficult, but Brooke was actually remarkably stoic. She could be so contradictory. When she looked helpless and vulnerable, inside she could be as tough as old boots. On the other hand, when she appeared to be unbreakable, she was like marshmallow inside and could cry quite easily if ever anyone said anything unkind to or about her.

For the rest of the day, she pottered about, thinking about Purses on Wednesday, Paige's party and hot tubs; how impressive and good fun it'd be if all their friends turned up to find one in her garden. Her day seemed to flash past as she mulled over her circumstances.

At around 6.30pm Dean walked in and knew he couldn't evade Brooke's questioning any longer. He'd braced himself and rehearsed a thousand times what he was going to say.

'Guess what? The hotel we're going to is The Hempel.'

Fuck. That's it. I've done it now. No going back.

'Oh…my…God!' Brooke bolted up from the sofa.

Suddenly her Willow front door didn't matter anymore. She ran up to him and gave him the most enormous squeeze.

'Oh, Dean, I'm so proud of you. This must be something special, I don't care what you say. That place is meant to be sick! It's crazy expensive! Like all the celebs go there!'

Dean was hopeless at this. He felt sick to the stomach and just wanted all conversation about it to stop. He laughed nervously and made his way rapidly up the stairs to hide his reddening face and to get changed. He planned to do the second coat on the front door. Brooke followed him, pursuing him relentlessly for more details and talking excitedly about The Hempel, as though she was the one going.

The next day she sent him fifteen questions about it at work. His phone was pinging constantly throughout the day and Brian the Lion kept peering over at him, watching him responding. At one point, he came up to Dean's desk and reminded him with a nod and a wink that he owed him a drink.

Oh God, that's all I need.

Wednesday evening was taken up with weeding and mowing. This was another job that was well suited to Dean's sense of perfection and order. He could get quite lost in his own thoughts and his razor-sharp focus on any patch of soil with so much as a pinhead of weed shooting up would have him plucking it out meticulously.

The lawn was mowed in immaculate straight lines using his own little grid system. He found garden shears not precise enough, so he always trimmed the edges of the lawn with kitchen scissors, centimetre by centimetre. And finally, he'd bring the Henry outside and hoover up the cuttings. His neighbour Mikey found all this extremely amusing and loved nothing better than to tease Dean about his OCD treatment of his lawn. Dean took it all in good humour, repeating his personal motto: 'If a job's worth doing, it's worth doing well.'

When he came in, it dawned on him that he needed to pack for The Hempel the next day. What should he take? What should he wear? He'd have to go straight to work from there on the Friday morning, so he'd need a fresh shirt, tie, socks and underwear.

As he packed his bag, he began to feel just a tiny bit excited.

10

Arrival At The Hempel

Dean was awoken on Thursday morning with a cup of tea from Brooke. This was unheard-of. She never brought him tea. He always brought her tea. That's just the way it was.

He was immediately suspicious and just knew it meant something.

'Dean. I've had a thought. Maybe I could come to The Hempel with you?'

Dean froze on the spot.

Shit shit shit!

With as much naturalness as he could produce, he came back quickly, 'Ah no, love, I wish you could but Dan already asked if his wife could come and they said no.'

It scared Dean how rapidly and easily that lie fell from his mouth.

Brooke slumped on the bed. 'But the room's paid for anyway, what difference does it make? I don't even need to come to the dinner, I'd just stay in the room. It'd be so fantastic.'

'That's exactly the arguments Dan put forward, but they still said no. I think it's because they're suppliers and want to focus on selling us a new telephone system and they know that it'll all become a bit of a jolly if wives and partners come along too.'

God, how am I doing this? Where's all this shit coming from?

To his utter amazement Brooke gave up and simply reiterated what a shame it was.

Unbeknown to Dean, in her mind she was thinking she didn't want Dean to risk upsetting the applecart at work: if she needed to sacrifice her usual pursuance of what she wanted for his (and their) future, then so be it. A wave of self-satisfaction overwhelmed her and she went downstairs to feed Paige.

Dean showered, dressed in his smartest suit, checked his overnight bag and came downstairs.

'Not that tie, Dean, please not that one. Spots and stripes - you can't mix them. Put on that silk plain navy one; much better with that shirt. You've got to look your best for tonight.'

He banged down his bag, shook his head, rolled his eyes, ran upstairs and changed his tie. Like an obedient schoolboy!

'That's much better. Have a fantastic time and don't forget to send me photos.'

'I'll try, but remember I'm working.'

At that, he embraced his wife and daughter.

'See you tomorrow night.'

***

Dean stood across the street from The Hempel, staring at the glossy painted black door. He'd been warned that it was difficult to find as it didn't have a sign of any kind outside, like most hotels. All very discreet and exclusive. He'd read and re-read the brief during lunch and knew to assess the Zen Garden in the square in front of the hotel first.

He stopped and inspected the planting in the garden and couldn't resist bending down to examine the straight, beautiful lines in the lawn. He ran over it with his hand, enjoying the smooth, soft finish of the grass.

's like a grade one.

Then he stood in sheer awe and admiration at how such a perfect lawn had been achieved. He'd read that the garden was used in the filming of *Notting Hill*. Brooke would've loved that. He shook his head in regret that she couldn't see it and then he remembered she'd asked him to take some photos, so he quickly obliged.

He walked across the busy road and towards the front door. He made a mental note of the impression he got from the outside and proceeded to the big black door with its polished brass handle. Was he meant to ring? Knock? Wait? Or just walk in? He hung around for a few moments hoping it'd become obvious what he was meant to do. Nothing.

So he took the plunge, turned the handle and walked in. As the door opened, he immediately became aware of the purity and simplicity of the surroundings and furnishings. In under thirty seconds he'd taken in the floor tiles, walls, lighting, reception desk ahead, reception staff, fireplace and floral display. His heart was pumping yet again. He'd done it. He'd managed to get here on his own and was going to enjoy every single minute of it. Part of him wished that Brooke was there, because she'd have been wild with excitement. He was desperate for a few more photos, but thought he might look a bit naff, so resisted. For a few moments he let it all sink in and enjoyed the thrill of just *being* in a place like this. He imagined that his favourite pop stars would've taken all this in their stride, but, for him, at that moment, he felt like a million dollars.

OK, look like you're used to this.

Dean strolled in a leisurely fashion to the reception desk. The two females standing behind it were dressed top to toe in black, mandarin collars on their jackets, their hair and makeup excellent. They reminded him of those air stewardesses on Virgin Atlantic's First Class adverts.

At once Dean realised that, despite wearing his best bib and tucker, he'd actually been at work all day and was looking somewhat dishevelled. He admonished himself for not thinking to check his appearance before entering.

The decidedly gorgeous brunette on the left asked if he'd like to check in.

'Yeah.' Dean responded casually as he took the opportunity to look around a little more and remember his visit brief.

With a serious face the receptionist said, 'You must be Mr Death. We're expecting you. Welcome to The Hempel.'

Oh my God. Why are they expecting me? What does she mean? Surely they can't think I'm the mystery shopper already? Please God don't let me have screwed up.

'Actually, it's De…'Ath.'

He took the bull by the horns as his heart raced with anxiety once more.

'Why are you expecting me?'

'Apologies, Mr De'Ath. Because we only have one person left to check in today and we know from our booking records that that is you!' The receptionist explained with a warm smile.

Dean was furious with himself. This stupid question revealed his inexperience of staying in hotels of this quality and standard. He wanted the floor to swallow him up.

He tried to brush it off with a laugh and a 'silly me, of course', but he felt most uncomfortable.

Get a grip, Dean. Think. Were the staff wearing the correct uniform and name badges? Please state who checked you in.

Dean looked at the brunette carefully. His eye caught her name badge, but he couldn't quite read the small writing. As she focussed on her administration for a few moments, he put his glasses on and peered down at the name badge which was inconveniently pinned on her right nipple area. 'Antonella'. He looked up to see her staring at him, staring at her nipple, with a look of disdain on her face. Dean had always been prone to going bright red at the slightest thing, and this minor episode turned him as purple as sprouting broccoli. She explained that his room wasn't quite ready yet and asked that he wait in the lobby until she called him over to check in.

She escorted him over to a white leather sofa, by the stone open fireplace, nestled in the centre of a dividing wall and offered to get him a drink. He declined and sat down. All around him was white and he mused whether this was what Heaven might look like. The flame flickering away in the centre of the fireplace was fake, he realised. He thought about Brooke again and how much she'd have adored the ambience of this place. Oh the guilt! He spent the next twenty minutes flicking through *The Times* newspaper nearby; not really reading it (it wasn't his bag), more just passing time. He took the *Daily Mail.*

After around twenty-five minutes, Antonella came over to him, apologised for the delay, said his room was now ready for him and invited him to the desk. He walked behind her as she strutted to Reception. Dean thought she had the most amazing bottom; made even more beautiful by the tight black skirt she was wearing. Now the room was ready, she dealt with him so efficiently that he was checked in, in less than two minutes. She offered a wake-up call, newspaper, key to his room and directions to said room, all at lightning speed. It was like listening to Angie. His mouth opened wide, trying to compute everything she'd said, like a typical man trying to remember six items his wife has given him for an emergency shopping list.

Were you asked if you wanted to book a table in the restaurant? If not please give staff an opportunity to do so.

Well he hadn't been. Or at least he didn't think so. She was so fast! Dean hung around awkwardly, pretending that he was searching for something in his pockets. He then opened his overnight bag, but still no offer of dinner was forthcoming.

'Are there any decent restaurants around here?' he finally blurted out.

'Several,' replied Antonella with a smile. 'What kind of food are you looking for?'

Dean hesitated. He couldn't describe what kind of food they served at The Hempel.

'Oh I don't mind, really.'

She went through an entire list of nearby restaurants and described them in detail, but at no time did she recommend their own. Dean was stumped.

I'll have to mark that as a 'No', but that's criminal. She was so helpful.

He mumbled something about how he'd have to think about it, but he was hungry and didn't want to go too far. At that point, she said that he could always eat in their 35 restaurant, here in the hotel.

Dean was relieved. He could change that to a yes.

He picked up his bags and headed in the general direction that Antonella had indicated to get to his room, but he couldn't see where he was meant to go. She pointed right ahead of him and said to 'just go through the door'. But there wasn't a door. He walked all the way along the wall and back. There was no door! It was just a wall. Oozing self-consciousness and panic, his eyes darted about to check that no-one was watching him.

I bet Bono doesn't struggle to find the fucking door!

He stood back from the white wall for a moment and analysed it, gradually becoming aware of an almost invisible line in the wall. He went back over to it and pushed where he saw the line. Something seemed to give, but not completely, so he just kept pressing up and down the line with his hand, like someone searching for a hidden compartment. Eventually, much to his relief, the wall opened up and let him in. The door was actually part of the wall.

Why the hell didn't they explain that at Reception? Well that's going down in the report. How bloody stupid is that? Making a door that doesn't even look like a door that no-one can even find?

As the door opened, he had to kick it to keep it from banging back again as both his hands were full. He'd declined luggage assistance.

Oh hell. Please don't tell me that was me. I'm positive they weren't there before.

What looked like a mass of black fingerprints suddenly came into focus. On the door. All round the opening. The gleaming white interior of this exquisite hotel had been infected with an unwanted display of black ink from the newspaper Dean had been reading. He took one more furtive glance around and thought it best to move on.

As he made his way through the airy corridors to his room, he began to feel guilty at leaving the handprints. He ran through all the options. He could go back and tell Reception, but that seemed a bit too keen or if he bumped into a housekeeper he could mention it.

Maybe I could try and clean it off myself later? But what if they caught me?

In the end, Dean decided to just leave it. He arrived at the door to his room and unlocked it with his key card. As he walked in, he started to laugh and dropped his bags on the floor as the door banged shut behind him. He stood near the door, legs apart, arms folded, mouth open, head shaking, perusing the surreal sight before him.

A huge high bed easily big enough for three people was positioned in the centre of the room. The height of it reminded him of The Princess and The Pea. Spotless, white linen, pillows higher than he'd ever seen, cushions plumped up to bursting and placed like a piece of artwork on the bed. His inner child escaped as he ran over, jumping up as high as he could, landing in the middle of the bed and laughing some more, ending up with his hands behind his head staring up at the ceiling.

Oh, Brooke. I wish you was here to share this with me.

Another wave of guilt flooded his heart. The fact that he *could've* got her to come, but chose not to, began to gnaw away at his conscience.

Was the bed correctly made, the linen clean, free from creases and cushions neatly placed on the bed?

Dean snapped out of his semi daydream and remembered why he was there and what he was supposed to be doing. He quickly jumped off the bed, as though this would restore it to its original state. He peered at the linen and cushions. He was in a dilemma. There were definitely creases, but he couldn't be sure if he caused them or if they were there before. He put his glasses on and gave the whole bed a more thorough inspection. He decided to give the hotel the benefit of the doubt and mark this question in the positive.

Was the bathroom clean and fresh-smelling?

Dean moved into the bathroom and found himself laughing out loud again. The bath was sunk into what looked like a marble floor; a strange-looking metal object at one end, which he guessed was the tap, gleamed; yearning to be turned on. There was a separate shower, with an array of taps and outrageously huge shower heads and Dean's mind went into overdrive imagining what you did with them all. Fancy brands of toiletries lined the bath and the sink surround.

He caught sight of his reflection in the mirror and stared at himself. He wanted to weep. He struggled to put his finger on his emotions but a combination of excitement, guilt, worry and loneliness probably just about described them.

He took numerous photos before trying to push his feelings aside, so he could continue assessing the hotel.

11

Dining At The Hempel

Dean couldn't decide whether to have a shower, get changed and freshen up *before* dinner, or have dinner first and then relax in a bath *afterwards.* He didn't much like the idea of wallowing in a hot bath after a big meal. But then again, he didn't really want to get all hot and sweaty in a bath before dinner. Mind you, he thought, he'd have to have a shower in the morning as well anyway. He felt he really didn't want or need so much time in water. He looked at the shower and the bath as if that'd help him decide and stared for some time at the contraption at the end of the bath, which he thought was a tap, but now wasn't quite so sure.

He decided that wallowing in hot water after dinner was the lesser of two evils. He'd shower in the morning. He freshened up, brushed his suit, tightened his tie, then took one more look at the questionnaire, checked what he needed to do and ask over dinner and then proceeded to the restaurant.

Considering the hotel was nearly full, the bar was completely empty, but then again, he realised that it was actually quite late; 9.30pm, to be precise. He did feel rather conspicuous when he went to the bar to order a drink, as the visit brief had required him to do before dinner.

You must ask for a recommendation at the bar and test the knowledge of the bar person.

'Hi there, what can you recommend?' Dean asked awkwardly.

The barman looked somewhat bewildered. 'What sort of thing would you like? Wine? Beer? Spirits?'

Dean hadn't really thought this through. He glanced quickly at the bar behind and noted an array of whiskies. He never drank the stuff himself but knew that some people really liked their whiskies. 'What whisky do you have?'

The barman's eyes lit up. 'Well, sir, we have one of the finest range of whiskies anywhere in London. Single malt, I'm assuming?'

Dean had no idea what he meant and, before he knew what'd happened, 'of course' confidently slipped from his lips without batting an eyelid.

Bloody hell, I never drink whisky, where did that come from? Such bullshit!

At once, the barman pulled eight different bottles forward onto the bar with an enthusiastic glint in his eye. As he placed them down one by one, he recited their names. It was only then that Dean became aware of his accent. Scottish.

Oh my God! What have I done? Why me?

'So what's it to be, sir? Or would you like to see some more?'

'Erm…erm…I'll have the…I'll have the…' Out of sheer desperation not to look idiotic, Dean chose the one that was easiest to pronounce. 'The Glen Grant please.'

Dean didn't know if he was imagining it or not, but the barman seemed surprised and appeared to raise his eyebrow slightly, in disapproval.

'Can I assume a double dram? And would you like water with that?'

Oh fuck. I dunno. Should I have? Is that normal?

He didn't like the sound of adding water to it.

'Er…no thanks. Maybe I could have it on the rocks?'

The barman stopped what he was doing and looked Dean square in the eye.

Dean was transported to the naughty corner at school.

Shit shit shit, he knows I don't know what I'm talking about. On the rocks? Is that even a valid expression nowadays?

The barman paused for the briefest of moments and replied. 'Glen Grant…on the rocks it is, sir.'

He handed over the malt with one lump of ice in a heavy-bottomed whisky tumbler. Dean stared at the amber liquid, anxious not to drink it. The barman waited. Dean picked it up, sniffed the glass, held his breath and downed it all in one. Isn't that what you're supposed to do? The barman smiled, turned away and emptied his glasswasher.

Dean decided he didn't like the barman. He was sure

he was laughing at him.

Did the bar person make you feel welcome and engage you in friendly conversation?

No. He made me feel like a dipstick.

The warmth of the whisky, despite not liking the taste at all, made him feel slightly fuzzy and very relaxed. In fact, he was amazed at the speed of his body's response.

By now it was 9.45pm and Dean recalled that the restaurant was due to shut at 10pm. He panicked and marched to the entrance, where the young woman standing over her reservations book looked alarmed. Her name badge looked like it said 'Kate'.

'Mr De'Ath? We assumed you weren't coming, sir. Are you still wishing to have dinner?'

Paralysed by indecision, he just didn't know what to do for the best but eventually confirmed that he *was* still having dinner, his smile hiding the sheer awkwardness he felt.

This sense of awkwardness only increased when he entered the restaurant, only to discover it was deserted. He looked around in dismay and casually said, 'It's De 'Ath, by the way; two syllables... Am I really the only one having dinner?'

Kate glared and stated that it'd actually been a busy evening and the kitchen was closing in a few minutes.

Oh God. The brief said I've gotta have starter, main, dessert and coffee.

With that in mind, he followed her closely and sat

down fast as she placed the menu and drinks list on the table and offered him a beverage. He was still feeling rather woozy from his whisky, but he had to test her knowledge on cocktails and wine.

As she went to walk away, he put his arm on hers to stop her and told her not to go. As he speedily glanced over the cocktail list the whisky sour caught his eye. Not only would it mean he was sticking to the same spirit but he could actually think of a question to ask. He ventured, 'I'll have a whisky sour, please. Would you happen to know if the egg you use in this cocktail is organic?'

She tried her best to act professionally, but curtly replied that all their eggs were organic. Dean could tell that she was irritated and that he'd ruined any prospect of her going home early. She was back in a couple of minutes with his cocktail and immediately asked if he was ready to order.

He took a deep breath as he ordered the starter that he reckoned needed no preparation – smoked salmon. Her face spoke volumes. Kate clearly assumed he wouldn't order a starter at all! He then asked for medium-rare steak with a salad – that'd mean no veg preparation – just turning over a steak for a few minutes. That'd be easy.

She wrote it down and almost ran to the kitchen; presumably to check that the chef hadn't already left for the night. A vision of a *Fawlty Towers* episode came into his mind where a guest ends up cooking his own dinner because the chef wasn't around. He smiled to himself and took a sip of his whisky sour. Vomit-inducing; he put the glass back down as though it contained some unknown poison. But it did look nice, so out came his phone for a snap!

Within only a couple of minutes the smoked salmon arrived. He ate it as rapidly as possible, all the time Kate's beady eyes watching him from the other side of the restaurant, although whenever he caught her eye she immediately looked down at her imaginary paperwork. Dean made a point of pushing his plate to one side to show he'd finished. She was over like a shot the moment his hand left the plate She removed it and was about to walk off when Dean remembered he was meant to order wine and test her knowledge. He'd barely even touched his whisky sour.

For God's sake; she's gonna think I'm some kind of alky!

'Could I possibly see the wine list?'

For a split second, it looked like the professional Kate was going to say something undesirable. Instead she smiled sweetly and said 'Of course, sir.'

She brought it and waited while he glanced through it quickly.

'What do you think would go best with my steak? I only want a glass.'

As sharp as a Wüsthof, she replied that they currently had a superb 2009 Argentinian Malbec, by the glass, which she'd highly recommend. Dean didn't argue; he simply agreed. He just wanted to get out of the restaurant pronto.

He was barely even thinking about what he should've been observing for the questionnaire.

She soon came over with his glass of red wine and, pointing to the whisky sour virtually untouched on the table, asked, 'Have you finished, sir?'

Dean immediately became concerned.

Why's she smiling? She knows I can't drink it. I bet she knows I'm the mystery shopper... Keep cool, just keep your cool.

'No, sorry, I'm just a bit slow!'

What a stupid thing to say, what the hell made me say that?

He picked up the glass and forced a few gulps down. She nodded and walked away. No sooner had she done so than Dean could hear a bell coming from the direction of the kitchen. She increased her pace and pushed the kitchen door hard, returning a moment later with Dean's steak. She offered all manner of sauces, but Dean stuck to English mustard. She returned to her observation spot.

Dean cut the steak right down the middle and was horrified to see that it wasn't just medium–rare, it was bleeding forcefully. The last time he tried to eat steak like that he was sick. He was torn between lengthening the assessment, keeping Kate and the chef from their bed, and being sick.

He motioned for Kate to come to the table.

'I'm really sorry but I can't eat this steak – it's too bloody for me.'

'Well that's how chef cooks medium–rare steak, sir, but I can ask him to cook it a little more for you if you prefer.'

'Yes please, sorry to bother you.'

That sounded way too grovelly. I bet the people who come here never say anything like that. I bet they just expect them to do whatever they want.

'No problem,' she lied and proceeded to rush into the kitchen with the steak. Through the toe-curling silence of the empty hotel restaurant, Dean heard raised voices in the kitchen. Never had he felt such a nuisance. The agony of it!

As he waited for his re-cooked steak, he glanced around the restaurant and became aware that virtually all the tables were set up for breakfast.

The steak arrived and, like the smoked salmon, Dean scoffed it down at speed, gulping large mouthfuls of red wine in between until everything was gone. He could feel Kate's eyes peering at him.

God, I'm stuffed.

Kate appeared at the table within a moment of him finishing, picked up the plate and asked him if he'd like the bill.

Oh shit!

He hadn't had coffee or dessert yet and couldn't answer this part of the questionnaire unless he experienced them.

'Actually, I'm still a tad peckish.'

'I'll bring the dessert menu,' Kate said in a manner that

suggested she thought he was probably a little disturbed. She dashed off again and returned with the dessert menu, which she proceeded to open for him and recommended the homemade granny smith sorbet.

'Done deal. I'll have that and a cappuccino please.'

By this time, it almost felt like a race; like that chap on the TV programme *Man Versus Food*. Kate went away to tackle the chef, who almost certainly had his coat on ready to leave. It was 10.45pm. Dean would never know the abuse she'd received when she asked for the sorbet.

She arrived with the bright-green mass of sorbet scoops, plus the coffee and bill all on one tray and placed them on the table.

'May I ask you to sign the bill, sir, so I can cash up please?'

Dean couldn't sign it fast enough.

She politely thanked him and disappeared. That was the last he saw of her.

He looked at his sorbet in despair and wondered if he could get away with not eating it, as it seemed likely Kate had probably finished and gone. But he was intrigued by its bright-green colour and tried a small spoonful of it.

Oh my God! This is delicious. Never tasted ice cream like this.

He quickly took a photo and then savoured the whole three scoops, after which he took one gulp of his lukewarm coffee and released a resonating burp. He automatically put his hand to his mouth and looked furtively around the restaurant, exclaiming out loud in an exaggerated fashion '*pardon me*!' – even thought there was no-one there to hear him. His mother had always taught him that table manners were important.

He stood up with a groan that demonstrated he'd eaten too much. His napkin was tossed onto the table and he strolled out of the restaurant rubbing his tummy as he began to think about his compulsory and imminent bath.

12

The Unexpected Visit

Now that dinner was over, Dean felt safe to turn his mobile back on. He was terrified that Brooke would call him during the evening and demand photos of the whole team and every dish they'd eaten. He was most surprised, if not a tad suspicious, that she'd not tried to message him even once.

As he scrolled through his other messages, one stood out. It was from Chloe in the office. She never contacted him. When he read it, his stomach dropped like on the Oblivion ride at Alton Towers.

Dean – am out with mates near The Hempel – fancy a drink? I'd love to see what it's like!

That message was at 10pm. It was now 10.50pm and Dean was ready for bed. Then he remembered that he had to have a bath yet. That was the last thing he needed. And he had to order room service!

Bloody 'ell. They'll think I'm the greediest bloke on the planet!

He decided to ignore the message and hope Chloe would assume that he hadn't picked it up. He walked through the lobby and turned to go through the doorless white wall when someone called his name.

'Dean…Dean!'

He turned round and there sitting in the foyer, looking both worried and excited, was the gorgeous Chloe.

Oh fuck! What the—

Dean looked around nervously and stepped over to the sofa.

'What the bloody 'ell are you doing here?' he whispered angrily.

'Don't be narked. Like I said, I was in the area with my mates and I remembered you were gonna do your…' Chloe lowered her voice, 'I mean, *be here this evening.* What's your room like, then?'

Dean was so terrified he'd be seen by the receptionists and that his cover would be blown, that he said firmly, 'The bar'll be shut now so, no, we can't have a drink. You shouldn't have come.'

Dean was incapable of not letting his angst show in his body language. He was becoming an expert in furtive looks and he'd begun to perspire.

Chloe couldn't stop herself from laughing as she watched Dean look so helpless and anxious. 'Keep your shirt on, Dean. No-one knows who I am or why I'm here. You might well be a businessman who's arranged to meet a colleague – or a hooker for a meeting!' She continued to giggle and Dean realised she was rather merry. He just wanted to get her out of the hotel, but he sensed that might turn into a bit of a scene. Maybe if he just quickly showed her his room that'd satisfy her and then she'd go.

'Right, come with me.'

At that, Dean became unusually aggressive, grabbed her by the arm and yanked her up roughly and quickly from the sofa.

'Ooooh, where are you taking me?'

Dean pulled her along quickly whilst he could see that the girl on Reception was occupied with another guest. 'You can see my room and then you've gotta go. I haven't finished my assessment yet; there's loads more I've got to do.'

He then pushed the white wall from Hell and pulled Chloe through it. He let go of her arm and walked at speed, urging her to hurry up the stairs to the second floor; he thought they'd be less likely to meet staff on the stairs than in the lift.

Just as they arrived at the second-floor landing, a housekeeper walked from around the corner straight into them. Dean immediately observed her name badge. 'Agnes'.

'Good evening, sir…madam.'

Why's she looking at me like that? I know what she's thinking. She definitely looked at me funny.

'Evening.' Moving his hand to point to Chloe, he said, 'this is a friend.'

The housekeeper smiled, nodded and walked on.

What a stupid thing to say, no-one would ever say that.

For fuck's sake, this is gonna end up bad.

'I've never been called madam before.' Chloe giggled.

Dean tugged her along the corridor until they got to his room. He fumbled around for his key card and swiped. Nothing happened. He swiped again waiting for the wretched light to turn from red to green. Nothing. He tried a third time and then got angry.

Why me? Why do these things always happen to me? I bet Chris Martin's key always bloody works.

Dean stood outside the door, shaking his head from side to side in frustration, with Chloe standing obediently and quietly by his side. Even she could see this wasn't the time to say anything sassy. Very sensible.

'Right, wait on the stairs while I go and get help.'

Before she'd a chance to argue, Dean bolted off down the stairs and into Reception.

Chloe walked awkwardly to the stairwell and waited there as requested, looking around her to make sure no-one was watching. As she stood there feeling quite tipsy, she started to lament coming. She'd seen a side of Dean she didn't normally see. The slightly cheeky Essex boy suddenly appeared to be a highly strung boring old fart with no sense of humour; not the Dean she knew at all. For a few moments she toyed with the idea of just leaving, but she really was desperate to see this place after all she'd heard.

Dean arrived at the front desk looking stressed.

'Sorry to bother you, but my door won't open with

this card.' Dean looked apologetic, as though it was his fault not theirs. This happened to Sylvie at least a dozen times a day.

'Are you sure you swiped it the right way round? It's an easy mistake to make.'

'I'm quite sure. I tried three times.' Dean wasn't in the mood for a battle and, uncharacteristically, he said curtly, 'Can someone just please get me into my room? I'm tired and just want to get to bed.'

Sylvie suddenly stood very upright in response to the abrupt comment. She hadn't had Dean down as a complainer. She'd thought she'd sussed him out quickly as someone on business who'd come up trumps with his employer, who'd probably got a deal on Lastminute.com. That lot were usually so overawed with the hotel that they weren't too fussed about anything else.

'Of course, sir, let me come up and try a new key card with you.'

She called quickly for Mohammed the night porter who was just about to come on duty, to cover her while she accompanied Dean upstairs to his room. She brought a new key card with her and went to walk the short flight upstairs, when Dean remembered that Chloe was waiting on the stairwell.

'Sorry, I've got a bad foot and I'd rather get the lift if you don't mind.'

'Of course. Not a problem, sir.' Sylvie looked down at his feet, clearly wondering which one was the problem and what the problem was exactly.

She escorted Dean to his bedroom and swiped her key card, which opened the door first time. Dean shrugged his shoulders and smiled stupidly.

'Well I can promise you that didn't happen with my key card. But thanks anyway.'

Chloe was listening out for cues as to when she could return to Dean's room.

Sylvie smiled, nodded, said good evening and walked off towards the stairwell.

Chloe decided she'd waited long enough; she left the stairwell and walked towards Dean's room. As she turned the corridor, she bumped into Agnes the housekeeper.

'Ohh…can I help you, madam?' Agnes enquired slightly suspiciously.

'No I'm fine, thanks. No worries.' Chloe thought she should just act nonchalantly. She made no eye contact with Agnes and minced her way along the corridor, smiling politely at Sylvie as she passed, until she got to Dean's room. Only then did she look around as furtively as Dean.

Agnes wasn't silly. There was nothing that she'd not seen before. Hookers (male and female), colleagues having one-night stands, full-blown affairs, lady boys, transsexuals, transvestites and those who clearly couldn't quite make up their mind.

Chloe knocked on the door and looked around, only to see Agnes staring at her as bold as brass at the end of the corridor. Dean opened the door and beckoned to Chloe to come in pronto, looking out of his room and also coming eye to eye with Agnes. She simply stood there motionless, emotionless and with just a hint of cynicism on her face. She turned around and walked away.

Chloe shut the door behind her and caught sight of the bed. 'Aaaaah! OH…MY… GOD!'

'Right, just have a quick look and you've gotta go.' The command came out in a slightly high-pitched and anxious voice.

'Oh for God's sake, Dean, don't be such a bore! Let's have some fun!'

That phrase utterly terrified Dean. He had a slightly odd relationship with Chloe at work. She was very flirtatious, but he had quickly realised that it wasn't just with him – she was flirty with all the chaps. The only way she seemed to be different with him, was that they'd talk in a more deep and meaningful way about personal issues. (Although he talked to her about his life significantly more than she ever talked about hers.) He didn't see her doing that with any of her other colleagues. Within a matter of seconds, his mind filled with all manner of things that she might mean and he became visibly distraught. Unfortunately for Dean that made his situation worse and Chloe's determination to get him to lighten up even stronger.

'Chloe.' Dean was doing his utmost to sound as serious as possible. 'You really do have to go. You can't hang around here – you just can't. I've got other stuff I've got to do for my assessment.'

'Like what?'

'Well, like ordering room service for a start.'

'Well I can help you out there. I've not eaten yet and I'm absolutely starving!'

Dean paused. He felt a bit sick after devouring so much and he had to admit to himself that the last thing on earth he felt like doing was eating and drinking any more.

Actually, that's a brilliant idea. I can test out the room service without actually having to eat anything.

'You know what, you've got a point. That could work. I'm stuffed and I've gotta order some food and a drink.'

Chloe jumped back on the bed and made herself comfortable by plumping up the pillows and cushions behind her. Without asking, she picked up the TV remote and switched onto Channel 4. Dean watched on, seemingly unable to decide whether to pursue this strategy or not. He looked totally helpless.

'Where's the room service menu?' Chloe enquired.

Without waiting for an answer, she jumped off the bed, searched through the drawers of the desk and found the hotel's guide. It was rather sticky and it looked as though a number of pages were missing. Those that were in the folder were rather creased. She grimaced.

'What's the matter?' Dean asked

'This folder is grim...really sticky.'

'Oh hang on a minute!'

Dean got very excited and grabbed the questionnaire

he'd been diligently filling in earlier on.

'Was the hotel guide easy to find, clean and up to date with all the information you needed to make your stay easy and enjoyable?'

'What the fuck are you talking about, Dean?'

'Sorry, that's one of the questions in the mystery shopping assessment.'

'Ah. Well in that case, no. Can I order some food now? I'm so hungry.'

Dean gave in and Chloe took his lack of response to the question as a disguised invitation to select something. She perused the short but delicious menu and was so hungry she didn't have the patience to really consider her choice fully.

'How about a funghi pizza and a glass of red wine?'

Oh God, is that OK? The brief doesn't really specify what I've got to order, just says some food and a drink.

Dean dithered, trying to think of any reason why this order may not be acceptable; but he couldn't come up with one.

'I'll take that as a yes, then,' Chloe said impatiently, as she stared at Dean waiting for an answer. She struggled to understand how hard he seemed to find it to make a decision about even the smallest thing.

Dean was gradually giving up the fight.

'OK, I'll order that, but as soon as you've finished it you've gotta get out of here, OK?'

'OK, pinky promise!' Chloe held up her bent little

finger.

Dean took another look at the questionnaire, to double-check that he'd asked all the right questions. He picked up the phone, dialled Reception and asked for room service.

'This is Kate speaking, how may I help you?'

Dean froze. He was sure that was the voice of Kate in the restaurant earlier.

'Oh hi, I just wanted to order a funghi pizza and a glass of merlot please?'

There was a moment of two of silence that made Dean hold his breath.

'Is that Mr De'Ath?'

Fuck,fuck,fuck! What do I say?

'Erm…yeah.'

'I thought I recognised your voice. I served you earlier in the restaurant.'

Oh shit! That's me done then! I've just eaten a fucking three-course meal and less than half an hour later I'm ordering more food!

'Oh…hi.'

Act blasé. Bono probably orders all manner of stuff at all times of the day and night. It's not that weird. It really isn't.

'How long do you think it'll take?'

'About twenty minutes, sir.'

'OK, thanks.'

'No problem at all. We'll be with you shortly. Bye.'

She definitely had a smirk in her voice. Dean could hear it. He pictured her on the other end of the phone imagining him as Homer Simpson. Dean put the phone down, looked at the floor, shut his eyes and shook his head.

'What's the matter? You look like your whole world's caved in.' Chloe looked quizzically at Dean.

'Nothing, just nothing.'

Chloe shrugged and took it upon herself to explore the bathroom. She opened the door and eyed up the toiletries she saw lined up next to the bath.

'Yippee! Molton Brown! Can I take some of these, Dean? You won't be using all of them, will you?'

'Er, yeah, sure. I do need to have a bath though, so just leave me some soap, will you?' He was weary.

Chloe grabbed all the mini bottles of body wash, shampoo, conditioner and body lotion and left just a small bar of soap on the side. She went back into the bedroom and threw them into her handbag.

'What do you mean, anyway, that you need to have a bath? No-one *needs* to have a bath.'

Dean took nearly ten minutes to explain in minute detail, all the things that he had to check and assess in both the bedroom and the bathroom; the whole questionnaire had 250 questions, of which 115 were about those two rooms alone. Chloe listened aghast, kicked off her shoes and then jumped on the bed. She snatched the questionnaire out of Dean's hand and flicked through it, stopping every so often, laughing heartily at what he was meant to check for.

'Bloody hell, who cares if the toilet roll end has been shaped into a triangle?'

Dean snatched the questionnaire back again, suddenly aware of the fact that Chloe was making herself rather too comfortable. She'd already been in his room at least twenty minutes and she hadn't even eaten room service yet. He just wanted her out ASAP.

There was a knock on the door. 'Room service!' Dean found himself with the increasingly all-too-familiar feeling of being frozen on the spot.

'Get in the bathroom, quick!' Dean hissed, leaving Chloe in no doubt he wasn't to be argued with. She leaped off the bed, dived into the bathroom and shut the door behind her. Dean opened the room door with an air of calculated indifference.

'Good evening, sir, where would you like me to put the tray?'

'Oh, anywhere will do – over there's fine.'

Dean motioned to the small round table in one corner of the bedroom.

The porter did as he was asked. As he left the tray to walk out of the room, Dean noticed a bright-red stiletto heel sticking out from under the bottom of the bed. Having partly defrosted, he froze yet again, but this time, his heart started thumping so fast he thought it would explode out of his chest and splat onto the wall opposite.

He saw the porter glance down at it and continue

walking towards the door. Dean followed him like a naughty child, begging to be forgiven. As the porter reached the door, he turned round and smiled, 'Thank you, sir, have an enjoyable evening!' And then he walked away.

What does he mean: have an enjoyable evening? What does he think I'm gonna be doing? Why did he say that?

Dean shut the door, held his head in both hands and screamed out loud. Chloe burst in from the bathroom looking extremely alarmed.

'What the hell's the matter *now*?'

'I'm done. That's what's the matter. I'm in deep shit!'

'Why?'

'He saw your fucking shoes, that's why! You've gotta go. Right now!'

'But I haven't had my pizza or my wine yet.' Chloe looked disappointed.

'That's too bloody bad.'

Dean picked up her shoes and handbag and handed them to her. He pushed her onto the bed and started putting her shoes on for her, as she was still clearly inebriated and such a delicate operation would take her a while without assistance he decided; and he didn't have 'a while'.

She giggled and let him thread the strap through the tiny loop and find the holes, as she leaned over to the table and grabbed the glass of wine from the tray.

'Keep still!' Dean demanded. Chloe ignored him and carried on anyway.

As he sat upright from her feet he banged his head right up onto the glass of wine and sent it flying across the room. In what appeared like slow motion it smashed and the contents sunk quickly into the exquisite cream carpet.

'Aaaaagh! No!'

Dean instantly abandoned Chloe's feet and ran over to the blood-red patch on the carpet. He wanted to weep and, indeed, the position of his body indicated he was doing precisely that.

Even Chloe realised her time was up, and she surprised herself that she could be brought so abruptly to sobriety. She quickly finished doing up her shoes, folded the pizza over and chomped away while checking that she hadn't left anything in the room.

'Dean. I'm really sorry. I think it's best I leave. Thanks for showing me up here and I'm really sorry if I've messed things up.'

She then staggered out, dripping mozzarella and chilli oil all the way down the corridor.

13

Bath-time, Brooke and The Missing Toiletries

Dean didn't even get up when Chloe left. He simply stared vacantly at the carpet and wondered why God seemed so set on punishing him. He was emotionally spent and he hadn't even finished his assessment yet. The visit hadn't turned out to be quite as relaxing as he'd hoped. He rose slowly from his all-fours position and sat on the edge of the bed trying to decide on his course of action.

Bath. I need to try the bath. Was the bath easy and pleasant to use? Were there sufficient toiletries for your needs?

Dean walked into the bathroom and at one end of the bath there was a metal contraption that he assumed was the tap. He peered into the deep oval tub and looked quizzically at the round chrome dome at the bottom. He gawped at the various knobs and tried to work out how to make the plug go down. The one he had at home that looked similar to this, was worked by a pull-up arrangement behind the main taps, but there was nothing like this here at all. He tried every combination of pulling, twisting and lifting, but nothing would make the plug go down. Dean was getting agitated, unable to accept that he was struggling to run a bath because he couldn't work out how to put the plug in.

Brooke. She'll know how to do it.

Brooke was always drooling over fancy bathrooms and kitchens in *Homes & Gardens*. Every time she bought a copy, he dreaded what she was going to require him to do next in the house.

But he had to prepare himself for this phone call. He knew it'd be like the Spanish Inquisition and he wasn't in the mood for that. He went back into the bedroom to get his phone and tried to think of an excuse he could give as to why he would have to get back off the phone quickly. The ceiling was his friend once again, but as usual came up with no answers.

Instead, he turned his phone on only to find a flurry of messages from Brooke. He didn't read them but took a photo of the plug and the collection of taps and sent a message asking how the plug went down – nothing else.

She sent a message back immediately. She must've been waiting by her phone all night. Dean felt an overwhelming sense of guilt and fear pass right through him.

What's it like? Where are the photos? What toiletries have they got? What's the food like? Can't believe u haven't rung me!

Dean ignored the messages and just hoped she'd answer his question.

After a moment or two, she replied.

Push the bloody thing down at the bottom of the bath. Why are you having a bath at 11pm? You never even have a bath at home.

Push it down? Just push it down?

It must've been the only thing he didn't try. He went back into the bathroom and pushed the chrome dome down and heard it click.

For Christ's sake, what's the matter with me?

He then went back to the taps. All he wanted to do now was run some hot water. But no water came. He pushed, pulled, turned, pressed and lifted. Nothing. Quite frankly he wanted to scream with exhaustion and go to sleep.

He took another photo of the contraption and sent it to Brooke asking how to turn the hot water tap on.

Back came the LOL emoji x 3.

OMG Dean, pull and twist to the right at the same time, left is cold. NOT HARD!!! Send photos of room!!!

Dean followed his wife's instructions and out poured the hot water. He was so happy. He suddenly realised why he loved his wife. She knew stuff. Despite not actually being a woman of the world, she was very worldly. While the water gushed out from a sort of spout thing overhanging the bath, he got undressed.

Dean was a creature of habit and a perfectionist about most things. How he removed and hung up his clothes – particularly his trousers – was one of them. He held them over one arm whilst trying to remove a hanger from the wardrobe. He tugged and twisted and pulled up and down but couldn't, for the life of him, get the hanger off the contraption it was attached to. In the end, he threw his trousers onto the bed, leaving both hands free to remove the hanger, after which he smoothed his trousers down again and hung them folded over at the crutch.

His jacket was also hung up on a separate hanger. The buttons were done up and he took a small clothes brush from his overnight case to brush it down. Brooke thought this was hysterical. She told him he looked like a butler from *Downton Abbey*. Dean wasn't perturbed in the slightest by her ribbing. He picked up his OCD habit of looking after his stuff from his grandad, who was very particular about such things, having been in the Royal Navy.

By now, his bath was almost overflowing. He was surprised at how quickly it'd filled up. He couldn't help but think about how long his bath at home took to fill up in comparison. They had a tiny water tank at Elephant Close and very low water pressure, which meant it took around forty-five minutes to fill. If they wanted a bath, they had to plan it at least an hour in advance, so they very rarely bothered. Brooke did have a thing about them though and was always trying to persuade Dean to join her. She was convinced that their bath was big enough for both of them, but it really wasn't. A couple of times they'd tried, but the water had flooded over the rim onto the floor and Dean couldn't sit comfortably with Brooke's size eights outside his hips without him getting stuck. She'd get so upset when her advances (made by candlelight and incense) were met with groans about how small the bath was and how she'd pulled the sealant away from the tiles; any ardour she had quickly dissipated.

Dean gingerly dipped his toe into the water, as though he was about to go swimming off Canvey Island. He smiled. It was so warm and inviting. He lowered himself into the water and groaned with pleasure. As he let his head fall back onto the pillow head rest and let his arms dangle outside, he gazed at the ceiling. For the first time since he arrived at The Hempel, he actually relaxed.

The whisky, the wine, the obscene amount of food, the heat of the bath, the surreal nature of where he was and what he was doing suddenly came over him in a warm fuzzy haze. He felt momentarily content.

It didn't take him long however, to decide he really did have to call Brooke.

He sent her a message to get onto Skype.

Brooke was in bed on her iPpad watching a documentary about Machu Picchu. She immediately stopped and picked up Dean's Skype call.

'Why haven't you called me? I can't believe you haven't even sent me any photos!! Where are you? You look like you're in the bath?'

'I'm in the bath and it's gorgeous. I didn't want to call you until I was alone. I feel as horny as hell and I really wish you were here. Just look at this.' Dean used his phone to show Brooke the bathroom, slowly panning the camera around so she could see everything.

'Oh…My…God…that's mental…where's all the toiletries? They always give classy toiletries away in those kinds of hotels. I can't see any.'

Dean glanced over to the side, where he was sure there were toiletries before.

'Your bath hasn't even got bubbles in it! Where are the bubbles?!'

'I'm so knackered I didn't even think about bubbles, to be honest, babe.'

'But they must be there somewhere. There's no way that hotel wouldn't have Molton Brown or something like it. You just need to look. I'm expecting a whole load of those little bottles when you get back! So what's it been like? What about the food?'

'Well to be honest, babe, I've not had much chance to do anything up until now. The meeting and dinner only just finished, so that's why I didn't pick up your messages before. I turned my phone off, 'cause no-one else was looking at theirs and I didn't wanna be the only one.'

Dean swallowed.

'That's why I didn't bother ringing. I didn't wanna embarrass you. You're *important* now! But I've been dying to hear all about it.'

With that, Dean turned the phone camera on to himself to reveal just how much he missed her.

'You are a right naughty boy, Dean De'Ath! Just wait

till you get home!'

'What happened to withdrawing me conjugal rights? Seriously, babe, I'm shattered, so I'm gonna get off the phone now, but I've got loads of photos, so I'll show you them all when I get home tomorrow. I really wish you was here.'

And at that moment he really meant it.

'Alright, love. Enjoy your bath – I wish we had one as big as that – then I might get you in more often!'

'Night, babe!'

'Night.'

Dean's head hit the pillow and he breathed a sigh of relief as he sank back under the water again. She wasn't as narked as he thought she might be.

His mind wandered and he started thinking about what he'd write in his report about the 'fucking taps and plug'.

And where are those toiletries??

At 1.23am Dean woke up in a bath full of lukewarm water. He'd been asleep for at least an hour. His fingers and toes looked like oversized sultanas. Despite his youth, he felt as stiff as one of his own hard-ons, but just about garnered sufficient energy to get out the bath. At least the towel had been hanging on a heated towel rail. It was heaven and he made a mental note they should really get one at home.

He wiped himself down and sat on the bed again, turned the TV onto Sky Sport and watched until he was dry. It had a soporific effect on him and it was as much as he could do to throw the towel off, set his alarm for 7am and crawl into the soft, clean, crisply laundered bed.

He went to turn out the bedside light, but all the switches by his bedside appeared to have gone on strike. He ended up turning the main light on, the hall light off and the desk lamp on, but no joy turning the entire room's lighting system off with one switch. Like a zombie, he reluctantly got back up out of bed and out of sheer exhaustion, took the key card out of the slot by the door. The room went dark and he felt his way back, knocking his shin on the wooden corner of the bedstead on the way.

He crawled back into bed for the second time and was out like a light within seconds.

***

At 7am, the harsh, grating buzzing of his alarm began and, despite having been in the deepest of sleeps, Dean awoke at once, scrambling about to turn the unbearable noise off. He was normally a light sleeper. Since Paige had been born, it'd got even worse. If that baby so much as breathed oddly, Dean could hear it and was up like a shot, inspecting her cot for signs that all wasn't well.

Dean knew he'd to have a shower, even though he was as clean as a scrubbed-up surgeon.

He had a bit of a head.

All that bloody whisky.

He decided he really should fill in the questionnaire before he did anything else. He was worried he'd forget the detail of the previous night. So, he went over to the desk where he'd left it and then as though a crossbow had been fired into his heart, his body went rigid and he came over cold and nauseous.

Oh Christ. Was that there last night when the room service guy put the food down? Oh God, if he saw that I'm well and truly screwed.

He sat on the chair at the desk – the one that nobody ever actually uses in hotels other than to sling their clothes onto – and stared down at the hard copy of the questionnaire opened at page nine and then in the mirror in front of him. He decided he looked rather worse for wear. This often happened to Dean. Once one negative thought had come into his mind, he couldn't seem to stop others from flooding in to join the party. It was as if someone else was responsible and had determined that he'd had things good for just a tad too long and that he really needed to feel bad for a bit. So, he started thinking about the disastrous night with Chloe, Brooke getting cross with him not phoning, being suspected of having a woman in his room by the housekeeper and then the room service guy maybe realising he was the mystery shopper. It was all too much for him. He started sweating and his heart banged against his rib cage with fear and distress. He found it impossible to concentrate on filling in the questionnaire, so he just turned to the page he needed next and checked what he had to answer for the shower.

Was the shower working properly? Were there sufficient toiletries for your needs? Was the shower screen and tray free from smear marks?

Dean looked with trepidation at the array of levers and knobs and his heart sank once again.

Please tell me these will be straightforward.

He nervously went for the most likely tap and, to his joy and delight, water gushed forth, albeit not quite the right temperature. He looked for a hot and cold sign to indicate which way he should turn the knob; he squashed his face right up to the dial and peered behind it to look for one. Not a dicky bird.

Why can't they just put a fucking hot and cold sign? Or a blue and red spot? Something?

Exasperated, he threw caution to the wind and turned it to the right. Within a second or two scalding hot water pumped out, burning his arm. He yelled loudly and promptly turned the knob hard in the other direction and withdrew his arm as if it were about to be bitten off by some rabid creature. He waited for a few moments, felt the water - too cold this time, so very, very slowly and gradually turned the knob round to the right again, but not as far as the first time. A few more moments went by and he meekly put his hand into the fall of water. It had to do. He got in and let the water tumble over him. In the corner of the shower on a small glass shelf, he spied some little bottles of Molton Brown, just like Brooke said there would be. He picked one up to wash himself and looked at the label to check what it was. He squinted and tried to read it, but the font was so small and pale against the liquid inside he simply couldn't. He picked up the others in turn and tried to judge by their colour which was shampoo, which was bodywash and which was conditioner. He sniffed them, squeezed a bit out onto his hand and felt it between his fingers, but it was no good he just couldn't tell.

I don't believe this, for heaven's sake, I just want to wash!

He was angry – so angry! He stormed out of the shower to get his glasses from the desk. It was so cold he dashed back in again and picked up the bottle he thought was bodywash. As he looked at it once more in the shower, his glasses steamed up. He bent down and grabbed the foot towel nearby and rubbed the steam off the lenses.

'Shampoo.'

He threw it on the floor of the shower tray and went for the other bottle with clear liquid and returned to the towel for another wipe of his glasses.

'Bodywash.'

Alle bloody luia!

By now, all he wanted to do was finish as quickly as possible and get out. Dean had never imagined this visit was going to be so stressful.

He bent down to pick up the shampoo he'd thrown into the shower tray and noticed a pinky, slimy lump of something at the very bottom corner of the shower screen. His puppy-like conscientiousness kicked in and he crouched on his hands and knees to inspect the mark properly. He wiped it, sniffed it and the sickly-sweet smell made him almost lick it before deciding that really would be too gross. He concluded it was food of some sort and dreaded to think how it got there; but it was definitely going in his report.

He finished showering and retrieved the large white fluffy bath sheet from the heated towel rail, threw it around his shoulders and then pulled it close to, with his arms underneath. For a few minutes, he felt like a small child. Being wrapped up like that and feeling so cosy and warm reminded him of his Mum patting him dry when he was little, playing 'this little piggy went to market'.

His short-term uplift in mood encouraged him to fill in his questionnaire calmly, so he sat back down at the desk with his towel now wrapped round his waist. Dean wasn't a man to hold back on the word count in his report. His face became stern as he tried to find the right words and phrases to use to describe his experiences. Frown lines appeared as he tapped his pencil between his teeth and periodically shut his eyes in order to help him recall details. By the time he'd finished, it was the *War & Peace* of mystery shopping at The Hempel.

He glanced at his watch and was alarmed to see it was now 8.15am. He was due in work at 9.30am, so he needed to get a move on as he still had to assess breakfast and check out.

He quickly dressed, packed his bag and checked his appearance in the full-length mirror. Finally, he looked around the room briefly to check he'd not forgotten anything; cautious, careful and thorough. At home, whenever he and Brooke went out, he always checked all the windows were closed, that the gas and grill were off and that the front and back doors were shut and locked. It drove Brooke insane.

Just as he reached the door, he remembered the toiletries in the bathroom. OK, so he'd used them; but he had to take something back to Brooke – she'd kill him if he didn't. So, he quickly ran back into the bathroom, picked them up and put them in his overnight bag.

As the door banged shut, he turned to look at it, smiled, sighed and wondered whether he'd ever stay in another bedroom like that at any time in the rest of his life. He strode down the corridor and as he turned the corner near the lifts, he came across a temporarily abandoned housekeeper's trolley. He took a swift look up and down the corridor, thrust his arm into the middle of the trolley and pulled out about twelve bottles of the Molton Brown toiletries, crammed them into his suit pocket and calmly walked into the lift.

You can take the boy out of Essex…

14

A Complicated Breakfast

Dean arrived in the dining room at 8.30am, the busiest time for breakfast in the hotel.

He was rather confused by the protocol. There appeared to be an arrangement whereby you had to stand at the entrance to the restaurant and wait to be ticked off some list and then seated. Several people in front of him were tutting impatiently and looking at their watches. Dean was particularly fascinated by one chap in the queue, wearing pink shorts, a black t-shirt with 'Death Fucking Metal' stamped on the back and whose neck and arms were covered with an array of indistinguishable tattoos. His ears were pierced all the way up and he was sporting flip-flops and square sunglasses. Dean felt decidedly uncool in his Marks & Spencer suit, which Brooke had absolutely insisted he bought when he got his job. She'd been told by a friend at M&S that the mens' suits were made in the same factory as Giorgio Armani suits. From that day on, she hadn't let him shop for suits anywhere else.

Dean took the queuing opportunity to remove the toiletries in his pockets into the less obtrusive home of his overnight bag, while glancing over at what looked like a buffet on the other side of the restaurant. After five minutes patiently waiting, Dean too started checking his watch.

Were you greeted and seated promptly for breakfast? No, I wasn't.

'303?' enquired the girl who eventually arrived at the desk.

'Sorry?'

'Are you room 303?'

'Oh, yeah. Sorry.' He wondered how she could possibly know that.

'Follow me, sir.'

The young woman marched to a table, invited Dean to take a seat, then promptly walked off.

303? That's hardly personal and friendly. What's wrong with my name?

Dean sat down, and observed what the other customers were doing, which was either eating, drinking or perusing the buffet.

Am I meant to just go up there? Where do I get tea? Perhaps I should wait a bit.

After a further five minutes and more anxious looking at his watch, he decided to wave down a staff member.

'Erm excuse me… But, er, can I have a cup of tea please… Oh and, er, do I just go and help myself at the buffet?'

'Do you want a cooked breakfast, sir?'

If you're asked for a cooked breakfast, please order one.

Dean had forgotten about that so had to ask for a menu.

Oh hell, I'll have to order something.

He scanned the cooked options and quickly chose the Hempel Classic, which seemed to be basically a full English.

Bloody hell, twenty-five quid for breakfast? It's £3.95 down Wetherspoons Dairyman!

'Please help yourself to anything from the buffet. Would you like tea or coffee?'

'Tea please.'

'Any particular type?'

He paused.

What does she mean? Tea's tea surely. Then he remembered.

Please test the server's knowledge of the beverages on offer.

'What types have you got?'

'English breakfast, Darjeeling, Assam, decaf, red bush, chamomile, peppermint, lemon and ginger.'

He bit his lip. He just wanted a normal cup of tea like he had at home.

'Do you do PG Tips?' he enquired uneasily.

The girl smiled. 'I'm afraid not, sir, but we do have Twining's English Breakfast tea?'

'OK, I'll have that. Thanks.'

He'd heard of Twining's but didn't really know what

she meant by English Breakfast.

Is that a tea you only drink at breakfast? Why can you only have it for breakfast?

'Would you like white or brown toast?'

'White please.'

She scooted off and left Dean to fend for himself at the buffet counter.

He wandered over, looking at whatever everyone else had on their plates on the way, so he didn't make an idiot of himself when it came to choosing. He took his time looking very carefully at what was on offer to make sure he could answer all the questions on the questionnaire.

Was the buffet well stocked and did the food look fresh and well presented?

He stared at the exotic range of foods on the counter. Weird fruits he didn't even recognise, an almost-empty plate of smoked salmon, olives, another nearly empty plate of salami and a couple of sad-looking pieces of an unidentifiable cheese. He decided this had to be the strangest selection of breakfast foods he'd ever seen. There was a bowl of something off-white and revolting-looking that had the label 'fresh, live Greek plain yoghurt'. It had a sort of watery layer on the top and it looked almost 'chunky'. The Ski yoghurts Brooke bought were smooth-looking. He was confident that something was wrong with the yoghurt and made a mental note for his report.

Who in God's name eats this stuff?

He spied a table with some cereals and fruit juice on

it and decided to play safe.

Where's the milk?

He looked around to no avail and came to the conclusion it must be on his table.

He returned to find no milk.

Ah maybe they'll bring it with my tea

So he waited...and waited... He'd now been in the restaurant over fifteen minutes and hadn't even had his cup of tea yet.

The waitress noticed some facial anxiety and scurried away to chase up his tea, returning a minute later with it... but no milk.

Dean was unimpressed and so he scoured the melee of uncleared tables all around him and picked off two very small but fairly full milk jugs and used those. No sooner had he done that than his waitress brought one.

Bit late now.

Dean smiled politely.

Just as he was about to put the first mouthful of cereal in, another waitress came over with his cooked breakfast.

Now what am I meant to do? Am I supposed to eat the cereal first or after the cooked?

He'd never had breakfast in any other hotel where they took an order for cooked. On holidays he was used to the typical bland stainless-steel dishes under hot lights with congealed baked beans, eggs floating in grease, bits of bacon that were either underdone or burnt and sausages that'd seen better days. That's what he knew and that's what he felt comfortable with. He'd never actually had to deal with this issue of whether to have cereal before or after. This new fancy way of taking an order was added pressure. He came to the conclusion that it should be eaten after, otherwise the waitress would've given him more time to select from and eat that selection from the buffet. So he put the spoon back down into the bowl and moved straight onto the plate of cooked food in front of him.

Was your cooked breakfast attractively served and the correct temperature?

As serving staff buzzed about keeping half an eye, Dean inspected every item on his plate comprehensively. He turned his plate round in stages to get a view of everything from all angles. He noticed on one side that there was grease around the rim of the plate.

Does that make it unattractive?

He tucked in. Halfway through, he stopped suddenly and out came his furtive look. Brooke would've been furious with him. He was scooping up his baked beans with his knife and fork rounded side down. She always said it was 'common' to do that and used to slap him on the back of his hand if he ever did it when they went out to eat. He turned his fork over and went through the painful process of piercing each baked bean individually and pressing them further down the fork with his knife.

What a waste of time.

Out of habit, he almost picked up a piece of toast to wipe it around the plate to soak up the last juices and ketchup, but chided himself; people in fancy places like this wouldn't do things like that. Instead, he stared longingly at the bacon fat pooled in the centre of his plate, before reverting back to his cereal. He devoured the entire breakfast in three minutes flat.

He looked again at his watch. It was 9.05am. He was going to be late if he didn't get a move on.

He sat for a moment, thinking about the questionnaire and whether he'd forgotten to do or ask anything. One question came to him.

Was the fruit basket attractively displayed and had all the stickers been removed?

He'd seen the display and thought how nice it looked but had forgotten to look for sticky labels. So, he returned to the buffet's massive fruit basket. He couldn't see any labels at first glance.

How do I know they aren't underneath?

He then proceeded to pick up every apple, plum, banana, nectarine and satsuma one by one, turn them over, put them back and then walk away. With a mixture of amazement and cynicism, the chef topping up the plate of smoked salmon on the other side of the buffet counter shook his head as he watched Dean.

Just as he was making his way back to his table, it occurred to him that he could save himself having to purchase lunch if he could take some food from the buffet. So he casually picked up a plate and picked two rolls, a large slice of smoked salmon, several slices of salami and a wad of paper napkins and returned to his table. As he did so, his server arrived to clear it. She appeared startled that he was seemingly about to devour yet another plate of food.

As soon as she'd gone, Dean made up the rolls, quickly wrapped them in the paper napkins and stuffed them into his pocket, before heading out of the restaurant. If he thought for one moment he'd not been seen, he was very much mistaken. Staff here had seen it all! The waitress who cleared his table watched him from her station, but she was hardened to such behaviour. She'd seen everything, including a well-known celebrity stuff her Chanel handbag full of mini jars of jam and one multi-millionaire businessman make no bones about taking as much food as he possibly could from the buffet as well as ask for a cooked breakfast with extra sausages and bacon, eat a tiny fraction of it and then ask for a doggy bag in which to take it all away.

Dean made his way to the public toilets just down the corridor. Just one last thing to do before he checked out.

Were the public toilets clean, fresh-smelling and sufficiently stocked with soap and towels?

He needed to go as it happened, so he walked in through the large heavy door and came face to face with an elderly Filipino cleaning lady who smiled, bowed and apologised, explaining in broken English she was just leaving.

'No worries.' Dean smiled at her.

There was no-one else in there so he took the opportunity to properly check every towel holder, both hand driers and all the soap dispensers – all perfect. He then peered closely at the huge mirror above the sinks and experienced a Narcissus moment. He'd no idea why, but his skin looked good and he just appeared slimmer than usual. Little did he know that soft lighting and skinny mirrors were this hotel's secret weapon!

Dean's bowel habits were as regular as episodes of *Friends*. As soon as he'd eaten breakfast, he had to open his bowels, but he'd waited to finish his inspection of the sinks. Then, he couldn't wait to go any longer and dashed into one of the cubicles. He was pretty desperate by now and hurried to pull down his trousers. Suddenly, he heard a splash. He'd been about to sit down but rapidly clenched his buttocks firmly together instead, turned round with his trousers round his ankles and peered into the toilet bowl to see his iPhone sitting at the bottom.

'Fuck fuck fuck, nooooo!!'

He held his head in his hands, paralysed by the choice confronting him. He went to put his hand in the bowl, but just couldn't countenance the idea. His OCD came to the fore when it came to hygiene. The mere thought of it rendered him a pathetic, withering imbecile.

He yanked up his trousers and sped out into the corridor where he saw the Filipino cleaner with her trolley outside the ladies. He tried to explain what'd happened and asked if he could borrow a pair of her gloves. She'd no idea what he was saying, but could tell he was distressed and so waved her hand towards the men's toilet, indicating to him that he should show her the problem.

She followed Dean who dashed into the toilet and pointed to his phone.

'THIS…IS…A…VERY…EXPENSIVE…PHONE.'

Dean clearly thought she was deaf as well as unable to speak much English.

'Ohhh!' she replied, smiling, and without hesitation thrust her arm down into the toilet and plucked the phone out of the water.

Dean gasped at her sheer bravery.

She didn't even have gloves on!

She went to give it to him but he automatically backed away and held both hands up in the surrender position. The woman cackled, took a wad of paper towels from her trolley and wrapped the phone up. She then said something – not in English – and laughed. She held up four fingers of her right hand and Dean frowned. After some toing and froing of semi English words and sign language, he finally understood. She'd already retrieved four phones from the toilets that week.

Well she'll definitely get a mention in my report.

She left Dean to finish his toilet. He took the wrapped-up phone, thanked her and went back into the cubicle to complete the job he'd set out to do. Afterwards, he made his way to the reception desk to check out. There were two people in front of him in the queue and Antonella was back behind the reception desk on her own.

More tutting and anxious looking at watches. Dean kept thinking about his phone.

What a dickhead.

He had no idea if it was ruined or if he might be able to fix it somehow. The paper towel was doing a reasonable job at absorbing all the water, but what the inside of the phone looked like was anyone's guess. Brooke would no doubt be furious. They couldn't really afford that phone, but as usual she was so concerned about Dean's image, she'd persuaded him he needed to be seen to be in possession of the latest gadgets, to show himself as a man who was ahead of his peers. She'd even sacrificed a better phone for herself so he could have the superior one.

'Checking out, Mr De'Ath?'

He'd got lost in possible iPhone recovery solutions and was at the front of reception before he'd really realised it.

'Oh yes please.'

'Did you enjoy your stay with us?' Antonella looked right at him. She was beautiful. Voluminous, black, curly hair neatly tied and that exquisite olive skin you see only on people from the Mediterranean. The black suit with the mandarin collar suited the shape of her face. Classy.

You don't see girls like that in Brentwood.

'Yes, fine thanks.'

In fact, there were a number of issues Dean could've raised with her, but it never occurred to him to actually tell her what they were. No, that'd be too difficult. He didn't want to cause a scene.

Were you invited to complete a feedback form?

Dean was presented with the bill and asked to check it. He went into his jacket pocket to get his glasses and plunged his fingers straight into a smoked salmon roll. He removed his hands quickly revealing a creamy, slightly fishy-smelling finger and remembered he'd put his glasses in his inside pocket to make room for the rolls. He looked embarrassed as Antonella wrinkled her nose up in bewilderment. He pretended nothing was wrong, put his glasses on and gulped hard as the sum of £827.50 stood out on the invoice like a pimple on the end of someone's nose.

Shit. I hope I've got enough credit on my card.

Yet another thing Dean hadn't thought about or bargained for at all. The expenses for the mystery shopping visits sometimes took a good few weeks to come through, so that was a worry too.

What if my card gets declined? Shit. What'll I do?

Being a master at body language, Antonella enquired, 'Is everything alright, sir?'

'Yes fine, fine. Sorry, I was miles away.'

He stood visibly agitated as she swiped the card through her machine. She waited. To his horror she looked perplexed and repeated the action. Dean held his breath and bit his nails. He had no other method of paying.

'There. All done.'

Dean finally exhaled and took the folded bill she gave him. He wanted to give her a good report, but she still hadn't asked him to complete a feedback form. He hung around for a few moments under the guise of sorting out his bags, but she never asked him so he said goodbye and left.

15

The Debrief

'You're late again.'

Brian watched Dean as he ran into the office with his overnight bag. He was slightly sweaty and out of breath.

'Sorry, Brian. I was delayed unexpectedly.'

'Has Brooke chucked you out eventually?'

He roared at his own joke.

Just as Dean got to his desk, a message came through on his phone from Brooke. He was gobsmacked that his phone still actually worked (albeit with a slightly weird screen in the top right-hand side) and also fearful of what Brooke might be wanting.

How dya sleep? Can't wait 2 hear all about it. Hope u got some lovely MB goodies?

Dean's mind turned to how he was going to handle another of Brooke's Spanish Inquisitions. She'd want a minute by minute breakdown of everything that'd happened from the moment he arrived to the moment he'd left. He had to figure out what he'd say about the 'dinner' and meeting'. He dreaded the thought; it all just seemed like so much effort.

Maybe I should just come clean and tell her? No way… I can't…She'd destroy me.

After a few minutes at his desk, he suddenly realised that Chloe wasn't around. He'd mixed feelings about her unexpected visit to The Hempel the previous night. On the one hand he was furious with her that she may have compromised his mystery visit, but on the other, when he considered how he behaved towards her, he was rather ashamed. He'd never normally treat a woman like that. He prided himself in being quite gentlemanly in his own way. He casually enquired of one of his colleagues who said she'd phoned in sick.

He wasn't entirely surprised. She had really had too much to drink. It made him suddenly recall the glass of wine on the carpet and how he'd forgotten to mention on checking out, that he'd spilled it. He'd intended to do that, but in his hurry to get to work had totally forgotten.

They're gonna think I'm such a slob. And a greedy, alcoholic one at that.

By mid-morning, Dean was yawning and finding it tough to concentrate on his work. He calculated that he'd probably only had about five hours' sleep. This was insufficient, because he was an 'eight or nine hours a night' kind of chap and would be grumpy in the extreme if he didn't get it.

During his lunch break, he got his questionnaire out again, read it over one more time and changed one or two comments until he was one hundred per cent satisfied with the report. It'd taken nearly four hours to complete. He then sent it through to Angie. He struggled through the rest of the day but logged off promptly at 5pm to avoid falling asleep at his desk.

On the train on the way home, he sat back and thought about the imminent conversation with Brooke. He rehearsed in his head what he'd say about the dinner and the meeting but would try to focus the conversation as much as possible on the hotel itself.

As he opened the gate, the front door sprung open and Brooke came running out and up the path.

He dropped his overnight bag and gave her a huge hug.

'Wow! You smell gorgeous. What's that?' Brooke asked.

'Dunno, just the soap in the hotel I think.'

Brooke held his hand and dragged him down the path, into the house and onto the sofa.

'I'll get us a cup of tea and then you can tell me everything. I haven't stopped thinking about it!'

'I hope it's Twining's English Breakfast.'

'You what?'

'Well that's what I'm used to now – no more PG Tips for me.' He feigned a plum in the mouth voice and a snooty face and then cackled loudly.

'Oh I see, like that, is it?' Brooke laughed and clapped her hands excitedly as she ran off into the kitchen to make tea.

While she couldn't inspect his face, he quickly covered the meeting and dinner element of the conversation, palming it off as the boring bit, wanting to get it over and done with ASAP so he could get on enjoying the hotel.

She shouted out from the kitchen, 'So who'd been invited exactly?'

Dean gulped and rambled off a list of random names plus the owners of TrussInUs – the only ones Brooke recognised.

'See, they must think great things of you if you were the only one in the call centre that was invited.'

'I wouldn't read too much into that, babe, I think they're gonna hold another one next quarter and take someone else from the centre.'

Brooke felt a pang of disappointment as she came in with the tea in mugs and sat down next to Dean.

He'd already got the hotel brochure out of his man-bag to show her and take her mind off the 'work' part of the hotel visit. Brilliant strategy! As soon as she saw it, she took it with reverence and then turned the pages of the exquisitely produced brochure as though it was made from tissue paper and would tear at any moment. Superlatives flowed from her mouth as she gave her opinion on the decor, overjoyed that her husband had been there. She couldn't wait to tell all her friends and show them the brochure.

The next hour was taken up with looking at the photos he took, reading through the menus, describing lumpy Greek yoghurt, telling her small details about the gardens and making her laugh at his inadequacy with plumbing fixtures.

'What on earth made you have a bath at that time of night?!'

Dean panicked inwardly as he'd not prepared for that particular question.

'Erm…well…how could I not? I've never seen such a huge bath and I wanted to try it out! I knew I wouldn't have time in the morning.'

'Actually, I don't blame you – I would've done the same.'

Phew!

'So, where are the toiletries?'

Dean delved into his overnight bag and retrieved first, several smoked salmon rolls, now soggy, squashed and unappetising in their paper napkins. He'd completely forgotten he'd put them in there.

Bugger, I could've had them for lunch today.

Dean hadn't spotted the look of horror on Brooke's face. She'd seen Dean do this before in hotels where they'd been on holiday; steal extra food from the breakfast buffet to avoid having to buy lunch, but she never dreamed he'd do it at this hotel.

'Dean. Please tell me they're not what I think they are?'

'Well it was criminal not to. There was so much stuff there. I thought you might wanna try some.'

'I can't *believe* you did that! In such a posh place? You're so embarrassing. I'm glad I wasn't with you. I really hope no-one saw you.'

Dean offered her one. 'No, I was very discreet,' he reassured her.

Brooke inspected it carefully and decided it was wasn't worth the calories so put it on the coffee table. After a minute more digging in his bag he yanked out all the Molton Brown Toiletries.

'Yay! Molton Brown! I told you they'd be Molton Brown!'

She then looked carefully at each label to see what she'd got. There seemed to be an abundance of body cream and conditioner, but a dearth of anything else.

Remarking on this disproportionate selection of toiletries, she asked, 'Why'd they put so much of the same thing in one bedroom? It doesn't make sense.'

'Ah. Well, they weren't actually in the room. For some reason there weren't any in my room. So when I left, I saw them sitting on a trolley in the corridor and quickly grabbed what I could. I didn't really look to be honest. Sorry, babe.'

Brooke shook her head and smiled.

'What are you like, eh?'

Then Dean brought out the bodywash he used. 'You can have this. It was in the shower. That's what you can smell. I tell you what though, those bloody labels were so small I couldn't read them. I had to go and get my glasses and then they all steamed up so I *still* couldn't read them!'

Brooke giggled and gave him a hug. She held him there silently for quite some time and wondered whether they'd ever be able to afford to go to The Hempel together some time in the future. She hoped with every fibre of her being that they would; that Dean's position in the call centre would improve and that maybe he'd soon get that promotion, a pay rise and the holy grail of a company car. She sighed longingly at the prospect, untangled herself from Dean and went back into the kitchen to start preparing the food for Paige's party the following day.

As Dean took his overnight bag upstairs, his phone went off. When he looked at it, he was alarmed that it was Angie from Sonny Global. He quickly shut the bedroom door behind him and answered it in a whisper.

'Dean, that report was brilliant! One of the most comprehensive we've ever seen here. Well done! Did you enjoy the visit?'

This was the first time Angie had come across quite that enthusiastic, so it took him by surprise.

'It was actually pretty stressful to be honest. I thought they might've guessed I was the mystery customer because the room service guy put the tray down right next to the questionnaire!'

'Well I don't think they did, or we would've heard about it.'

Dean, not for the first time during this whole saga, breathed yet another sigh of relief.

Angie went on to say that he was one of the best new assessors they'd come across. Normally, she told him, they made errors – big ones – in their first few visits, but he seemed to have a penchant for detail that made him very well suited to the job.

Dean was pleasantly surprised, flattered and reassured.

Ha! OCD rules!

'So why are you calling now? It's a bit late on a Friday afternoon to be working, isn't it?' He glanced nervously over to the bedroom door.

'I've an urgent job for you. It's not too far from you and the visit needs to be done between 12noon and 2pm tomorrow. Is that OK? Someone else was meant to be doing it, but they let us down at the last minute and this client gets very miffed if we miss one. It's the Burger King in Basildon shopping centre.'

'You are joking? You're gonna pay me to go to Burger King?'

'We have to; we can't get assessors to go otherwise. It's not exactly like The Hempel – there isn't quite the same incentive, if you know what I mean!' At that she laughed heartily down the phone. 'It's for two people. We'll pay you ten pounds to do the visit and you must each have a different burger, fries, different flavoured ice-creams, a different cold drink, a coffee and a tea, for which we'll reimburse you as usual.'

'Ten quid? Is that all?'

Dean's shoulders dropped.

'Out of interest, is Burger King the only client who pays?' he enquired curiously.

'No, we've got some car showrooms and banks that pay.'

Dean's mind went into overdrive.

Car showrooms? Banks?

He couldn't conceive what kind of assessments they must be. But before he had a chance to ask, Angie went on to finish her verbal briefing and promised to send him all the details immediately as the visit was the next day. She went on to say she was so glad she'd managed to get hold of him before she went home, or there would've been trouble. She thanked him and asked that he send the completed questionnaire back by Monday and put the phone down.

'Dean, Dean? I've just remembered you didn't pick up Paige's birthday cake for the party, did you?'

Brooke was running up the stairs as she was talking.

Oh holy shit.

'What time's the party tomorrow?'

'It's not 'til one o'clock but the baker shuts at twelve tomorrow, so you'll have to pick it up before then. They'll be shut now and I'll be far too busy to go myself.'

By this time Brooke was in the bedroom.

'Who were you talking to just now?'

Dean's heart raced. 'No-one.'

'I'm sure I heard you talking just now?'

'Oh, I was ranting at my phone that's all. I was trying

to send some Hempel pictures to Martin and couldn't seem to send them – files too big or something. No worries about the cake, I'll go and get it tomorrow.'

He turned away as he spoke, as casually as he could, unpacking his clothes and hanging them up. Brooke was pleased to get that job off her list and went straight back downstairs again to finish tea.

The second she'd left the room, he tried to ring Angie back to tell her he was sorry but he couldn't do the visit after all, as he'd completely forgotten about his daughter's birthday party.

Angie's extension rang and rang and eventually it clicked over to an answer machine message, explaining the office was now closed and that office hours were Monday to Friday 9am – 5.30pm

Dean sat on the bed, shut his eyes and screamed silently inside.

16

Race Against Time

As soon as he woke up, Dean messaged Martin and asked him if they could meet at the baker's in the high street at 11.30am.

Martin was unsurprisingly perplexed at the request.

Why?

Just tell me yes or no!

OK yes.

Brooke was fussing about with putting the chicken drumsticks into its marinade and wanted help setting the garden furniture up outside. She'd also ordered a bouncy castle which had yet to be delivered. She'd invited about twenty-five other children and all their parents and it was quite a big deal for her. She'd never entertained that many people in her life. Cooking wasn't exactly her strong point. If it could be bought at Marks & Spencer or Waitrose, she'd buy it from there, much to Dean's despair. What's wrong with Aldi, he'd always say?

Brooke shouted out to Dean to help with the furniture.

'I'm just off to pick the cake up, babe.'

'But that's not necessary right this minute, this needs

to be done now.'

Dean ran out to the garden. It was a glorious hot and Sonny day. Mikey, his neighbour, looked over the fence and laughed, as Brooke ordered Dean about like a dog. 'Stay there…fetch this…go over there…move quickly!' Dean glanced over at him and smiled a sickly-sweet smile. A sudden need to exert his authority overwhelmed him and he boldly declared that he was done, that he had to go now and she'd have to finish it herself.

Brooke stood uncharacteristically speechless as Dean stomped through the kitchen, accidentally on purpose leaving his phone on the side. He knew that if he took it with him, he'd be hounded to get back ASAP.

'Don't be long, Dean, there's still loads to do!' Brooke shouted from the back garden. As Dean was reversing out the drive, she came running out the house with Paige. 'Take her with you, Dean, so she's out my way while I set up.'

Without warning, she opened the back door and clipped her into the car seat.

'But, Brooke, she'd be far better off here than stuck in a car and I don't know how long I'll have to wait at the baker's. Let her stay here with you,' he pleaded, but she was already walking back down the path.

He looked up to the sky and made the sign of the cross. The guilt of deserting her while he not only picked up the cake, but went to Eastgate Shopping Centre to have a Burger King meal with Martin, all before 1pm, was almost too much to bear.

As he sped to the baker's, Paige started crying.

Oh Christ, this is all I need. Please God let Martin be there.

Dean screeched up outside the baker's on a double yellow line and, with the engine still running, got out the car. Martin was lurking outside.

'Thank God you're here, mate, can you get in and sit with Paige for a minute, I've just got to pick a cake up?'

'Alright, mate.'

Martin opened the front passenger door and was met with screaming from the back seat. He looked aghast at Paige and then for Dean, but he'd already gone inside the shop. He turned round and leaned over to try and appease her. He rattled a toy in front of her face, tickled her feet, poked his tongue out, played peekaboo – all to no avail. She just carried on screaming. Her face resembled a tomato, so he took off her little white cotton sunhat and blew right at her. She stopped momentarily when the breath hit her face, but then carried on where she left off. Martin's attempts to stop the screaming continued for almost five minutes, at which point a traffic warden appeared in the distance. Martin quickly got out the car and tried to wave at Dean through the shop window. He turned around and the two of them became very animated.

Within a minute, Dean walked out of the shop with a huge cake box. He saw the warden and indicated to him that he was just leaving. The warden started to take down his car registration details.

Fucking hell! Just give me a minute!

He opened the car door at the back and as gently as he could at high speed, put the cake down next to Paige's car seat. He then sped off, wheels spinning as he went, avoiding a ticket by a whisker.

Inside the box, the enormous green, red and black caterpillar cake had received a sharp jolt and all its legs, which looked rather delicate, snapped off.

Paige continued to scream in the back.

'SHUT…UP…PAIGE!' Dean yelled.

Martin was taken aback. His friend wasn't partial to shouting and he'd certainly never heard him shout at the baby.

'Hey, mate. Calm down. What's going on? Why the hurry? Why d'ya want me to meet you here?'

Dean took one of Paige's music CDs and put it into the system.

'Humpty Dumpty sat on a wall, Humpty Dumpty had a great fall…'

Almost instantly, Paige stopped screaming.

'Whoah! How d'ya do that?!' Martin asked, amazed at the change.

'It's one of her favourites, but you'll be sick to death of it by the time we get back. OK so…you know this mystery shopper programme I'm involved with? Well, they rang me late yesterday and said they had a visit that needed to be done and as it was near me would I do it?'

'Not another Nous Geraldine; we haven't got time. Isn't Paige's party at one o'clock?'

'That's the bloody problem, I completely forgot about the party when I agreed to do it. By the time I realised, their office was shut, and I couldn't cancel the visit, so I've got no choice I've gotta do it and PDQ.'

'I wouldn't worry, mate. They'll understand. I'd go home if I were you – I bet Brooke's going mental.' Martin knew her well.

'Well that's the difference between you and me, Martin. If I commit to doing something, I do it. It's only a Burger King, in Eastgate in Basildon, but it's gotta be two people and I didn't think you'd mind.'

'You are joking? Basildon? There's no way you're gonna be back for one, mate – the traffic at this time of day on a Saturday'll be horrendous.'

'All the kings' horses and all the kings' men, couldn't put Humpty together again…'

It was by now 11.45am and traffic was busy in Brentwood. Dean put his foot down and Martin saw yet another side of his friend that he'd not witnessed since Paige was born – fast driving. He'd become very cautious behind the wheel – in fact Brooke called him Captain Slow. It was such a hot day that Dean had opened all the windows and at one point on the A127 when there was no queue, he reached over 90mph and the 'baby on board' sticker flew out the window. The Vauxhall Astra driver behind got it right on his windscreen. Clearly unhappy about this interruption to his vision, he raced up beside Dean on the inside lane and made a hand gesture. Martin quickly thrust his arm towards the back seat, covered Paige's eyes with one hand and gestured back with the other.

'Baa Baa Black sheep, have you any wool? Yes, sir, yes, sir, three bags full.'

Paige began her crying fit again.

Martin watched with amazement as Dean deftly skipped this and the next four tracks.

'Mary, Mary quite contrary see how your garden grows…'

Paige stopped crying.

Vauxhall Astra man (well 'boy' if truth be told) and his pal made a point of singing along with Dean's music at unnaturally high decibel levels as he cruised at the same speed and as close to Dean's car as he could physically get.

'Banging tunes, mate!'

'How d'ya do that? She was screaming a minute ago,' Martin asked.

'She doesn't like four of the tracks, but I know she likes this one. What an arsehole.'

Dean carried on until he hit traffic further down when he came to a grinding halt and Vauxhall Astra man pulled up right beside him yet again. Dean wound up all his windows and ignored him, but he could still hear them singing nursery rhymes.

By just before midday, they'd got to the multi-storey

and parked up in the first space they found.

'We haven't got long, mate. Let's go.'

Dean speedily unstrapped Paige from her car seat; she seemed happy to get out being red, hot and sweaty but, most importantly, she smelled worse than Brentwood Dump. Dean hadn't got any of her nappy changing gear with him at all. She'd just have to wait.

Martin and Dean (with Paige in his arms) legged it to Burger King, passing a group of middle-aged women with hair so perfect it looked like a wig convention. They glowered at Martin and Dean, clearly believing that they must've abducted this poor baby.

When they got into Burger King, Dean had to try and remember the brief as he'd forgotten to bring it with him. They marched straight up to an empty counter and Dean blurted out, 'I'll have a whopper with regular fries, chocolate ice cream, a coke and a cup of tea please.'

'I'll have the same,' Martin offered helpfully for speed.

'No. You can't,' Dean replied firmly, remembering that they had to eat different things. The young lad at the till called 'Luke' looked strangely at Dean, wondering what right he had to dictate to his friend what he must eat.

'Why not?'

'I'm gonna order for you. A cheeseburger with small fries, vanilla ice cream, lemonade and a coffee for him, please.'

'I don't want that. You know I don't like cheese and I never drink coffee.'

'Too bad. It's what you're having. Now shut up and let's get out of here.'

Was your server friendly and efficient?

Was he wearing a name badge?

(Luke had worked at Burger King only for around six months and yet had seen it all. Well, so he thought. As he observed Martin and Dean, he became fascinated, wondering what on earth their relationship was. Maybe they were gay and one was a feeder – one was pretty fat and the other was more slender. But then what's with the baby?)

As Luke was putting the order through the till, Paige started pointing to something and trying to pull away from Dean. Her eye had caught the kids King Junior meal packaging and she made an assortment of grunting noises as she became perilously close to starting another screaming fit.

'Could I possibly have one of your kids' boxes? I don't want the food, just the box?'

Luke said he'd have to go and find the manager to check that was OK.

'Oh forget it then, we're in a hurry' said Dean in an exasperated tone.

They hung around for their food for five minutes and twelve seconds. Dean knew. He was timing it.

Was your order served within four minutes? No it bloody well wasn't. Why can't they just hurry up? So much for 'fast food'.

Then Dean dumped Paige into Martin's arms.

'I've gotta check the loos,' Dean whispered.

With that he ran to the lavatories. They were disgusting – smelly, dirty, no paper, water all over the floor. He couldn't forget them in a hurry.

Martin, meanwhile, was trying to appease a screaming Paige. He couldn't believe how much strength such a tiny creature could have as she arched her back and tried to wriggle free of his grasp. She wanted a King Junior box and she was going to have it. He resorted to holding her away from his body so people could see he wasn't doing anything to her. He was getting very flustered and sweaty.

When the order was ready, Luke handed it over to Martin and obviously felt so sorry for him he slipped a King Junior meal box into his hand and winked at him. 'Here you go, mate – good luck with that one – rather you than me!'

Martin grabbed the bags with one hand and just about managed to hold onto Paige with the other arm, all the while wondering how women possibly did this sort of stuff on a daily basis.

Within a minute or two, Dean had marched out of the lavatories, straight up to Martin, took Paige from him without a word and made his way through the crowded restaurant to the exit door. Martin followed like a tourist trying to keep up with their guide, with his two big bags of burgers and drinks in his hands and an empty kid's meal box, which he finally gave to Paige when she held out her hands for it.

Was the restaurant clean?

Were the tables being cleared regularly both upstairs and downstairs?

Shit – I need to have a quick look round.

With no notice, Dean turned around, went downstairs and walked around the entire area at high speed, assessing the tables, with Martin following, demanding to know what the hell he was doing. He then scaled the stairs two at a time and did the same thing, Paige being thrown up and around like a rodeo cowgirl. He whizzed aggressively close to the tables of various diners, who looked up whilst holding burgers in their mouths, convinced they were about to be mugged. Martin was already hot and bothered, but this extra, unexpected bit of exercise all but finished him off.

Were the staff knowledgeable about the food? Shit!

By this time, Dean was near the exit door again. He walked straight up to one of the staff clearing the tables. ''scuse me, love, d'ya know what oil your chips are cooked in?'

Martin stared at him as though he was completely deranged.

'Poppy' the table clearer looked at him with a sort of 'you're having a laugh' face. She said she didn't know and reluctantly offered to find out if he really wanted.

Dean told her not to bother. By this time it was about 12.20pm. He, Martin and Paige, chewing the kids' meal box, ran back to the car, coffee and tea spilling everywhere along the way.

'You're bloody mad you are! I can't believe you just did that. You do know you looked like a madman on speed?'

Dean was so preoccupied about getting home he didn't even respond. As he went to put Paige into her car seat, she did that back-arching thing again and recommenced her screaming. Dean carefully placed his hand along where the top of her legs met her tummy and pushed firmly to try and stop the arching. She was having none of it and continued to make life very difficult.

Without being asked, Martin got into the front seat, put the burger bags in the foot well; then he turned on the music system, found 'Humpty Dumpty' and pressed Play. Within seconds, Paige had stopped. Martin laughed out loud, incredulous at his newfound ability to halt the noise.

'Well done, mate – you're learning! One day you'll make a good dad!' Dean joked as he finally managed to click Paige's seatbelt, get into his own seat and drive off.

What woman on earth would want him?

Over the next thirty minutes, Martin fed Dean and also Paige, whenever she made a noise or arm gesture indicating she wanted a chip; licking his fingers in between. Dean drove at over ninety miles per hour whenever he could, back down the A127 towards home, slowing down only when he knew speed cameras were coming up. They'd forgotten to pick up any napkins so a combination of grease, ketchup and salt covered their hands, until Dean remembered he had some hand wipes in his glove compartment.

He asked Martin to get them out. Martin opened the glove compartment to find not only wet wipes, but a small bottle of hand gel, hand cream, lip salve, a packet of tissues, nail file, a pair of fold-up scissors, vanity mirror and a clothes brush. Each item clearly had its own little place. Martin laughed out loud.

'Oh, my hands feel *so* rough, I *must* put some cream on and my nail keeps getting caught in my hair, where *is* my nail file?' Martin did a brilliant impersonation of Brooke and made Dean laugh for the first time this stressful morning. What Martin didn't realise was that it was, in fact, Dean's grooming kit.

Just before 1pm, Dean screeched up outside the house, whisked Paige out her car seat and asked Martin to bring the cake in. There was a huge vehicle parked outside the house with its back doors open. Dean really hadn't thought too much about how he was going to explain his absence. What Brooke thought was going to be a twenty-minute trip to the baker's had turned into a disappearance of an hour and a half.

He took a deep breath and opened the front door.

'Where the bloody hell have you been, Dean? You were only meant to collect the birthday cake, not bloody well make it!'

Brooke came marching into the hall with her hair in heated rollers, arms waving and with one of those 'Brooke looks' that could kill. She was beyond furious. Dean apologised and went to kiss her on the cheek while Paige was still in his arms. Brooke backed off.

'God, you stink of McDonald's, Dean, and so does Paige! Where've you been? What's this?'

She snatched Paige's Junior King meal box out of her hand and a couple of French fries out of the folds in her t-shirt and held them up in an accusatory manner.

'I'm so sorry, babe, but I saw Martin near the baker's and he fancied a Burger King. I didn't think it'd take that long but the traffic was bloody horrendous.' Dean sounded apologetic and terrified all at the same time and he felt like his life depended on a good defence. He also averted his eyes away from Martin, whose mouth dropped open as he gaped at Dean wide-eyed and then dumped the cake box onto a little table in the hallway. He didn't want to be in Brooke's bad books. He'd experienced that too many times before and he knew that she thought he was a bad influence on Dean.

'WHAT? You've been to bloody Burger King while I've been left to sort everything out here? I can't *believe* you'd do that! Are you stupid or something? People'll be arriving any minute now and I'm not even ready! Neither is Paige. Just go upstairs and change her nappy. You need to put her into the dress that's laid out on her bed and wipe her down with a nappy wipe to get that stink of chips off her. As for you, Martin,' she prodded him in the chest, 'you can make yourself useful now you've pissed me off. Go and sort out the bouncy castle people who've just arrived – they're bloody well late as well. They should've been here half an hour ago. ERRRRRGH!!!!'

Brooke stormed upstairs to remove her rollers.

Martin was about to speak when Dean raised his hand, palm facing towards Martin.

'Don't say a word. Not a bloody word. I'll make it up to you…alright?' Dean sounded stern and not to be argued with.

He went off upstairs with Paige, photographed his hands before wiping off his notes, while Martin was left to organise the bouncy castle people.

17

Paige's Party

'Helloooo! 'ow are *you?* And 'ow's this little dinkum? Happy birthday, sweetheart! Where's Brooke?'

Stacey was one of Brooke's best friends but Dean hadn't seen her for a while. She was one of those larger-than-life characters; loud, exuberant, gregarious and 'in your face' as Brooke once described her. She was voluptuous, but didn't let that stop her from wearing the most figure-hugging, revealing outfits. Every time Dean saw her, he found his eyes drawn to the two enormous mounds of spray-tanned flesh plumped up and spilling over whatever low-cut top she was wearing at the time. Bosoms 'til Tuesday, he used to say. Brooke once told him that on a friend's hen night, in a drunken stupor, Stacey told them all that her head fitted neatly into one of her bra cups. No-one believed her, so she took it off on the spot, put it on her head and paraded round Duke's nightclub singing 'Milkshake' by Kellis, just to prove it. He never looked at her the same way since.

'I bet you'd like to sink your face in there, eh, Dean?' she screeched with laughter and strutted on through.

He ignored the comment and followed her through to the garden, where Martin was helping the guys set up the Princess's Bouncy Castle in their tiny garden. It took up virtually the whole grassed area, leaving only the patio for the tables, chairs and BBQ. Dean stared at it for a few moments, horrified at the size of it.

And she thinks she can get a bloody hot tub in here?

Stacey took Paige from him and started playing with her, throwing her up in the air and making her laugh. She then gave her an enormous helium-filled balloon in the shape of a unicorn with 'Happy 1st Birthday!' in pink, silver and yellow, on a long ribbon with a weight at the bottom. Paige's angelic face lit up and she wriggled to get to it. Stacey put her on the floor and let her fiddle about with trying to pull it down.

Paige's birthday outfit, chosen painstakingly by Brooke from Monsoon, consisted of a pale pink full netting skirt with a sequinned camisole, topped off with a little plastic tiara and pink satin ballerina pumps.

'So, where's Brooke, Dean?'

'She's running a bit late 'cause the bouncy castle people only just arrived. She'll be down in a minute. Help yourself.' Dean motioned to the back corner of the patio.

Stacey walked over to a large recycling bin full of ice and booze and helped herself to white wine in a glass so obscenely large that it took almost three-quarters of a bottle. It was to be one of many that afternoon. She sat down near Paige and the unicorn.

Within a few minutes, at least another half a dozen couples had arrived with their broods and presents for Paige. They were all local, good friends of Brooke and Dean and needed no introductions, nor prompting to help themselves to the alcohol on offer in the bin. They all brought their own too and added it into the mix.

Brooke's mother Jackie and father Rick arrived next. Brooke was a chip off the old block. Her mother's hair was coiffured to within an inch of its life and sprayed to minimise all risk of movement, nails manicured to death and spray-tanned to resemble a Spanish expat. Rick carried a colossal box wrapped up in bright-pink wrapping paper and a big bow and Jackie clearly couldn't wait to get it to a place where it could be unwrapped by her only grandchild. Brooke immediately called over to Paige, who caught sight of Nanna and held her arms to the heavens as a sign she wanted to be picked up. With glass of wine firmly in hand Stacey followed behind; she was nervous that the precious Paige might get hurt on her short journey across the garden. She smiled warmly at Jackie.

''allo, Jackie, long time no see. 'ow are you?' Stacey gave her a quick peck on the cheek before Jackie picked Paige up.

'Not too bad, love, not too bad. Trying to keep Rick's wretched diabetes in check. It's a full-time job! He's so laid back about it he forgets how important his eating and drinking habits are. I'm dreading this party; he'll be heading straight for all the things he's not allowed.' Jackie had a habit of giving people way more information than they actually wanted to hear.

'Blokes, eh?' Stacey laughed and moved away quickly towards Rick, before she had to listen to some gory story about his diabetes.

Rick walked up to Brooke and gave her a cuddle and a kiss on the cheek.

''allo, love, 'ow are you and 'ow's that little granddaughter of mine then?'

'I'm alright, Dad, thanks. She's right here, waiting to see her grand-daddy-daddy! Aren't you, Paige?' Brooke's voice took on a sickly-sweet sound; the sort that the world overuses when talking to a small child.

Stacey gave Rick a hug and he slapped her bottom in full view of his wife saying, 'And 'ow's my favourite girl, then?'

'I'd slap 'im round the face if I were you, Stace.' Jackie was used to her husband's affectionate bottom slaps of other women.

Rick had a soft spot for all Brooke's girlfriends – but an especially big one for Stacey. Something to do with bosoms almost certainly.

'Oi! That's enough of that, Rick Smith!' Stacey joked, though she didn't actually mind in the slightest.

Rick moved towards Paige with his arms out and his eyes wide open, 'Come to Grand-Daddy-Daddy!'

Paige clung resolutely to Jackie and put her thumb in her mouth – a sure sign that she was tired and probably about to have one of her infamous screaming fits. (Even the neighbours along the road had come around to complain one night.) Rick didn't mind. He ruffled her hair instead before heading to the beer.

One of Dean's other friends Mick, sauntered over to Dean and shook his hand.

''allo, mate, 'ow are you? 'aven't seen you for ages, what you been doing with yourself?'

'Oh not much. Just working really. Paige is a bit of a handful; doesn't sleep that well to be honest, mate, so I've been a bit knackered and I've not been going out that much.'

Mick was hard-core Essex. He sold caravans and mobile homes on the A127 and had made a fortune. You'd never know it by the way he dressed; more like a black cab driver. Dean knew him from school. He was almost a millionaire and had made his money very quickly. He used to have a stall on Romford Market as a teenager, selling car parts and learned the gift of the gab there. He could've had any car he wanted, but belonging to Essex Rebels Classic Car Club (as did Dean when he owned his Dolly), he had a canary-yellow 1973 Ford Escort RS1600. He was obsessed with that car and being without wife or children, he'd spend eight hours every week cleaning and polishing it.

'Come and look at the car. See what I've done to it.'

He walked back out and Dean followed like an obedient dog.

'See?'

'Err…no, Mick. It looks the same as last time I saw it.'

'Look at the lights.' Mick walked round the car and pointed to the headlights – great round bulging bits of plastic that'd been attached to the front. 'Beautiful, just beautiful.'

'Dean! What are you doing? We've got guests. You should be getting their drinks, not sodding about looking at cars – no offence, Mick. Can you get Dull Dave a cuppa? He's driving.' Brooke walked off as quickly as she'd arrived. Modelling a skin-tight pair of white cropped jeans, gold gladiator sandals and a bright-red crop top, she showed off her flat washboard tummy; admirable after having a baby. She also sported gold hoop earrings the size of side plates, her head was piled high with ringlets and it was all topped off with her trademark makeup. Dean and Mick obeyed and went back into the garden, where they opened a couple of cans of Foster's with a 'cheers', Dean completely forgetting to go round offering other people any.

The sun was burning down on the whole party and the children were purple after only a few minutes expending energy. Brooke had prepared jugs of Ribena with ice for the toddlers, who drank the entire lot within twenty minutes. All the men had gathered round the BBQ and were debating which supermarket sold the best sausages and how best to light the charcoal. The girls all sat together round the tables under a large umbrella and periodically broke off from their conversation with each other to nurse a bouncy castle wound, or break up a fight. Jen had asked for an ashtray, much to Brooke's disgust. She couldn't stand smoke or smoking and so found the grottiest container possible and placed it on the farthest corner of the table to make a point.

'Blow the smoke away from the kids, Jen.' Brooke said it in that very matter-of-fact way that only the diplomacy-free people of Essex could get away with.

Jen rolled her eyes. As one of the only smokers in their social circle of friends she felt like a leper sometimes. She also indulged in the odd joint now and then – another thing Brooke strongly disapproved of.

Brooke brought out a large pile of chicken drumsticks ready for cooking and asked Dean to put them on the BBQ. Over the next half an hour or so, he turned them while Brooke added sausages and burgers where she could fit them in. There were bowls of pre-made salad from M&S and garlic bread ready to put in the oven and those dreadful turkey Twizzlers for the children. Condiments were on the tables, along with paper plates, plastic knives and forks. They didn't have enough china plates or cutlery for everyone and Brooke didn't like washing up anyway, so she thought paper and plastic would suffice.

The drink flowed, the conversation and laughter grew, the children got hotter and redder and the adults became more inebriated and tried to stay in the shade.

'Come on, Dean! We're bloody starving over 'ere. Something must be ready by now. The 'ammers'll have won the league by the time we get fed!'

Dean poked one of the drumsticks and it looked good to go, so he emptied them onto a large plate, took one for himself and put them in the middle of the table. Anyone would think that their friends hadn't been fed for weeks. Within minutes all the chicken drumsticks were gone, along with all the garlic bread and they hadn't even had any burgers or sausages yet; only the salad remained resolutely untouched. Dean wasn't even hungry, and he couldn't help but notice that Martin was the first to dive into the plate of chicken.

God, that man can eat.

Brooke suddenly came marching up to Dean with one of her looks. She was doing that thing with her arms (like Usain Bolt in the 100m) and clearly on a mission of some sort.

'Dean, I can't believe it, we're running out of booze. They're like bloody gannets. Can you pop up to Tesco and get some more lager, white wine and Prosecco?'

'Babe, I've had a couple of Foster's. I don't think I should be driving.'

'You'll be fine, two's OK. Please, Dean, it's embarrassing. Anyway, you owe me.'

Dean knew Brooke well enough to know that it wasn't worth arguing with her, so he simply walked away without saying a word and drove the five minutes to Tesco.

Back at the party in the garden, the chaps were becoming a tad lairy and started singing their beverage requests in the style of West Ham fans at home.

'Where's the booze, where's the booze, where's the boooooooze? Where's the booze, where's the booze, where's the booooze?'

Brooke was trying desperately to play the 'hostess with the mostest', handing round bowls of crisps. At one point she bent over the BBQ to check the food and suddenly there was a roar of laughter behind her.

'You paid way too much for 'em, Brooke. There's nothing of 'em. You was robbed!' Porno Gazza was the joker of the pack.

With a reaction time Gordon Banks would've been proud of, Brooke stood bolt upright and turned round to find a sea of faces laughing at her. She had a bad feeling about this. Her cheeks flushed and her eyes darted about looking for reassurance from one person to another, the girls as well as the chaps, but none came.

Stacey strolled over to let her in on the joke.

'Turn round, you daft cow.'

She yanked hard at something and Brooke felt her jeans waistband pulled down and a clicking noise. Stacey handed her the TK Maxx reduced label that'd been attached to her lacy thong and hanging out over the back of her jeans. £8.95 down to £2.95.

'Oh my God, Stace, why didn't anyone tell me?'

'They just did!'

Brooke was mortified. Image was everything to her, but in legendary Brooke style, she laughed it off publicly and waved the label at everyone insisting she'd got a bargain and that they were a bunch of lingerie philistines.

She and Stacey then took the sausages and burgers over to the table. They were almost black on one side and pale on the other. No-one cared and yet again they were all snatched before the plate even hit the table.

''ang on a minute! The kids need something too, you know!' Brooke pleaded.

But it was too late. She dashed into the kitchen where she retrieved the turkey twizzlers she'd put in the oven but forgotten about. They weren't quite black but a very, very dark brown. No-one cared. She put them on a plate, went back into the garden and placed them on a rug just in front of the bouncy castle. The children immediately stopped bouncing and slid onto the rug. They tucked in with no preconceived ideas about plates, knives or forks. Fingers would do nicely. Several more jugs of Ribena were brought out and they gulped it down like they'd been deprived of liquid for months. Dawn, pint of cider in one hand, staggered over with Paige in the other and put her down. Brooke felt grateful to have such a reliable mate – except when she'd had too much to drink, that is. She thought Dawn deserved to let her hair down once in a while, so she didn't judge. Brooke scooped Paige up and played with her on the bouncy castle for a bit while it was empty.

'Come on, Brooke, give us a somersault, we wanna see if you've got a matching bra!' the chaps all cheered. Much to their amazement, she turned a perfect back somersault. More cheers.

Dean arrived into the back garden to jeers of 'What were you doing? Pressing the grapes and picking the 'ops?'

He unloaded all the bags into the recycling bin and grabbed another beer for himself. Brooke saw him and mouthed, 'Thanks, babe!' and blew him a kiss. He wandered around chatting to his chums who were well and truly intoxicated by now.

It got to around 4pm and Brooke suddenly remembered the birthday cake. Dean found the box on the table in the hallway, where Martin had left it. He carefully lifted the lid off and a sharp intake of breath followed.

Fuck fuck fuck! She'll kill me! How in God's name did that happen?!

Dean was confronted with a caterpillar who, to all intent and purposes, was doing the splits, had lost his eyes and broken its back. It'd definitely been standing up when he picked it up from the baker's. He pushed the eyes back in and smoothed the icing over the broken back area. He fetched the birthday cake candle Brooke had bought specially and placed it strategically around the broken back area so he could blame it on putting the candle in if he got caught out. But there was nothing he could do about the legs. Twelve chocolate legs splayed out on each side.

A gymnastic caterpillar – that's what I'll call it.

Before Brooke had a chance to inspect it, Dean lit the

candle using the gas flame on the cooker and brought it through ceremoniously.

'Happy birthday to you, happy birthday to you, happy birthday dear Paige, happy birthday to you!'

Everyone joined in and clapped at the end. Brooke walked towards the cake to show Paige how to blow the candle out. Dean panicked, blew it out and, purposefully, cut the cake in half badly – at the point of the broken back.

'Oi! Dean! Paige needs to blow out the candle! Light it again!'

Dean walked towards Brooke, meeting her before she reached the cake. Jen looked smug as she was called upon for her lighter. He grabbed Paige and quickly re-lit the candle, hoping to keep his wife as far away from the cake as possible – she had eyes like a hawk. He demonstrated to Paige what she needed to do, whilst ensuring that he allowed her foot to press down on the caterpillar's back, which could explain the caterpillar's splits. Paige tried, but the candle refused to go out. Porno Gazza got up from his chair, marched over to the cake and blew the candle out to protests from everyone present.

'*Now* can we 'ave some of this cake then?' he roared and cut himself a clumsy great big slice without being asked.

Dean breathed a sigh of relief and walked towards Brooke, still holding Paige, whose little ballerina pumps were now caked in chocolate icing underneath. He asked Dawn to take a photo of the three of them. Genius strategy!

That put Brooke off the scent; she wiped Paige's pumps, preened herself for a few seconds and then beamed a huge smile.

'Cheeeeeeese!'

Done.

Thank Christ for that!

Dean pecked Brooke and then Paige on the cheek and told them he loved them. A lucky escape indeed!

He cut the rest of the cake into slices, like a professional chef slices carrots, and then handed them round on a plate. It was only after it'd all gone, that he realised he hadn't given any to the little ones.

Just keep quiet, keep calm and hopefully Brooke won't notice.

He needn't have worried. The children soon saw they'd missed out on chocolate cake, but simply ran over to their respective parents, stole their piece and ran off back to the bouncy castle, which by now had a small puddle of vomit pooling in one corner.

As the afternoon wore on, Dean grabbed his friend Steve who was a builder.

'Steve, can I have your opinion on something? Have you got a tape measure on you by any chance?'

Steve grinned and pulled one out of his back pocket. 'Always prepared, me! What d'ya want measuring? It won't cope with anything microscopic…hahahahahaha!'

Dean ignored the innuendo and casually sauntered towards the corner of the garden, pointing as he walked.

He was determined to establish whether a hot tub would actually fit into the garden.

'Do you think that a hot tub would fit in this garden? And DO NOT under any circumstances tell Brooke I asked you that question!'

'Well, I'm not being funny, mate, but that depends on the size of hot tub. Are we talking for four or twelve people?'

'Christ…are you saying that hot tubs actually exist for twelve people?'

'Too right they do.'

Oh God, Brooke's bound to want one of them. That girl never does anything by halves.

'Well I can tell you now that an average eight-seater is gonna be around 240cm x 300cm'.

Without any prompting from Dean, Steve expertly pulled out the measuring tape and walked around the garden laying it out on each side. Brooke glanced over and looked rather quizzically at them both.

'Your garden's 3.5m x 2.5m so, no, you couldn't get one in.'

'That's what I thought. Brooke wants one.'

'Oh her ladyship does, does she? Well good luck with that one, mate! I tell you what, though…' Steve got his tape measure out again and discreetly measured the patio. 'You could squeeze one on your patio and you've already got your concrete base, but it'd be pretty crammed. You'd probably best get one of them plug 'n' play ones.'

Steve pretended to zip up his mouth and laughed, then made his way back to the beer and yanked the lid off a bottle of Budweiser with his teeth. He always did that. No-one had figured out how he had any teeth left.

Brooke made her way over to Steve. 'What were you measuring, Steve?'

He was caught by surprise, but remembered Dean's strict instructions.

'Oh…erm…we were having a bet as to who had the smallest garden. I won.'

Blokes, thought Brooke.

Dean was sneaking a cheeky sideways glance as Brooke was talking to Steve and was reassured he'd stuck to their agreement.

Job done.

The party progressed and there came a point late afternoon when Brooke realised that Paige hadn't opened any of her presents and that people were bound to be going soon. She put them all on the patio and brought Paige over to open them all in front of everybody.

First had to be the colossal one from Nanna and Grand-Daddy-Daddy. It was a sight to behold. A miniature dressing table, fully equipped with Hollywood-style mirror, drawers and pretend bottles of perfume, makeup and nail varnish. There was even a tiny set of GHD straighteners.

Brooke clapped her hands and squealed with delight.

Dean's eyes connected with Rick's, as his jaw dropped

open and his eyebrows raised to the roof. He'd already witnessed his wife early that morning playing shops with Paige, using the present they'd bought her – 'Let's pretend to go to Lakeside' – it was truly frightening.

God what will that girl be like when she's a teenager?

Rick's face and body language suggested *Mate. This has got nothing to do with me.*

For the next hour, Mick and Dave started a game of five-a-side using a scrunched-up Foster's can, while Dawn was being egged on by the girls to down a pint of cider in one. To the side, the children were pretending either to go to Lakeside or having their nails painted.

But by 6.30pm everyone had gone, bumbling off to their cars; most way over the limit, no-one offering to help clear up. Dean and Brooke were shattered. The garden looked like a bomb site and the kitchen like a student flat. Paige was fast asleep in her carry cot. Someone had put her in there but neither Dean or Brooke knew who.

They decided they'd clear up in the morning. Instead, they showered, changed into their pyjamas and vegged out in front of the TV. They discussed the success (or not) of the party and came to the conclusion that everyone had a great time. They poured themselves another drink, put Paige to bed and congratulated themselves.

Flowers that people had brought for Brooke had been neglected and had drooped or died. Entire plates of food and side dishes that people had brought as a contribution to the party hadn't even been seen, never mind opened.

As Brooke and Dean went to go upstairs to bed, they came to the little table in the hall and stopped.

Underneath it, like pretty maids all in a row, sat twenty-five Pretty Princess party bags.

18

Poison, Puke and Posh People

Jackie didn't quite make it to the toilet.

The explosion came from her backside first, followed by projectile vomiting of such force that the bathroom window resembled stained glass.

Over in Romford, Martin had been on and off the toilet all night and used so much toilet paper he'd run out and resorted to folding bits of kitchen roll to make do.

For the second time in as many weeks, Dean held up Brooke's hair as she retched into the toilet bowl. He was doing his best to hold in his own feelings of nausea, but after an hour he relented and vomited violently in the bathroom.

By 9am Dean and Brooke had received at least two dozen calls from friends saying how sick they all were and just wanted to let them know…you know…just in case it was anything they ate at the BBQ.

It was hard to escape the painful fact that the chicken drumsticks were almost certainly responsible.

'I thought as long as the juices ran pink then they were cooked!' exclaimed Dean.

'IDIOT! They have to be running clear – that's when you know they're cooked. What'll everyone be thinking? They'll never come to one of our parties again!'

Dean was astonished that she could still get so mad in between bouts of vomiting and diarrhoea.

He picked up the phone to Jackie to ask for help with looking after Paige, who kept crawling into the bathroom to watch Mummy and Daddy put their head into the toilet. She tried hard to join in and stood with them in solidarity, trying to get her head over the bowl too. All they could do was keep batting her away. Dean was gutted when Jackie revealed that she, too, had fallen prey to the chicken drumsticks and was in no fit state to help.

'No worries, Jackie. I'm really sorry it got you too.'

Dean sat ashen-faced, legs outstretched in front of him, arms hanging limply by his side.

One fucking chicken drumstick!

He realised that probably most of their friends would be in the same state, so it wasn't worth asking anyone for help. How on earth were he and Brooke going to get through the day like this? They were struggling to look after themselves, let alone a one year old.

That Sunday was purgatory. Brooke and Dean yearned for it to be over. They'd put a playmat out with as many toys as they could find easily and simply placed Paige there in the hope she'd occupy herself and disturb Mummy and Daddy as little as possible. From time to time, Paige would pretend to be *their* Mummy and Daddy and clearly thought the whole thing was one long glorious game. They'd managed to bring in the dressing table set from Jackie, but Paige was far more engrossed in the wrapping paper, the ribbon and the cardboard box it came in.

Sunday drifted by in a haze of retching, puke, diarrhoea, groaning and attempts to look after Paige. The garden and kitchen both remained untouched. Brooke just about managed to get Paige a jar of pureed fruit and half a Weetabix and as she lay on the floor and fed it to her, Paige actually seemed to understand that her mother wasn't capable of giving it to her in the normal way in her high chair. So, she crawled over to the spoon Brooke waved about, opened her mouth and slurped it messily.

By around 7pm Brooke and Dean's sickness and diarrhoea had finally abated and they were in need of sleep, as was Paige, who was unceremoniously plonked into her cot in the same pyjamas she'd been in all day, without a wash or tooth brush. The only thing Dean managed to do was change her nappy, which had been on all day.

Dean couldn't bear the thought of the next day being Monday and having to go to work, and leave Brooke with all this clearing up to do on her own. Maybe he'd take the day off? He'd not had a sick day for over ten years. Mr Conscientious, he was nicknamed by his colleagues who always seemed to fall ill on Mondays and Fridays for as long as he could remember. Remarkable, that!

In the event, the next morning, Dean felt fine and

decided he really should go into work. He fully expected Brooke to try and persuade him to stay at home and was rather put out that she didn't. In fact, he was surprised, to say the least, when Brooke brought him up a cup of tea – the second time in a week.

'C'mon, babe, you need to get to work. Here's a cuppa. This'll make you feel better.'

Brooke tried to look and sound casual, but her insides were like jelly. She was due at Mrs. Townsend's at 9.30am and if Dean didn't leave on time she'd be late. She merrily and speedily started clearing the kitchen from Saturday's party.

'Babe, I feel so bad not staying to help. Are you sure you don't want me to stay? I could pull a sickie.'

'No. You're alright. I'll get this lot done in no time. You get off to work. You won't get a promotion, or my hot tub, if you start taking days off sick now!'

Dean looked unsure until his phone went off. He glanced quickly at the many messages clearly left by miffed and poisoned friends. Then he checked his emails. There was a message in his inbox with the subject line 'URGENT MYSTERY SHOP – Golf Club.'

As he was reading his email, Brooke's phone vibrated. She pulled it out of her dressing gown pocket and glanced at the text that'd just come through. It was from Lady Townsend.

Brooke, Hugo is unwell today and I need help with a talk I'm giving in London at midday. Are you able to

come a bit earlier this morning – say 8.30am? I need you to come with me to the venue to help me set up. There will be a rather nice lunch afterwards if that helps your decision! And I'll pay you double for the day! LT

There it was. After knowing her for just one week, Lady Townsend had essentially got Brooke sussed.

Brooke had to re-read it twice before it fully sunk in. She tried to look normal yet was feeling anything but.

Dean's shoulders slumped.

Really? A golf club?

There were probably many more assessors who'd rather play golf for free than him, so given all the circumstances he emailed back quickly to say 'No'. Within a minute Angie had come back to say they were absolutely desperate; that the owners believed there was some sort of theft ring going on at the club and they needed independent evidence if at all possible to give to the police that staff were systematically stealing from the club. They'd pay him one hundred pounds to do it.

For fuck's sake. Why now? Why today? And a monkey?

'Is everything alright, Dean? You look angry.'

'No, it's fine. I've just been asked to get into work ASAP for some sort of crisis. So that's my decision made then.'

He reluctantly got ready 'for work' as Brooke hopped about itching for him to leave. About ten minutes later, he came downstairs and gave her a hug. 'OK, babe, I'm off. Sorry to leave you with all this mess. I'll see you tonight.'

Brooke embraced him, but the second he left, she checked her watch. 8.15am.

Mrs T I can be there at 8.45am but no sooner. Hope this is OK?

OK that'll do – please look smart. Heels would be good on this occasion!

'OH MY GOD!!' Brooke screeched out loud; partly frustration at not having more time and partly excitement at what the day might entail. It didn't occur to her for even one minute to say she couldn't do it. She messaged Dawn immediately.

Need to bring Paige over a bit earlier – I'll be there at 8.30amish

She stopped the façade of clearing up and immediately got Paige dressed in less than a minute – her personal best – and put her in her playpen. She lobbed a bunch of toys in a huge supermarket bag and threw it by the front door, along with the nappy changing bag. Then she focussed on herself, while Paige played. She sniffed both armpits.

Thank God I showered last night! What to wear? Why heels? Does that mean smart? Posh? Trendy?

She took a deep breath and looked in her wardrobe quickly. She spotted an understated LK Bennett blue shift dress she'd found in a sale but which she'd never actually worn. She was panicking and in a hurry, so she pulled it on and decided it'd have to do. She found a pair of white kitten-heel slingbacks from Hobbs and slipped them on. She achieved that glorious thing women dream of –

roughly piling her hair up and it looking fabulous first time.

That'll do.

She gathered her trademark makeup into a bag and slung it in her handbag.

Is it better to be on time and unmade up or fully ready and a few minutes late?

She decided she'd put her makeup on in the car as she was going along. There was bound to be a bit of rush-hour traffic. Paige was moulded, against her will, into her car seat.

Within ten minutes of Letitia Townsend's text, Brooke was in the car driving to Dawn's, leaving a semi-cleared-up bomb site behind her. As she suspected, no sooner had she left, than she was in rush-hour traffic. Out came the cosmetics bag and with the accuracy and skill of an artist with an alcohol problem, she painstakingly managed to make up her entire face over the course of the journey to near on her normal standard. The mascara was the trickiest part and required a long gap in the traffic in front of her, but she managed.

She let Paige ring Dawn's doorbell. Nothing. She rang again and eventually Dawn came to the front door, unbolting and unlocking it in her dressing gown.

'Why are you here so early? You're not due till quarter past nine?' Dawn looked dreadful. Then Brooke remembered that Dawn was likely to have suffered from the terror of the chicken drumsticks.

'Oh God, Dawn. You look rough. Did you get food poisoning as well? We've all had it. We think it was the chicken drumsticks.'

'Yeah I've been throwing up and had the shits all Saturday night. But why are you here so early? And why are you dressed like that? You look weird.'

'Love you too! Well, Mrs Townsend's asked me to go with her to some posh do in London today 'cause Hugo's ill.'

'And?'

'Well I didn't think you'd mind having Paige a bit early – I'll see you right. Honestly. She's paying me extra to do it 'cause it's short notice.'

'Well it doesn't sound like I've got much choice! What time will you be back?'

'God knows, but I must get home before Dean. The house is still a tip. I'll message you when I'm leaving to let you know what time I think I'll be back.'

Dawn smiled, plucked Paige out of Brooke's arms and shook her head as Brooke threw the toys and nappy bag into the porch and darted off back to the car. Dawn had always believed there was more to Brooke than met the eye and she had a funny feeling that this Lady Letitia Townsend, whoever she was, would be responsible for its manifestation.

***

'Oh good you're here. Well done, Brooke. This has helped me out enormously. Thank you so much.' Lady Townsend was visibly delighted.

Brooke had run to the staff entrance from the car rather than be later than she said. She was panting.

'You look very nice dear. Very…appropriate.'

'Do you mind me asking where we're going? I didn't know what to wear.'

'Well you look perfect. We're going to a private members' club in St James's in London called Brooks's.'

Brooke thought that was rather funny. 'Ha! Brooke goes to Brooks's!' she laughed out loud and Mrs Townsend joined her.

'Do you know, that hadn't even struck me! Anyway, as my late husband was a member of the club all his life and a past member of The Society of Dilettanti, I'm giving a talk to members on the paintings that are housed in the club.'

Brooke clammed up, out of her depth. She'd no idea who Dilettanti was, or what Brooks's was. Lady Townsend seemingly understood her feelings of inadequacy. She could read Brooke's face as her demeanour shifted noticeably. Lady Townsend had been there herself many years ago.

'But none of that matters, right now. All I need from you is a pair of hands, a charming personality and an ability to connect the projector to my laptop. Can you manage that, do you think?'

'First two no problem. Not so sure about the projector, but I can certainly have a go. I've learned a fair bit from Dean over the years, to be fair.' She crossed her fingers behind her back.

'How are we gonna get there?' asked Brooke

'Oh they're sending a car at ten-thirty.'

OMG – sending a car!!!

'In the meantime, I need help getting my notes finished and all the equipment in the car. The wretched club is like a dinosaur – it doesn't have any audio-visual equipment whatsoever. I've had to hire it all out myself!'

You alright, babe? Keep thinking about you and all that tidying up!

As a notification came through on Brooke's phone, Mrs Townsend didn't bat an eyelid but carried on what she was doing, saying, 'Do you need to get that, dear? It's quite alright if you do.'

Brooke looked stony-faced, turned it off quickly and said she'd deal with it later. She didn't feel at all guilty but knew she couldn't deal with anything else other than what she had going on right in front of her.

She spent the next hour or so getting coffee and pulling books from the library shelves as and when Mrs Townsend asked for them. Most of her talk was ready, but these were last-minute amendments. Brooke had never seen books anything like them and had never heard of any of the authors. This really was another world; one that she felt miserably excluded from. She was both anxious and enthralled at being part of it – even if it was only for one day. She made a real effort to examine the photographs of the paintings that Lady Townsend was going to be talking about and trying to memorise them; it'd at least prove she was curious and could pick things up.

Brooke was asked to go through the PowerPoint one last time – just in case there was anything glaringly obviously wrong, like the slides were in the wrong order or something. Lady Townsend made it clear that she didn't expect Brooke to pick up on any spelling or grammar. Hugo had taught her how to put together a PowerPoint slideshow. He'd offered to do it for her, but she wouldn't hear of it, determined to learn this 'new-fangled technology'.

As Brooke went through each slide, she noticed that the date on one of them was wrong. Or at least wrong from her memory of something she'd just seen in the books in the library. She was very nervous about bringing it up. She didn't want to look a fool and she was sure that Lady Townsend wouldn't have let such a basic error slip through unnoticed. But when Lady Townsend asked Brooke if she'd spotted any errors, she had to speak up.

'Well…erm… Actually, I think this date might be wrong.' She pointed to the slide of the group portrait of The Dilettanti Society by Sir Joshua Reynolds that hung in The Great Subscription Room – the one with hidden saucy overtones. It said 1797 and she was sure it'd said 1779 in the book she'd seen.

'I'm probably wrong, but I seem to think it said 1779

in the book you had out – not 1797.'

'Oh my goodness, you're quite right. Well done, Brooke. See. You've paid for yourself already!'

Brooke was secretly pleased and the PowerPoint was duly changed. Lady Townsend went to freshen up while Brooke started loading all the equipment and notes into the smart Daimler car that'd come to collect them.

By about 10. 15am they were ready to depart. They both sat in the back seat and yet again Brooke found herself smiling at the totally bizarre and unexpected place she found herself! The butterflies in her stomach flapped wildly, ready for take-off! Her thoughts turned to Dean's earlier message and she discreetly got out her phone to reply.

'You don't have to keep hiding your phone, dear. I do understand that young people do everything by phone these days and it's fine by me.'

Brooke smiled at her and now feeling a tad guilty, sent a brief reply to Dean.

Hi babe – out right now at Dawn's. Kitchen still a mess. Felt rough and came here for some TLC. C u later.

***

Dean read the message and was taken aback. It was unheard-of for Brooke to leave the house without cleaning it first. A bit like her makeup, it was simply something she never neglected – even though she *despised* housework.

Dean was perplexed, but had his own issues to sort out, so he could give it no more thought.

He'd arrived at work only to tell them he needed to go back home as he felt so ill. Brian had taken one glance at him and, knowing his one hundred per cent attendance record, let him go immediately. He did look a little ropey.

By midday Dean was at Wendle golf course with an old friend Nigel, ready to conduct a mystery visit. Dean didn't see him very often, but Nigel did like golf, so was his first choice for partner. He had to bring some suitable attire for Dean, which then required a tricky explanation. As soon as Nigel started talking, Dean remembered why he didn't see him very often. He was *so* negative; 'a mood-hoover' Brooke would've called him. It was the last thing on earth Dean felt like doing, but one hundred pounds was too good to turn down.

The next five hours were like being sidekick to Inspector Morse. Dean made the fatal mistake of explaining to Nigel why he was asking him to come and play golf with him at this particular club. Well, that was all Nigel needed to get out his mobile and start taking notes on every single aspect of the course, the clubhouse and the staff. You name it, Nigel had it covered. In a way, it took pressure off Dean to be as alert as he would normally have been. On the other hand, he didn't shy away from accepting he was ultimately responsible and didn't want to miss anything really important that'd be helpful to the police investigation. So, although he let Nigel take the notes, he remained ultra-alert.

Within ten minutes of being in the bar, they ordered two pints of beer. Lo and behold, a young girl called Danuta took a twenty-pound note from them, gave them change but didn't ring the amount up into the till. The note was slid very discreetly into front pocket.

Oh shit! They're right!

Dean said nothing and they walked to the outside patio and sat down.

'Nige. Did you see that?'

'You mean twenny quid in the pocket? Yeah. I did.'

They both stared at each other hoping for inspiration as to what to do next.

'I think we should order something else later, after our round, just to check if they do it again.'

Nigel agreed. Nigel had no friends except Dean. And even then, Dean was only friends with him because he felt sorry for him. He'd no personality, no drive, no opinions of his own, no job, no money, no girlfriend; the loser of their social group. Dean just had more compassion and empathy than the rest of the lads.

***

The Daimler arrived outside Brooks's, the driver got out, opened the door for Lady Townsend and Brooke, and helped them out of the car. The driver started to bring the equipment in and Brooke automatically went out to help.

'No, dear. Leave it to the driver.'

Brooke waited uncomfortably in the hallowed porter's hall of Brooks's as the head porter shamelessly looked Brooke up and down. She felt like Julia Roberts in *Pretty Woman.*

Lady Townsend appeared immediately behind and shouted, 'Don't worry, Marco, she's with me.'

'Good morning, Lady Townsend. How delightful to see you again. I understand you're giving a talk today?'

'Yes and this is my assistant Brooke.'

Blimey – I'm her assistant now!

Marco glanced at Brooke's face somewhat disdainfully. 'You're a little early, Lady Townsend, so would you mind awfully taking a seat in the drawing room until the Oval Room meeting is finished? Then I shall get one of the porters to take the equipment upstairs.'

You alright, babe?

Dean was experiencing pangs of guilt, leading him to eventually send Brooke a message.

Brooke, on the other hand, was beginning to feel as though she were living in some kind of parallel universe.

'I'm afraid mobile phones are not allowed anywhere in the club,' said the porter snootily, so Brooke stepped onto the pavement for a moment.

Yeah – all good, babe. Are you feeling better? Did you get your crisis sorted?

Yeah all sorted.

C U 2 nite.

Love ya xxx

Brooke stepped back inside and took a few minutes to absorb the surroundings. She felt like she'd gone back a couple of hundred years. There wasn't one thing she was looking at that was familiar to her. Ancient and threadbare carpets and worn leather sofas, wood panels, silk wallpaper, card tables, oil paintings, huge fireplaces, stuffed animals. It all seemed so surreal. She found herself smiling again. She was also painfully aware that Lady Townsend was watching and alert to any discomfort at her surroundings. She'd wanted to make Brooke feel as welcome as possible.

They were offered tea which came in solid silver teapots, real tea leaves, a strainer and a cup and saucer, along with solid silver milk jug and sugar bowl. Brooke didn't dare touch any of it. She was terrified of doing something wrong. One of the staff came to pour after a few minutes.

Eventually they were shown up to the Oval Room in which Lady Townsend was giving her talk. The porters, with an average age of around ninety it seemed to Brooke, helped them with all their equipment but left sharpish when it came to connecting the data projector with the laptop. Brooke got down on her hands and knees and, to her joy, successfully connected everything. While she was still on the floor, a gentleman came into the room and was confronted with Brooke's bottom.

'I say, Georgina, do you need any help down there, sweetheart? That's quite a sight for an old man!'

He slapped her bottom.

Brooke shrieked and banged her head on the table above as she tried to get up and complain. By the time she'd risen above the table, he'd gone.

'What a bloody cheek! Who's Georgina?' Brooke asked, flustered.

'You mustn't worry about him, dear. That's the Duke of Albemarle.' Lady Townsend sounded her usual calm, assured self.

'But he called me Georgina!'

'He would, dear. He frequents the club over the road; the club for aristocracy and royalty. In that club they call all the female staff Georgina and all the male staff George. That way it doesn't tax their memory. It's just what he's used to.'

Brooke was dumbfounded.

'You're 'aving a laugh! You mean they're too old or too posh to be bothered to remember the staff's names?'

'Sadly yes, dear. Now let's get cracking and get everything set up.' It was quite clear that Lady Townsend was used to all this.

Brooke felt she needed to go with the flow even though something felt inherently wrong about ignoring such behaviour.

She very naturally took charge of getting Lady Townsend's notes in order and handouts of her talk collated in case anyone wanted them. Lady Townsend spoke to a series of gentlemen who came to talk to her.

They clearly knew her well.

It came to the allotted time for her talk and the room gradually filled with men. All men.

They all sound like Prince Charles.

She couldn't help but stare; their suits, their haircuts, their mannerisms. The way they spoke to each other; it was all just extraordinary. Brooke had to keep reminding herself that this was real. She was mostly ignored by the men, who spoke only to Letitia. But Letitia's manners were exemplary and she always introduced Brooke. Some nodded and moved on, others shook her hand. Several made vaguely sexist comments.

Remember bone crush, bone crush!

One or two actually deemed her worthy enough to speak to.

'Well, what do we have here?' followed by a loud guffaw.

'Letitia, where did you find this pretty little thing? Your assistant, eh? Well, she can come and assist me any time hahahaha!'

Then they merely walked past her.

She wasn't quick enough, or clever enough, or witty enough to retort, so she just smiled sweetly, as shame and humiliation enveloped her.

One gentleman actually picked up her hand and kissed it. 'If they let women like *you* in here we wouldn't complain! Hahahaha!'

(For years there had been a battle. Should Brooks's let

women into the club or not? There was a unanimous 'No' from all sides.)

Brooke actually found that quite funny, dug deep, found her mischievous self and winked at him, immediately regretting it.

Oh God, I shouldn't have done that. Big mistake.

'Oh, Letitia, let me take this little sweetie home – please!'

'Leave her alone, Charles. She's taken.' Lady Townsend said in a more serious tone.

He pulled a face at her, winked back at Brooke and sat down.

'You have to watch that one. He's got a history of affairs. Now, I think we're about ready, so if you want to sit up at the front with me with the clicker, and when I indicate, just move the slide on to the next one. Is that alright? I may ask you to go back at some point as well.'

Brooke sat down on a beautiful carved mahogany chair with dusky-pink silk upholstery and played nervously with the clicker in her hands. The chair was very uncomfortable and she was relieved she didn't have to sit on it for any length of time.

She became aware of the number of men staring at her; no compunction whatsoever. It was as though a strange, exotic creature from another place had landed in their midst. There were a few hidden snorts of laughter and heads turning, making her decidedly ill at ease, which was strange really. In her normal life she loved it if she got attention from men! She couldn't quite pinpoint why this particular situation made her feel so uncomfortable.

She decided she needed to assume a serious look on her face as she watched the screen and listened to Lady Townsend talk about The Society of Dilettanti. She was such an inspiration to listen to and it made Brooke wish she'd listened more and worked a smidgen harder at school.

She found herself looking so intently at one particular painting – looking for the clues to the fact that the gentlemen in it were allegedly staring at a 'lady of the night' and making visual jokes about her genitalia – that she was oblivious to Mrs Townsend's instruction to move onto the next slide.

'Next slide please!' Then, a little louder, 'Brooke, dear, next slide please!'

'Oh sorry!'

Brooke panicked and quickly moved onto the next slide and looked around the room to see how badly she'd mucked up. No-one appeared bothered.

The rest of the talk went without any issues and Lady Townsend was clapped heartily by all those present. The club secretary got up to thank her and presented her with a small gift exquisitely wrapped – professionally – Brooke could tell. She'd once been to Harrods and watched from a distance to see exactly how they did it, so she could copy it back at home.

She thanked them all and then the club secretary

called them in for lunch in The Great Subscription Room, where some of the paintings Lady Townsend had been talking about hung majestically on the walls.

'Brooke, you come and sit next to me. I don't think you're quite ready to cope with this lot on your own, even though I'm quite sure they'd find you utterly fascinating.'

Brooke didn't understand why would they find her fascinating. She was quite sure she'd be as dull as dishwater to these men, who quite clearly led such privileged lives and must've been used to mixing with the most cultured women, who Brooke could only dream about aspiring to.

The room was set up in round tables of eight and there were six of them. They gleamed with silver cutlery, cut crystal glass and crisp, white, starched linen tablecloths and napkins.

Brooke did nothing until she'd watched someone else do it first. She sat down and permitted the waiter to place a napkin across her lap but frowned as he did so.

I'm not a bloody kid! Oh, they're doing it to everyone.

After a few minutes, the gentleman to her right introduced himself.

'Good afternoon, I'm Geoffrey D'arcy. And you are?'

Brooke gave her best bone-crushing handshake to date and Geoffrey D'Arcy winced.

'Hello, I'm Brooke. I'm Mrs…er…Lady Townsend's er…'

Can I really call myself her assistant? I'm not really. I'm just a fill-in.

'Executive assistant?'

OMG! Brooke De'Ath – what're you thinking?

'Well at least for the day anyway!' She laughed and retrieved herself.

'Well it's delightful to meet you, my dear. You used that clicker to perfection!'

Are you taking the piss?

Brooke didn't know how to take that comment.

'And where are you from, my dear?' Geoffrey D'Arcy enquired.

'You probably won't know it.' Brooke didn't like the thought of revealing or talking about it really.

'Try me!'

'Brentwood. It's in Essex.'

'Well I never. I do indeed know it very well. My grandfather was the commander-in-chief of The British East India Elephant Army Training School there.' He laughed out loud.

Yet again, Brooke didn't know whether he was teasing her or not. He sensed her disbelief and went on.

'Truly! He was there from 1901 to 1956.'

'Are you seriously telling me people trained elephants in Brentwood?'

Brooke was incredulous.

Oh…My…God…Elephant Close. I wonder if it's got anything to do with that? Should I mention it?

She took a deep breath and took the risk.

'I live in a road called Elephant Close.'

'Well it's almost certainly been named after the school; a nod to the wonderful men and women who served there.'

'Bloody hell!'

Brooke had forgotten herself for a moment and quickly put her hand up to her mouth.

'Sorry – that just came out! I can't believe it. I didn't know anything about that. I've never even heard anyone else talk about it either.'

A bowl of some kind of soup was suddenly placed in front of her. She stared at it anxiously.

'It's Cullen Skink,' Geoffrey offered helpfully.

'Right.' Brooke continued to stare at it, then tucked in and hoped for the best.

God, this is gorgeous.

For the next hour over lunch, Brooke enjoyed a delightful conversation with Geoffrey D'Arcy about the East India Elephant Training School. She was fascinated and suddenly forgot who she was, why she was there and, most importantly, where she was from. She asked question after question and Geoffrey was thrilled to talk about it. No-one had taken this much interest in what he'd had to say for years!

The main course was poached salmon with hollandaise sauce, with baby new Jersey Royal potatoes, spinach and baby carrots.

There were two knives to her right. One a weird shape she'd never seen before. She waited until Geoffrey D'Arcy had picked up his and then she followed suit, carefully examining the polished silver fish knife in her hand. Geoffrey D'Arcy smiled, sensing her lack of knowledge and used his most gracious way of speaking. He'd no desire to embarrass or humiliate her.

'It's a fish fork – used especially for fish. Before the use of detergents, the smell of fish would stay on the dinner knives so they always had a separate set to be used for fish dishes only.'

'Thank god for Fairy Liquid, eh? Imagine having to find room for all them extra knives!' Brooke laughed out loud at her own thoughts. Geoffrey D'Arcy laughed at her straightforward manner.

She enjoyed her main dish, with the exception of the sauce. Although she'd had all the things on her plate before, they'd never tasted as good as this. It had to be about quality. A vision of the two for one offer in Tesco's on baby potatoes came to mind and she recalled how they'd gone mouldy after a couple of days.

I bet these don't go mouldy that quick.

Dessert was Pear Condé. Brooke was clueless as to what this was but felt she'd built up sufficient rapport with Geoffrey D'Arcy to ask him.

'It's cold rice pudding with a pear purée.'

'Oh god, I can't stand rice pudding – never mind cold rice pudding!'

'Ah, but I'll bet you'll never have tasted rice pudding like Brooks's rice pudding. Nowhere else on earth do they make it like they do here. Do you know that a new chef once took it off the menu and there was a revolt amongst the members. It was put back on again the next day!'

Brooke really wasn't convinced and the waiter put it in front of her before she'd even had a chance to say no thank you! She stared at it like a spoilt child; sullen, sulky, insistent she didn't even want to try it. Rice pudding reminded her of school dinners, which she'd despised. And rice pudding, in particular, made her feel physically sick.

Geoffrey D'Arcy watched her face carefully and could see she was genuinely repulsed at even the idea of eating it. But he knew something she simply didn't. She'd love it. It was creamy, cooked to perfection, the perfect consistency and temperature.

'I tell you what. In a nod to the betting history of this place, I formally place a bet of twenty pounds that you'll like it. No; love it. But you've got to be honest!'

Brooke didn't know what he was talking about, but found herself agreeing to the bet.

She picked up the silver teaspoon. As she did so, she suddenly remembered the expression 'born with a silver spoon in their mouth'. It'd never really meant anything to her before. Three hours at Brooks's gentlemen's club was enough to educate her. Not only about that expression, but about so many other things.

'Oh my god. This is fabulous. It's so creamy! It doesn't taste anything like rice pudding.'

Geoffrey watched carefully at the expression on her

face as she gradually worked her way through the entire dessert and scraped round the sides as a child would do with a knickerbocker glory.

'That'll be twenty pounds please!' Geoffrey demanded in mock menacing style.

Brooke laughed. 'You've won fair and square! I owe you!'

She reached for her purse in her fake Louis Vuitton handbag.

'Blimey, I haven't got any cash on me!'

'I've heard that one before! If you make a bet at Brooks's, you absolutely have to honour it. It's the Brooks's way. There's no getting out of it.'

Brooke was unsure whether he was joking or not. She just couldn't tell.

'Don't worry about it now. Here, take my card.' He handed her his business card. She took it without reading it properly but immediately observed it was gold-embossed lettering on heavy white vellum with some sort of crest on the top, along with contact details.

'You can send a cheque or bring cash. Up to you, but all bets must be paid. Now, it's been quite delightful speaking with you, Brooke, but I must dash now, I have a meeting with my stockbroker at three o'clock.'

Geoffrey D'Arcy stood up, shook Brooke's hand, thanked Letitia and walked out of the room.

By this time, Brooke urgently needed to pay a visit to the powder room. She stood up to go and find it and all the men suddenly stood up. Brooke stopped in her tracks and assumed that someone was about to make a speech or something and so turned to face the room. She waited. The men waited, all the time looking at Brooke. She didn't know what was going on and glanced panic-stricken over to Lady Townsend, who remained seated, smiled in a very reassuring way and waved her hand at her as if to say 'Don't worry, just carry on doing what you were doing'.

Brooke expressed confusion, left the room and asked where the ladies was.

'Please follow me, madam.' The member of staff escorted her personally to the ladies and pointed it out.

Brooke opened the door to find a rather shabby toilet. The whole thing needed a good makeover, she thought, as she sat there looking intently at everything. There were cartoons on the wall, chipped paint everywhere, yet more threadbare carpet.

Who has carpet in the toilet?

And there were flowers, tissues and fancy soap. She washed her hands and looked for a drier or paper towels. Nothing. She checked the little cupboard underneath the sink. Nothing. There was a basket on the top with what looked like rolled-up flannels. She couldn't imagine what they were for, but decided to use one to dry her hands anyway. She searched for somewhere to put it after she'd finished and when she found a bin and opened it, to her relief it had a couple of used flannels in it. She felt quite proud of herself having navigated the ladies at Brooks's.

As she found her way back to the Great Subscription Room, she walked slowly, soaking up every single thing she set eyes on. She felt like a naughty schoolgirl; looking in the headmaster's office when he wasn't there; doing something she wasn't supposed to be doing; being somewhere she wasn't supposed to be.

She found herself back outside the Great Subscription Room. She stroked the ornate doors and took a deep breath; the wine she'd consumed was catching up with her and making her feel a little woozy. As soon as she entered, all the men stood up again. She looked over to Lady Townsend for guidance, who beckoned her to come and sit back down, which she did. All the men then sat down.

'What are they doing?' Brooke asked quietly and with some anxiety, leaning in towards Mrs Townsend.

'It's etiquette, my dear. These men are some of the most wealthy, influential, well-educated men in the country. This is how they've been brought up. Their way of showing respect to a lady is to stand when she enters or leaves a room.'

Yeah right – like these are the same blokes who smacked my bum and laughed at me.

Brooke decided it was probably best not to have a discussion about that right now, so sat down dutifully.

By 2.45pm lunch was over and all the men started to leave the room. Some came over to Letitia and spoke before exiting. None said a word to, or even acknowledged Brooke.

'Right. Let's get packed up. You probably need to be getting back now. I don't want to make you late.' Mrs Townsend started gathering up all her things and Brooke swiftly and efficiently began taking everything back downstairs, with help from one of the porters.

As they descended the staircase, there appeared to be some sort of commotion ahead. There, lying spread-eagled across the black and white chequered hall floor, blocking the entrance, was a long-bearded priest dressed in what looked to be red and purple religious robes, demanding money for his church and shouting at Alastair, the Assistant Club Secretary. One or two members had come out of the card room to see what was going on. They stood to one side staring at the priest trying to make out what denomination he was from.

'I say, do you need any help, Alastair?' asked Sir Henry, who was just leaving the club.

'Thank you, Sir Henry, but it's all under control.'

At the head end of the man, Alastair – a welcome barrier between the members and the normal world – stood in his black morning suit with grey-striped trousers and waistcoat. His sense of calm was admirable in such an extraordinary situation. His hands were firmly clasped behind his back, his head tilted upwards in disdain, but he was serious and unwavering in his determination not to let this man ruin the members' afternoon tea. Alastair, having worked at the club for donkeys' years, was quite frankly as essential to the members as their own wives.

His familiar face, loyalty, reliability and discretion meant he was trusted by all the members and had indeed handled many undesirable situations – and people – at the club.

Sir Henry stepped over the body to retrieve his umbrella from the rack on the other side and checked the events board to see who he was playing next in the bridge tournament. Humphrey Furness-Jones and Alastair exchanged a few words over the priest about the club grouse shoot in a few weeks' time.

Lady Townsend and Brooke had stood back as the scene unfolded, but, once Alastair had reassured them that it was all in hand Lady Townsend walked forward to leave.

'Come along, dear,' she called back to Brooke.

She looked down briefly at the priest on the floor, clearly trying to decide which part would be easiest to cross and chose the head end. Brooke followed, but looked down as she stepped over the priest, trying hard not to touch him and apologising for catching his beard under her foot. Lady Townsend didn't look back, but at the door Brooke couldn't stop herself. She saw Alastair continue to politely but firmly encourage the priest to leave. Brooke waved at Alastair, who smiled kindly at her.

'Goodbye, Ms De'Ath.'

'Byee!' she shouted cheerily as she walked towards the waiting car.

By just gone 3pm they were on their way out of St James's Street and back to Warley.

Almost as soon as they were in the car, Mrs Townsend spoke.

'You know, Brooke, you did remarkably well today. They're not the easiest people to socialise with and you did brilliantly. Thank you so much for agreeing to help me at such short notice.'

Happiness, pride and contentment engulfed Brooke like The Great Wave off Kanagawa.

'Well thank you for asking me to come with you and help. Especially as you've only known me a week! It was a bit of a risk bringing me here!' Brooke laughed.

'There was little, if any, risk as far as I'm concerned, Brooke. You need to have more faith in yourself. I knew from the first time I met you that you're capable of doing so much more. When Hugo couldn't come today, I had no hesitation whatsoever in asking you. I knew that if you were able to make it, you wouldn't let me down.'

'It's another world though, Mrs Townsend. Another *planet*!'

'I know, dear. I was in your place once.'

Brooke looked at her quizzically as Lady Townsend made herself comfortable in the back seat of the same Daimler that'd picked them up. She shut her eyes and had a nap.

Brooke also sat back. Had this really happened? She giggled quietly to herself and shook her head. What would Dean say? What would any of her friends or family say if they knew where she'd been and what she'd done today? Then she suddenly thought about her phone. All afternoon, she'd not given it a second thought. But now, when she'd nothing else to do, it burst forth into her brain like a shooting star that landed at her feet and demanded attention.

She turned it on, fully expecting to see a flurry of messages from Dean wondering why she hadn't responded. Nothing. There was nothing from him at all. She was surprised but undeniably relieved.

Then she suddenly thought about Paige.

Shit! I haven't thought about her once all afternoon!

She felt guilty for a few seconds and then messaged Dawn to let her know she should be back to pick Paige up at about 4.45pm.

She then sat back and relaxed, wallowing in the afterglow as she was chauffeured back to Warley and began to think that Elephant Close wasn't such a bad address after all.

19

Mystery Golfing and A Near-Miss.

Nigel and Dean stayed in the clubhouse for half an hour, during which they ordered another drink each. It was blatant. The staff were nicking from the club. The money from their round was pocketed immediately.

Dean so wished he could talk to Brooke about this but, of course, he couldn't. He was naïvely astounded that staff would do this to their employer. No matter how distressing Dean found the whole thing, he knew that he had yet to actually play a round of golf.

He and Nigel tried to find the visitors' changing rooms. It wasn't entirely clear where they were – or indeed if there *were* separate changing rooms for visitors and members. In the absence of anything obvious, they tailgated into the members' changing room; behind an old boy that looked as though he wouldn't be even be able to hold up a club, never mind play a round of golf. They took their time, diligently inspecting every single shower, shower tray, soap dispenser, hand drier, towels, locker, toilet bowl, toilet roll dispenser and door locks. They tried their best to be discreet, but the old boy glanced over suspiciously at them a couple of times before mumbling something to himself and leaving while Nigel and Dean were in the toilets.

Dean was rather alarmed at Nigel's over-zealous approach to the assignment. Dean was aware *he* was careful, but he'd never met anyone who'd quite matched up to that. Now that he'd witnessed Nigel in full force, he was rather perturbed at the thought of being put in a similar category.

They made their notes, changed and went to go out onto the first tee, but they simply couldn't find a way out of the changing rooms. They tried going back in through the door through which they'd just come, but it was automatically locked. The door which appeared to lead out onto the first tee had an entry code system for which they didn't have a code. They waited and waited in the hope and anticipation that a member would eventually enter. After fifteen minutes, no-one had come in. They were stuck inside with no known way out. Dean tried to phone the pro shop, but there was no signal inside the clubhouse.

'For fuck's sake!' Dean shouted out in frustration. 'This is bloody ridiculous!'

They waited ten more minutes by which time their booked tee time had well and truly been and gone.

'I can't believe this,' Nigel stated in a tone that sounded exactly like he'd locked himself out of his own house.

There was a small window on the same wall as the exit door that led to the first tee. Out of sheer desperation, they opened it and Dean shouted out to anyone who happened to be nearby.

'Hello? Hello? Is anybody out there?'

So much for Goddamn mystery golfer discretion.

A very large unfriendly man came up to the window. 'What're you doing? You just need to press the key code.'

'But we haven't got the key code,' came Nigel's voice back – slightly apologetic.

'Why not? All members have the key code.'

'I know, but we're not members,' explained Dean, as though he was fully expecting to be given a lecture.

'Then what're you doing in the members' changing rooms?' asked the fat chap indignantly. He was clearly far more concerned at the fact that his precious members club changing rooms were being infiltrated by non-members than he was about ensuring visitors to the club had a lovely 'Warm Wendle Welcome'.

'Well, if you let us out, we can explain,' Dean pleaded.

'I'll get the club secretary. I think he'll want to know about this.'

'Fine, but can you please let us out so we can at least get on and play our round of golf? We can talk to the club secretary afterwards.'

'No. You can explain it to the club secretary directly. Lifetime honorary members of this club, such as myself, don't come here to play golf or socialise with the likes of you.'

He proceeded to waddle off towards the office.

Dean and Nigel looked at each other flabbergasted. They'd no choice but to wait, like rule-breaking staff waiting to be seen by HR. They sat speechless on the wooden slatted benches.

After a few minutes, the club secretary arrived in the changing rooms.

'Gentlemen, you really shouldn't be here. These changing rooms are for members only. Can I see proof of purchase of green fees, please?' He sternly held out his hand, exactly as a father would do if he suspected his child had taken something he shouldn't have. He looked at them over his glasses, eyebrows raised and lips pursed.

Make a complaint about any aspect of the club and make note of how your complaint is handled.

It took all he had, but Dean was actually very genuinely annoyed, so he found his 'puffy-out' chest and set to.

'We were recommended to come to this club by a friend. We've been shocked, appalled and bitterly disappointed by the way we've been treated since the moment we stepped foot in the place. At no point did anyone let us know which changing rooms we should use or where they were and there are absolutely no signs anywhere indicating that there are any other changing rooms than the members'. To add insult to injury, once we did find ourselves locked in here, one of your members – instead of helping us – actually kept us forcibly trapped in here as though we were some sort of criminals.'

To Dean's astonishment, the club secretary's reply

was simple. 'Well that's because you shouldn't be in here. I'll let you out now but you need to use the visitors' changing rooms next time. And I'll need to see your proof of purchase of green fees.'

Dean and Nigel had no words.

'Did you understand anything that my friend here was just explaining?' Nigel asked incredulously.

Next time? Does he seriously think that after how he's treated us that we would ever step foot in here again? Recommend any of our mates to come here? He's got to be taking the piss. What a tosser!

'So where *are* the visitors' changing rooms?' Dean enquired with exasperation in his voice.

The club secretary finally let them out, and as they followed him like puppies after their master, he pointed to a rather old, tired and slightly dilapidated outbuilding.

'They're in there. Now, please can I see proof of purchase of green fees?'

Dean took out his receipt from the pro shop; the secretary glanced at it, mumbled that it was all OK and then off he marched back to his office.

Was your complaint handled to your satisfaction?

No it fucking well wasn't! No wonder the staff are stealing from him. If any of my team behaved like that, I'd have given them the sack by now!

The starter looked at his watch disapprovingly as Dean and Nigel announced themselves. He tutted and made some comment about visitors always being late but then let them through anyway. Dean was so mad that he played golf terribly for the entire eighteen holes. He couldn't stop thinking about the club secretary's response to his complaint.

At one point during his round, they were waiting for some greenkeepers to finish their work on the green. They waited and waited but the greenkeepers seemed to be completely oblivious to the visitors trying to tee off. Dean got so cross he shouted,

'Oi! Can you get off the green? We're trying to take our shot?'

The greenkeepers looked up, rather surprised. They were clearly not used to golfers shouting at them in this way and they were none too happy about it. They made a point of very slowly picking up their equipment and walking off the green with no acknowledgement or apology for keeping Dean and Nigel waiting.

Please tell us your overall impression of the club and how likely you'd be to recommend it to your friends and family?

Right. You asked. You're gonna get!

As they approached the eighteenth hole, Dean told Nigel that he really wasn't in the mood to go back into the clubhouse and that, if he didn't mind, he'd rather just go straight home. He was still shattered from the weekend and was just not in the right frame to socialise.

Nigel was fine with that. He was so grateful that Dean had asked him at all. No-one ever asked him to anything.

He secretly knew that the lads didn't particularly like him. But he remained grateful that they let him hang out with them.

It was about 4.30pm and Nigel took Dean back to his house in Hornchurch, where he'd left his moped and work suit. Before he left, Dean got all the notes that Negative Nigel had made, along with his own observations and went to town, listing every single minuscule thing that the club did wrong. He delighted in informing them that the secretary was being robbed – probably on a daily basis. Every so often, Dean would ask Nigel if he'd any other comment to add about a particular aspect of the visit and he'd add in his two penneth. His report was another tome. It couldn't be said that he wasn't thorough. Once he'd finished, he got changed back into his work suit and headed off home.

Dean thought it'd be nice to get back a bit early for a change, although he'd have to come up with some sort of an explanation for Brooke as to *why* he was back so early.

Maybe I could say that I asked Brian if I could leave a bit early to make up for Brooke having spent all day clearing up the party mess. Yeah, that'd be good. She'd like that.

***

The Daimler arrived at Purses at around 4.30pm. Brooke was frantic about the time, but nevertheless helped Mrs Townsend bring in all the equipment into the library.

Brooke thanked her again and promised she'd sort it all out when she was next in

as she had to pick her daughter up from the childminder's.

'Not a problem at all, my dear. Thank you again. See you on Wednesday.'

Brooke ran in her high heels to the staff car park and climbed delicately into Edna. She'd noticed earlier that when Lady Townsend had got into the Daimler that she had this slightly odd way of doing so. She turned away from the car and sat down facing the outside with her legs dangling on the pavement. She then swung her legs round ninety degrees – they looked like they'd been glued together – as her bottom also moved round ninety degrees at the same time and her body finally faced the front of the car. When she'd noticed Brooke looking at her, she said, 'It's to avoid anyone ever being able to look up your skirt, dear. It's the proper way for ladies to get into and out of a car.'

'Oh right!' Brooke had said and chuckled to herself.

The proper way for ladies! Not me then!

Brooke was a fast mover and, to get into a car, she normally opened her legs as she would for sex. Despite being in a hurry, she tried Lady Townsend's method and actually found it rather easier than her usual manoeuvre.

She drove like a rocket to Dawn's and even though there was traffic, she arrived at about 4.45pm, leaped out the car and rang the doorbell. Dawn answered it with

Paige, toy bag and nappy bag ready and waiting at the door.

'Don't tell me. You're in a rush. It's all 'ere. We'll catch up tomorrow. Paige has been fine, except she kept pretending to be sick over the toilet!'

'Thanks a million, Dawn. Don't forget. I'll see you right!'

Paige was grabbed, put in the car quickly and Brooke broke the speed limit several times on the way home. She kept running through everything she had to do when she got home; feed Paige tea, give her a bath and clear up the entire house from the party all before Dean got back. Oh the stresses of a double life! She felt exhausted just thinking about it. But she was focussed and ready.

She arrived home at just before 5pm.

She'd just finished bringing everything into the house when she heard Dean's moped pull up outside. She walked over to the front bedroom window and saw Dean riding up onto the gravel and park his moped.

What the f...?

Adrenalin gushed through her body like a tsunami. She stood still, holding her head, eyes moving from side to side. Out of sheer desperation she yanked her dress and shoes off and dived into bed with Paige, who clearly found the whole episode very amusing. She decided with remarkable speed that she'd been *'so ill that after I got back from Dawn's earlier, I went straight to bed, taking Paige with me, and we both fell asleep. So, nothing's been done in the house.'*

That'd have to do. Shit! Why's he back so early?

Dean walked straight into the lounge and to the same mess he'd left that morning. He was instantly worried.

This isn't like Brooke. I hope she's alright.

'Brooke? BROOKE? Babe, is everything alright? Where are you?'

A weak and feeble voice came from upstairs. An Oscar-winning performance!

'I'm up here. I'm in bed with Paige!'

Dean leaped up the stairs two at a time and dashed straight into their bedroom.

'Oh, babe! You poor thing!'

Dean always turned soppy when Brooke looked so vulnerable. It's when he loved her the most. His need to smother her with protection and to care for her would always overwhelm him in those moments. He bent down to kiss her and couldn't help but notice she was fully made up and smelled gorgeous.

'I felt *so* ill that after I got back from Dawn's earlier, I went straight to bed, taking Paige with me, and we both fell asleep. So, nothing's been done in the house I'm afraid. How come you're back so early?' The big fat lie tripped off her tongue.

Dean didn't quite know what to think and remarked, 'Well considering how ill you are you've done a great job on your makeup!'

Brooke panicked. 'Well I didn't feel *too* bad after you'd

left so I thought I'd go and see Dawn for a bit of TLC. I thought I might perk up a bit but she was still on and off the loo while I was there and then I started to feel rough again so I came home.' Oh dear, another whopper!

What was the crisis at work? You wouldn't make us a cuppa, would you, babe?'

She wanted to change the subject.

Dean panicked. 'I'll go and make you a cuppa and then I'll tell you all about it.'

He was grateful for the few minutes he'd have to get his story straight. He'd forgotten he'd said there was a crisis that morning. He gave Paige a peck on the head as she was playing with Brooke's hair, splayed out all over the pillow.

He ran downstairs, all the while trying to concoct a reasonable story. He took a leaf out of the book of the mystery shoppers' training manual and tried to keep his 'legend' as true to real life as possible, which made it much easier to carry on the story if necessary. All he could think about was that they were genuinely having problems at work with a new IT system that'd just been installed. He decided on: *'There was a problem with the new IT system and Brian's crap at anything to do with technology, so he needed me to go down there and sort it out with the IT company at their head office. I said that as it'd probably take some time could I go straight back home afterwards rather than come back into the office as Brooke wasn't feeling too good.'*

He practised sounding casual as he made the tea

in Brooke's favourite mug. Dean's nan had bought it for Brooke for her last birthday. 'Lady Muck' it said on the front.

He took it upstairs and placed it on Brooke's bedside table. He wasn't capable of lying directly to her face so he immediately turned his back on her to get changed.

'So what happened?' Brooke enquired, desperate not to go back to Dean asking her anything else about her day.

Dean's rehearsed big fat lie was successfully delivered while getting into shorts and a t-shirt.

'Oh you're such a clever bunny. If they don't give you that promotion soon, I'd be surprised.'

Flattery always worked with Dean. He liked it when Brooke said nice things to him.

'Well I wouldn't hold your breath if I were you. Right. I'm going to wash my moped. I'll leave you in peace. Do you want me to take Paige downstairs with me? She can hold the hosepipe.'

Without waiting for an answer, he plucked Paige from the bed, gave Brooke a kiss and went downstairs, relieved not to have to talk about his day any more.

Thank God for that!

Brooke breathed a sigh of relief.

Thank God for that!

She sat upright to drink her tea, and, to her horror, realised her dress was draped over the chair. She waited until she heard the front door close and then bounded out of bed, picked up the dress and hung it up quickly on the hanger.

Just before she put it away in the wardrobe, she held it up in front of her and smiled.

20

As Time Goes By

After a promising start with a number of mystery visits, Dean was somewhat disappointed when they seemed to come to a halt. After his lengthy report about Wendle Golf Club, he'd not been asked to conduct any more visits and he wondered whether he'd gone too far with his comments. He thought he might give Angie a ring and check. Then again, she'd once told him how pissed off the team used to get when assessors phoned up whingeing that they hadn't been given a visit for a while – as though they were somehow entitled. He ummed and ahed about it; Dean being Dean, he didn't really want to rock the boat, so he left it.

Chloe had been right about the money, of course. He certainly wouldn't be buying a hot tub anytime soon with money he made from it. Brooke made the odd comment about the hot tub now and then, but seemed to have calmed down about it. Of late, she appeared to have got more of a bee in her bonnet about Dean's much-hoped-for promotion and seemed to have convinced herself that this really was imminent and how different their life would be once he got onto that next rung of the ladder. This had taken over as her main goal to be pursued over the coming weeks and months.

Dean decided that he was just going to have to work even harder for the promotion, which was realistically the only way he was going to earn more money. He was going to have to indulge in some serious sycophancy towards Brian the Lion; the thought of it alone made him shudder.

Dean was daydreaming about all of this when his phone went off.

Mate whats happening? U fancy a pint?

Martin messaged Dean yet again. He normally heard from Dean at least once a week, but he'd barely had anything from him at all recently; just the odd non-committal message claiming he was too tired to go out. Martin had enjoyed their jaunt at Nous Geraldine and kept saying to Dean that when he needed someone to go with, he'd be delighted to oblige. Martin had a feeling that Dean wasn't being honest and that he'd probably had several other mystery visits, but just hadn't asked him. He was such a sensitive chap. He'd been down to The Hungry Horse in Hornchurch not long after the golf club visit. Negative Nigel had been in there boasting about playing golf with Dean, despite being instructed categorically by him not to tell a soul and never to talk about what he'd done on the mystery visit. Martin was miffed and a tad upset.

Yep – how about tonight after work? Corney &

Barrow in Canary Wharf around 6.30pm?

Dean could tell that Martin was pleased if not relieved. He then thought about Brooke.

I suppose I'd better tell her.

Dean popped outside the office into the corridor and rang Brooke from his mobile. Her phone rang and rang. No answer. He'd lost count of the number of times he'd rung her in the past few weeks and she hadn't picked up.

What the hell's that girl doing?

He was mildly exasperated, but just messaged her instead.

Babe where r u? No reply? Again! Going out for a drink with Martin 2nite. Back about 9pm

Brooke subtly glanced at her silenced but vibrating phone as she listened to Hugo giving her instructions about the library. He'd been off sick for a while and had only just returned today and to a backlog of work to sort out. He was very specific about what Brooke must use in this room, because it was filled with precious objects as well as ancient leather-bound books, some of which she had of course already had a peek at. She momentarily got distracted as her mind wandered off to her recent visit to Brooks's. It seemed like ages ago and she smiled at the somewhat unreal memory.

'A penny for them.'

'Sorry?'

'Penny for your thoughts. You looked miles away,' replied Hugo kindly.

Brooke analysed his features and again thought how elegantly he dressed and how good-looking he was, with those piercing eyes.

'Oh sorry. I *was* listening. I was just thinking about Brooks's. I still can't believe I went to a place like that. It seems like so long ago now.'

'Oh yes, I heard about that!' Hugo gave a broad and genuine smile.

'That sounds a bit ominous! Did I mess up that badly?'

'Quite the contrary. Mrs Townsend was very impressed with you.'

Brooke found that hard to believe.

'Really? Why? I forgot to click the clicker and I bored the pants of this geezer, asking him loads of questions when he started talking about elephants in Brentwood!'

'Well I heard that that you spotted an error in Mrs Townsend's PowerPoint presentation, that you worked hard to get everything ready and packed up in the car, you sorted out the computer and connection in the Great Subscription Room, that you were engaging with those members that spoke to you and you did it all without any fuss whatsoever. You just got on with it…and that you looked very elegant.'

Elegant! Someone thinks I'm elegant!

Brooke was so taken aback, her mouth opened slightly as she struggled to find the right words to say.

'Wow! No-one's ever called me elegant before! Ha ha ha!'

'Well I wish I'd witnessed it; I've only ever seen you in jeans! But I've been assured that you do, in fact, have legs!'

Brooke laughed out loud and found herself blushing.

Is he flirting with me?

'Trouble is, Hugo, it was all a different world. I thought it was amazing – really fascinating, but I don't belong in it, so I don't expect I'll ever get the chance to do anything like that again. It was only 'cause you were ill. No way would she have asked me otherwise.'

'Well yes and no,' Hugo replied. 'Yes, she asked you because I was ill and she was desperate for help, quickly. But no, because she knows plenty of other people she could've asked, but she chose to ask you. She chose to give you a chance and show her what you could do. You succeeded and I'm in no doubt the next time she needs help and I'm not here, she'll ask you again.'

Brooke feigned seriousness.

'Well can't you just bugger off now, then?'

They both laughed. Hugo fixed his gaze on her as he did so. He'd never met anyone like Brooke before. She lacked confidence in some ways, had it in others, was funny and down to earth and a bit of a rough diamond, which he rather liked.

He made her feel a tad uncomfortable, the way he was staring at her.

'Right, well, *I'm* going to bugger off now and leave you to your work!'

'Yes, you do that!'

'Anyway, *this* is me. This is the work *I'm* cut out for. See you later!'

She smiled, got back down on the floor, bent over and carried on with her work. Hugo stared at her divine derrière.

Brooke waited until Hugo had left the room and then rang Dean straight away.

'Hi, babe, only me.'

'Where were you? I tried loads of times and you didn't pick up.'

'Sorry I accidentally left my phone on silent… I'm in the library.'

There was a nanosecond of awkward silence.

'You what?'

Brooke found it slightly easier to tell half-truths.

'Yeah, I thought it was about time we introduced Paige to books.'

Another slightly awkward nanosecond of silence as Dean let this statement compute.

'Blimey! Well yeah, good idea. Just can't imagine you in a library.' Dean laughed out loud.

Although she knew he meant no harm, it was a stinging comment.

'Why not? Don't you think I can read?' Brooke retorted in a narked voice. 'I want Paige to do better at school than I did.'

This was just not the sort of conversation that Dean ever expected to be having with his wife.

'Course not, babe! You're right, the earlier she starts with books the better.' Dean knew he needed to change the subject. 'So, I'm going out with Martin tonight, is that OK? I haven't seen him for ages.'

To his surprise, she didn't kick up a fuss at all – most unlike her. She secretly breathed a sigh of relief that he fell for her story – well half story – she was in a library and she did want Paige to do better at school, but she wasn't going to be borrowing *The Complete Works of Shakespeare* any time soon.

They finished the call. Brooke went back to her work and Dean went back to his desk where Brian The Lion was waiting for him.

'Where have you been, Dean? Can you come into my office? I've got something I want to talk to you about.'

Dean's heart sank. What'd he done now? He followed Brian into his office.

Why does he always make me feel like a naughty puppy?

Brian sat behind his desk and put his feet up on it.

Christ, he looks just like Ricky Gervais in The Office.

'So. Dean.'

'Yes, Brian.'

'Well done.'

'Eh?'

'Well done. I got a call from the IT people a few days ago and they said that your help the other week was invaluable and you showed them a few ways round some problems they were having which meant they came up with a solution much quicker than they'd otherwise have done.' Brian shifted his position to facilitate a tête-á-tête across his desk. 'As you know, IT isn't exactly my strong point, so I just wanted to say thanks. You got us all out of a bit of trouble with this one.'

Dean couldn't help but wonder what Brian wanted. He never praised anyone. He must want something.

'Is that all?'

'Well yes. But I was thinking, how about I buy you a pint tonight – my way of saying thanks. You did agree to that drink!'

Oh shit, not this again.

'Ah, would love to but I can't tonight and, besides, you don't need to buy me a drink just for doing my job. It's no problem.'

Brian looked disappointed. He so desperately wanted to be invited to the drinks and socialising that went on amongst the team in the office, but he was never asked. The sad thing was, he just didn't get why not. He was so lacking in self-awareness that he'd no idea that most people in the office couldn't abide him. His smarmy manner, his way of speaking to people and his most unpleasant bad breath and body odour. What was there to like?

'C'mon, Dean, just a quick one? We'll leave the office early so you can still get away on time.'

Regrettably poor Dean couldn't think of a single reason why not, and he knew that getting Brian on his side would be important in his recommending him as his replacement. The sucking up started here and now.

'Alright then, but I need to leave by six latest. Thanks. It'll be nice. See you later.' Dean tried to sound genuine and forced a smile as he got up and walked out.

Brian sat back with his feet still on the desk, placed his hands behind his head and smiled. At last he was 'going out with a friend from work'. That was what he heard people saying all the time. Only it was never him who was saying it. Now he could. Not that he'd anyone to tell particularly, but he didn't care about that; just basked in the warm glow of satisfaction and went about his work with a smile on his face that gravely worried the staff.

At 4.30pm on the dot, Brian appeared at Dean's desk. He made a big show of saying, 'C'mon, Dean, let's go down the pub for that pint.' He looked around as he said it, but no-one was watching Brian The Lion.

The two of them walked out and within three minutes were inside The Ship Tavern's glorious, dark, Victorian interior. For Dean this was something to be got over as soon as possible. For Brian, this was what he hoped would be a last-ditch attempt to befriend a work colleague before he retired, so that he'd someone to 'go and have a pint with' after the novelty of retirement had worn off and when he was desperate to do something other than go shopping and eat his Sunday roast at his local on his own.

They sat down on the ageing velvet banquette seating and put their pints down on the stained beer mats that were scattered on the sticky wooden table.

'Well this is nice, isn't it, Dean? We ought to do this more often.'

'Yeah, well, life is busy right now and expensive with the baby and everything.' Dean was looking at the floor and shaking his head as he described the situation.

'It must be, it must be.'

'I really am hoping that I have a future in this place, Brian.' Dean went straight for the jugular and stared hard at Brian.

'Oh you have. TrussInUs!' Brian guffawed like a gameshow host. 'Your home life might cause a few issues but the customers, all our providers and the staff here seem to love you. So, a good word in the ear of the big bosses from Uncle Brian here and all is well.'

God, he makes me want to vomit.

Dean just didn't know what to say to the man. He loathed him. So, he just smiled. Brian smiled back. They sat there awkwardly with their pints. Smiling. Looking around at the rather eclectic bunch of people in the pub; booted and suited, trendy creative types and builders.

'You did a good job there with the IT people, you know, Dean.'

'Yeah, so you said. But it's really not a big deal, Brian. I was just doing my job.'

'Ah yes, but that's the point. It was more than your job, really.' He leaned forward in a way of exaggerated confidentiality.

'I can safely say that I've recommended you to take

my place when I retire.'

'Well that's very good of you, Brian, but, like I said, no need.' Before hastily adding, 'Not that I wouldn't like the promotion. Like I said, things are a bit tough right now with Brooke and the baby.'

'I know. I know. Well. You should know that I'm bringing my retirement forward by a few months. The big bosses agreed to let me go a bit earlier on full pension if I wanted. When I mentioned the work you'd done on the IT project, they seemed very keen to get you in post ASAP.'

Well bloody hell!

Dean was speechless. He'd not been anticipating this at all and, quite honestly, was at a loss as to what to say next.

'Blimey, Brian!' was all that came out.

Brian had a rather smug and self-satisfied look about him and he wallowed in it for a while.

Dean sat back and, for once, felt a genuine warm, fuzzy feeling radiate all over him as he briefly contemplated the future.

A company car. At long last, a company car!! And a hot tub! Brooke can have her goddamn hot tub!

'So, what do you think, then?'

'Oh, Brian. I'm a bit gobsmacked, to be honest, mate. Is this official or does it have to be…between us for the moment?' Dean leaned forward as he said it.

Brian grinned. No-one had ever referred to him as 'mate' before.

'Well, mum's the word, for now, but I think Dave and Jules are going to want to come in and announce it all to the staff soon. I'm just not sure when.'

OMG! This is real. This is actually real. I'm actually going to be promoted!

Dean messaged Martin to say he'd been caught up at work with a colleague and couldn't make drinks after all.

Then he swiftly finished his pint and turned to Brian with a gleaming smile. 'D'ya fancy another one?'

***

Dean made the train journey back to Brentwood station asleep and managed to ride his moped home, despite being two pints over the limit. In Essex, no-one seemed to worry much about drink driving unless they were really legless. Unless you were Brooke, of course. She never did and hated it when Dean did (unless it was convenient for her, of course), so he knew he'd be in for a hard time when he got in.

He tiptoed into the bedroom and discovered her in bed, watching TV. It was an auction of paintings at Sotheby's of all things.

Blimey, she must be bored.

'Hello, babe. Sorry I'm a bit late.'

'Dean De'Ath. Tell me you didn't drive that moped home. I've been expecting a call.' Daggers came flying out of those beautiful eyes, piercing him hard.

'Oh c'mon, babe. It's only a few minutes away and I haven't had that many.' He looked woefully at the floor.

She turned off the TV and shouted at him. 'Dean. I've told you. I'd rather you ring me to come and pick you up or get a taxi than drink and drive. You could kill yourself or someone else. You've got Paige to think of now. How many times do I have to tell you. Just don't do it! That *bloody* Martin is such a bad influence on you.'

Poor Martin, he didn't know the half of it!

She lay down and pulled the duvet cover right up to her neck. Dean said no more. He knew that mood and that tone of voice; no point. He got undressed, and, despite the late hour, still diligently hung his trousers and jacket up. He brushed his teeth, washed his hands and blew his nose. It never ceased to amaze him how much filth came out of his nostrils after a day in London. He looked in the mirror to see the dark stubble that'd sprouted up gradually throughout the day and evening. He rubbed his hands round his chin and neck to see how painful his shave was likely to be tomorrow. Then he sniffed himself.

Mmm, bit beery.

As soon as he crept into bed, Brooke turned over so her back was to him. He snuggled up to her in the spooning position and nuzzled his lips into her neck, gently licking and kissing all around. He kept saying sorry for smelling of beer and asking for forgiveness. Initially, she pretended to be in a half sleep, but he kept going until she gradually melted and her libido came bubbling to the surface. She wrapped her left leg backwards over and round his back and her left arm back round his neck as she pulled him towards her.

'Oh, Dean De'Ath, what am I gonna do with you?'

'Restore me conjugal rights?'

21

Ingatestone Hall

Dean sat at his desk wondering yet again why he hadn't been given any more mystery visits. He frowned and chewed the end of his pen, unable to settle down or concentrate on his work. He decided to ring Brooke, just for a chat, as he had a few minutes to spare.

Her phone rang and rang, but no reply.

Where is that girl? What the hell is she doing?

Brooke felt her phone vibrate in her pocket. She was listening to Mrs Townsend talking about a trustees' meeting she'd just attended. Brooke had no idea why she felt the need to speak to her about it, but felt it would be impolite not to listen, even though she'd a lot of work to do. She smiled and nodded politely, but was feeling impatient as the minutes went on; she was getting further and further behind in her work.

'Geoffrey D'arcy mentioned you,' she said quite suddenly. 'He said that you owe him some money.'

Mrs Townsend looked Brooke straight in the eye and waited for a response.

Brooke had no idea what she was talking about and

looked suitably aghast.

'He what? He said I owe him money? I don't know what he's talking about!' Brooke inexplicably turned to jelly and her stomach hit the floor.

Mrs Townsend looked at her with mild suspicion.

'He said you made a bet with him in Brooks's…and lost. He said you owe him twenty pounds. Something about rice pudding.'

Brooke was flabbergasted. She'd thought it was a joke. She'd not believed for one minute that he'd been serious in insisting that she repaid this supposed debt.

'Blimey. I thought he was joking!'

'Brooke. Bets at Brooks's are an institution. They are real, serious and debts must be paid.'

Brooke couldn't digest this, but then remembered that Geoffrey D'arcy had given her his card and invited her to bring him cash or send him a cheque. She'd assumed it was all just high jinks.

'I'm happy for you to leave early today so you can take him what you owe. I don't want to get on the wrong side of Geoffrey. He's an important man and a vital trustee to one of my most important charities.'

Are you for real?! Do you people really believe this ridiculous bet actually matters?!

Brooke was speechless and looked sternly at her watch. It was 2.45pm.

Lady Townsend could read her like a book.

'Go on, dear, it won't take long to drive there and it'll

save you and me a lot of hassle in the long run.'

'Right. Well. I'll get going then, but I haven't finished my jobs for the day – just so you know.'

'Not to worry, dear. This is much more important. You go and I'll see you on Wednesday. Don't forget Geoffrey's a baron.'

What's a baron?

***

Like a zombie, Brooke got into her car, took out the business card and entered the postcode for Geoffrey D'arcy into her sat nav. She'd not looked at the card since he'd first given it to her, having forgotten it was in her bag at all. It was only now that she saw the title: 18th Baron D'Arcy. Brooke laughed out loud and assumed it was impressive.

Hahaha! I'm going to see a baron!

She was soon on her way to Ingatestone Hall. She was rather confused as she'd a vague memory in the back of her mind that she'd been there as a child. The name was familiar to her. She had to be quick or she'd be late picking Paige up again; a habit she was beginning to develop, much to Dawn's exasperation.

Twenty minutes later, one junction along the A12, through the village of Mountnessing, fields on the left and the Ladybird Cattery on the right, Brooke arrived at the magnificent entrance to Ingatestone Hall. She stopped the car and stared at it for a bit. There was a tatty sign in front of the gate stating that entrance fees were £7 for adults and £3.50 for children. She'd definitely been here, but she couldn't recall when and certainly had no idea why.

She drove into the car park in the field next door and positioned Edna as far away as possible. She looked at her feet and was glad she had decided to wear flats as she strolled through the black iron gates and along the path leading to the hall. It struck her that everything looked rather old and tired; the buildings on either side, the paintwork and the outbuildings. Despite its grandness, it all looked very lived-in'. Her eyes were drawn to the beautiful old clocktower above a dusky-pink timbered and brick archway. She immediately recognised the paint as Little Greene Carmine. The path was surrounded on both sides by tall, deep forest green hedging that had been cut formally, but not very precisely in her view. As she entered the section close to the house it became a courtyard and she looked longingly at the flat tree that'd been trained up the brick wall to the left of the entrance door. It'd developed the outline shape of a Christmas tree and Brooke smiled as she imagined what one of these would look like (a smaller one, of course) trained up one side of her front door. She opened the large black entrance door and found herself in the reception area. There were schoolchildren everywhere, making an almighty racket. Two gentlemen were trying to herd the children together and it dawned on her that she'd probably come here many years ago on a school trip.

Surely he can't live here?

As she waited for the receptionist to become free, she observed a rather unusual oriental ornament, which caught her eye. She walked over to it and looked at it carefully to catch it from all angles.

This is fabulous.

Since Brooke had been working for Lady Townsend, she'd learned a great deal about antique paintings, mirrors, furniture, lighting, fabrics, furnishings, tiles, flooring plus a myriad of other accessories found in country houses all over the UK. She'd become quite an expert. If only she realised! She was a sponge; soaking up anything and everything in 'her new life'. In fact she'd secretly been sneaking copies of *Country Life* into her handbag at the end of each week to take home and read. When Dean was out of the house, she'd have a bath and take a large glass of Chardonnay and *Country Life* in with her. She'd light the Jo Malone candle that her mother had bought her a couple of years previously and spend a couple of hours flicking through the pages, between sips of wine. Deep down she believed she had an eye for such things, but her low self-worth and feelings of inadequacy and inexperience inevitably hijacked her brain and put those thoughts down to delusions of grandeur.

She'd watch *The Antiques Roadshow* and BBC's *Bargain Hunt* whenever she could and she frequently got the final price right and also seemed to have a knack of knowing whether the items being offered were valuable or not.

'I've come to see Baron D'Arcy, but I'm not sure if I've come to the right place,' Brooke declared unconfidently.

The lady at the desk ('Mrs Brompton' on her name badge) looked at her with a smiley face. 'Is *Lord* D'Arcy expecting you?'

'It's Baron D'Arcy, I think, not Lord. Or is he the same man?' Brooke replied, suddenly worried she'd made a boo-boo.

The lady smiled knowingly, just as Mrs Townsend had when Brooke wondered why all the men at Brooks's kept standing up and sitting down.

She stared, not unkindly, at Brooke, with a sort of 'poor you' look about her and leaned forward in that way of confidentiality and whispered, 'One never uses the title Baron verbally – only in written legal documents. A baron is always called "Lord".'

Brooke could tell she was being kind, but she felt as if she'd been unexpectedly flicked with an elastic band. She developed a tomato face, like a pupil who's discovered she's unwittingly broken the rules on her first day at big school.

'May I ask who's calling?'

'Oh…er…well…um…if you can just tell him it's Brooke De'Ath.'

'May I ask what your visit is in relation to?'

'Oh. Well…er…I've come to repay my debt?' Her intonation at the end of the statement turned it into a question, intimating she was unsure if this was an acceptable reason. She grinned and fingered her handbag nervously as she waited for a response.

The woman showed no outward signs of being unimpressed, but merely smiled sweetly, picked up the telephone and explained to whoever was on the other end, that Lord D'Arcy had a visitor.

Brooke stood there feeling like she did at her first-ever interview. She couldn't get her head around the fact that a) she was in this place at all and that b) she was actually having to repay a debt that she thought was a joke. It was all just daft.

'If you'd like to take a seat in the tea shop, Lord D'Arcy will come and collect you himself. He'll be with you presently. In the meantime, Mr Bolter will see to you.'

Presently?

Mr Bolter was a rather intimidating-looking man. Tall, large and wearing a black formal suit, he looked like a mix between a butler and an undertaker.

'Please follow me.' His voice sounded kinder than he looked and his accent reminded her a bit of Hugo's.

He escorted her into the tea shop to her left and to a table for two. She sat down in her newfound delicate manner, then adjusted her legs, locked them tight and leaned them over to one side.

This is how Kate Middleton sits.

Mr Hunter motioned for one of the waiting staff to come over and take an order.

'Ms De'Ath is here to see Lord D'Arcy. Please would you get her a drink while she's waiting?' He smiled, nodded and returned to the little monsters who were all over the gift shop like a bad rash. It could hardly be called a gift shop really. It was a mish mash of odd items such as scarves, jugs, keyrings and the ubiquitous tea towels.

A slim lady with blond hair in a ponytail, bright-coloured lipstick and wearing an apron, came over. Brooke observed her rather glamorous black mules with a diamanté buckle on the front.

She placed a menu in front of Brooke and asked her if she'd be eating.

'Oh god, no. I haven't got long really, so just a cuppa'll be fine. Bog-standard builders' tea, please.'

Brooke took a peek at the menu while she was waiting. The most divine-looking proper English tea was on offer; photos of delicately cut sandwiches and cakes on a three- tiered stand looked delightful, but twenty-three pounds per head.

Blimey, that's a bit steep for a few sarnies and some cake!

She sat in the tea shop area with phone in hand, ready to contact Dean, but actually her attention was purely focussed on the scene in front of her. Her eyes wandered over the enormous oil portrait paintings on the surrounding walls. She then looked carefully at the table which had been covered with a plastic washable tablecloth in a sage green colour with white flowers.

Fancy using a plastic tablecloth in a gaff like this!

There was a pretty old green glass jar of some

description which was being used as a vase for a small bunch of pretty white gypsophila. She was brought a white china teapot, cup and saucer and milk jug by a chubby red-faced teenage lad in trainers. She mused how she couldn't recall ever having used a teapot or drunk tea out of a cup and saucer at any time in her life – apart from now and at Brooks's. She thanked him and watched him walk back to the sideboard, which was full of the most delicious homemade cakes under huge glass domes. Temptation won and she went over for a peek. It'd said on the menu that a young lady called Taya had baked them all – she was a student at Westminster's catering college.

I'm sure that's where Jamie Oliver went. Good old Essex chefs!

'Would you like to try one?' said the chubby-cheeked chap. 'They really are jolly delicious.'

'Oh no. Thanks all the same.'

Blimey, he certainly didn't go to Gaynes!

Brooke thought the atmosphere of the whole place was so serene and intimate; quiet, but not museum quiet, and old fashioned, but in a good way. It was actually like being in a posh person's house for tea.

She sat back down, poured herself some tea and took the opportunity to check her phone; she was alarmed that she'd missed yet another call from Dean. Lately, she kept missing calls from him and he was beginning to get both annoyed and sometimes suspicious.

She'd no idea how long Geoffrey D'Arcy would be, so

she didn't dare start a phone call, so she chose to message instead.

Hi Babe sorry I missed you. Hope nothing urgent. Been busy. C U later.

'Brooke, how delightful to see you! My, you look in fine fettle!'

Brooke snapped out of messaging mode and stood up as though she'd been ordered to by a police officer.

Geoffrey D'Arcy was standing at the entrance to the tea shop and laughed out loud at Brooke's response. He wasn't stupid, or naïve. He knew how Brooke must have felt, and, in a rather perverse kind of way, it gave him a power over her that he quite enjoyed.

Brooke walked awkwardly towards him, but panicked about whether she should shake his hand, curtsey, give him a kiss or a high five. She dithered for a respectable amount of time before Geoffrey decided for her and walked towards her with both his arms out open wide and welcoming in front of him, followed by a gentle but firm kiss on both cheeks as he pulled her in and held her by the waist with both hands.

Brooke was rather alarmed at such assertive physical contact and blurted out rather inappropriately, 'I've just come to repay my debt.'

'So I hear. Well I'm glad to know that you take paying your gambling debts so seriously. Not everyone does.'

Even then, Brooke was shocked at how clearly serious he was. She was dumbfounded, but delved into her handbag, retrieved the twenty-pound note she had in her purse and handed it over with her head bowed down like a teenage shoplifter who'd been caught out. Geoffrey took it without ceremony.

'To be honest, Geoffrey, I thought it was a joke. I'm really sorry you didn't get your money sooner. Had I realised… I…'

'Brooke. Please forget about it. Now, would you like me to show you around the house?' He seemed keen to and she couldn't deny she was completely intrigued. She was in two minds about being late for Dawn again, but in the end her curiosity won the day.

Dawn'll understand when I tell her.

She put on her bravest smile, pulled herself up tall, lifted her chin slightly and closed her eyes momentarily.

Of course I bloody well would!

'That'd be lovely. Thank you, Geoffrey. But I honestly don't have very long. I have to pick my daughter up from my childminder.'

'Well we're not going around with that bloody lot!' He motioned to the monsters still causing havoc in the gift shop. 'Come. You can have your own private tour, but I'll make it quick.'

'Actually, I've been here before.'

'Really?' Geoffrey seemed surprised.

'Yeah. I came on a school trip years ago, so of course I don't remember any of it except the entrance.'

'Ah yes – those lovely school trips and delightful

pupils we host every day! Well much work has been done since you would have been here.'

He marched up to another butler cum undertaker cum child herder man. 'Bassiter, please can you delay your tour for fifteen minutes, old chap? I'm taking Ms De'Ath around myself and I don't want to be disturbed by this motley crew. Well done. Good man.'

Having issued his instructions, Geoffrey held his arm out towards another large wooden door which led into the Stone Hall, leaving Mr Bassiter looking horrified at trying to keep the monsters contained and not stealing for yet another fifteen minutes.

Brooke stepped through into the Stone Hall. Geoffrey started giving her all the history in a manner that indicated he'd done so hundreds of times before. She couldn't take it all in, but wandered around regarding the various objects and paintings, with Geoffrey following close behind, stopping his spiel each time she showed interest in a particular piece. When she moved on to examine a different item, he'd then change his spiel, rather like an overly eager car salesman following a prospective purchaser around a showroom.

She marvelled at the carved wooden thrones and she couldn't help wondering why anyone would need that many walking sticks. Her eye caught a painting of a man that looked very recent in comparison to all the others. She stared at the photos of Obama and Queen Mary and listened gleefully as Geoffrey revealed some of the shocking antics that Wanstead Girls High School got up to during the war when they were moved to The Hall.

She was whisked through the study and was fascinated by the priest hole. Geoffrey dutifully gave her an explanation of the Reformation. She caught sight of a leather-bound book on the desk with the word 'Game' stamped on it in gold leaf.

'What's that book all about?'

'Ah, that's where they keep a record of all the hunting, fishing and pheasant shoots. But the current Lady D'Arcy doesn't like these blood sports at all.'

'Too bloody right. It's disgusting! So unnecessary.'

Geoffrey smiled at her innocent honesty – just like Lady Townsend, he liked her for it.

The drawing room was full of horns from such shoots; they literally covered all four walls. She screwed up her little nose at them before moving on.

'Oh my God, Geoffrey, this is so tatty! Why don't you get it repaired? It looks awful!'

Geoffrey sprung immediately back into good form as he moved over to the badly faded, ripped red sofa suite at the end. Years of light and wear had rendered it barely recognisable as a sofa.

'Ha! You try affording getting that renovated. Brooke, it costs a fortune to keep this place going. You've no idea. That's why we have to open it to the public.'

She smiled as she knew he was probably right. She couldn't imagine the time and money it must take to keep this house clean, never mind fully renovated and repaired. Ingatestone Hall was ten times bigger than Lady Townsend's house and that was bad enough.

'And all this stuff to keep clean and polished? Unreal!'

'This is only a fraction of what we've got; we have an entire outbuilding full of stuff that we can't display as we just don't have the room, as well as a ton of other bits and pieces that we haven't had the time or resources to look through or properly catalogue. We have two full-time cleaners just for the house.'

They moved into the dining room and Brooke gasped at the sheer volume of knick- knacks that filled the table and the room. She looked at the huge candelabra in the centre of the table and thought it was quite funny that it was decorated with little silver pigs. Why would anyone do that, she wondered? She was also quite taken with the horn and silver cigar lighter on the table; so unusual. The walls were made from wooden panels; to her they looked quite unique and Geoffrey explained they were linen fold panels. She inspected the tapestries and nodded.

'I bet Johnson's won't take those in for dry cleaning!'

Geoffrey laughed at her humour and proceeded to talk about them.

He took her quickly through the kitchen, where she spied eight bottles of Gordon's gin on the table.

'Who's the lush then, Geoffrey?'

He laughed again and claimed it was for an event that'd been held there.

The humungous fireplace was begging to be walked in. Brooke was so tall she had to duck down, but could stand up inside it. She turned around and looked up.

'Holy Mother of Gladys!' thought Geoffrey, eyes firmly fixed on Brooke's bottom, which was the most perfectly round specimen he'd ever had the pleasure of witnessing. She reversed out, which was even more loin-tingling.

She was told about the secret tunnel that went under the house and Geoffrey pointed out the family motto under the clock which could be seen from the kitchen.

'Sans Dieu Rien – that's Latin for Nothing Without God.'

'Blimey, I was never clever enough to do Latin at school.'

'Rubbish! You could easily learn Latin. You're a clever girl it seems to me.'

'Haha! If only! Geoffrey, I'd love to see more but I do have to scoot now. I'm really sorry.'

Even though Brooke was loving every minute of her private tour, she was getting worried about the time and started walking out the door and towards the car park as they spoke.

'Only if we have one more bet. Twenty pounds that you can't tell me the scene being depicted on the tapestry in the dining room?'

Brooke kept on walking. 'The trojan horse being dragged into Troy. Ta-da!'

Geoffrey had already taken the twenty-pound note out of his pocket to give her.

'Well done. Here, I owe you twenty pounds.'

Brooke roared laughing.

'You mean I've travelled ten miles and left my job early to come and repay my debt and now I don't even owe you any money?'

'OK, let's have one more bet then, but we'll up the odds. I'll bet you thirty pounds that you can't remember what the Latin is for Nothing Without God? No looking!'

'Oh hell! I can't remember that!' She closed her eyes and thought hard, but to no avail. No… Sorry, Geoffrey… no can do. And I definitely don't have another ten pounds on me to give you.'

'Well in that case, you'll simply have to come back again another time and repay your debt. I might let you off *if* when you return, you can answer the question and have learned some more Latin! Now. Let's get you back to your car.'

Brooke froze.

'No!'

Geoffrey looked alarmed.

'I'm fine, thanks…thank you. I can walk myself. I'm sure you're really busy anyway. Just one thing I forgot to ask you. I hope you don't mind, but…do you actually live here?'

'Oh yes, of course, I didn't show you my private wing! I'm so sorry. It's over there. Maybe next time.' He pointed to the south wing of the house and a feeling of privilege and importance at merely having *associated* with the person who lived there overcame Brooke as she looked longingly at the red rusty bricks and old leaded windows in all their summer sunshine glory.

She said thank you as she went to shake Geoffrey's hand, but he grabbed her by the waist and pecked her on both cheeks again.

'It was entirely my pleasure, sweetheart. See you soon. Cheerio!'

Brooke trotted back to her car, giggling.

I wonder if he's got a hot tub.

22

It's All About Family

Brooke drove fast back to Dawn's to collect Paige. She was over an hour late and was apprehensive. Dawn was so good to her and helped her out so much she didn't want to lose her as her childminder, never mind friend.

As she turned into Woodman Road, the difference between where she'd just come from and this tiny, cramped car-lined road hit her like a truck. Cars were bumped up on pavements so moving vehicles could barely get past. She had to park in front of Dawn's car in her drive. As she did so, the perv from next door stared out of his window, making no secret of the fact he was checking she didn't invade his parking space.

Before she'd even got out of her car, the front door opened and Dawn was on the doorstep holding Paige, who was covered in makeup. Brooke extracted herself from the car awkwardly in the tiny area she had available to her.

'Thank God you're here. She's just discovered my makeup bag! Why are you so late this time?'

Dawn wasn't exactly angry, but Brooke did sense a tone of resigned acceptance that this was always how it was going to be as long as Brooke kept working for Mrs Townsend.

'You won't *believe* me when I tell you. This will take some beating.'

'Well you'd better come in. You got time for a cuppa?'

Brooke checked her watch. It was just gone five o'clock. 'Just a quick one then.'

Brooke took Paige and gave her a huge kiss and cuddle and tickled her belly until she squealed, then put her on the floor in Dawn's toy corner. They sat down on the sofa, Brooke kicked off her shoes and tried to tuck her feet under her legs. Those poor toes had nowhere to go!

She proceeded to tell Dawn all about the bet, Lord D'Arcy and Ingatestone Hall. She laughed as she did so because she herself could barely get her head around the way her life seemed to be heading.

Dawn sat there listening intently, hanging on Brooke's every word. Every so often she'd shake her head, eyes popping out of her sockets and exclaiming, 'No! No!'

'You've gotta tell Dean now, Brooke. You can't keep all this stuff from him! He'd think it was mental!'

'No! You must be joking! I can't! He'd be so mad, Dawn, if he thought I was working. He was only banging on about my blood pressure the other day. And can you even *imagine* me telling him I had afternoon tea at Ingatestone Hall and then a private tour with the baron! Talk about making him feel inadequate! He'd be well narked.'

'Well when *are* you gonna tell him? He's gonna find

out sooner or later!'

'I dunno. I've gotta find the right time. Maybe once I've proved to myself I can earn my own money.'

'But why does that matter? You don't need to. Dean likes you being at home not working.'

'But that's the point. I used to like it, but I've got to thinking it's not very… I dunno…modern, I suppose. I feel a bit trapped sometimes, like I'm so dependent on Dean. If anything bad happened, I'd be up shit creek without a paddle. And, to be honest, Dawn, I'm bored.'

'Yeah, I suppose.' Dawn sipped her tea and looked thoughtful. 'But you've already proved you can earn your own money. You must've made a fair bit already, 'aven't you?'

'Yeah, not bad. Mrs Townsend pays me in cash so I've had to find somewhere to hide my secret stash!'

'C'mon, where's it, then?' Dawn was wide-eyed, jokingly motioning with her fingers as if to get Brooke to hand something over.

'Let's just say it's inside an old toy I don't use anymore!'

Dawn screeched with laughter. 'You little devil! Well, 'e certainly won't go looking in there!'

Brooke stood up, laughing. 'There's nearly two grand in there!' She turned to pick Paige up and realised that, as they'd been talking, she'd emptied the entire contents of her handbag all over the floor. She'd successfully demolished Brooke's favourite 'just launched' Charlotte Tilbury lipstick. (She'd read about the new makeup brand

and had gone up to Selfridges just to take a look and, of course, ended up coming away with a package that she could ill afford, all put on credit card.)

'No! Paige – you little devil!'

'Like mother like daughter!' Dawn retorted.

Paige looked up at her mother with the most gorgeous eyes, with lashes to die for, and smiled mischievously. Brooke couldn't be cross. She got a wipe out of the nappy bag and wiped it gently all over Paige's face to remove her makeup, then picked her up.

'I gotta go, Dawn. Thanks so much and I really am sorry I was late, but hopefully you can see why now!'

'Too right! No worries.' Dawn stood up and gave her a hug, squeezing Paige in between them both, then waved them off at the door, glancing briefly at her neighbour's house to check the perv wasn't looking. He was, so she unceremoniously stuck her middle finger up at him then slammed her door shut.

Brooke drove back to Elephant Close and chatted away to Paige all the way home, telling her all about her day.

'Maybe Mummy isn't so ditsy, eh?'

By the time she'd bathed Paige, given her tea and got her ready for bed, Dean had walked in.

He put his bag down and shouted upstairs, 'Babe, I'm home!'

Brooke shouted back down, 'Do you want to come and read her bedtime story?'

Dean was shattered and could've done with just crashing out on the sofa, but knew it was his fatherly duty, which he wasn't always home in time to do. In fact, he made sure he wasn't always home in time to give her a bath and read her a story, as he found it all rather stressful.

'OK, coming!'

Dean trudged up the stairs and spied Brooke playing with Paige in her cot. He kissed them both.

'How was your day, babe?' Dean asked, as he did every single day, often not listening to the answer as it was usually the same: 'Oh I went to Lakeside/up the high street/over to Dawn's/to the mum and toddler group/had my hair/nails done.' The only recent addition to this long list of places she spent her time was the library, which he still found quite funny. Martin had nearly choked on his pint when Dean told him. He'd said that Brooke wouldn't know what a book was if one dropped in front of her. Dean was annoyed by that and had defended her to the hilt.

Brooke often used the library as her alibi, because she could use the excuse that she had to have her phone on silent, which helped explain her frequently not picking up when Dean called.

Brooke felt herself sounding slightly strange as she lied. 'Yeah, good thanks. Didn't do much. Went for a walk in the park, then went over to Dawn's for a bit.' She turned away from Dean as she said it, pretending to fold some clothes and tidy up.

'You've been going over there quite a lot lately. Is she OK?'

'Yeah she's alright. She's Dawn. We have a laugh. If I get bored, I can always have a giggle with her. And she's so good with Paige. Not everyone can take that level of screaming.' She remained turned away from Dean as she spoke.

'How was your day?' Brooke then turned to look at Dean while he answered her.

Dean looked away and at Paige as he spoke. 'Yeah fine. Same old, same old.'

'When's Brian bloody well going to retire? You deserve his job now, especially after that work you did on their IT.'

Dean had decided not to tell Brooke until it was absolutely official and, even then, he wanted to surprise her.

'God knows, not too long hopefully.'

There was a split second of silence that somehow felt awkward. In a marriage that normally flowed with natural conversation, it seemed to insinuate something.

Brooke got up. 'Right, I'll leave you two to it. D'ya fancy a brew?'

'Yeah that'll be great, thanks. I'll be down in a few minutes.'

There was something about their conversation that made Dean feel uneasy. He couldn't pinpoint it, but he knew his wife so well that the slightest abnormality in her speech or behaviour was very noticeable to him. He put the thought to the back of his mind and tried to focus on Paige.

She was actually lying down flat in the cot – a first! He went to bend over and give her a kiss when she suddenly sprang up and her head wacked his forehead. He yelled, she yelled and screaming ensued. Brooke came running up the stairs. 'What the hell happened? I'm only gone for a minute and there's a crisis!'

She plucked Paige from the cot and immediately saw that she had a nasty cut by her eyebrow, which was bleeding. Dean was rubbing his forehead but seemed otherwise OK.

'For God's sake, what happened?'

'We banged heads! Is she alright?'

Brooke examined the cut and quickly decided it was really rather deep. She held her up in front of Dean 'What do you think? I think it she might need a stitch in that.'

Dean also examined it and reluctantly agreed she needed to go to A&E, although the thought of having to sit in that Godforsaken place for four hours made him groan out loud. He watched as Brooke cleaned the cut carefully and put a small Elastoplast over it. Unnervingly, Paige stopped screaming at this point. Dean then gathered up a few things for the nappy bag, wrapped Paige up in a blanket and took her downstairs into the car. No arching her back this time, she just sat there holding her teddy bear mournfully.

'How come she's not screaming?' he asked Brooke. He was perplexed and became concerned. 'It's not normal. She screams when she shouldn't and when she's got a right to scream, she doesn't. It don't make sense!'

'Kids *don't* make sense!'

They got into the car and Dean drove at speed along the A127 towards Queen's hospital, Romford. They got as far as Gallows Corner when Dean's foot suddenly went flat to the floor and Edna gradually began to slow down, eventually coming to a halt on the A1203.

'I don't fucking believe this!' Dean shouted as he hit the steering wheel several times. 'What the hell are we gonna do now?'

'I HATE THIS CAR!' Brooke screamed.

'SO DO I!' Dean screamed back. Brooke quickly examined Paige's wound, which was looking worse and still bleeding. 'Well I don't think Paige's eye can wait. You'll have to wait here for the AA and I'll walk to the retail park and get a cab from there – taxis can't stop here. It's only a few minutes away. Can you find a local cab company and get them to meet me outside Next ASAP? They should be there by the time I get there.'

'You can't walk from here! It's dangerous. There's way too much traffic. It's not safe for Paige, Brooke. And it'll be no good for your blood pressure. And you can't walk in them heels! Have you got your insoles in? Why don't I go with Paige and you wait here for the AA?'

'No! I can't not go with her, Dean, she'll scream if I leave her now, then you'll wish you'd stayed here. I'll be fine. I don't expect it'll be quick though, so just come and find me in A&E once the car's sorted.'

It didn't occur to Brooke for a minute that the car mightn't be able to be sorted. She took her seatbelt off and got Paige out. She looked around outside the window to determine the best way of getting to the shops.

'You've got a point but I'm not happy about this, Brooke. Not happy at all. Please be careful. I can't bear to think of anything happening to either of you.' Dean's face was contorted with anxiety.

'Stop fussing! We'll be fine. We just need to get a move on.'

Dean rang for a cab, while watching helplessly as his precious wife jogged over towards the lights of the retail park, injured daughter bouncing about in her arms.

Luckily it was a warm, balmy evening; the short walk to the retail park would've been horrendous in wet weather so Brooke was grateful for small mercies. Just as she arrived outside Next, a Smithy's Cars cab pulled up at the front doors. The driver was rude and abrupt. Brooke wasn't in the mood for it and was equally rude and abrupt back.

His loss. No tip.

Paige was silent for the entire journey.

On arrival at the hospital, as Brooke got out the car, she was confronted with the dreaded sign outside.

LONGER WAITS IN A&E – WE ARE EXTREMELY BUSY TODAY WHICH IS RESULTING IN A MINIMUM WAIT OF SIX HOURS.

Brooke swore out loud, much to the obvious disgust

of an elderly couple who were walking in at the same time. They tutted as they stared at Brooke and her toddler covered in blood.

'What you staring at?' Brooke snapped at them. The prospect of being in that place with Paige until gone midnight made her want to weep.

She carried her into the A&E entrance.

Are you there yet?

Yes. 6hr wait ☹

Oh shit!

***

At 12.15am, after a very brief and worrying call from Brooke, Dean asked the AA man how much longer he'd be.

'I'm just finishing up now. Your accelerator cable snapped. I've repaired it, but it's only temporary. Still, it should get you home. You'll have to get it replaced ASAP.'

Fifteen minutes later, Dean screeched up to the entrance of A&E to find Brooke outside sobbing. She eventually stopped shaking as he put his arms around her as best he could, squeezing hard and kissing her neck, back and head, continuing to ask what was the matter, despite deep down realising that she was unable to answer him right at that moment. Paige was out for the count so he put her in her car seat.

'Babe? What's the matter? What's happened? Why are

you crying?' Dean was now panicked and clasped her face between his hands and drew her close to his. In between sobs, Brooke went on to explain how the nurse and doctor in the hospital had implied she'd hurt Paige and that her injuries weren't consistent with her story. Dean's reaction was more measured than Brooke's, but he was nevertheless quietly furious that someone had made his wife feel like this.

'How could they possibly think that we'd ever harm our own daughter?' Dean asked, looking quite incredulous.

'I know. That's what I said.' Brooke's sobbing gradually subsided and Dean's care, love, physical affection and support for her took over, helping her to feel vaguely human again.

What would I do without him?

'C'mon, I need to get you home.'

They drove back in silence. Paige was so profoundly tired that when they got home, Brooke was able to undress her down to her vest and change her nappy with barely a murmur and she felt eternally grateful for that.

'You need sleep, babe. Let's talk about this more tomorrow.' Dean stroked Brooke's hair and face with so much heartfelt love it hurt.

'Yeah. I'm overtired now. I just hope I can sleep at all. 'Night, babe. Love you so much.'

Brooke eventually succumbed to the warmth of her bed and the comfort of Dean next to her and slept like a baby.

***

In the morning, Dean brought Brooke a cup of tea. He sat on the edge of the bed and held her hands tenderly as he looked into her eyes with genuine concern.

'Brew for you, babe. How are you feeling?'

Brooke stayed lying down, but opened her eyes. They were red and puffy and she could feel it without even having to look in the mirror.

'Sorry about last night, babe. I was just tired and emotional.'

'With every reason, if you ask me. Please just take it easy today and try and forget what happened last night. I was thinking, it's not like they stopped you taking her away from the hospital, so they couldn't have been that worried.'

'I guess so. We're bound to hear more if they want to see you or me, but I doubt it. I wish you'd have been there. It was just awful. I felt so…I dunno…just so alone. D'ya know what I mean?'

'God, I knew I shouldn't have left you both. I should've left the car and come with you. It was my fault and I'm so, so sorry.'

'No, babe. It wasn't your fault, it was just sod's law you couldn't be there, that's all.'

'At least they managed to fix the car – well, temporarily anyway. We should be grateful for that, I suppose. But we've got to get it properly fixed ASAP. More bloody money.'

Brooke sat up and they hugged and kissed passionately on the bed; a force of togetherness against…they didn't know what against. But against something or someone; and nothing was going to divide them. They'd deal with it together. Whatever 'it' was.

Brooke felt reassured by Dean's presence. He had a calm and mature way about him and he always made her feel that he'd protect her, come what may. She thought about this as she lay in bed for a while after he'd left for work. Her musings were interrupted suddenly by a message from her mother.

Fancy going down Romford Market today?

Brooke thought about it for a few moments. She wasn't sure if she was in the mood. Then again, she thought it might cheer her up. She couldn't imagine what her mother would say when she told her about the incident at the hospital. Ordinarily Brooke would've rung her straight away, but it was so late by the time she'd got out of the hospital, she just didn't feel she could. Jackie phoned her daughter every single day and sometimes twice a day. Nothing urgent. Just to chat. Dean was always at a loss as to what they could possibly find to talk about. To him it was just banal rubbish, but they could easily talk for an hour on the phone.

Brooke got up slowly and made her way into Paige's room, still trying to decide whether to go or not. Paige's little head looked so red and sore, but she was as happy as Larry playing quietly in her cot. Such a rare sight and sound! Brooke smiled and got down on all-fours and made her way over to the cot pretending to be a tiger, making growling noises and lifting her arms up as though they were huge cat paws. Paige squealed and giggled, jumping up and down and pointing at her mother, half fearful until she smiled and made it obvious it was a game. Paige appeared oblivious to the cut and dressing on her head.

Brooke plucked her out the cot and tenderly touched the area around the wound. It didn't register with Paige at all, who carried on playing with her favourite white rabbit. 'Shall we go out with Nanna today? What d'ya think? Nanna doesn't know all about your poor little head and those horrible nurses in the hospital. We can tell her all about it, can't we?'

'Naaanaaa.'

Brooke got excited. 'Nanna.'

'Naaanaaa.'

This went on for some minutes, after which Brooke messaged Dean.

Paige just said Nanna!

It was her first word. Up until this day she'd only ever uttered screams.

Fab! Bet that cheered you up. Give her a kiss from me!

'Daddy says to give you a kiss!' Brooke opened the middle poppers of her babygro and gave her a raspberry kiss on her tummy, which sent Paige into another fit of giggles and squeals. This did cheer Brooke up, so she decided she'd see her mother, but she fancied a relaxing soak in the bath first. Paige needed one too, so they had one together. Hopefully Paige would say Nanna when she saw her!

OK 12 noon at Wimpy end of market?

Suits me fine. C U there.

What I wouldn't do for a hot tub right now.

After an hour of bathing, soaking and playing in the bath, they got out and Brooke cuddled Paige inside her huge fluffy dressing gown to help dry her off. She took a selfie of her and Paige naked on the bed, both grinning at the camera, and sent it to Dean.

See, I've cheered up! Going down Romford Market with Mum.

Dean thought about Brooke all morning at work and messaged her numerous times to check she was OK., pleading with her to check her blood pressure on her monitor at home. He hurt for her and could only imagine how she'd felt. He'd do anything to cheer her up. He was so obviously preoccupied that Chloe, Brian and a couple of other colleagues asked him if he was OK. He tried hard to perk up after that; he didn't want Brian to think he couldn't handle difficult situations – wherever they came from – he was still waiting for his promotion to be announced. He was sure it wouldn't be long now.

Late on that morning, he got a call from Angie at Sonny Global asking him if he could do a hotel visit in a couple of days' time. Dean said no straightaway and explained that he needed to be at home at the moment. Angie pushed him, as it was another urgent visit, but he was unusually assertive and made it quite clear that he simply couldn't do it this time – but thanked her for asking him.

***

Angie came off the phone a bit stuck. She wasn't used to Dean not being a pushover. Although he was relatively new to mystery shopping, he was one of their best assessors and was so willing to do difficult visits at the last minute. He was one hundred per cent reliable and extremely diligent. He also gave really detailed feedback in his reports, which the clients loved. He didn't realise how good he was compared to some of the people Sonny Global had to deal with. Like the assessor who went to Chobham instead of Cobham and another who actually drove five hours to St Ives in Cornwall instead of St Ives in Cambridgeshire and one who went into his bathroom in a hotel only to discover all his clothes had somehow been stolen from his room while he was in the shower and so had to reveal himself as the mystery shopper, while in his birthday suit, to the hotel manager. She thought about them all as she considered who she'd ask instead.

Just before lunch, Dean went in to see Brian.

'Brian, I know I've had a bit of time off lately, but is there any chance I can leave early today? I'll stay later tomorrow. It's just I'm a bit worried about Brooke.'

'I thought there was something wrong. You definitely haven't been yourself this morning. I don't want to pry, but is she alright?'

Prying was exactly what Brian wanted to do.

'Not really, but it's not anything I want to talk about right now. So…can I leave early?'

'Of course. I hope you get sorted out, whatever it is.'

Brain's face was screaming *tell me tell me what's the matter* but Dean ignored it.

'By the way, Dean, before you go, you'll be pleased to hear that Jules and Dave are wanting to make the announcement to the team about your taking over as Operations Manager next week. They confirmed your salary increase, which will take you up to £40,000 pa (not quite what I earn, but I have been here for over twenty years) plus the target-based bonus we talked about and a company car, of course. You'll be needing that in this job.'

Dean's face lit up. He hadn't banked on that piece of news today, but it would make his afternoon even sweeter. He thanked Brian and walked out of his office in a daze.

At 3pm, Dean shut down his PC, packed his things away quickly and marched out of the office. He'd been unable to get down to any real work today and was anxious to get home. But he decided to take a small detour first.

23

Romford Market

Jackie turned her nose up at the pile of vomit in one of the many doorways nestled in the alley from the car park to the marketplace. She held her breath as she walked past it and shook her head at the piles of rubbish that'd built up in the corners of every graffitied exit and entrance she passed. She tiptoed around so as to avoid the soles of her elegant heels from getting dirty. She breathed out again as she entered the marketplace. Under the clocktower of Tollgate House, she waited for Brooke to arrive, as she was a few minutes early. Her eyes wandered over and around the market. As she surveyed the scene in front of her, it dawned on her just how much the market had shrunk over the years. Stallholders had come and gone and there were only a few of the originals left. She'd lived in the area all her life and had been a regular visitor to the market, but for one reason or another she'd found herself going less and less.

Well it just ain't as big or good as it used to be.

Her eyes swept across to the entrance of Romford Shopping Hall. The facia was the sort of faded pink that you see on red cars that have been through the car wash too many times.

When was that last painted?

On the opposite side was an entrance to The Liberty Mall, which had at least made an attempt to update itself with more contemporary branding. Another hive of shopping activity was also close by; The Quadrant Arcade where the metal shutters had been pulled only partway up and the entrance just looked a mess.

There was something else that was different from how it used to be but she was struggling to think what it was. Then she laughed to herself as she remembered. Of course, it was the smell; the pungent stink of hops that pervaded the air from the brewery at the other end of the market place – it was no more! It had closed thirty years ago to make way for yet another shopping mall. Even Jackie, who lived for shopping, began to wonder if Romford really needed yet another arcade.

The marketplace was white van man territory. Rows and rows of them, neatly parked behind their stalls.

If only they drove as thoughtfully as they parked, the M25 would be a much happier place.

A multitude of young women (girls, even) pushing prams with one or more babies, wandered about aimlessly. Some were accompanied by young men (boys, even) but most by their mothers. They were everywhere. Jackie also noticed four people in motorised scooters who were so overweight they clearly couldn't walk properly.

Hmph. Morbidly obese.

Their bellies escaped and hung like sand bags over the sides and it was hard to tell where their legs ended and their crotch began. This horrified her, although they seemed jolly enough.

Never used to see people like that years ago. How can people let themselves get that fat?

Jackie watched one young girl, no more than sixteen years old, leaning against a pillar talking on her phone. She looked odd in a navy-blue tracksuit with red stripes down the side, with a fake-fur brown gilet over the top, open-toed furry mules and huge sunglasses that seemed to cover half her face. Her gold hoop earrings were so enormous they swept her entire cheeks. She looked as though she might've been a refugee who needed to accept whatever clothes had been donated to her. Dark black roots shamelessly poked through her bleached-blond hair as it sat flat and greasy against her head. She was smoking in a very odd way, taking short drags and puffing them out quickly, like she was getting ten pounds for every drag she took. Next to her was a toddler, no more than eighteen months, in a pushchair. A little girl dressed top to toe in vibrant purple. She had the remains of something chocolatey around her cheeks and mouth, which was occupied by a dummy, and she had several gold studs in her ears.

Jackie shook her head at the sight and inadvertently heard the girl talking.

'I ain't goin'. I 'ate 'er. You tell 'er from me…she turns up and I'll fuckin' kill 'er.'

After a minute or two, the girl was surrounded by a group of her friends. Jackie couldn't understand a word they were saying. It might as well have been a different language.

Brooke suddenly appeared, pushing Paige in the pram, looking immaculate as always. Tight pair of denim shorts, pretty white broderie anglaise off-the-shoulder top, brown leather belt and matching brown leather sandals. Fake tanned to perfection, hair straightened, full makeup and bright-red talons.

Jackie admired her daughter; slim, sexy and stylish, not like the riff-raff she'd been watching for the last ten minutes.

''allo, love.' Jackie gave her daughter a big hug. 'You look lovely. 'allo, gorgeous! 'ow's my favourite granddaughter, then?'

Jackie bent down over the pram and pinched Paige's chubby little cheeks. As she did so, she noticed the cut.

'What's happened to her 'ead, poor little mite?'

Brooke took a deep breath. 'Let's go and have a cuppa and I'll tell you all about it. Let's go to Greggs. None of that fancy stuff, just a proper brew.'

'Alright, Greggs it is,' agreed Jackie. They moseyed through the marketplace, briefly glancing either side as they went, agreeing that they'd come back and look around properly after their tea. Within a few seconds they heard a wolf whistle and turned around.

'Hey! Doll! Your arse looks good in them shorts! Fancy some slap and tickle?'

'Andy – *shut it!* You wouldn't like it if some bloke shouted that at your Anna!' Jackie walked over and gave him a hug. Brooke followed and in mock indignation said, 'Cheeky bugger! So 'ow are you, Andy? 'ow's Anna?'

'Long time no see, both of you! Yeah, we're all good. Anna's good, only world domination ain't 'appening quickly enough for 'er! Where've you been? I 'aint seen you for ages.'

Andy Kidd was well known round these parts and somewhat of a Romford legend. A real 'diamond geezer', Brooke called him. He'd had all manner of stalls for donkey's years here in the market and was a natural born trader. He and Jackie chewed the cud for a bit and from time to time Brooke carefully observed all the comings and goings around her. It must've been at least a year since she'd been to the market. Lakeside had become her shopping centre of choice for quite a while now. Jackie and Andy's voices faded into the background as Brooke focussed on the people around her. She noticed how cheap the clothes were, how blingy the bags were, how young the mums looked, how there was a distinct lack of…what was the word she was looking for? She felt odd. A bit like she didn't quite fit into this world anymore. Yet there was something comforting about it at the same time. This all had a strange effect on her.

'C'mon, Mum, we ought to get going!'

'OK, yeah I know. Sorry, Andy. Nice to chat. Take care of yourself and send my love to 'er indoors!'

'Bye, Andy, send my love to Anna next time you see her!' Brooke said it half-heartedly, turned around with the pram and moved on. Anna Kidd had done so well (TV celebrity and TOWIE superstar) and yet she didn't seem to be anything special in Brooke's opinion – just a lucky break. Maybe Brooke resented her? Jealous, perhaps? She couldn't work out her own feelings at all. She just knew she felt uncomfortable.

Jackie led the way with a speedy march to Greggs. They ordered two cups of tea, two iced donuts and sat down at a table inside that'd just become free. It was full of rubbish from the previous inhabitants and, without fuss, Brooke quickly put it all on a tray, moved it over to a nearby empty table and sat down.

She and her mother sat there for nearly two hours discussing the detail of Brooke's unfortunate visit to the hospital with Paige, who was by now fast asleep. Jackie was – as Brooke had predicted – absolutely livid.

'You should make an official complaint, Brooke. It's well out of order.'

'No, Mum. There's no point. Just leave it.' Brooke sounded a mix of resigned, worried and fed up.

Jackie wasn't convinced and it was as much as she could do to stop herself driving over to Queen's straightaway and giving them a piece of her mind.

'C'mon, let's go back to the market, there's a few things I wanna get.' Brooke stood up and pushed the pram outside. Jackie followed.

They walked past Lindsay's shoes without looking and onto Michelle's clothing stall. A cornucopia of dresses, jackets, t-shirts and skirts were all hanging up in an attempt to show them off. Fake fur, polyester, diamanté, denim, stretch, big buckles and lots of studded t-shirts flapped around in the breeze and you had to swerve or duck to miss them. Brooke flicked through the racks and that niggling feeling came back again.

What am I doing, looking at this stuff?

She thought about Lady Townsend and wondered what she'd make of this place. She imagined her standing on the cobblestones – a vision in her exquisite Jaeger trousers, John Smedley cashmere sweater, Salvatore Ferragamo shoes and her silver-grey hair neatly cut in a bob. Understated, stylish and classy.

'Paand only! Paaand only! C'mon, paand only!' Brooke was jolted out of her thoughts by a coarse female voice. Toni from the fruit and veg stall was shouting to persuade the punters to buy at a reduced price. Brooke automatically looked over and observed her. A black t-shirt with two flamingos facing each other on the front hung off her scraggy frame. The birds looked like they were made out of pearls, so the whole thing protruded and it must have been heavy to wear. Her black hair was scraped back in a ponytail and she was smiling.

That's a hard face. You look like you've seen life. I bet shit stuff's happened to you.

She watched as Toni bagged up some reduced items for a customer.

'Thanks, mate,' Toni said as she handed over her plums.

Once upon a time Brooke wouldn't have thought twice about that; but now she smiled to herself as she imagined how it would sound if Lady Townsend called *her* 'mate'. It just seemed so wrong now somehow; a woman calling another woman 'mate'.

Jackie had passed Penny's stall full of household goods: cleaning liquids, dusters, brushes, scourers and batteries lined the table. Opposite was the underwear stall; hung high above it were beige panty girdles for grannies, oversized white pants for post-menopausal women, and oversized bras for those with exceptional mammary glands. Brooke strolled between the two stalls and began thinking about some of the articles she'd read in Lady Townsend's magazines. There was one about the market in Aix-en-Provence in France, with the most alluring photographs of whole tuna fish being sliced with a double-handled saw by a young girl, stalls with glistening black and green olives in terracotta bowls, freshly made bread in the most appealing shapes and sizes, piled high in baskets, gorgeous huge blooms of cut flowers and stylish wicker and raffia bags for shopping, being sold by a woman who looked like a supermodel. It all looked simply glorious to

Brooke.

And in Romford we sell big knickers and tea towels.

'Hey, Brooke, come and look at this!' Jackie shouted from a stall a bit further along, holding something up and waving it at Brooke. Storky's children and babywear was one of the oldest stalls on the market. It'd been there for over seventy years and was a family-run business.

Brooke walked towards it, quickly forgetting about whole tuna fish. As she got closer, she could see her mother holding up a tiny pink-check woollen overcoat, with huge buttons and a pink furry collar.

'Can't you just see Paige in this? Oh my God, she'd look so gorgeous, Brooke. What d'ya think?'

Brooke took it from her and looked over it. It was really cute. But then everything on that stall was really cute. Row upon row of the most adorable outfits split with no thought for current political correctness into the blue side and the pink side. There was no room for any mother who wanted her baby brought up gender neutral. In fact, anyone believing anything other than girls wear pink and boys wear blue would likely have been removed swiftly and violently from the stall.

''ow much?' Jackie asked.

'Twenny-five quid' came the response. She too had a hard face, she didn't smile and her hair was scraped back off her face, which was free of makeup. Her tanned skin glowed and there was ample flesh showing. She wore a black t-shirt with Balenciaga Paris in gold letters on the front. The irony didn't escape Brooke.

'Let me buy it for 'er, Brooke. It's so lovely!' Jackie pleaded, knowing that money was tight. She'd always had to be careful about buying things for her daughter and granddaughter. She'd noticed an independent streak in Brooke that meant she didn't like accepting gifts or money from her parents. She viewed them as handouts and would often retort with 'I don't need you to buy me stuff. I can buy it myself, you know.' Anything not to feel inferior; a trait ironically brought on by Jackie.

On this occasion she wavered. It was so pretty. She put it against Paige in her pram. She and Jackie peered in and cooed. The stallholder looked over.

Kerching! Done deal.

While Jackie was paying, Brooke looked around again and noticed two young men slumped down on the pavement, leaning against the wall in front of the church. They were drinking Stella from a can and looked like they hadn't washed for some considerable time. She was shocked and actually a little sad. She didn't know why. She didn't know them. Yet again, she thought about the area where Lady Townsend lived and she couldn't help think about the fact that within six miles of Purses there could be people living lives so far removed from the life of her employer.

'Thanks, Mum!' Brooke gave her a hug and smiled, suddenly very grateful for having such a generous mother.

They moved past the 'Real Leather' stall and the

watch repair stall with a sign so badly weatherworn that entire letters had peeled off so it actually said:

WTCH REAIRS, STRAPS & BATTERIES TED WHIL U WAIT WE USE BEST QUALITY REPIA ME E GIVE GUARANTY RE AIRS

Again, the irony wasn't lost on Brooke.

They sauntered slowly down the middle of the marketplace glancing one way and then the other, but Brooke found herself more interested in people-watching than shopping. Coming towards her were Janet and Jean – infamous amongst the locals, but especially the market traders in Romford. Brooke remembered these two alright – they hadn't changed how they looked in all the years she'd seen them around. Mutton dressed as lamb and never apart. Two women who claimed to be fifty years old but who looked 'just really good for our age'. They had to be seventy if they were a day. As they looked over one footwear stall, chock-a-block with diamanté mules and flip-flops, one said to the other in a voice Brooke deemed worse than on East Enders,

'The cleaner probably wears 'em! Know what I mean?' Janet agreed and they dismissed the entire footwear collection as far too gaudy for themselves.

What do they look like?

Just as she was thinking that, another vision appeared; one that she fast came to the conclusion epitomised Romford. Coming out of the Bull pub was a couple in their late sixties. Both the man and woman were covered in tattoos: arms, legs, chest, back and neck. Only the faces had been judged too special to be given over to Aaron at Cult Classic Tattoos over in North Street. The man wore shorts, a black skull t-shirt with a black leather waistcoat over the top and she wore jeans and a low-cut t-shirt revealing plenty of cleavage. Brooke was so shocked at the sight of this woman that she didn't even notice what was on the front of her t-shirt. All she could see were her overblown trout lips Botoxed to kingdom come and she was made up as though she was going pole dancing in town. Poor Brooke failed to see the irony there! As the lips passed right in front of Brooke, followed a minute later by the rest of the woman, she tried to pretend she wasn't looking, but as soon as the couple walked past her, Brooke turned around. She saw that the man had the word 'Family' written in script all up one forearm and a Smurf tattooed onto each calf.

Why would anyone do that?

Suddenly Brooke spoke. 'Actually, Mum, I think I'm done in the market, I wanted to go to Beauty By Zara before we go. Do you mind?

'No, course not.'

So they made their way back through the market, into South Street and into Beauty by Zara; an Aladdin's cave of all things to do with hair and makeup. Brooke looked around helplessly as she struggled to see any way of getting the pushchair through the narrow aisles which were packed with women of every shape, size and colour imaginable. Paige had miraculously been asleep from just before they got into Greggs – probably because of her exceptionally late night the day before. Jackie offered to stay with her at the front of the shop while Brooke went around on her own.

She marvelled at the way they'd utilised every millimetre of space in the shop. You could see no wall, only products. From floor to ceiling and across three walls were every type of wig, hairpiece and hair extensions known to man, in every conceivable human shade, and one or two that didn't actually look human at all. All the way along the floor were ten-litre containers of shampoo in red, green and white.

Who the hell needs ten litres of shampoo at a time?

Then there was the makeup. Brooke was fanatical about makeup. She had 'more pots, tubes, jars, palettes than I've had hot dinners', as her father would say, and she never threw any away. Her mother had bought Brooke her special dressing table with two huge acrylic compartmentalised storage holders, which was purely for all her makeup. One day when Dean was particularly cross at having no room to put his deodorant and talcum powder, he decided to count it all. There was almost one thousand pieces and when he confronted Brooke with the reality, she'd simply remarked, 'Is that all?'

She spent at least ten minutes browsing through all the lipsticks and nail varnishes, just in case there were any that she'd never seen before. This of course was highly unlikely!

She picked out a bright orange and cherry-red lipstick and a turquoise nail varnish. Turning the corner, she was faced with shelf upon shelf of shampoo, hair conditioner, mousse, hairspray, dye, serums and treatments by manufacturers that were mostly unknown to anyone except residents of Romford – with the exception of Redken. She pulled some Redken shampoo and conditioner off the shelves, looked at the price and had a sharp intake of breath. It'd been a while since she'd bought this shampoo. TRESemmé in Tesco was about as fancy as her shampoo got these days. She noticed they had a deal on the hair colour that her mother always used, so she shouted for her to come and have a look. Jackie left Paige still asleep in the pram just for a moment and popped round the corner to the hair dye section.

Within a minute there was the most almighty scream. Sadly, Brooke recognised it straight away. She marched back round to where the pram was. It took less than ten seconds to get there, but there were half a dozen women surrounding the pram, including a punk with a bright-green mohican, a lady in a full-length burqa and an elderly Chinese woman who had more deep lines in her face than the Himalayas, all clearly wondering where the child's mother was.

'Don't worry! I'm here! I'm here! She's mine!'

Brooke appeared and casually dumped her stuff on the counter and immediately yanked Paige out the pram, revealing the cut on her head. She continued to scream with a vengeance.

'You really shouldn't leave her alone like that,' the woman in the burqa said.

Brooke felt the colour rise on her face, the fury rise in her body, her chest start heaving and her blood pump hard. She turned around shaking, stabbing her finger at the woman who'd spoken and screamed, 'YOU! You lot probably scared the living daylights out of her! Why don't you mind your own business and FUCK RIGHT OFF?!'

All the women looked aghast at each other and then back at Brooke. All the nearby customers fell silent and looked over at Brooke. Jackie was taken aback at her daughter's language. She'd never heard her speak like that before and she felt compelled to apologise in a sort of half whisper, on Brooke's behalf.

'I'm so sorry, ladies. She didn't mean it. It's just she had a bad incident happen last night and I think your comment reminded her of it. She's also a bit tired. Didn't get out the hospital 'til around midnight. Like I said, I'm sorry.'

All the women said nothing and went back to their business.

Brooke continued to shake as she tried to pay for her shopping whilst holding onto Paige, whose scream was so piercing that Brooke had to move her ear away from the source, for fear of damaging her hearing. She felt stressed now and anxious. The total came to sixty pounds. Sixty pounds which she really didn't have. She dithered before finally handing over her credit card.

'Love, let me...'

'No! It's my stuff. I'm perfectly capable of paying for my own stuff.' Brooke shot her one of her infamous looks.

Jackie sighed, knowing there was no point in arguing.

They bundled Paige back into the pram, put it up as a pushchair and tried to strap her in. The ubiquitous back arch followed, then more screams all the way down South Street. As they passed Palace Amusements, Brooke noticed two women, probably about the same age as her, dressed in grey joggers, t-shirts and trainers drinking cans of Foster's, while trying to persuade a security guard to let them inside.

She'd seen sights like this all her life and never thought anything of them, but today she was finding it all very disconcerting. It was as though she no longer belonged here. She felt...out of place. That was it...out of place. Discombobulated.

I hate this. I hate this cheap, tacky place. These people.

Brooke hated herself for hating the place and the community here; she knew they were good-hearted, hard-working, friendly people who didn't have an easy life, but she couldn't fathom her own emotions. She thought about her outburst and suddenly felt deeply ashamed.

Mrs Townsend, Hugo and Purses came and steadfastly stayed in her mind; then Ingatestone Hall appeared and she tried to imagine Lord D'Arcy here in Romford Market. The mere thought of it made her recoil in embarrassment.

Then the penny dropped. *That's* what this was all about.

Class.

24

Hot Tub Heaven

'Hot Tub Heaven'. The brightly lit and flashing sign glowed garishly from the car park on the industrial estate. An unfortunate selection of bulbs had gone out on both 'H's, so it actually read: ot Tub eaven. The very epitome of style and irony!

Dean alighted his moped and stared at the gargantuan metal warehouse in front of him.

How can they fill this place just with bloody hot tubs?

As he wandered in, a chime rang round the warehouse, indicating to the hidden salesman that his next prey had just arrived. The noxious smell of chemicals overpowered Dean, as did the tinny version of 'Copacabana' playing in the background.

He stood for a few moments, scanning the floor for some sort of useful signage that'd advise him where he should be heading. All he could see were row upon row of hot tubs, seemingly in no particular order.

Dean, being the rather particular chap that he was, decided to take it logically and walked to the nearest corner, in order to make his way up one aisle and down the next, rather like his lawn-mowing routine.

He stopped for some time at the first one – The Benidorm model. It was made for four people and it had a glitzy black-glitter effect around the outside. He looked intriguingly at the jets inside and wondered how forceful they were and what their actual purpose was.

I bet they're a mare to get clean when they get blocked. And them seals'll all end up dry and cracked with the first bit of sun. Then there'll be no stopping the water coming in.

He bent down and read the guidance sheet stuck on the side to check the measurements.

'It's our bestseller, that one!'

The salesman appeared out of nowhere. Ryan was his name, according to his badge. He wore a grey slim-fitting jacket and eye-wateringly skinny trousers, pink shirt and a blue tie with Bart Simpson on it. He had an excuse for a moustache and a spot on his chin so large it had its own passport. He grinned enthusiastically.

'I can see you've got good taste.' Ryan winked at Dean. 'Have you got any experience of hot tubs?'

'Well that depends what you mean by experience. I've seen a few but never been in one.'

Ryan rubbed his hands gleefully and looked pleased as punch; eager to impart his extensive knowledge of hot tubs to his unsuspecting prey.

'Well, welcome to Hot Tub Heaven! Let me enlighten you on the joys of the hot tub!'

'Actually, I think I'm already enlightened. My wife's

been wanting one for ages.'

'So, you're buying it for her as a present?' Ryan looked ecstatic, clearly thinking about all sorts of exciting sales techniques he could deploy.

'Well I haven't definitely decided yet, but I've come to have a look round, see what you've got and get an idea of price.'

'Will you be looking for finance?'

Like Greta Garbo, Dean actually just wanted to be left alone and not interrogated in this way. He didn't have a huge amount of time.

'I don't know yet. I'm quite happy to be left to wander at the moment, if you don't mind.'

'Course! No worries! I'll be around. Just let me know if you've got any questions.'

Dean smiled, nodded and continued walking around the glitzy hot tub, stroking the smooth, warm-to-the-touch acrylic with his fingers. He noticed out of the corner of his eye that Ryan hadn't moved and was just staring at him. So Dean slid over to the next hot tub in the row. This was a twelve-seater – The Sag Harbour model no less – and looked as though it'd house the whole of Elephant Close. He strolled around it, peered into it and, out of sheer curiosity, glanced at the price.

£15,750. Plus VAT.

Fuck me.

Ryan came up behind Dean. He'd somehow swooped across from Benidorm to Sag Harbour, just like an owl, neither seen nor heard, taking Dean completely by surprise and making him jump.

'Hah! Didn't mean to scare you! I do that sometimes. Jack-in-the-box they call me!'

More like Dick-in-the-box.

'Imagine sitting in there with all your mates, beer in one hand and…well, who knows what in the other, eh? Hahahaha! Take a look at this!'

With that, Ryan picked up a remote control, pressed a button and suddenly a TV screen rose up from within the casing of the hot tub.

'Blimey!' Dean exclaimed.

'That's nothing.' Ryan looked around cautiously. 'Just think, mates, beer and…' He winked again and pressed another button which made the screen come to life. Within seconds Dean was faced with a completely naked redhead being lightly spanked by what looked like her identical twin, wearing a fig leaf and oh-so-tasteful red, shiny, thigh-high boots!

Being on the prudish side, Dean looked up at Ryan, disgust written all over his face.

'It's for my wife and our friends, actually,' he said indignantly. 'I don't think they'd appreciate that somehow.' Anxious to move the conversation on, Dean added, 'Besides, this one's way too big for our garden and way too expensive.'

Ryan's face dropped as he realised he'd misread young Dean. He'd assumed he was like every other hot-blooded young chap from Essex, with basic needs and horny as a goat. He quickly switched it off and they both watched on in silence, as the TV sunk back into the hot tub like a coffin being lowered into a grave.

Ryan, not being one to give up quite that easily, swiftly moved on and changed tack as though nothing awkward had happened at all! His revised sales pitch was a stroke of genius.

'Well, how about this one? For eight people – the lovely Barcelona model. Imagine lying in this with your friends, a glass of wine in hand and looking up at the stars?' He beckoned to Dean to follow him, which Dean reluctantly did, because of course he didn't want to appear rude.

'Sorry, I didn't catch your name?'

'Dean.'

'Hello, Dean. I'm Ryan.' He put out his hand with a big grin on his face. Dean very reluctantly shook hands.

'So, Dean, this beauty has a great feature, which they don't all have.' Ryan again pressed a button on the nearby remote control. A few seconds later, 'Careless Whisper' boomed out from the surround speakers embedded in the hot tub. Dean stood there trying to separate the dulcet tones of Barry Manilow from George Michael, with great difficulty.

This is doing my head in.

'Why don't you get in? See what it feels like?'

'No…you're alright.' Dean shuffled from one foot

to the other feeling very uncomfortable, like teenagers do when they've been asked to give a relative they barely know a kiss goodbye.

'Go on! Get in! No-one's looking!' Ryan laughed and beckoned in an exaggerated fashion for Dean to climb right in.

Dean remained insistent that he didn't wish to get in.

'Well I'm getting in, even if you don't!' And at once Ryan leaped over the side and lay down at one end as you would getting into a dodgem car.

'See? Great fun. Imagine how relaxing this is, how much your friends would love a hot tub, but that *you're* the geezer who's got one? You'll be the envy of all your neighbours!' Ryan held out both his arms palms up and looked at Dean, imploring him to heed the logic and reasoning of his argument.

'Yeah, maybe,' Dean said unenthusiastically.

'Come oooon! Get in, why don't you?'

Just to shut him up, Dean climbed tentatively over the side and sat down at the opposite end to Ryan. He examined the layout and shelving arrangement.

How the hell would you get eight people in here? Stacy and Martin alone would take up four of these spaces.

'What kind of music do you like, Dean?'

'What?'

'What music do you and your wife like to listen to?'

'Oh God, I dunno, Olly Murs, Maroon 5, Rhianna – loads of different stuff really. Why?'

Ryan immediately grabbed his phone out of his pocket and typed something in at such speed Dean couldn't fathom how it was possible. Barry Mannilow stopped and Olly Murs took over with 'Dear Darlin'' blasting out the music system all around them.

'God I love this song!' Dean said with the first bit of enthusiasm he'd mustered up since he'd been there. Without thinking, he lay back, shut his eyes and commenced singing (of sorts) just as he did when languishing in the bath at home. Ryan allowed himself to feel a moment of hope and confidence. He watched Dean for a few minutes before taking the next step.

'Do you realise you could have this in your back garden tomorrow for only a hundred and fifty quid a month?'

Dean sat bolt upright.

What the hell am I even doing? I must be mad!

'Woah! I was getting all carried away for a minute there – sorry!'

'No need to apologise, mate! You were enjoying yourself. That's what a hot tub lets you do!' Ryan leaned forward and patted Dean on the arm.

Dean started to relax and stop being so anti-Ryan, who didn't seem such a bad chap after all (porn aside.)

A hundred and fifty quid a month. That still seems like a lot of money.

Ryan could read him like a book.

'Why don't you have a look at a six-seater? I've got an

ex-display model – The Ibiza, which we're selling reduced 'cause they've brought in a newer version.'

'I've always wanted to go to Ibiza,' Dean let slip.

Fateful schoolboy error!

Ryan leaped out the hot tub, ran over to the other side and helped Dean (who reacted like a fiercely independent OAP) out the tub. They walked side by side, glancing at the plethora of hot tubs all around.

Ryan stopped at a deep purple round six-seater model.

'This one is round and some people really prefer round. I've got a round one myself.'

How the hell can you afford a hot tub?

'I suppose you get a discount working here?' asked Dean as he automatically climbed in after Ryan.

'Yep! Anyway, this one's got a fab feature I've just gotta show you!' He got out his phone again and, to Dean's astonishment, made a phone call. Ryan wasn't going home tonight without a sale to this man.

'Johnny, do us a favour, mate, can you put the shutters down and turn the lights off and give us night?'

Dean sat forward alarmed.

What the hell's going on?

A few seconds later, the metal shutters at the windows started to come down and block out all natural daylight.

'What's happening?' said Dean, a bit concerned by now.

'Nothing to worry about, Dean. You just wait and see.'

A minute or two went by for them to fully shut and then the entire warehouse went pitch black. With no talking or announcement of what was to come, Ryan turned on the flashing LED display around the hot tub and told Dean to look up to the ceiling.

A dark black and navy velvety sky with twinkling stars and a glowing moon enveloped the warehouse; 'Dear Darlin'' still serenading him in the background.

'Wow! That's beautiful! How d'ya do that?'

'Well that don't matter, really. What really matters is that you can picture yourself in this hot tub of an evening with your wife, enjoying the hot bubbling water, relaxing and inviting your friends over for a little party. Don't you think? I bet your wife deserves it. I bet she looks after you. It's one small thing you could do for her that'll make her really appreciate what a fantastic husband she's got.'

Ryan was good. Really good.

'Well it's gorgeous, but—'

'We could probably do you a deal on this one. I reckon we could get the payments down to just under a monkey a month. She must be worth that, no?'

Ryan had Dean sussed.

Dean thought about Brooke. He couldn't help but picture her next to him in this hot tub, her glorious curvy body clad in that bright-yellow polka-dot bikini with a glass of Chardonnay, singing along to Taylor Swift at the top of her voice. Happy! So happy to have her longed-for hot tub. Showing off to all her friends. And she'd tell them as she hugged and doted over Dean that her husband had bought it for her as a birthday present. That really made his heart start thumping. So often he'd thought that his wife wasn't proud of him. She so often seemed discontented with what he'd done or achieved. This was his moment to show her he could provide – and more than the basics.

'I'm not sure it'll fit in my garden. It's tiny.'

'Well have you got the exact measurements?'

'Yeah, I brought them with me but I can't see them in this light.'

Immediately Ryan called Johnny again. 'Off, Johnny.' This was a well-rehearsed routine.

Up came the shutters, off went the lights, out of the hot tub Ryan leaped and marched purposefully round towards Dean, who'd retrieved a bit of paper from his suit pocket. Ryan put out his arm to help Dean out, who was more amenable than first time round.

'Let's go over to the desk and look at what's possible. So, what are the measurements of your garden?'

They walked towards the office by which time it was 5.15pm and the store was due to close at 6pm. Dean was no longer really even wondering if he should do this, more wondering how he should do this.

'Well the patio's where we'd put it and that's 4.5m x 3.5m.'

'Mmm, that is small, you're right. Smaller than most gardens where we install hot tubs. What about access? Are there any issues with getting to your back garden?'

'Well we've got a side gate and an alleyway about 1.5m wide although I'd want it to be a secret so we'd have to work out delivery and stuff.'

Ryan proffered a seat in front of his desk and Dean sat awkwardly waiting, while Ryan tapped into his computer. He had a calculator on his desk and embarked on several calculations.

'OK, well according to my sums, we could just about squeeze the round hot tub in, but I've gotta be honest, mate, you won't have hardly any room around it. I could do it for one hundred and twenty a month.'

Dean sat there paralysed. It was such a monumental decision. He'd never, ever normally take such a major decision without Brooke. They'd discuss it, argue about it, prove each other wrong and eventually come to some sort of compromise. To do this without her seemed so wrong. Never mind dangerous. Very, very dangerous!

'What are your concerns, Dean?'

'Oh I dunno, it's a bit more than I thought and I just don't know whether it'd satisfy my wife. She's very fussy about stuff, you know?'

'OK. Well what's affordable to you?'

'Well I got excited when you said a hundred quid a month, 'cause that's probably just about affordable.'

'OK, Dean, I tell you what I'm gonna do. I'm gonna talk to my manager. I'm gonna see if he can do anything for you. So, you just sit here for a minute and I'll be right back.'

Dean sat on his chair which was at least fifteen centimetres shorter than Ryan's, he noticed. He felt like a student waiting for the head of year to come and tell him whether he'd been let off detention.

A few minutes went by and Dean's brain went into overdrive thinking about Brooke and her reaction. For the first time since he'd arrived in this place a genuine smile of excitement crept over his face.

Ryan returned with a look of self-satisfaction.

'Dean. You'll be glad to hear that my manager has agreed a one-off opportunity to buy this today at a reduced price that can take your monthly payments down to just under a hundred pounds, but you've got to sign the agreement tonight. The offer won't be there in the morning.'

Dean's natural instinct was to panic. Ryan could smell it.

'Why don't you just take a wander round the rest of the showroom on your own, just to reassure yourself that it's a good deal and that it's what you want? I'll be here preparing the finance agreement.'

Dean thought that sounded reasonable enough and readily agreed. He spent the next half an hour admiring all the other hot tubs in the showroom. They were vastly more expensive than the one he was about to purchase.

I wonder why? Maybe there's something wrong with it? What'd happen if something did go wrong with it? Would they refund or repair it or replace it? Does it have a guarantee? What if Brooke doesn't like it?! That'd be a disaster. But she won't. She'll love it. I know she will.

Dean talked himself round in circles and arrived right back to where he started. He'd come here today to do something lovely for his wife who'd been through some unfair treatment by others and had been really disturbed and upset. He wanted to be the person to rectify that situation and make her feel good again. It was just about affordable after his pay rise, although there would be very little left over for anything else. He could sell his moped now he was going to be getting a company car so he could make a bit of money that way.

Dean returned to Ryan's desk and bombarded him with his questions, which Ryan handled like a pro.

With a grin on his face, giving away the fact that he'd resigned himself to it, Dean stated firmly, 'OK. Let's do it!'

The paperwork, installation and delivery details were completed efficiently; no surprise really considering this sale meant that Ryan would take his quarterly sales over the point at which he got a higher bonus.

It was 6.15pm before everything was completed, but neither Ryan or Dean were complaining and they shook hands for the second time, once Dean had signed on the dotted line.

Dean left on a high.

Ryan left rubbing his hands.

25

Latin, Lies and Love

Brooke stood by the large window overlooking the garden while polishing a large table full of silver, while Lady Townsend sat on the sofa engaged in sorting through some papers.

'Have you ever thought about getting a hot tub, Mrs Townsend?'

'Oh no, dear. They're positively vulgar; all those sex parties. Urgh! I've a friend over in Chelmsford and she's beside herself at the weekends in the summer because her neighbours have one and they invite all their friends. She says it all ends up in one big orgy and she has to keep her children out of the garden to protect them!'

Brooke looked crestfallen. She believed Mrs Townsend was actually really good fun (very misleading to look at) and Brooke was positive she'd think hot tubs were the most wonderful invention. She looked up to her and took her lead from her now on so many things since she'd been working for her; from how she sat to what she wore, to how she introduced herself. As usual, Lady Townsend sensed Brooke's disappointment.

'But I suppose there are people who have them that aren't like that. It's just that one does tend to associate them with a certain "type" of person, if you know what I mean.' Diplomacy personified.

'Mmm…yeah… I guess so. I read that there's health benefits to using them.' Brooke spoke like someone who was engaged in a personal damage-limitation exercise. She so wanted Lady Townsend to approve of her, although why that mattered, she didn't really understand herself.

'There may well be. I suppose if you've got arthritis or something; the heat might be beneficial, but it's rather a dramatic way to get warm joints!'

Brooke's eyes glazed over, lost in her own thoughts about the merits or not of hot tubs. As she mindlessly polished a candlestick, it vaguely reminded her of a candlestick she'd noticed somewhere in Ingatestone Hall and she suddenly remembered, to her horror, that she still owed Geoffrey some money; another unpaid debt – yet again. Unforgiveable! But she wasn't worried about it this time, having experienced his humour first hand, so to speak.

Maybe I could go over later and give him his money?

She rather fancied the idea of turning up there without being asked or reminded by Lady Townsend – as though Lord D'Arcy were simply a friend of hers. He did say that she was welcome to come back at any time. It was thirty pounds she owed from memory, but he'd said he might let her off if she could recite the Latin motto under the clocktower and he'd also challenged her to learn some more Latin.

'Mrs Townsend, do you know any Latin?'

Considering this bizarre question had come completely out the blue – hot tubs to Latin in two minutes – Lady Townsend didn't bat an eyelid. But then again, she'd decided a while back that she'd take it upon herself to surreptitiously act as Brooke's unofficial mentor. Her mind was open to answering anything that Brooke asked her and she absolutely adored Brooke's natural, child-like curiosity. Lady Townsend never had children, but there was something about Brooke that she warmed to and she always looked forward to the days she came to work at the house. There was something about her lack of pretentiousness that she found so refreshing.

'Et venerunt ad debitum referre.'

'Oh my god, Mrs Townsend, you're *so* clever! I wish I could speak Latin. What does that mean?'

'It means, I've come to repay my debt.'

'Hahahha! Why did you say that?! I can't believe it! Do you know that I got myself into another bad debt situation with Geoffrey D'arcy again! He said he might let me off if I can prove to him that I've learned some Latin! Bloody cheek!'

'I know, he told me about your visit. He thinks you're quite delightful.'

'Really? He said *that*? About *me*?'

'Brooke, you need to stop underestimating yourself.'

Lady Townsend stood up and asked Brooke to follow her into the library, where she climbed carefully up the wooden ladder resting against one of the bookcases and plucked a book from the shelves.

'Here, take this, Brooke. You'll be amazed at what you can understand once you've learned Latin. Ordinary English words that you don't know the meaning of, you can work out with knowledge of Latin.'

Brooke took the book, but looked doubtful. It was a well-used old dark-green leather-bound book entitled *Learning Latin*.

'It's very old and very precious to me, so please look after it. Keep it for as long as you need it, but I'd like it back eventually.'

'I'll never be able to learn it. I know I won't. But thanks for the book – I'll certainly take a look.'

'Don't say no before you've even tried. You can do it.'

Lady Townsend smiled an encouraging smile.

'OK, thanks. I'll have a go, but I'm not promising anything. Can you write down what you just said for "I've come to repay my debt?" I might impress Geoffrey if I can remember it right!'

Lady Townsend wrote it on a piece of paper and Brooke said it out loud just to check she was pronouncing it correctly.

'Beautifully said, my dear! Now. Back to the silver!'

Then, with a mischievous twinkle in her eye, 'Oh wait. Look. Hugo's coming. Test out your Latin on him and see what he says!'

Hugo marched in with his air of casual professionalism, which Brooke tried hard to emulate but never got quite right. 'Ah there you are, Brooke. I was just looking for you.'

'Et venerunt ad debitum referre,' Brooke said it perfectly and grinned at Lady Townsend.

Hugo raised his eyebrows, smiled, looked at Lady Townsend and then back at Brooke.

'Pecuniam non debes.'

'Oh my God, not you as well. You all know it. It's an exclusive little club of people in the know! What did you just say?'

'I said, "you don't owe me any money!"'

'Well blow me down! Right. I'm gonna have to get in on this!'

Hugo and Mrs Townsend laughed – but not at her – with her.

'How come you know Latin, Hugo?' Brooke was fascinated.

'I learned it at Eton. It was compulsory.'

Brooke shook her head. She'd heard of Eton. That was the posh school where all the boys wore those funny uniforms, she seemed to think. She thought about her time at Gaynes and how the teachers struggled to get any of the pupils to take any language at all. Brooke took French, but never learned it seriously and couldn't wait to drop it. She thought how ironic it was that her wish to improve herself was so strong now, that she was seriously going to have a go at learning Latin.

Latin! Hahaha!

The thought made her smile.

Hugo smiled and gave her yet another list of jobs to do. They were never-ending. No sooner had she finished one lot, than he or Mrs Townsend would give her another. She'd never have dreamed that working at Purses would involve so much. But virtually from the beginning, both Hugo and Mrs Townsend had realised that she could do much more than she was originally brought in to do. It was clear she wanted to learn all about the house, everything in it and the history, as well as about Lady Townsend's background. Over the months she'd been there, she was also gradually being introduced to all manner of people who had cause to visit the house, such as the auctioneer, art and antique valuers, delivery companies, event planners, personal shoppers, racehorse trainers, gamekeepers and charity trustees. It was actually very convenient for both of them that Brooke was happy to take on whatever responsibility they gave her. She didn't see it as them dumping their work on her at all; only very occasionally did she object to what they asked her to do. Like the time Lady Townsend had asked her to ring Fortnum & Mason's and complain about a food hamper that'd been delivered. Apparently, the foie gras wasn't up to standard and Lady Townsend wanted them to know about it, but was going out and didn't have time to ring them herself, so she'd asked Brooke to do it. Brooke didn't even know what foie gras was, so she'd googled it first so she didn't say anything stupid. She was appalled.

How on earth can they do that to those poor little ducks? That's awful! I wonder if Mrs Townsend knows about how they make this stuff? I bet she doesn't. She wouldn't buy it if she knew, I'm sure.

She did make the call, but it was clear by the tone of voice on the other end of the telephone that they wondered who on earth they were talking to; it certainly wasn't Lady Townsend, who'd been a regular client at Fortnum's for over thirty years. They made Brooke feel small and she didn't like it.

Apart from that, she loved her work there and was very fond of both Hugo and Mrs Townsend. She was very disciplined and conscientious with her work because she absolutely didn't want to lose the job. It paid her very well (at least well in Brooke's world) and her savings had got to the point where she was beginning to feel financially independent.

***

Babe? Ur not picking up again?

That morning Dean had had a call at work. It was Angie from Sonny Global; aka Queen of Mystery Shopping in the hospitality industry throughout the UK. She was adored by her team for her sense of humour, highly regarded by clients for her ability to get mystery shops organised at the last minute with brilliantly detailed reports afterwards, and worshipped by all the sycophantic mystery shoppers so that she would dole out the best assignments to those people who did their job properly. She was also quite partial to a bit of arse-licking!

Dean was glad to hear from her, although he was beginning to feel that it was almost always when they were stuck for someone to do an assessment or if another assessor had let them down. But he'd always quite enjoyed what he'd been given (perhaps with the exception of the golf club.) He'd all but given up being paid anything worthwhile, but lived in hope that he might be given another hotel visit or two at some point in the near future, so he could get a night away from Paige. But he'd been warned not to push, because the assessor coordinators really hated that.

'How far is Cambridge from you, Dean?'

'Oh, I dunno, about an hour I guess, why do you ask?' Dean was curious. He'd never been to Cambridge.

'Well, we've got a really nice visit that needs to be done on a weekday in the first week of September, to Wimpole Hall.'

'Never heard of it. And that's next week.'

'Well, it's a National Trust property and the reason I thought of you is because you need to take a small child. There's also a farm on the site which is a family attraction and they really want to see how well the little ones are treated. The schools will have gone back by then and so it's a bit more difficult for us to get someone. And yeah, it's next week.'

'Well, my daughter's only fourteen months, so I don't know whether you consider that too small?' Dean was typically diligent in his response.

'Oh I'm sure that'd be fine.' Angie didn't have any children of her own, so she was clueless about the different stages of children's development.

'What would I have to do? I've never been anywhere like that before. Is it one of them fancy historic houses?'

'Yep! You got it. It doesn't matter if you've not been before. All you need to do is buy tickets for you, your wife and child, to the hall, farm and gardens. You need to visit all three areas and you must have lunch in the restaurant, visit the toilets and make a small purchase in the gift shop. That's it. So, d'ya want to do it?'

Dean had never heard anyone speak as fast as Angie. It was remarkable and he had to be very alert when she rang or she made him feel like an idiot for asking her to repeat it. He could hear the sighs of exasperation on the other end of the phone.

Dean had to think about this.

'Do I have to take my wife? Could I just take my daughter?'

'No, sorry. There have to be two adults. You're assessing how they treat the whole family unit. But it doesn't have to be your wife. If you have a mistress you're more than welcome to take her.' She sounded dead serious.

'Ha ha! I didn't mean that. I just thought it might be nice to have some quality time just with my daughter and let my poor wife have a rest,' he lied. What he meant was, how can I conduct this visit without letting onto Brooke what I'm *really* doing?

'Well it's up to you, Dean, but most people like these visits, so I'm sure your wife would really enjoy the day. It should be really nice; not stressful at all.'

Dean thought about the practical reality of how it could work. Could he get away with conducting the entire visit without Brooke noticing what he was doing and just fill in all the paperwork later? The woman had eyes like a hawk and didn't miss a trick. Having said that, he was naturally observant and diligent in his everyday life at home, so he may not come across any differently.

'Dean, sorry to rush you but I've got a lot of visits to allocate today, so is it a yes or a no?'

'OK. It's a yes.'

'Great. Will do. Cheers, Dean. Speak soon. Bye.' Angie was gone.

Dean took a deep breath and immediately started thinking about how on earth he was going to suggest to Brooke that they went to Wimpole Hall in Cambridgeshire on a weekday when he should be at work. He knew full well that she'd question him about why on earth he suddenly wanted to go there, why take a day off work to do it when they could go at a weekend and wouldn't Paige just be bored stiff and kick off? He thought long and hard about how he was going to overcome all those objections before putting it to her.

***

Brooke saw Dean's message and excused herself from the room to ring him back.

'Sorry, babe, I didn't hear my phone ring. Is everything alright?'

'Yeah, it's fine, just wanted a chat. Where are you?'

Pause.

'In the garden.' Well it was true. Just not their garden.

'Can you put Paige on?'

Brooke panicked.

'Er…no. She's at Dawn's.' It slipped out.

'That kid spends more time with Dawn than she does with you! Why's she there this time?'

Brooke froze and tried to come up with something feasible. She was staring at one of the gardeners planting a tree while trying to keep his madcap springer spaniel from running around it and getting in his way at the same time.

'I wanted to plant this tree I bought, but it was gonna be difficult to do with Paige around, so I popped her over there for an hour. I'm picking her up shortly. I'll put her on the phone to you when I get there.'

Tree? What made me say tree? Oh God, now I've got to go and buy and plant a bloody tree.

'What tree? Where? We haven't got room for any trees.

I wish you'd ask me about these things, Brooke, before you just go off and do them.' Dean sounded cross.

Brooke had to think on her feet.

'Oh I don't know what it's called. I just liked the look of it. Don't worry about it! I've gotta go, some delivery driver wants me to take a package or something I think.'

Brooke felt herself getting red, hot and bothered and she just wanted the phone call (aka lies) to end.

'OK. See you tonight. We'll talk about it then.' Dean sounded mildly exasperated.

As soon as Brooke got off the phone, she cursed herself for making up such a plainly absurd excuse. Now she was going to have to drive to the wretched garden centre on her way home and buy a tree. Of all things! And she certainly wouldn't have time to go to Ingatestone Hall. She'd have to do that tomorrow.

Why didn't I just say plant? Why did I have to say tree?

It got to around 4.30pm and Brooke asked Hugo if it'd be OK for her to leave a bit early. He said that was fine and she could either come early or stay late next time. That was another reason Brooke liked this job. They were so good to her about being flexible. She didn't think she could've done it unless they had been.

She ran out to her car, wheel-spinned out the car park at high speed like a seasoned Essex boy and stopped off at Bonnett's Garden Village. She ran to the tree section and hurried up and down the aisles looking for a tree that she liked the look of. She saw a trained Fagus Sylvatica that reminded her of the one that grew up the side of Ingatestone Hall.

Hah! That's Latin! That'll do nicely! Oh God. Thirty-six quid!

Brooke ummed and ahed. It was a lot of money. Money she didn't really have and definitely shouldn't be spending on a tree. Time was marching on, Dawn would be waiting for her to pick Paige up soon and she had to get home to plant the damn thing.

She raced up and down the tree aisles one more time looking at price tickets but they were all pretty expensive. If she was going to have to buy one, she may as well buy one she liked.

Oh sod it. I'll have to get it.

***

'What's that sticking out your window?'

Dawn was peering over at Brooke's car as she held Paige in her arms at the front door.

'Oh don't ask. It's a bloody tree. I've gotta go home and plant it now.' Brooke was looking up to the heavens exasperated as she took Paige from Dawn and strapped her into her car seat.

'Since when have you been into gardening?'

'Since never, that's when! I'll explain another time. I've gotta go, Dawn. How was she today?'

'Next question?' Dawn looked and sounded weary.

'Oh no, really? That bad?' Brooke was concerned.

'I've looked after a lot of kids in my time, but none of 'em have ever screamed like this one. The neighbours must think I'm torturing her or something. But she can go from being like that to silent as a mouse a few seconds later. It's so bloody weird.'

'Are you sure it's still OK to keep bringing her?' Brooke didn't really want to know the honest answer to that question.

'I need the money, Brooke. Besides, there's a pint of cider with my name written on it in the kitchen waiting for me. That always helps!'

That really wasn't the answer Brooke was hoping for. She knew Paige was difficult, but she'd always admired Dawn's stoic character. There was no way Brooke could've worked in secret like she had for the past three months without Dawn's help. She'd been not just her childminder but alibi as well.

'One day I'm gonna be a millionaire and then I'll see you right!'

They both laughed out loud at the mere thought of it.

'Enjoy your cider. See you next week.'

As Brooke drove home, her thoughts turned yet again to the big dilemma.

To have a hot tub? Or not to have a hot tub?

That was the question.

***

'Paige, please just stay away for a few minutes!' Brooke sounded on the edge.

She was desperately trying to dig a hole in ground that was hard, dry and seemingly not designed for planting trees of any kind, while batting Paige away with one hand, who was determined to help her mother at all costs.

She plunged her hands into the bag of compost, stole Brooke's trowel and hid it, plucked the leaves off the tree that was about to be planted, knocked over the full watering can and, to top it all off, ran out into the road at a critical moment, forcing Brooke to leap up and run after her, decorated in mud and looking somewhat stressed.

It was late. Dean would be home shortly; Paige hadn't been fed or bathed and Brooke was stressed and exhausted. The next thirty minutes were a manic rush to get everything done and in order, before Dean would be back.

At 7pm, he walked through the front door.

'Hi, babe!'

Brooke posed in her dressing gown, holding Paige in her pyjamas and trying her utmost to look happy, smiling and relaxed, like a 1950s housewife waiting for her husband to come home from work, but inwardly feeling rather ruffled, anxious and guilty. 'We just had a bath together, didn't we, my little pickle?'

'Nice! I saw the tree outside. It looks a bit of a mess out there. What happened?' Dean put his keys on the hall table, took off his coat, hung it up by its little gold chain on the coat rack in the hall and placed his moped helmet carefully on the floor, with the chin strap neatly folded inside. He became most agitated if Brooke ever moved it or hung it up or did anything different with it.

'Well. She's a clever girl is our daughter. After I got her back home from Dawn's, she noticed that something looked different out the front. She kept pointing at the tree and she started playing around with it, so now it needs a bit of tidying up.'

Brooke turned around and walked away into the kitchen to hide her face.

'D'ya fancy a brew?'

'Yeah, that'd be great, thanks. I still can't think why you bought a tree and for that tiny little space too, it seems mad!'

Dean was too weary to risk asking about Wimpole Hall. He was worried he might say the wrong thing, so he decided to speak to her about it the next morning. But he did want to suggest something else to her that he'd been thinking about ever since he'd been told about his promotion and pay rise.

Brooke just wanted to change the subject. In fact, she was beginning to realise that she was finding herself in more and more situations where she wanted to change the subject.

What is going on with my life?

'Babe, I was thinking. It's your birthday soon and… I wondered if you fancied having a party?' Dean kept his voice quite casual and calm as he talked through the doorway to the kitchen where Brooke had gone to make the tea.

Brooke was flabbergasted. Dean was usually the one to list all the reasons why she couldn't have a party. She poked her head round the doorway.

'Wow! What's happened? You normally avoid having parties like the plague.'

'Well, I was thinking the other day that things have probably been a bit tough for you lately. You're here all day every day with just Paige for company. You must get bored. No wonder you've started to go to the library. That really made me realise how desperate you must be when you first told me that. And I feel so bad about not being with you in A&E after Paige got hurt and having to put up with all that crap, I just want to make it all up to you.'

Brooke felt a shiver up her spine and the colour in her cheeks start to form. She carried on stretching out the process of making the tea as she said, 'Oh it's not all bad. I do have some nice days, you know.'

Then, as smoothly as a TV presenter trying to make a link to the next topic, she said, 'But I'd love to have a party. Funnily enough, I was thinking about that after our last disaster, but I didn't think you'd agree to another one after that.' She poked her head into the living room.

'Well I am agreeing to one. The twenty-eighth of September falls on a Saturday as it goes, so, good for your birthday!'

Brooke walked out of the kitchen with two mugs of tea and brought them over to the sofa. The red had left her cheeks and she'd forgotten about the first half of what Dean had said and was able to focus her mind entirely on the party part. No surprise there!

'Oh my god, Dean, it'd be fabulous. I've got some great ideas of things we could do!' Brooke leaned over to him and hugged him tight, looking up at him smiling and with a special feeling in her heart. Such a wonderful husband!

'Well we've got a few weeks to organise it all, and I know how much you love doing all that stuff, so I'll leave it up to you. The only thing I'd say is it can't be a BBQ, not only 'cause of what happened at the last one, but it'll be too cold to sit outside. So, we might have to limit numbers a bit so it's not like a sardine tin in here.'

'Mmm. Need to have a think.' Brooke chewed the inside of her mouth and started curling a ringlet of hair around her forefinger as her brain went into overdrive.

Since that now-infamous BBQ earlier in the summer, Brooke's world had opened up somewhat and what might've once made a great party in her eyes wouldn't make a great party now. She'd seen, heard, read and experienced things that in three short months had fundamentally begun to change things for her.

'I've been saving a bit of money for it, so I'll give you five hundred quid to make it a great night.' Dean fell back into the sofa, hands behind his head and smiled, feeling terribly chuffed with himself. The primitive man in him burst forth and his role as breadwinner was safe. He loved her so much and he finally felt secure in the knowledge that he was able to provide for his wife and make her proud of him on what was going to be a special day.

Brooke mentally ran through a list of all their friends as she began to consider all the possibilities open to her for holding what she was determined would be the best party of the year – if not the best party ever, for her and all their friends.

Roll on twenty-eighth September!

She went to bed that night thinking about what she'd done earlier that morning. She'd sat on the bed and reached underneath to pull out her special toy. She unwrapped it from the silk scarf in which it lay, opened one end of it and carefully extracted a wad of notes from inside the battery compartment. She quickly thumbed through the pile. Three thousand five hundred and forty pounds.

Wow! This is going to be one helluva party!

26

Lord D'Arcy's Naughty Secret

Brooke unstrapped Paige from her car seat and set her down on the grassy field where she immediately toddled off to explore this place she'd never seen before.

'Paige! Come to Mummy!'

Brooke bent down, smiled and held both her arms out encouraging Paige to run to her. Brooke prayed that she'd not have a screaming fit here but hoped that she'd be a well-behaved little girl and show her mother in a good light. She couldn't bear the thought that Lord D'Arcy might view her as one of those 'types', unable to control their brood.

Paige held Brooke's hand as they strolled up the driveway to Ingatestone Hall. As she walked, she kept repeating to herself 'Et venerunt ad debitum referre, Et venerunt ad debitum referre, Et venerunt ad debitum referre', determined to get it right.

She took a deep breath before entering the big black door again and squeezed Paige's hand for reassurance. It was quiet. No schoolchildren in sight. Paige pulled away from her mother's hands and made a move towards the gift shop area, where the array of glittering and hanging objects was too much for her to resist. Brooke yanked her back again and picked her up.

'I've come to see Lord D'Arcy.'

It was a different lady behind the reception desk from the one who was there the first time she came.

'May I ask who's calling?'

'It's Brooke De'Ath.'

'And may I ask what it's regarding?' As she looked at Brooke's ripped jeans, she couldn't hide her curiosity.

'It's just a personal visit.' Brooke tried to sound casual but assertive.

The woman scrutinised her. Brooke knew she was thinking 'what business can a girl like you possibly have with Lord D'Arcy?'

'One moment please.'

Brooke explored the gift shop holding Paige, pointing out all the interesting things and talking about them in her 'Mummy' voice. Paige was itching to get down, so Brooke finally let her pootle about for a few minutes while she waited for Lord D'Arcy. She followed her around closely, bent over and at the ready in case she went to pull anything over.

A booming voice suddenly reverberated around reception. 'Brooke, my dear, how lovely to see you!'

Brooke immediately went to pick Paige up, who didn't want to be picked up and so let out the most appalling scream, which led to the receptionist and Lord D'Arcy to physically jump from the shock. Brooke had devised a plan for such an incident. She whipped out an unwrapped Chupa Chups lollipop from her jeans pocket and thrust it into Paige's mouth. She didn't believe in dummies, but failed to see the irony of her alternative. Silence. She turned to face Lord D'Arcy and managed to compose herself momentarily before proudly announcing 'Et venerunt ad debitum referre.'

The receptionist's mouth dropped to the floor.

Lord D'Arcy looked absolutely delighted and replied, 'Bonum tibi est mulier puer honestus.'

The receptionist looked wide-eyed and mouth agape, from Brooke to Lord D'Arcy and back to Brooke again, utterly perplexed, but clearly in excited anticipation of more conversation.

Brooke laughed loudly, partly because she was relieved to remember what she was meant to say, but partly because she'd no idea what Lord D'Arcy had replied.

'Well you got me there, Geoffrey. No idea what you mean, I'm afraid!'

He laughed and walked over to greet her warmly as before with a kiss on both cheeks. Paige stared at him with those huge blue eyes, but continued sucking her lollipop. She reminded Lord D'Arcy of a girl version of Damien in *The Omen*.

'And who's this little sweetheart?' Geoffrey went to pinch her gloriously chubby cheeks, nervous about what she might do.

'I wouldn't do that if I were you, she might bite,' Brooke replied with a deadpan face. Lord D'Arcy had no idea whether to take her seriously or not as his blank look revealed and so he quickly retracted his fingers. Brooke smiled.

One all!

'This is Paige, my daughter. Sorry about the scream. I'm afraid she's got a habit of doing that. The lollipop's my emergency last resort. I didn't want her screaming in here!'

Geoffrey laughed and joked that it couldn't be any worse than the ghastly school parties that regularly descended upon the place. He looked Brooke straight in the eye and held her gaze.

I wish he wouldn't look at me like that.

'Do you have a few minutes to spare?' he asked.

For what seemed like the first time in ages, she wasn't in a hurry, so confirmed that, yes, she had some time to spare. Geoffrey smiled broadly and rubbed his hands.

'Jolly good! Well…last time you came, I forgot to show you which part of the Hall I actually live in. Would you like to see the "Inner sanctum"?' He spoke with mock reverence.

'Well as long as you don't mind your gaff being decimated by madam here.' Brooke tried to sound nonchalant, but was secretly thrilled to be asked and petrified at what Paige might do.

'I'm sure she'll be fine,' he lied. 'Follow me!'

He marched rather than walked, Brooke noticed. She

wondered if he'd been in the army. She couldn't help but observe his clothes as she followed.

What do you look like, Geoffrey?

Lord D'Arcy sported an outrageous pair of red trousers, a sort of yellow checked farmer's shirt that was badly frayed at the collar, no tie and a brown tweed jacket with leather elbow patches, one of which was hanging off. He wore brown lace-up brogues. The sunshine and heat were clearly irrelevant in his choice of attire that morning. His hair was styled in that combover fashion that balding men attempt when they're desperate to utilise every last hair on their head. He wasn't a bad-looking man, apart from a slightly red nose that indicated he might enjoy a tipple rather too frequently.

The fashion police certainly missed you this morning!

With Paige still in her arms, they went outside and meandered over to the south wing. It was another sunny day and it looked just beautiful from the outside. They entered through another door, which was shut off to members of the public. She walked through, head held high. Once in, Brooke was surprised at how different this part of the house was – quite ordinary in comparison. It had many more contemporary pieces of furniture and accessories than the main house, although there were still some exquisite antiques dotted around. There was an elegant Smallbone of Devizes kitchen, a TV, computer and printer revealing that it was impossible to live as his ancestors had done. She thought it rather sad that this idyllic place had been forced to come into the twenty-first century in order to survive and sad for Lord D'Arcy that he'd been unable to afford to maintain the building himself and had to rely on members of the public to keep the place going.

Fancy being chucked out your own gaff just 'cause you can't afford to stay in it!

Lord D'Arcy pointed out certain important items and talked about them if Brooke showed any interest. She smiled to herself as it reminded her of being shown around a house by an estate agent! He made her feel very relaxed and she chatted away when he asked her about Paige and Dean and Dean's job. She found him staring right at her again. He looked at her very intently and with a slight smile as he spoke. She got the distinct impression that he was flirting with her, which was flattering but a bit worrying.

God, I hope he doesn't want to show me up to his bedroom! Thank God I've got Paige with me!

'So, where's Lady D'Arcy then?'

'Oh, she's gone out for the day. She won't be back until er…much later.' Again, he stared at her and said it as though there were some deeper meaning.

'Oh right.' Brooke felt just a tiny bit concerned and wanted to change the subject.

'So, have you got your own separate garden from the main hall then?'

'Of course! Come. Let me show you.'

He led the way out of the French doors into a large and beautifully landscaped garden. She could see all manner of individually designed areas that'd all been separated by hedging or trees. It looked like lots of miniature gardens inside one big garden. Just like in the hall, there was clearly a particular route that he took when showing people his garden. One area had a rectangular pond with a tall yew hedge all around it and a fountain in the middle of it. Brooke gently encouraged Paige to follow her by playing a sort of hide and seek as Geoffrey watched, seemingly enchanted by the two of them. They moved on to an inviting herb and vegetable garden, where Paige headed for the little strawberries temptingly hanging down from their branches.

'Do you eat this lot yourself, Geoffrey?' Brooke enquired earnestly, wondering how on earth two people could get through so much fruit and vegetables.

'Good gracious, no! Jack, our main gardener, has ensured we produce way too much for just us to eat!'

'So who gets the rest of it then?'

'Heavens, I've no idea! It probably gets composted!'

This geezer's not for real! How the other half live!

'What?! Geoffrey! That's well out of order! There're people starving all over the world and you're just chucking this stuff in the bin?' Brooke was shocked and most upset by this casual revelation.

'You know what you should do? You should take it to the local foodbank. They've recently set one up in

Romford in Collier Row.'

'What a jolly good idea! I'll talk to Jack and my wife about that. Why didn't we think of it?' Lord D'Arcy seemed genuinely enthusiastic about the idea.

Brooke walked on, somewhat perturbed by Lord D'Arcy's apparent indifference to the privileges he enjoyed. The third area they wandered into was a rose garden still with many bushes in full bloom and whose smell was overpowering. Brooke snapped out of her self-righteousness immediately.

'Oh the smell! It's just gorgeous! I've never smelled roses like this before. The scent is so strong.'

'That's because we only plant old roses. They have the best perfume. Do you know it takes four tonnes of roses to make one kilo of rose oil?' Lord D'Arcy delighted in teaching Brooke this little-known fact.

'Wow! No. I didn't. That's unbelievable! No wonder my Jo Malone rose perfume's so bloody expensive! Four tonnes?!'

Brooke had been given some London Velvet Rose & Oud by Dean for Valentine's Day and swore she'd never smelled a perfume more divine. This rose garden reminded her of it and it made her close her eyes and sniff slowly and deeply.

Paige went running ahead into the next hedged-off area, but reappeared within seconds, looking very animated and babbling away. She seemed to want Brooke to join her so she could show her something. Brooke laughed and apologised to Lord D'Arcy for being usurped. Paige dragged her behind the tall topiary leaving him behind.

'OH...MY...GOD...GEOFFREY!'

Lord D'Arcy jogged over to the topiary hedge, imagining the worst. As he appeared, Brooke shrieked out again, 'No! You've only got a hot tub! That's so sick!'

Lord D'Arcy was panting from his short sprint and was alarmed. 'Why is it sick?'

'No. Not that kind of sick!'

'Well what other kind of sick is there?' His face was one of genuine confusion.

Brooke roared. 'Oh, Geoffrey, you're *so* funny! Sick means cool – you know...good...fantastic!'

He looked relieved and gave a half-hearted laugh.

'Well that's alright then. Do you like it? It's my naughty little secret. My wife can't stand it. Says it's vulgar! I'm not allowed to tell anyone we meet that I have one. She even made me put up topiary to hide it! She didn't want anyone coming to visit us to be able to see it from the house! Only our closest friends know about it and they give me such a hard time I can't tell you!'

Brooke felt chuffed and excited and couldn't resist probing him more. 'So...what made you buy a hot tub then, Geoffrey, when your wife obviously doesn't approve?' She sounded like Stacey Dooley at her inquisitive best.

'Well, I have arthritis and my doctor said it'd be good for me,' he replied simply.

'Ha! That's exactly what I told Mrs Townsend. But she thinks they're vulgar too. But I'd read about the heat being good for joints.'

'Quite right too. But just so you know, Letitia is one of those friends who doesn't know I've got one, so it's entre nous…yes?' He bent forward and tapped his forefinger on the side of his nose a few times.

'Well I dunno what entre nous is, but your secret's safe with me! I just can't believe you've got one. So *you* don't think they're vulgar then?'

'Well I don't really know. I don't know why my wife thinks that. I mean why would warm water be considered vulgar? I just don't get why they're so hung up about it?'

'Maybe it's because *certain people* have given them a bad name.'

'Like who?'

'Well I dunno; people like…Joey Essex from *TOWIE* and all that lot on I'm a *Celebrity Get Me Out Of Here*!'

'Where's Towie? And what's "I'm a celebrity out here?"'

Brooke roared, laughing again, and Geoffrey looked rather bemused and a tad hurt.

'Why are you laughing?' he asked innocently.

'Oh my God, Geoffrey, are you seriously telling me you haven't heard of *TOWIE* or *I'm A Celebrity*?'

'No. I haven't.'

'Where have you *been*? Don't you watch telly?'

'Not a lot, no. I watch the news, *Daily Politics* and

David Attenborough documentaries. Sometimes I watch *University Challenge*.' He seemed vaguely perplexed and worried about his answers.

'Holy moly! I bet you're a right laugh down the pub! Well, I'm gonna have to get you a bit more streetwise, Geoffrey. So…TOWIE stands for *The Only Way Is Essex* and is about a group of friends and family who live in Essex, what they get up to and all that, and the TV camera is on them the whole time. *I'm A Celebrity* is about a group of twenty-somethings who get put in the jungle together and get given crazy stuff to do like lie in a snake pit or eat spiders and stuff and the public vote them out if they don't like them.'

'Good lord, that sounds ghastly! Why on *earth* would anyone do that?'

'Because it's a laugh! I tell you what, I can get you an episode up on YouTube and you'll see what it's all about! Come on, take me to your computer. Please tell me you've a computer.'

'Of course I do…but what's YouTube?'

'You're 'aving a laugh! Right…I'm on a mission now. Let's go.' Brooke shook her head in disbelief.

She picked up Paige and they started walking back to the house. Geoffrey led the way to his computer and looked mildly offended when they arrived at his desk and Brooke laughed at it.

'Geoffrey, this should be in a museum! This computer's gotta be at least five years old.'

'What's wrong with that?!'

'Never mind. Let's just get this clip up.'

The next ten minutes were a complete revelation to Lord Geoffrey D'Arcy, 18th Baron of Ingatestone. Never in his life had he ever seen such behaviour. Never before had he known that he could find such things on the internet. He displayed amazement, shock, horror, amusement and yet felt embarrassed, ashamed, concerned and… what was it? What else did he feel? Oh yes. That was it! Embarrassingly highly aroused. All those glorious girls half-naked, frolicking around in their bikinis in a hot tub and throwing themselves at those chaps. He couldn't take his eyes off them, as his aristocratic member stood to attention.

Brooke watched Lord D'Arcy watching YouTube. A smile crept across her face as it dawned on her that just as she'd been introduced to a whole new world, of which she wasn't a part, she was introducing Geoffrey to a world of which he was most definitely not a part – and quite frankly never would be. But it was fun to watch, anyway.

'So…can you see why some people *might* think hot tubs are "vulgar"?' Brooke said the final word in an exaggerated fashion while holding her fingers up to indicate she was putting quote marks around the word.

He seemed rather anxious and at a loss as to know what to say. It was as though he was afraid to speak for fear of incriminating himself, so he remained silent. Brooke examined his every facial movement. She didn't want to be pushy, but she really did want to know the answer to her question. She looked at him quizzically, making it clear to him that she really did require an answer.

'Brooke. Would you like to join me…in the hot tub?'

Oh my giddy aunt! No no NO! Please don't say he's misread all this.

Lord D'Arcy was totally oblivious to what Brooke was thinking and went into self-absorbed mode.

'I had no idea that this sort of thing…' He waved his hand at his computer screen 'went on anywhere, never mind in hot tubs.'

Oh shit shit shit! What have I done?

She mustered up every ounce of diplomacy she possessed. She thought about Lady Townsend and how much she admired her ability to deliver bad news in the most charming way. Now was her time. Now she had to do this on her own, without help or advice.

What would Lady Townsend say in this super awks situation?

She composed herself for a second time the same morning and spoke slowly and carefully.

'Geoffrey. I feel…'

What's that bloody word?

'privileged…that you've asked me to share in your… enjoyment…of your hot tub, but I really don't think it'd be…it just wouldn't be…'

Got what's that word Lady Townsend always uses at times like this?

'Appropriate.'

Geoffrey's body language changed palpably. He suddenly looked like a pathetic man, devoid of influence or power, driven only by the organ dangling between his legs and the most primitive desire known to man. No amount of status, money, knowledge, intelligence or contacts mattered at this moment. He was just a man. An ordinary man.

Up until then, Paige had been playing beautifully with some toys that Geoffrey had in a box in the corner of his living room for when his grandchildren visited. But as was Paige's way, she suddenly ran over to Brooke looking for all the world as though she was about to have one of her screaming fits. Oh what joyous luck!

For the only time in Brooke's life, she was grateful that Paige was about to scream.

'Geoffrey, I've gotta go. I can tell that Paige is about to have one of her screaming fits. Thank you for inviting me to see your inner sanctum.'

No that's not quite right. That's not how Lady Townsend would've said it.

She stood up, racking her brains for a better way of saying what she wanted to say. 'Really. You've been *most* kind. Thank you *so* much for a lovely morning. We've both had *such* a wonderful time.'

Gracious. That's what she was trying to be – without actually knowing that that was what gracious meant and she even *sounded* a little like Lady Townsend, emphasising certain words.

Lord D'Arcy reverted from a stance of humiliation, to his more usual upright demeanour surprisingly easily. His sort were a dab hand at brushing emotions aside; at least on the face of it. You don't get buggered to Kingdom Come at Eton and survive by being emotional. He put up the usual old barriers and responded in the only way he knew how. Self-deprecation.

'Forgive me, Brooke. I'm just a silly old bugger lost in today's world. I do so hope that I haven't offended you. Please forget that I ever made such an appalling suggestion. I don't know what I was thinking.'

Brooke felt so sorry for him and just wanted to give him a cuddle, but she knew instinctively that she mustn't. So, she changed the subject; something at which she was fast becoming an expert.

'Nothing to forgive, Geoffrey. Honestly. It's fine.' These words came very naturally. She delved into her handbag and retrieved the thirty pounds that she'd got ready to give him.

She handed it over. 'Well. Here it is, Geoffrey. Thirty quid.' She hoped that this would mean an end to their betting games, once and for all.

'Well I'd love to take it, but you appear to have forgotten part of our bet. What's the Latin motto underneath our clocktower?'

Brooke shut her eyes and recited, 'Sans Dieu Rien.'

'And what does it mean?'

'Nothing Without God.'

'Nunc nihil mihi debes.'

Geoffrey looked her straight in the eye and wouldn't look away.

'I believe that you just said "Now you owe me nothing"', Brooke said.

Lord D'Arcy shrugged his shoulders as if to say, "There is nothing else I have to offer you, nothing else I have to say."

'Brooke. You're always welcome here. I hope you know that. You're such a refreshing person to have around.'

She nodded and said, 'Thank you.'

Paige indicated that she wanted to be picked up. So Brooke plucked her from the floor and said, 'Say bye-bye, Lord D'Arcy.'

'Baaabaaaalerdsee.'

Brooke and Lord D'Arcy both laughed at her bold attempt to pronounce his name.

Lord D'Arcy dithered for a moment or two before deciding to go for it. He placed his hands firmly around her waist and kissed her lightly on both cheeks.

'Goodbye, Brooke. It's been a pleasure. As always.'

Brooke smiled and walked away, holding Paige tightly and thinking of Dean.

And trying to decide whether a hot tub was so bad after all.

27

Visit To Wimpole Hall

'Babe. Have you ever heard of a place called Wimpole Hall?' Dean knew she wouldn't have, so he felt he'd be safe in his approach.

'Yeah, that's near Cambridge, isn't it? It's one of them National Trust houses. I think that the poet Kipling's daughter owned it once and then sold it to them. Why?'

Dean was floored. Completely floored!

'How the hell do you know that?' He simply couldn't hide his surprise.

Brooke shrugged her shoulders and said, 'I dunno. I must've read it somewhere. What about it anyway?'

The concept of Brooke reading anything apart from *Hello!* magazine was one which Dean couldn't get his head around at all. Little did he know that her penchant for *Country Life* (who'd recently carried an article about Wimpole Hall) meant that Brooke had prior knowledge.

'Well. Someone at work mentioned that they'd been with their kid and reckoned we should go. He thought we'd really enjoy it. So, based on the fact that I'm owed a day in lieu, I made an on-the-spot decision to book us tickets for Monday next week! How about that?'

Brooke stiffened. She'd be at Mrs Townsend's on Monday. 'I can't, Dean.'

'Why not? It's not like you're busy!' Dean retorted sharply and looking confused.

'I've got something else on.' Brooke was rapidly, silently, inwardly racking her brains to think of what to say next; she knew Dean would pursue her about her answer.

'What something else?'

'I can't remember, but that day rings a bell, I know it does. Let me check the calendar.' She walked into the kitchen.

Think, Brooke. C'mon, think! What can I say? What can I say? Tell him about the job? I just can't, he'd be livid!

She just couldn't do it. Her heart pounded. She had the same excruciating blank that used to come over her in exams at school. It was like her brain was paralysed, unable to shake out of its frozen position; caught in a loop that just went round and round. She took a deep breath (she'd read that could help with de-stressing), then gave herself a moment to think rationally.

Maybe I can just take the day off? Maybe Mrs Townsend won't mind?

She relaxed. She had to be quick, or Dean would soon suspect something.

She made a play of flipping over the calendar pages noisily and then shouted out 'Ah, no! Wrong day. Sorry. In that case, yes! Let's do it! What a nice idea!'

Brooke said all this in the safety and comfort of the kitchen. Out of sight of Dean thank God, for her eyes and body language would surely have given away her culpability.

***

As Dean drove up the grand drive, the car spluttered and made a banging noise as they headed towards the car park. Brooke stared wistfully out the window. Something about this was punishing for her. What was it? The lies? The guilt? Or was it the fact that she seemed to be drawn in and towards these historic places for some inexplicable reason? Why was her interest piqued so, by this world? In her heart she felt a strange sense of fate. Poor Brooke! She couldn't really explain it; not even to herself, let alone anyone else. It made her feel both excited and anxious. It was like she belonged, yet didn't belong.

Get a grip, you're just Brooke De'Ath from Brentwood. An Essex girl.

Dean parked, got out, dived under the car to check that the exhaust hadn't fallen off, and then immediately went into assessor mode.

Was the car park clean, tidy and well maintained?

He looked around, walked over to a bin and noticed it overflowing with rubbish.

'What are you doing, Dean?' Brooke shouted impatiently as she struggled to get Paige out of her car seat.

'This bin is disgusting and it's only eleven o' clock.'

'You're unreal, you are! Is that all you can say? We drive over an hour to get to this place and all you can talk about is the bloody rubbish bin!' She rolled her eyes.

'Sorry, I just couldn't help notice it, that's all.' Dean rapidly got out his phone and made a note, strode back to the car and helped Brooke.

Mr Conscientious had read and re-read the visit brief about twenty times the night before, so he didn't have to refer to it at all on the day. He was going to have to dig deep into the recesses of his mind to ensure he remembered every single thing he had to do.

First buy tickets.

They strolled over to the courtyard which housed the ticket office, toilets, the gift shop, a second-hand bookshop and a cafe.

Ask for tickets and note if they invite you to become a member of the National Trust.

'Why don't you and Paige have a wander round the shop and I'll go and collect the tickets?' Which of course he'd not actually bought.

That suited Brooke well, so she happily made her way to the gift shop with Paige, while Dean went to the ticket office.

'Two adults and one toddler please for the house, farm and gardens.'

A very jolly lady in twin set and pearls smiled and asked, 'Are you a member?'

'No.'

'Well would you be interested in joining? You can get family membership for only sixty pounds today – it's normally a hundred and twenty. That gives you free unlimited visits to any National Trust properties all over the UK for a year. There are some lovely places to go for walks and, if you have any little ones, there are so many activities and events that we put on, you'll never be short of anything to do at the weekends and school holidays.'

If you're asked, please join so we can assess the efficiency of the process. (The direct debit will be cancelled by us shortly afterwards.)

'Well that sounds pretty good as it goes, so yes. I think we will join!'

'Splendid. Do take a seat and I'll just get all the paperwork. It won't take long.'

God I hope not, or Brooke'll wonder where I've got to.

Even though Dean was quick, it wasn't quick enough and sure enough Brooke appeared in the ticket office.

'What you doing, Dean?' She went over and looked down at the direct debit form he'd almost completed. Her eyes enlarged.

Dean had been caught. He couldn't think on his feet, so he said simply. 'I thought we ought to join. It's a bargain!'

'God, Dean, can we really afford it? It's hardly a priority at the moment, is it? What with my party coming up.' She was totally flummoxed as to why Dean would want to join something like the National Trust. If only the poor girl knew!

Dean could sense her bewilderment. 'This lady has just told me about the great things they've got for kids, all over the country, and I know you've been trying to make sure that Paige gets a…a…er better education than we had. So, I thought it was a bonza idea.'

Clever Dean. He knew precisely which buttons to press!

Brooke looked at the lady, stood a little taller and smiled proudly. 'My mum and dad would never have taken me to anywhere like this. My husband's right. I want our daughter to experience things and go to places we never did and learn about history and stuff. I was interested in history at school, but I was rubbish at it.'

Phew!

Dean breathed a sigh of relief as he completed the paperwork.

Brooke analysed the lady, who reminded her a little bit of Mrs Townsend. She had the same neat bob and that demeanour! Oh how she longed to have it! What was it about these people? How did they achieve it? That sort of effortless, elegant graciousness. Brooke always felt such a common tart!

As soon as Dean was finished, they were given their book and their stickers to wear for the day. They had a very quick cup of tea in the courtyard cafe and then decided to tackle the house first while Paige was seemingly content.

It was a beautiful early autumnal day, still quite warm

for this time of year and Wimpole Hall looked impressive.

'D'ya know what this reminds me of? The big house that belonged to that bloke in that TV series *Pride and* something or other – what was his name? Mr D'Arcy… or something?' Dean was soaking up the magnificent frontage in wonderment. 'Isn't it beautiful?!'

The mere mention of the name Mr D'Arcy sent Brooke into a tizzy. Only, of course, she was thinking about a different Mr D'Arcy. She felt a combination of terror and thrill at the memory.

'Yeah, it's gorgeous. I can't wait to go inside.'

With well-rehearsed precision, they lifted the buggy up the steps and into the entrance hall, where the charming guide explained how to navigate around the house and gave them a mini guidebook.

Please ensure you ask all the guides you come across questions to test their knowledge throughout your tour of the house.

The first thing Dean noticed was the word SALVE! It was formed from floor tiles at the entrance to the hall on the right. The guide was right next to him and she saw him looking at it.

'What does Salve mean?' Dean enquired, pretending to be interested.

'It's Latin for hello!'

Dean stopped dead in his tracks and stared at Brooke. The guide smiled.

'There's no need to ask me. Your wife clearly knows

the answer!'

To say that Dean was surprised was an understatement.

'How come you know that?!'

Brooke secretly enjoyed a rather warm glow of superiority (a most unique experience), but she also found Dean's reaction extremely funny and couldn't help laughing.

'Seriously, Brooke, how d'ya know that?'

She resorted to the standard 'I dunno, I must've read it somewhere.'

'I'm getting a bit worried about you and all this reading malarkey. What's happening to my ditsy blonde wife?'

All three of them laughed, but inside Dean felt inexplicably uncomfortable. Brooke, on the other hand, began to realise for the first time in her life what people meant when they said 'knowledge is power'. And it felt good. Very good indeed!

He'd have to ask the guide another question.

'So, who lives here now?' Dean asked.

The guide went on to explain, but encouraged him to look at the various exhibitions in some of the rooms that gave more detail.

Well she's very impressive.

Dean got his phone out and pretended to be replying to a message, but he was actually typing in his comments about the guide. Brooke had already made her way into the hall and was looking attentively at the paintings. Paige was playing with her white rabbit in her buggy, so all was good.

They moved around the house, into the ante chapel, then fairly swiftly into the Inner Hall and Brooke examined the Roman marble busts. She tested herself and recognised Augustus. She smiled. Dean had found the cards that explained who all the busts were but he was more bothered about the battered condition of them than he was the content. More surreptitious notes were made. They moved onto the Saloon and felt compelled to gaze out at the large bay window looking out onto the parterre hedges. Being symmetrical and neat, like well-groomed soldiers standing to attention, this was most appealing to Dean's perfectionist tendencies, so he took a photo through the window.

Maybe we could do something like that in our garden?

Soon they strolled through to the magnificent Yellow Drawing Room. Paige came alive in her buggy the moment they entered this exquisite yellow space and pointed at the huge dome and the gasolier hanging down from it. She babbled away and became obviously desperate to get out of her buggy, banging around and jumping up and down on her bottom.

'Shall I let her out? I'm worried she might do a runner!' Dean bit his lip.

'Oh she'll be fine. At least she's not screaming. I think we should let her out, but keep hold of her hand.'

Nervously, Dean unstrapped her and plonked her

down on the floor. Paige instantly ran over to the dome and looked up all the while pointing at it. She held out her hand and opened and closed her fingers several times. He walked over and she grabbed his hand, continuing to chatter away, Dean clueless as to what she was saying. He laughed as she proceeded to lie down on her back waving her legs and arms in the air, still pointing and looking up.

'Maybe she's trying to tell us when it was built!' Brooke joked. They laughed as they watched their daughter completely captivated. The guide in the room looked on kindly and made a comment about what a lovely daughter they had.

God, if only they knew!

Brooke glowed with pride whilst praying that she didn't start screaming.

Although Dean showed some genuine curiosity, he was more focussed on asking the guides questions, giving Brooke an entirely false notion about his level of interest in paintings, antiques and history.

She was really rather pleased. She hadn't thought of Dean as someone with any interest in anything to do with the past, but began to think that he might be more cultured than she'd given him credit for. She decided that this could work to her advantage in the future and at some point she could actually introduce him into her newfound other world.

Brooke looked around at the colour of the walls. This yellow was like no other yellow she'd ever seen.

This would be the perfect colour for if and when we ever get a summer house.

They walked through the Red Room into the Long Gallery, where Paige saw a long run of space in front of her and tumbled all the way down and back again, thankfully not knocking anything or anyone over in the process. Dean found out from one of the guides that they still held concerts in this room.

They wandered through the Book Room and Library fairly rapidly, as Paige was beginning to flag. Brooke held her in her arms as she pointed out the porcelain figurines in the South Drawing Room and the Ante Room, all the while explaining to her what they were. Dean occasionally looked over and was enamoured with the way his wife talked to and tried to involve their daughter.

They moved through the Breakfast Room and into the Grand Dining Room, where Brooke visibly gasped. She asked Dean to hold Paige's hand for a moment while she walked around for a proper look. Brooke was in her element. She wandered around the enormous dining table looking carefully at the place settings, trying to date the various items. The candelabras and other pieces that adorned the centre of the table were of particular interest and she spent a good fifteen minutes there until Dean chivvied her along. They went up the grand staircase looking at the magnificent paintings along the way. Paige ran up and down several times, forcing Dean to follow in case she fell.

In the Lord Chancellor's bedroom, Paige looked perplexed and excited as she pointed to the rather gaudy domed top to the bed and babbled for some minutes with the most expressive face, showing what appeared to be disdain and contempt one minute and delight the next! Dean and Brooke both laughed out loud, as did several other visitors who clearly found her chatter amusing. Oh how easy it was to get a false impression!

Dean found himself staring at a most unusual chair in Mrs Bambridge's bedroom. It had a large strange-shaped hole in the back of it and he couldn't work out what it was for. The guide came over to him, having perfectly read his body language.

'Do you know why there is a hole in that chair?' she asked Dean.

'No. I'm just trying to work it out.'

'The bustle of a lady's dress in those days was so large that this hole made room for them to tuck it through.'

'Blimey, that must've been uncomfortable!'

'Comfort wasn't really what they thought about back then!'

Dean was impressed yet again. He looked around furtively, took out his phone and made a quick note. He liked the way the guides were secretly educating him without making him feel stupid. By this time, he was so interested in what he was seeing that he forgot why he was there in the first place.

They arrived in the Print Room and Brooke

recognised some of the artists; Geoffrey D'Arcy had others at Ingatestone Hall.

When they got to the Bath House, Paige squealed with delight and bent over to look into the now-empty plunge bath. It was almost as if she instinctively understood that it was meant to be filled with water. She was itching to go down the steps and kept trying to escape Dean's grasp. When he didn't give in, she did the only thing she knew to get her parents' full attention. As the assortment of visitors gathered around the top of the bath, she let rip the mother of all screams.

'Oh for God's sake!' Dean exploded.

'Just get her out of here, Dean! Please! I just wanna finish off the house quickly and I'll join you at the end, outside.' She shooed him away as if he were a dirty fly and he scarpered with Paige in his arms, who by this time was reaching decibels unknown to mankind.

Brooke abruptly became very aware of everyone staring at her, but smiled. 'It takes all sorts!'

She tried to walk ahead of the pack, so she didn't have to face them throughout the rest of the house. She was intrigued by the illusion created in the chapel, but as soon as she saw the rest of the people catching up, she left and trotted down to the basement corridor. She laughed as she looked at the rows of bells in the servants' quarters. It made her think of Hugo and how Mrs Townsend would shout very loudly in order to be heard and how Hugo came running but always appeared unruffled as he entered the room. She decided she might recommend to Lady Townsend that she install this rather quaint bell system.

Brooke loved the Housekeeper's Room and the Butler's Pantry, but she was particularly taken with the Steward's Room where she spied an original Louis Vuitton set of luggage. Good heavens! She nearly wet herself with excitement! She spent several minutes poring over it in detail and at the luggage label with Mrs Bambridge's name clearly handwritten on it.

She could've stayed another half an hour easily, but was conscious that Dean would be waiting for her outside with Paige, so she left feeling short-changed and with a huge sigh.

Why am I so interested in this? Where's it come from?

'Thank God you're out! Paige is hungry, love. We need to go and have something to eat.'

Dean looked and sounded highly anxious. He'd strapped Paige back into her buggy and started pushing it towards the Rectory Restaurant, which is where the visit brief had instructed him to eat lunch.

'Sorry. Yeah, that's cool, I'm starving too! This place is just fantastic, don't you think?'

'Yeah, it's pretty impressive as it goes. I wasn't sure I'd enjoy it really, to be honest, but I thought you might.'

'Well I did and I'd love to come back when I've got a bit more time and maybe without madam here! Where are we going?'

'There's a restaurant here called The Rectory. I thought

we'd eat there.'

'Won't it be a bit expensive? Maybe we can just grab a sarnie and a cuppa and eat it out on the grass here?'

Dean hadn't thought about this. He'd not expected Brooke to interfere with his visit brief.

'Naaah! It'll be fine! It's a treat! Let's just enjoy the day!'

Brooke was bemused, as this was so unlike Dean. Mr Cautious, Mr Careful, Mr Don't Spend Beyond Your Means and yet here he was, seemingly nonchalantly splashing out on a load of mediocre food and over-priced drinks!

'OK. You're the boss!' she replied with a tone that implied he would have to take all the blame if anything went wrong.

As they entered the restaurant, they appeared to catch the last of the hot food before they started serving afternoon tea. As they were choosing some jacket potatoes with fillings, the staff were clearing dishes away.

Was there a good choice of food on offer?

No. It's crap!

Was the food attractively presented?

No. The jackets look dry and stale and the fillings look like they've been eaten already and spewed out about four hours later.

Were the staff friendly and helpful?

'Would it be possible to just have some baked beans mashed up for my daughter?'

'No. We don't do that. She can have it with a jacket

potato for four ninety-five.'

'Well she's only fourteen months and can't possibly eat a whole jacket potato. Can't she just have the beans and you charge us for those?'

'No. We can't do that. Sorry.'

'But why not? You've got the beans. You just need to make up a price for beans.'

'No. We can't do that. The till has got all the prices pre-inputted and we can't change them.'

Dean sighed and ordered another jacket potato with baked beans. They then ordered two teas and a hot chocolate for Paige. Dean watched on as the girl walked over to the back of the counter at the pace of a snail. She chatted to a colleague as she loaded four heaped teaspoons of chocolate powder into the mug and added water and milk with no attempt to give it a proper stir. She brought it aimlessly to the counter.

'We ordered two teas as well.'

'Oh yeah.'

She walked back to the counter again, even slower than before and stood talking to her manager for a minute or two as Dean waited with his hot chocolate.

'Excuse me, but my hot chocolate's getting cold!' Dean complained.

'Yeah, I won't be a minute.' She turned back round to carry on speaking with her manager in the most blasé fashion.

Dean couldn't bear it. He could barely hold back from

leaping over the counter and making the tea himself.

No. She was utterly miserable, inefficient, unhelpful, a jobsworth, infuriating and she couldn't give a shit.

Not that he'd write it exactly like that, but these people weren't going to get a good assessment and he hadn't even eaten anything yet. More notes.

Brooke just glowered at Dean the whole time with one of her looks. The silent message was clear. 'What did I tell you? Waste of money. We should've brought our own sarnies.'

Brooke managed to find them a table to sit at. She retrieved Paige's Tommy Tippee beaker from the bag and poured the hot chocolate into it. At the bottom of the mug was a large, dark, glutinous mass of undissolved chocolate powder. She tutted and swirled it around violently to try and pick up some of the gunk. Instead she succeeded in swirling it so hard it came flying out the beaker and all over Dean.

Dean being the fastidious chap that he was, went a bit crazy, like he'd been stung by a wasp or something. Paige started giggling, which in turn made Brooke laugh, although she knew Dean well and knew he'd not see the funny side of this at all. Several other people in the restaurant were watching him, including the restaurant manager.

Do nothing to bring attention to yourself. The last mystery shopper was recognised. You won't be reimbursed your expenses if you're recognised.

Suddenly Dean stood perfectly still, stopped speaking and sat down calmly with a forced smile on his face. Brooke appeared confused at this sudden turn of mood. For the rest of the time they ploughed through their almost inedible twenty-five-pound lunch in near silence.

Was your food the correct temperature and tasty?

No. It was shit.

Was your beverage the correct temperature and tasty?

No. It was shit.

Would you return to this restaurant or recommend it to friends?

Over my dead body.

They spent less than half an hour in the restaurant and Dean went straight to the loo afterwards where he made detailed comments about the restaurant. He carried out his usual microscopic evaluation of the toilets before leaving.

'What was your loo like?' Dean enquired of Brooke

'You what?'

'The gents was pretty good, I was just wondering what the ladies was like, that's all.'

'You're weird, you are. Why do you care? They were OK as loos go. No soap left though.'

Were the toilets clean, fresh-smelling and well stocked with soap and towels?

God, how do I answer that? They were clean and smelled OK, had plenty of hand towels but they didn't have soap in the ladies. But I'm the assessor, not Brooke. So is that a yes or a no?

'Come on, let's go to the farm. Paige is gonna love this!' Brooke forgot about everything else that'd gone before and pushed Paige quickly in her buggy as though it were a race, shouting, 'We're going to see the sheep! We're going to see the little piggies! We're going to see the horses!'

Paige giggled as she bounced up and down in her buggy.

Were there signs warning you to wash your hands before and after dealing with the animals?

Oh God, I didn't see. I'll have to look on the way out.

Were the guides alert to visitors who weren't sticking to the rules?

Will have to wait and see.

Were the guides knowledgeable about the care and feeding of the animals?

Did the guides speak and behave appropriately with your children?

Dean began to feel under pressure. This was the part of the visit that Angie had told him was most important. He had to remember everything.

As they approached the goats, pointing at Paige, Dean asked a guide, 'Can she stroke the goats?'

'Yes, but she needs to be careful as they can bite sometimes.'

'Come on, Paige,' said Brooke in her Mummy voice. 'Stroke the little goatees!'

Paige looked up at her mother, confused. Brooke demonstrated what she wanted Paige to do, then placed her hand on top of the goat's head and helped her stroke it. Paige pushed away Brooke's hand so she could stroke on her own. She was firm. Very firm. Too firm. Within less than a minute she wailed as the goat decided that her fingers made for a tastier lunch than its usual fayre.

All the staff came running over immediately and one dived inside to get a first-aid kit and the accident book. All the other visitors had moved at least fifteen metres away to rid themselves of the inhuman noise emanating from this angelic-looking infant.

Paige went purple, Brooke went red and Dean went pale as they tried to calm her down – an impossible task, given the circumstances.

Oh my God, how the hell am I going to write this up?

'I think we need to take her to the first-aid office for a plaster, if that's OK?' said the animal guide.

Brooke had that resigned face. She'd been here before. Nothing ever really surprised her with Paige.

'OK. Well let's just get it over with so we can get back to seeing the animals.'

'We can't stay now! She needs to go home! She should have a tetanus,' Dean exclaimed.

'Why? She'll be fine. It's just a bite! There's loads more for her to see yet!' Brooke was laissez-faire.

'But she's hurt! She needs to rest and recover!' Dean was mortified.

'Rubbish – kids go through far worse than that and survive!'

'Actually, we need to take her to get some first aid. We also need to compile an accident report,' said the guy who they'd been talking to prior to the incident.

Dean was thrown into a state. He was beside himself with worry about his daughter but he hadn't yet finished the assessment. He was thoroughly torn.

'Well OK, let's get her sorted and just see how she goes.'

Do nothing to bring attention to yourself. The last mystery shopper was recognised. You won't be reimbursed your expenses if you're recognised.

So they all trudged off to the office, serenaded by Paige's world-class screaming, and where (thank goodness) they had lollipops. The moment she was offered one by the staff the screaming stopped. She grabbed it, smiled, babbled and shoved it unceremoniously in her mouth. Purple wet face, tears, screams, tantrums – all gone in a split second.

If you had a problem or complaint, did the staff deal with it appropriately?

Considering they were all at risk of losing their hearing, I think they did brilliantly!

While the guys were finishing off the bandaging of the finger, Dean took the opportunity to make a few more notes on his phone.

'Dean. What you doing on your bloody phone? Our

daughter is at death's door, according to you, and you're sitting here texting!'

Dean quickly put it in his pocket and apologised, lying that Martin had just messaged him about going out for a drink.

The entire episode was over and done with in less than twenty minutes, after which they went back to where they left off, but with Paige nursing a goat bite. Persuading her to stroke or even go near any other animal after that was a challenge. She was happy to look from a distance but no more than that, so the rest of the visit was somewhat subdued.

By about 3pm Paige was getting very grumpy and Brooke decided it was time to go home. Dean willingly agreed. His mind was bursting with information that he'd not been able to get down and he was very worried he'd forget it. They got to the car park and Dean suddenly remembered that he hadn't visited the gift shop.

Oh shit shit shit!

'Babe, I need a slash. Sorry, I don't think I can hold on for an hour. I won't be a minute.'

Without waiting for a response, he chucked her the car keys and ran to the gift shop.

Were all the staff wearing a name badge?

Dean walked quickly round the shop looking only at name badges of all three staff. He was satisfied.

Was the gift shop well laid out?

He walked very quickly around it again and decided

yes.

Were the shelves filled with stock?

They look alright to me.

Were the staff knowledgeable about the items in the shop? You should make a purchase under ten pounds.

'Excuse me, but do you know if these biscuits are gluten-free?' It was the first question that came into Dean's mind as he brought a tin of what looked like shortbread to the till.

'I'm so sorry, I don't know. But don't worry, I can find out for you.'

'No, please don't worry.' Dean was aware he should already have been back at the car.

'It's no trouble, I just need to make a quick phone call.'

'Oh it's fine, really. I'll take the risk and get them anyway.' Dean shifted from one foot to the other as his desperation to make a purchase and leave grew.

'Oh no, I couldn't possibly sell them to you if there is an allergy problem.'

Fuck fuck fuck!

Dean waited patiently and diligently for the lady to come back and reassure them that the biscuits were indeed gluten-free.

He said he'd take them and speedily put his debit card into the card reader.

'I'm sorry, sir, but your card has been declined.'

'What? Are you sure? There's nothing wrong with my card!' Dean displayed wide-eyed horror.

'Perhaps sir would like to try again.'

Dean's heart was palpitating as he put his PIN in a second time.

Long pause.

'OK, well it seems to have worked this time.'

Thank Christ!

'Great. Thanks.'

As soon as the transaction went through, he grabbed the biscuits and ran back towards the car. As he ran, he tried to remember if there was anything he hadn't done or asked.

Did they make any efforts to sell anything to you?

Oh hell, I can't go back. I'd say yes, 'cause she did all that phoning stuff to get the sale.

'Dean, seriously, is there something wrong with your bladder? You've been ages!'

Dean was in no mood to find another excuse, so he chose to ignore Brooke's comment, got into the driver's seat and threw the biscuits over into the footwell of the passenger's side.

'Ouch! What d'ya buy these for?' Brooke asked incredulously as the tin of shortbread landed on her feet. Sadly, it was impossible to miss them!

'I just thought it might be nice to have a memento of our day, that's all.'

Brooke picked up the tin, glanced at the clichéd imagery on the front and thought it was a sweet thing to do.

'You're so funny, Dean. I just don't get you sometimes! But I've had a lovely day; really enjoyed it, thanks! Apart from madam being bitten, of course!'

Phew! Bloody got away with it!

Dean had miraculously pulled off an entire day doing a mystery customer assessment and successfully kept Brooke in the dark. All he had to do now was write up and send his report.

As he drove back to Brentwood, he reflected on the day and realised that they'd actually had a really nice time – apart from the curious incident with the goat in the daytime!

28

Onwards and Upwards

'Where's my Ben Sherman striped shirt?' Dean asked as he flicked through the wardrobe for a suitably smart outfit for the office.

'I dunno. Maybe I ironed it in a moment of madness?'

'You'd better bloody not have done.' Dean retorted jokingly. Only he wasn't joking. After they first moved in together, Brooke successfully ruined just about every good shirt he ever had. She never ironed properly and he'd been humiliated at work more than once in the summer months when he took off his jacket, only to discover in full light that she'd only ironed the front. She decided the sleeves and the back didn't need to be done, as they couldn't be seen under a jacket. This meant, of course, that he could never take his jacket off! Since then, he'd banned her from ironing any of his shirts. He'd told her he'd rather do them himself. And he did. Diligently. Any professional would've been proud of his ironing skills.

He ran downstairs whistling. He definitely didn't want to be late this morning. He found his shirt under a pile of towels and ironed it speedily, but thoroughly. It stressed him being rushed.

Brooke furtively removed her toy from under the bed and, as fast as Ronnie Biggs, counted the cash inside. She heard Dean coming back upstairs and quickly stuffed the cash back in the toy and pushed it back under the bed.

He handed Brooke a cup of tea and gave her a big kiss.

'For you! What're you up to today?' It was an innocent enough question, but Brooke's guilty state of mind caused her to leap into a defensive mode.

'What do you mean by that?' she asked accusingly.

'Nothing, babe!' Dean was quite put out by the way she'd taken his simple question. 'I just meant: are you doing anything nice today?'

'Oh.' She looked down, slightly ashamed of her response. Even she realised it was an over-the-top reaction to a simple question. 'No. I think I'll just stay at home today. I need to get stuff sorted out for my party, which I'm *very* excited about, by the way! Thanks, babe!' She pulled that out of the bag with perfect timing, ensuring Dean's chest swelled with pride. The party had been his suggestion *and* he'd given her some cash to help with it.

'OK, well I'm off – see you tonight!'

Another kiss and stroke of her cheeks and he was gone.

She sat up in bed drinking her tea and for the next hour she browsed the internet on her tablet for ideas for her party. DJs, lighting, entertainers, magicians, disco balls and karaoke machines. She wondered about a theme or fancy dress. After a while she started thinking about Lady Townsend. She pondered on what her opinion would be of all these ideas. She hoped that she wouldn't consider them to be vulgar – a bit 'Essex'. She tried to imagine what she might've done for *her* twenty-fifth birthday. She tried to envisage her boss as a twenty-five-year-old and struggled. It would have been in the mid–late 1960s.

I expect it was in some fancy place in London surrounded by rich men. I bet she looked fabulous.

She really couldn't decide what to do for the best. Her musings were cut short anyway by Paige's high-pitched scream, letting Brooke know it was time to get her out of her cot. She reluctantly put her tablet down, sighed and went to see to her daughter.

***

In the meantime, on the train, Dean was preparing a little speech in his mind before the big announcement. Brian had texted him the previous night telling him it was going to happen the next day. Jules and Dave were coming into the office to let the team know of Brian's retirement and Dean's taking over as Operations Manager.

He went to the gents as soon as he arrived in the building and made sure he looked the part – sharp. He made his way to Brian's office just to check it was still on and what time it would all happen. Brian confirmed it would be just before lunch.

Dean breezed over to his desk and glanced around the office. This was the first time it'd actually occurred to him that he was going to be responsible for managing this motley crew. This melting pot of personalities, work ethics and opportunities disguised as problems.

Well I'm gonna do a damn sight better than Brian, that's for sure.

The morning dragged and he struggled to get down to work. He just wanted the announcement to be made so he could get on. He checked his emails. He answered some calls. He shuffled bits of paper from one side of his desk to the other. He read and re-read the same article three times and took none of it in whatsoever. He messaged Brooke.

How r u babe? Thinking about you.

Yeah all cool. Just looking at party lights.

Although he was delighted that she actually returned his message immediately (an almost unheard-of occurrence these days) he became concerned.

Where for?

Dunno just looking generally. 4 party.

Well don't forget got very limited space.

IM JUST LOOKING!

'Paige, look at the camera and stick your tongue out at Daddy…like this!'

Brooke captured her daughter with a tongue that hung out as if it'd been burnt.

That'll do.

Brooke sent it to Dean

He backed off straight away. He didn't want to spoil this special day.

OK luv ya. Gotta go! Kiss Paige for me.

XXX

Brooke tutted, shook her head and kissed Paige on top of her head.

'There! That's from your silly daddy!'

Paige crawled around the bed trying out the duvet poppers, pulling the fur out of the fluffy wool cushion and yanking the sequins off another cushion as Brooke went back to looking at LED-lit planters and cube chairs for patios. She investigated multi-coloured uplights for the few trees she had, large solar lights on poles for the three-metre-long garden path. In fact, she got very carried away. Had she actually ordered it all she'd have been at serious risk of her garden resembling Adventure Island in Southend.

***

Finally it got to midday and Jules and Dave walked into the office unannounced. Normally Brian would warn the team they were coming, so that everyone would be on their best behaviour and ensure the calls were being answered in a timely fashion. Everyone was taken by surprise and the sense of impending doom was palpable.

Chloe looked over to Dean and whispered, 'What's

all this about then?' They all looked around at each other with inquisitive looks on their faces. All except Dean of course! He remained calm, looking ahead and with just a hint of a smile on his face as he caught Jules's eye.

'OK, folks, can you all please gather round? Jules and Dave have an announcement they'd like to make. Janice, you need to man the phones, just for the next five minutes.' Brian indicated he wanted people to come over to where he was standing and slowly everyone left their desks, except poor Janice who looked decidedly miffed at being left out of something so clearly important.

Jules started. 'Dave and I want to let you know that Brian has finally decided to retire at the end of this month.' She paused, waiting for some sort of reaction – anything at all – but there was none, so she carried on. 'We want to thank Brian for being here from the beginning and for the hard work and effort he's put into the growth of this company over the last twenty years. We couldn't have done it without him.' She waited again and looked a little disconcerted when nobody said anything. Jules seemed utterly oblivious to the fact that he was despised by the team. 'We know that all of you will want to say goodbye, so we'll be having a drinks party in the office on Brian's last day and we're sure you'll all want to be there.' She turned to Brian and clapped her hands, after which everyone reluctantly joined in with half-hearted applause.

Dave picked things up from there. 'So…I'm sure you all want to know who'll be taking over, am I right?' There were mumblings and whisperings which Dave let go on for a moment or two. 'Well. I'm going to put you out of your misery and tell you all that me and Jules are delighted to announce that Dean here is being promoted to Operations Manager of TrussInUs as of the beginning of next month. He's come personally recommended by Brian and our own experience with Dean, as well as some fantastic feedback from our clients and suppliers – particularly on that last IT project – meant we felt entirely happy to hand the role over to Dean.' Instantly the team stood up and cheered and clapped for several minutes, much to Dean's delight. He'd not anticipated they'd respond with such genuine affection and he was quite touched by it. Several of his colleagues came up and shook his hand, others patted him on the back and Chloe sidled over and gave him a squeeze and kiss on the cheek and said, 'Well done, Dean. How about that, then? No need for any more mystery shopping for you now, eh?!'

There was some good-humoured heckling from the team: 'You gonna give us longer tea breaks, then? I suppose you're gonna sit in Brian's big fancy office now you're not one of us? Ooooh! *Who's* going to get a company car then?!'

Dean decided to say something, because he felt a bit embarrassed that Brian's retirement announcement got not a squeak from anyone and he felt really sorry for him. Billy no mates.

'Thank you so much, everyone. I don't know what to

say, really. One thing I must say though is a huge thank-you to Brian,' he lied.

Power-crazed perv.

'He's helped me so much since I've been here; you know, really shown me the ropes.'

That bastard made my life utterly miserable.

'I hope I can help take the business on to the next stage of growth and hope you'll all support me along the way. Thanks, Dave and Jules, for having faith in me. I'll try not to let you down.'

'Three cheers for Dean!' cried Paddy 'Hip hip hooray, hip hip hooray, hip hip hooray!' Everyone joined in and more clapping and cheering followed. Paddy was the office joker. Always full of banter and practical jokes and as Irish as they come, with a bright-red face and nose from a drink habit that'd followed him all the way from the Guinness factory in Dublin.

'OK, back to your desks and back to work!' Dean joked in a stern and overly dictatorial voice and waved them all back in the general direction of their desks. They laughed and did as they were told, with Chloe stopping by Janice to have a gossip about the announcement.

Dean's heart was thumping. He was on such a high he couldn't stop grinning. He felt very, very pleased with himself and for the first time in a very long time, knew that his wife would be proud of him. The mere thought of the surprise he had in store for her made him giggle. He allowed himself a minute of daydreaming; he imagined his wife in her leopard-print bikini, lounging in the hot tub with her fulsome breasts bouncing about on the water with a glass of bubbly in her hand and a smile to die for.

Dean had been on autopilot and wandered back to his desk.

'Oi! Dean!' Dave was shouting to him from over the other side of the office. 'Can me and Jules have a quick word?'

'Blimey! He's in trouble already and he's only been in the job two minutes!' Paddy shouted out. The whole office laughed.

Dean looked up, realised his error and sprinted back over to Brian's office, where Dave and Jules were sitting. Dave was quite an imposing figure, well over six foot and with a gut to match. He was a self-made man who'd started this business twenty years ago with his wife, from a tiny office in Tilbury and gradually built it up to a three million turnover business with sixty staff. He seemed streetwise and smart. Not an intellectual, just very savvy. Jules was a plump, round-faced jolly-looking sort, the kind of person you see making tea at jumble sales up and down the country. Only she was the financial brains of the business. Dave did Sales and Marketing and she did Finance, HR and Administration; all back of house stuff and she only came into the office once a week, if that. The rest of the time she worked from home in their footballers' wives'-style house in Chigwell, so she could do the school runs and indulge her love of chocolate and biscuits all day without being judged.

'Well done, Dean! Well deserved!' Dave shook hands with Dean and smiled. 'My new Brian.'

God forbid!

'You were obviously the popular choice if the reaction from the guys out there was anything to go by. But take my advice and keep your distance from now on. You can't be their friend and their governor. No more piss-ups after work with them all. They'll find the chink in your armour and ruthlessly exploit it.' Jules had the most discerning, disarming way of communicating. She was the only person Dean had ever come across who could talk to you in the most sickly-sweet way with a lovely smile on her face but you'd walk away realising that she'd actually told you off. Dean always described Jules to Brooke as a razor blade dipped in cream.

Dean hadn't thought about this side of becoming the manager at all, other than the brief look around at the team that morning. He'd not ever received training of any kind in how to be a manager. His responsibilities as Brian's assistant, with special responsibility for IT, involved primarily the day-to-day running of the team, handling any escalated complaints, ensuring there was always enough staff manning the phones and using his skills in IT to sort out computer, telephone system and printer problems, because no-one else had a clue. He also did a fair bit of client and supplier liaison work. He thought and just hoped he'd be a good manager. He knew that the team liked him and that would help. What Dean didn't understand was that it was more important to be respected than to be liked. But he'd learn!

'Well thank you and I'll do my best and take your advice on board.'

'Great. I'm sure you will. OK, one last but important thing. Your company car. You've got a choice of a Ford Focus or a Seat Leon. You don't have to decide now but whichever one you go for, let me know within a week and I can have it ready for you to pick up on Saturday 28th September.'

Dean grinned all over again and had to hold back a child-like scream of joy. That was Brooke's birthday. What a present!

'You have no idea just how fantastic this is right now! Thanks, Dave. I'll have a think and let you know.'

'OK, well we need to get going now. Lots to do!' Dave shook Dean's hand again and then he and Jules left the office.

A company car.

He'd made it.

***

Brooke walked in the building as though she were on a mission, straight over to the reception desk, and asked for Alan. She was holding Paige by some reins as she toddled about still navigating her own legs and working out what they could and couldn't do. Brooke didn't dare let her loose, but she couldn't leave her in the car.

The receptionist disappeared out back and almost immediately Alan came out of his office and over to Brooke. 'You must be Mrs De'Ath.'

Brooke had no idea how he'd know that; they'd only spoken on the phone, but she ignored the fact and said she was here to pay for her order. He invited her to sit down at his desk as he leered at her cleavage while pretending to look up her order.

Alan watched with some alarm as she plonked Paige on the chair in front of Alan's desk, and tied her to it with the reins, while she took out three thousand five hundred pounds in cash and counted it out on top of his desk. Paige tried to stand up but couldn't and leaned over the desk trying to touch the wad of money. Brooke looked for signs of an imminent scream, but it didn't materialise.

'There. That's the lot. Three and a half grand – as agreed. You've got all the other details yeah?'

Alan smiled. 'Yeah. All's clear. You strike a hard bargain, if I may say.' He thanked her and leaned over to talk to Paige 'Aren't you a lucky girl? I bet you'll have a lot of fun, eh?'

'Oh that she will – that's for definite! Thanks for all your help.'

She untied Paige, scooped her off the chair, into her arms and marched out, bouncing her up and down and laughing quietly to herself.

29

An Interesting Revelation

The next couple of weeks saw Brooke research every conceivable idea for her party. She spent a disproportionate amount of time browsing the internet. Both Lady Townsend and Hugo had caught her looking at her phone when she should've been working. Initially she tried to hide what she was doing, until one day Lady Townsend actually asked her:

'Brooke, my dear, is everything alright? I've never seen you on your phone as much as I have in these past couple of weeks.'

Brooke was embarrassed and hadn't really realised that she'd been spending quite that much time looking at her screen. Although now she thought about it, Dean and Dawn had also commented.

'I'm sorry, Mrs Townsend. I've been a bit preoccupied, to be honest, but not with anything serious. Quite the opposite.'

'Well perhaps you'd care to enlighten me?'

Mrs Townsend sat down on the sofa in that royal way she always did, put her hands in her lap, slanted her head slightly, raised her eyebrows and maintained direct eye contact.

'I'm all ears.'

'Well. It's my twenty-fifth birthday next Saturday and I'm having a big party to celebrate. I've been looking at so many ideas on the net trying to decide what to do and trying to organise everything. I'm having to do so much chasing. It's all getting a bit on top of me, to be honest.'

'Oh how marvellous! A party! Oh how I wish I were your age again!'

Brooke was somewhat relieved at her reaction.

'I don't suppose you remember what you did for your twenty-fifth, back in the day?'

'Well, as a matter of fact, I remember exactly what I did and with good reason. I went to Ronnie Scott's Jazz Club in London with a group of my friends. That was THE place to be seen in those days; so exciting! It's where I met my husband. It was probably one of the best nights of my entire life. And a turning point in it too.'

This was the first time that Lady Townsend had ever spoken about her husband. All Brooke knew from Hugo was that he died seven years ago and that's why she hired him. She simply couldn't manage the house and gardens without help. Her husband had organised everything to do with the house and gardens. He'd preferred his wife to spend her time organising charity events, being a charity trustee and hosting parties and private dinners. Hugo indicated that his death was still too painful for her to talk about, so Brooke had never asked, but she'd often wondered.

'Oh I'm sorry. I didn't know.' Brooke bowed her head thinking she'd put her foot in it.

'That's alright. Why should you know? I even remember what I wore! A Biba dark- green, velvet mini-skirt with high-heeled, suede, up-to-the-knee boots and a Mary Quant satin, halter-neck top, with beads and fringe hanging around the bottom. I saved for months to buy those boots! I even painted glitter around my eyes and wore huge false eyelashes! I bet you can't imagine that, can you?'

Mrs Townsend's eyes lit up at the memory and she appeared to come alive in a way Brooke had never seen. She laughed at the picture Mrs Townsend was conjuring up. She'd always been a woman of class, obviously!

'I can't believe you ever had to save for anything!' Brooke laughed casually.

Suddenly Lady Townsend's face changed and she looked very seriously at Brooke.

'You've absolutely no idea. No idea at all just how hard things were for me back then.'

Brooke felt herself going red and she wished she'd not started this line of conversation.

'My life hasn't always been a bed of roses, you know. I actually came from a very poor background. My mother was born in a workhouse in the East End of London. I grew up in Bow.'

'Gordon Bennett! I'd never have guessed that. I'm really sorry.' Brooke was dumbstruck.

'She was a cleaner all her life and my father, who worked on the docks, died when I was young. I had no brothers or sisters, so it was just me and my mother.'

Brooke didn't quite know how to say what she was thinking. She unconsciously bit her lip before curiosity won the day and she took the plunge.

'God, that's terrible. But you sound…and look…so…so…posh?' She made the statement like a question while she looked nervously at Lady Townsend, as if she thought she might be insulted by this.

Lady Townsend laughed out loud.

'Of course I do! My husband's family sent me to finishing school in Switzerland.'

'What's that, then?' Without thinking, Brooke removed her cleaning apron as though she were done for the day, which she most certainly wasn't!

'It's a place where they send young ladies to learn how to dress, behave and be a good hostess in society and usually to learn how to bag a rich husband.'

'What?' Brooke was astounded at this revelation.

And I always thought you were a strong bad ass woman!

'I always assumed you were wealthy in your own right, but you're saying that *he* was the rich one then?'

'Most definitely. His great grandfather was Sir Charles Townsend, one of the earliest members of The Dilettanti Society, which is where the connection is to Brooks's.

Membership of the club was passed down through the family.'

'So how come you're *Lady* Townsend? I don't get it.'

'William was a Lord when I met him. I really was a bit rough for someone of my husband's standing. But it was practically love at first sight when we met at Ronnie Scott's. We couldn't keep our eyes off each other.' She leaned forward and whispered in a confidential manner, 'And he couldn't keep his hands off me either! Six months later, he proposed.'

'Crikey! So what did your husband's parents think of you? Weren't they like…expecting someone a bit posher to marry him?'

'They were absolutely horrified,' she said matter-of-factly. 'I was taken to be introduced to them just a few weeks after we'd met and although they apparently liked me, it was inconceivable that someone from my background could possibly marry their son!'

'So what happened?' Brooke was so intrigued at this point, she sat down next to Mrs Townsend, completely forgetting where she was, who she was talking to and the fact that she was meant to be explaining her excessive mobile phone use whilst at work.

'William wouldn't budge. They even threatened to disinherit him if he married me. In the end, the compromise they made was that they'd pay to send me to finishing school in Switzerland in the hope I'd polish up a bit and become a more acceptable society wife.'

'That's terrible! To be made to feel…not good enough like that…it's awful.'

'Not really, dear. As far as I was concerned, I'd only ever been to Spain once and the prospect of going to Switzerland for a jolly, paid for by someone else, was extremely exciting. I couldn't wait to go! I had an absolute ball. More importantly for William's parents, it worked; I came back a well-spoken, well-dressed, well-behaved, cultured young lady (well on the surface, anyway, hahaha!) and so they reluctantly gave the marriage their blessing. I automatically became a Lady.'

'Well I'll be buggered!' Brooke quickly put her hand up to her mouth realising her faux pas. 'So what did *your* mum think of it all?' Brooke was seriously struggling to imagine Lady Townsend's mother as an East End cleaner.

'She was a bit in awe of it all really, but I did take William to meet her and they got on like a house on fire (although she took the mickey out of his accent and took the mickey out of me even more for mine). At Institute Villa Pierrefeu I had to have elocution lessons to destroy my London accent! I took my mother to Selfridges to buy her 'Mother of the bride' dress. She'd only ever bought her clothes from a market stall, or for a special occasion she might've gone to Littlewoods or C&A. It was an absolute hoot, the poor sales assistants just didn't know what to make of the two of us at all, but sadly she died two weeks before the wedding.'

'Oh my God, no! How did she die? That's just tragic.

You poor thing.'

'She had a heart attack and well... I just had to get on with it. My life had already changed beyond my wildest dreams at that point.'

'So did you have a job, then?' By now Brooke had well and truly forgotten about everything else and was one hundred per cent focussed on her conversation with Mrs Townsend.

'I did before I got married. I was a receptionist at a fancy art gallery just off Carnaby Street. I loved it, even though I gave most of my earnings to my mother. I met and mingled with some very wealthy, famous and interesting London people.'

'Wow! That must've been so exciting in the sixties.'

'It was. But after I married William I had to leave.'

'Why?' Brooke was astonished.

'Ladies like me married to men like William simply didn't work. It wasn't the done thing at all.'

God – sounds like Dean.

'You must've been bored out your tiny mind!'

Lady Townsend laughed. 'Well I used to sneak out during the day when William thought I was at flower arranging classes or some other godforsaken activity it was deemed acceptable for me to do! I'd take the train to London as soon as he'd gone to work and spend the day at the National Gallery or the V&A and hurry back before he got home. I had no children so it wasn't too difficult!'

That all sounds a bit familiar – except for the kids.

'Crumbs! Well I'm a bit shocked, to say the least, Mrs Townsend. I don't know what to say, really.'

Brooke realised they'd been talking for quite some time.

'I'm sorry, I've been talking for way too long. I must get back to work! I only wanted to know if you did anything for your twenty-fifth birthday!'

'Well now you know! And a whole lot more. Well, if you need any help organising your party or if you'd like to borrow anything from the house for it, please do ask. I'd be delighted to help!'

Brooke was overwhelmed by Mrs Townsend's kindness and tears welled up in her eyes as she thought about her life. How Brooke had assumed! How she'd believed that she could never be like Lady Townsend. And yet this conversation proved just how much it was possible to change the trajectory of one's life in just a couple of generations.

Except that I'm married to Dean; from Brentwood in Essex.

'Thank you so much. That's really kind of you. I'll let you know if I think of anything.'

Lady Townsend smiled, got up and left the room.

Brooke tried to carry on with her work, but her mind kept going back to what Lady Townsend had told her. She kept putting her hands to her mouth, with incredulity every time she thought about it. She periodically looked around her to see if there was anything she might be able to use for her party, but she thought none of it would really fit in, at her modern little house. Her phone buzzed in her pocket.

Hey Babe

Babe??

R U there??

Brooke didn't dare look at her phone again, in case Hugo or Mrs Townsend came in, so she just ignored Dean's messages.

Dean stared at his phone.

Where's that girl? Why the hell isn't she picking up?

He was feeling a tad lonely and just fancied a chat. It was tough at the top and he'd just had to discipline Janice for being late once too often. He was virtually sent to Coventry by all the women in the office who tried to tell him that she was having 'women's problems' and that he ought to show a bit more compassion.

Of course, he couldn't actually tell Brooke anything yet because she didn't know about his promotion yet. He'd decided that she'd find out about it on her birthday when the hot tub arrived and he drove up to the house in his brand-new company car. It was the hardest secret he'd ever had to keep in his life! He'd told Martin because he knew he might need his help when he picked up the new car. Martin had been dead impressed and a tad jealous, truth be known.

Every day, for the previous fortnight, Dean had had to double-check that Brooke hadn't gone overboard with spending on her party. He knew what she was like. Give her an inch and she'd take a yard. She'd get cross if he questioned her choices of fancy dress, food or decorations and he certainly didn't think that a magician was necessary. But she only had to give him one of her looks and he'd walk away with his tail between his legs.

Worst-case scenario and my pay rise'll cover it.

So far, fancy invites for a 'Characters From a Film' fancy dress party had gone out to their friends and most replied that they'd be coming, she'd got a DJ, lights inside and out, garden heaters 'in case people wanted to go outside for a fag', matching tablecloths and napkins, a three-tier cake made from multi-coloured muffins, all the food had been ordered from Marks & Spencer and she'd splashed out on buying a couple of cases of sparkling wine from Majestic along with copious bottles of Becks. Glasses had been hired. Oh and of course she'd rented the most fantastic outfit for herself and chosen one for Dean on his behalf.

Dean had been given his usual list of jobs. It felt like only yesterday they'd had Paige's first birthday party and he'd had another list of jobs to get through. At least this time it didn't involve any painting. It was mostly moving furniture into different rooms, to make the living room and tiny conservatory as big as possible for dancing and the DJ in the corner. Brooke wanted Dean out the house on the morning of the party so she'd told him that he needed to pick up various party items. This would leave her at home for her 10am delivery, get herself ready and make sure everything was perfect for the moment their friends started to arrive at 7pm.

The countdown to Brooke's twenty-fifth birthday party had begun.

30

Double Trouble

Early on the morning of the party, Brooke ran down the stairs in a panic, with two fancy dress outfits folded over her arm.

'Dean, Dean, quick, I forgot, you haven't even tried this on yet. You need to make sure it fits! We should've done this days ago!'

Dean had no input whatsoever into his costume. To be fair, Brooke had tried to get him interested, but he'd seemed so not bothered. Little did she know that he was finding his feet in his new role at work and was almost permanently preoccupied. So, when she'd asked him if he was happy to let her choose something suitable, he'd blindly agreed. Oh dear!

Dean pulled out the hanger from its dry cleaning bag to reveal a pair of long red baggy dungarees, white shirt and huge pale-blue bow tie with yellow spots, all in glorious 100% polyester. He put it down on the sofa and looked back inside the bag again. Nothing.

'Where's mine then?' He looked up at Brooke.

'That *is* yours. And the ears. You forgot the ears.' She

retrieved them from deep inside the bag and handed them to Dean, who simply glanced at them and watched as his wife slipped on a long red glittery and very revealing tight-fitting dress with a huge slash up the side, long purple satin gloves and a long red wig, all topped off with a pair of six-inch red stilettos. 'I tried mine on when I bought it, so I know it fits but I'll put it all on anyway so you can see it and so we can see what we look like together. C'mon, get into your costume!'

'You're 'avin' a laugh. I'm not wearing that! What am I meant to be?'

'Well surely you must know – just looking at *me*!' Brooke pointed both hands at herself.

'No. I haven't got a clue.' He was genuinely in the dark.

'Just put it on and stand next to me. You'll soon get it.'

Dean shook his head, stripped off in the lounge and pulled the outfit on. Brooke placed the ears carefully on his head.

They turned to look in the long mirror in the hall. Brooke excitedly linked her arm through Dean's arm and grinned at the sight in the mirror. Dean just stared blankly, mouth ajar.

'Brooke, you look stunning and I look like some retarded fucking Mickey Mouse. Whatever I'm meant to be, I'm not wearing this.'

'Dean, you're Roger Rabbit!'

'Who the bloody hell's Roger Rabbit?'

'Dean, you can't be serious. Roger Rabbit? I'm Jessica

Rabbit? From the film *Who Framed Roger Rabbit*?

'Never heard of it. When did it come out? Who was in it?'

'God, I don't know, Dean. Sometime in the 1980s. Bob Hoskins was in it. It's such a famous film. How can you not know about it? It was a mixture of cartoon and real life people. You *must* know.'

Brooke was exasperated. She couldn't accept he'd never heard of the film. Even though it came out the year she was born, it was her parents' favourite film; they had it on VHS and watched it frequently. Brooke remembered, even at a young age, how she loved the long red dress.

'Well I don't and I'm not wearing this! Simple as.'

He began to take it off.

'Dean De'Ath, don't you dare. I *asked* you *weeks* ago if you wanted to choose something and you couldn't have cared less. You said you'd be perfectly happy to let me choose something on your behalf. Now I have, you don't want to wear it! You're stressing me out! I haven't got anything else and there isn't time to get anything else and we're meant to be going as a couple, which means I can't wear my Jessica Rabbit outfit, which took me ages to find I'll have you know. Not everyone's got size eight shoes!'

Brooke's voice got louder and louder until she was virtually screaming with anger and frustration at what she saw as Dean's completely unreasonable behaviour.

'Babe! Don't get so upset. You'll get your blood pressure up. It's only fancy dress!' Dean became increasingly alarmed; he'd never heard Brooke get so mad.

'Yes, but it's my birthday party and it's meant to be *fun* and you're ruining it by arguing about something that can't be changed. It's *pointless*. You need to go as you are… no matter how much you hate it.' She did that sort of stompy thing with her feet and flung her arms about like a toddler having a tantrum.

'OK, OK. I'll wear it! Now calm down. Honestly, love, you should sit down and take your BP. Remember the doc said you mustn't go over one forty over ninety.' Now his voice was raised, eyes wide open; he was desperate to stop her from getting any more het up than she already was. She was right about one thing – it was meant to be a nice day.

Brooke stomped off upstairs, clearly furious with Dean. She wanted him to have fun at the party, not spend the whole night miserable as sin because he didn't like his outfit.

'Hello? Hello?' a voice shouted through the letterbox.

What the fuck?

For some reason known only to himself, Dean knelt down and spoke back through the letter box. He was so annoyed he really wasn't thinking about what he was doing at all.

'Yes? What is it?' Dean sounded so irritated, the man on the other side was startled and he jerked back, surprised.

'Sorry, is that Mr De'Ath?'

'Yes. What do you want?'

'I did knock, but nobody answered. Sorry to bother you,' the man said very apologetically, fearful that he was disturbing Dean at a bad time, 'Keith here, delivery associate; we've got a delivery here for you.'

Oh fuck!

'Oh god yes, sorry, hang on.' Dean stood up, tried to gather his thoughts and opened the door.

The man fought back the urge to stare full on at Dean and sensed that to laugh wouldn't be a good idea right now.

'I'm sorry, I hadn't realised it was this late. OK, just hang on a minute.'

'Well we've got two more deliveries to do this morning, so we can't 'ang about. If you can just show us where it's gotta go and then we can get on with it.'

Dean was torn. He looked upstairs and shouted to Brooke.

'Babe? Babe?'

Brooke didn't respond and wasn't in the mood to either. It was her birthday after all. It'd started off so nicely, with Dean bringing her up tea in bed first thing and a beautiful bunch of red roses and a card the size of a small TV. And yet not one hour later, here she was, sat on the bed upset and angry when she should've been happy and excited about her party. Paige was pootling about in the bedroom taking advantage of her mother's preoccupation by delving into her makeup bag on the floor, emptying it of all its contents and trying each palette, jar and tube out one by one.

'BROOKE?' Dean took a few steps back down the hallway, leaving the front door open.

For God's sake.

'Sorry, mate, I've gotta get cracking,' Keith shouted back to Dean and walked back to his lorry and pulled up the shutter at the back while his mate Rod got out to help.

Dean ran out and asked them to try and get it round the back as quickly as possible and indicated the gate at the side of the house.

'I'll meet you in the back garden in a minute.'

As he turned to run down the side alley, his neighbour Mikey pulled up outside his house, got out of his car and came pretty much face to face with Dean. He looked him up and down and shook his head in that way that shows you feel really, really sorry for someone. 'I won't even ask, Dean. What you do in your own private life is your business.'

Dean said nothing, but slammed the front door shut and ran around the side alley into the garden. He looked up at their bedroom window, but the curtains were still shut, much to his relief.

Suddenly, there was a knock on the front door.

Brooke screeched from the bedroom, 'Dean! DEAN! DEEEAN! Can you answer the door?' She didn't want to answer it dressed as she was.

Dean couldn't hear her and he couldn't hear the

knocker bang again and again.

Still exceedingly stroppy but not quite as mad (she'd been staring at her beautiful roses), Brooke scooped a well-made-up and naked Paige into her arms and stomped down the stairs, continuing to call Dean and irritated that he didn't answer.

She opened the door looking completely divine if not decidedly strange, considering it was only just after 10am.

'Mrs De'Ath?'

'No. Jessica Rabbit.' Brooke put her free hand on her hip and slanted her head with an attitude and look that could shrink a man's testicles instantly.

The man looked confused and laughed nervously as he pretended not to notice her rather unusual mode of dress.

'Delivery for you?'

She noticed his name was on a magnetic badge on his shirt, 'Albie'. And it'd slipped, so was hanging in a wonky fashion.

'Oh Christ, I hadn't realised the time!' She automatically put one hand up to her forehead and was visibly shocked. Paige put her hand up to her own forehead and looked up at her mother for approval.

Brooke looked over Albie's shoulder into the road and then back into the house to make sure Dean wasn't looking. She frowned and tried to make out what the two huge lorries were, parked up the road. As she was doing so, Keith and Rod climbed out of the first one and lowered the back plate to slowly reveal a beautiful six-seater hot tub.

'What the hell's that?' As she walked towards it, she pointed at the shrink-wrapped hot tub being brought out of the first lorry.

'Dunno, Mrs De'Ath. That's not our truck. Our delivery is in the lorry in front,' replied Albie from lorry number two, as he ran behind after her.

'What?' Brooke was so confused now, she marched further along the road, glancing at the hot tub coming out of lorry number one but moving swiftly past to see her ten-seater hot tub nestled inside lorry number two. The back plate was already down so she climbed inside and looked over the hot tub to check it had no more scratches on it. She'd negotiated harder than Alan Sugar and until she'd ground the poor salesman into submission, but it was an ex-display model and had a number of marks on it as she kept reminding him. As Brooke walked around it slowly, a smile crept across her face and any remaining anger dissipated. She caressed it with her free hand as Paige tried to climb into it.

Meanwhile, Keith and Rod from lorry number one carried their hot tub on its side into the back garden, squeezing their stomachs in as they walked it down the alleyway and placed it on the square patch of lawn that was the De'Ath's garden.

Mikey had gone straight into his garden and peered over the fence to observe what was clearly going to be an interesting morning. 'What's this then?' He motioned to Keith and Rod as they ensured the tub was on flat ground. 'You gonna start the Elephant Close swinger's club, then? Hahahaha!'

'Fuck off, Mikey, just fuck off!' Dean wasn't in the mood to listen to any wisecracks. He needed to sort this delivery out PDQ.

'Well I dunno who that other one's for, but this one's mine!' Brooke said gleefully. 'Bring it round the back. Quickly. I dunno where my husband's got to. I'd better go back in and get changed.'

Brooke trotted back inside with Paige, to put on some normal clothes, while Albie and his delivery mate Gary from lorry number two struggled to get their hot tub off the back. By this time Keith and Rod had made their way back and saw them having trouble.

'That's out of order, if you ask me. A ten-seater and only two of you? That's gotta be against health and safety regs.' Keith adopted his most militant trade union voice.

'D'you wanna hand, mate?' he added.

'Oh cheers, mate, that'd be great. Yeah, we told 'em that but they never listen to us,' Albie moaned.

As they all approached Dean and Brooke's house with the ten-seater on its side, the first two delivery drivers gave each other a sideways look.

'Are you sure this is the right place? We literally only just delivered a hot tub here,' Rod enquired, looking a bit worried.

Albie checked the delivery note. 'Yep. This is it. Number 6 Elephant Close.'

'Blimey, maybe they're having an orgy! Hahahaha! Well good luck finding space for this one!' Keith warned him and sneered.

After some minutes and much moaning about the size of the alleyway and lack of suitable access, they finally got through into the back garden and were met by Dean, who'd been wondering what all the commotion was.

'STOP! What the fuck's that?!' Dean froze on the spot and pointed at the huge hot tub they were carrying.

'It's your hot tub, Mr De'Ath. Where's it goin'?' Albie responded.

Jessica Rabbit heard a commotion outside, opened the bedroom curtains and suddenly appeared at the window, wondering what on earth was going on. She opened it and peered out into the back garden.

For the next few minutes, Keith, Rod, Albie and Gary as well as Mikey looked for all the world as though they were at Wimbledon, moving their heads first in the direction of Brooke and then back to Dean and then back to Brooke again.

'What the hell's going on, Dean? What's that…*thing*… doing in our garden?' She looked over at the six-seater hot tub on the lawn and pointed her finger at it while waving her hand at it dismissively, with a mortified expression on her face.

'This "thing" is your birthday present!' Dean shouted

up to her hopefully, not knowing quite what else to say. This wasn't exactly turning out the way he'd envisaged. 'Happy Birthday, babe!'

'But you couldn't *afford* a hot tub! How come you got one?' Brooke sounded annoyed and panicky.

'I got promoted! A few weeks ago…I was keeping it a surprise until today…I've got a brand-new company car as well…a Seat Leon. I'm picking it up later on.'

He desperately searched her face for a crumb of evidence of joy, but it remained frozen in place.

'It's banana yellow. That colour you love,' he added hopefully. Dean looked up at Brooke in a scene reminiscent of the balcony part in Romeo and Juliet, only he was grinning with primitive male pride.

Brooke made the foolish error of letting out a scream of delight combined with shock, after which Paige merrily copied her mother sticking her head out the window and screaming her little heart out. 'OH…MY…GOD, Dean! *Why* didn't you tell me?'

'More to the point though, what's *this* thing?!' Dean pointed to the ten-seater on its side on the patio, there being nowhere else to put it. It was barely visible from the bedroom window.

Brooke leaned out to see the corner of her hot tub.

Oh God, what do I say? What do I say?

'*That* one…*that* one…is *mine!* I ordered it!'

'WHAT?!' Dean went pale and looked as though he were about to pass out. 'Are you fucking mad? How the hell? I can't afford one that size…and it won't bloody well fit in the garden anyway, Brooke.'

'It's my birthday present to myself! And you don't have to pay for it. *I* bought it!'

All eyes were on Dean. Keith made that facial expression at Dean that all men know means 'better you than me'.

'Yeah and pigs might fly.' Dean buried his head in his hands as it dropped forward and his bunny ears fell to the ground. Without thinking he automatically put them back on again. He felt desperate.

'I *did*, Dean! With my *own* money!' Brooke stood up straight, dead serious, and was the picture of defiance.

'But you haven't *got* any bloody money!' Dean yelled at the top of his voice, no longer able to hide his sheer exasperation as he threw both his arms up in the air, knocking his humungous blue and yellow spotted, clip-on bow tie flying. Brooke's wicked sense of humour meant she couldn't help laughing out loud as it hit Albie in the face.

'Delivery for Brooke De'Ath? Sorry but no-one was answering the door and I could hear people round the back.' A man appeared at the back gate with a case of Bollinger Champagne. On top was balanced an enormous silver champagne cooler with round lion's head handles either side. He carefully placed it all on the ground. Brooke craned her neck forward and frowned.

Dean's mouth was wide open.

God she's gone fucking mad this time.

There was a little tag hanging off the champagne bath and he automatically walked over to it and read it.

'Have a divine birthday, my dear – you can bring it back on Monday. Best wishes Lady Townsend.'

'Brooke, what's this? And who the fuck is Lady Townsend?'

All eyes were now on Brooke. She took a deep breath, blew it out slowly between pursed lips and looked at Dean long and hard before declaring, 'Dean…I think we need to 'ave a little chat. There's something I need to talk to you about. I'm coming down.'

Caelum mihi, caelum mihi!

Thank You

Thank you for reading my debut novel and I really hope you enjoyed reading it as much as I enjoyed writing it! If you're bursting to know what happens next, you can visit the link below, where you can get a free book to download that will reveal all!

www.helenefield.com/free-download1

As a new author, reviews are a vital way for our books to be discovered by readers, so if you can possibly spare a few minutes to leave a review on Amazon and/or Goodreads, I truly would be most grateful!

② Acknowledgements

I would like to thank Anna McFadyen, Marianne Acs, Jill Foxley and Jo Terry for giving me the confidence and courage to go ahead and publish this book. I must also thank Domini Atkin and Liz Coleman for finding me great beta readers and to Terri Hampton, Zoe Godbold, Tina Friend and my eagle-eyed daughter Georgia for giving up their time to read the manuscript.

My copy-editor and proofreader Nicola Lovick was a patient source of professional knowledge and I am grateful to her for that, as well as advice that went above and beyond her brief.

I also have to acknowledge the wonderful contributions of my husband Nic to some of the dialogue!

I owe a huge gratitude of debt to Alastair Curbuun, who is the real Assistant Club Secretary at Brooks's and who facilitated my working with all the gentlemen's clubs in London for many years – a truly fascinating and enjoyable part of my career in hospitality.

Finally, I must thank all the people in my life in Essex – especially those during my teenage years. They have unknowingly inspired many of the characters and incidents in the book!

Printed in Poland
by Amazon Fulfillment
Poland Sp. z o.o., Wrocław

65371534R00270